The Last Heiress

A Novel of Tutankhamun's Queen

Stephanie Liaci

authorHOUSE®

AuthorHouse™
1663 Liberty Drive
Bloomington, IN 47403
www.authorhouse.com
Phone: 1-800-839-8640

Published by AuthorHouse 1/30/2012

ISBN: 978-1-4520-6308-9 (e)
ISBN: 978-1-4520-6306-5 (sc)
ISBN: 978-1-4520-6307-2 (hc)

Library of Congress Control Number: 2010913077

Printed in the United States of America
This book is printed on acid-free paper.

For Cassidy, brave and beautiful

PART ONE

1342 BC-1333BC

Chapter One

Spring
Year Ten Akhenaten

I pull my bedroom door open just as my older sisters drift past. "Mayati! Meketaten!"

I call to them, but they hardly look over their shoulders. The echo of their giggles trails them through the hall. My sisters, nine and seven years old and close as twins, step as lightly as gazelles in their jewel studded sandals. Their myrrh scented gowns swirl around them with deliberate and rehearsed grace. "Wait for me!" I cry, even though they won't.

"Run, run!" Mayati calls over her shoulder. Her laughter stings like wasps, and she keeps on going, arm in arm with Meketaten.

"You know I can't," I say quietly, to myself. I don't want to anger my eldest sister, she has the temper of a viper and she could easily tell me that I can't sit in the garden with them, which means I cannot swim. I love swimming best of all things, swimming and horses and singing, and of course playing with my baby sister, who is too little to taunt and tease.

Mother says that I was hurt when I was born, and it rules every moment of my life, but not because I'm in pain. The midwife broke my foot, and I had to wear a cast for a long time.

1

I was also-and still am-very small for my age. After seeing her tiny third daughter injured and bandaged as a baby, Mother determined that I must be guarded and held back every day. She tells me every day that I didn't heal well enough, that I can't dance or run through the gardens with my sisters. My nurse Tia holds my hand tightly as my sisters rush off to whisper together, and I wish more than anything to be free like them. My older sisters dance and twirl like flower petals in the wind, they ride horses and drive their own chariots, and whenever I can catch up, Mayati can't resist hissing at me like a nasty cat.

Mother shares her clever laughter with me when I cry. She says Mayati is cruel only because she is jealous, and I should be flattered. I'm mewed up like a falcon in the stables, but *she* envies me, because-my mother says-I am the prettiest girl in Egypt, lovelier than all of my sisters. When Mother comes to see me, she rubs cream into my cheeks and onto my lips, telling me that I must always take care of my gifts, that they are greater even than hers. She says I shouldn't give a fig about running after them because it's much better to be the most beautiful. She would know. My mother is called the most beautiful woman in the world, just like her name says: *Nefertiti, the Beautiful One has come.* I'm not sure if I'm the most beautiful girl in world, but I know I hate being left behind, and it happens just about every day.

Alone, I walk past our bowing servants. Even at four years old, the women who clean our home must bow to me as they would to Mother. I step gingerly over their abandoned rags and their buckets of lemon scented water. If Father were here, they would have to press their faces to the floor in prostration.

I have always known that my father was an important man, and very different from other men. Now that I am big, I know that he is the *greatest* man in the world. He is Pharaoh Akhenaten, and all of Egypt, and everything in it, belongs to him. He must always tell everyone what to do, and it must be done just so, because he knows so much more than other men do. His clothes are always very fine, with thread of gold woven into his soft linen, and he eats off gold plates and sleeps in a gilded bed. But he also has a very friendly laugh and a lovely smile, a smile that makes everyone happy right along with him. And when he comes to see us girls, his big ringed hands are always full of candied dates or little gifts, and then he asks after our little troubles. Father is fierce, too. He is called the son of the great Sun God Aten, our god, and so sometimes he can be very frightening when he is angry. But he is never angry with me, and I wouldn't dream of displeasing him.

I don't see Father-or Mother-as much as I would like. My father is a very busy man, because of the bad priests. There once was another great god in Egypt, but I dare not even think his name. It is a crime to speak it, a capital crime, which means you can have your head cut off for it. That forbidden god angered Father and Aten, and so did his priests, who were nothing but thieves and traitors. Father banished them from the land, but the priests lied to many people, people who don't want to worship Aten as they should, and so Father must work very hard to make sure Aten is honored properly. Sometimes I am frightened of these bad priests. Mayati doesn't tease me about that, like she does when I am frightened of the dark. She knows how scary they are, she knows that our food must always be tasted before we eat it, because the heretics want to hurt us.

Father says we must be brave, like him, and help him on his mission. Aten is not only the patron god of our house; he chose Father of all Pharaohs to tell his truths, so that Father could bring a great new age to Egypt. When we all eat together, Father and Mother and us girls, our parents speak of this mission with bright eyes and excited words. I'm not sure I understand it all, but I pray to Aten as I should, and I know that he is my father too.

And what do I pray for? Other than for the health and prosperity of Pharaoh and my mother and my sisters, and the safety of our family, it is the same thing every time: I pray for a true friend, someone who can be like Meketaten for Mayati, but all mine.

The dim, torch lit hallway brightens as I approach the

3

courtyard garden. The gilded cedar doors are wide open, as if waiting for me to pass through them. Palms, pink hibiscus, and creeping vines threaten to spill over the threshold and into the palace itself. Beyond the doors, a portico of fluted columns lines the huge garden, and my sisters are stopped in its shadow. I hurry to them.

"Someone is here!" Mayati declares, sitting her gold-bangled hands on her hips. She pouts her lips indignantly. I look through the flowers and trees, finding a tall, slim woman standing with her back to us. "It is *her*, again, and that means the little prince will be with her. In *our* garden! I will tell them to leave."

I look between my sisters in excitement. They must speak of another of Father's children, by one of his lesser wives. I always like to see these children, and I wish we could play with them; but Mother is too conscious of our status to allow that.

Meketaten, who often cringes when Mayati is mean or imperious, warns, "*Can* you do that? Wouldn't Father be furious?"

Mayati flips her braids over her shoulder. "No! *Our* mother is his chief wife, his Great Royal Wife, and we ought to have privacy! It is bad enough that boy must live in the palace with us!"

When they both rush away, I step down from the portico onto the white limestone walkway that borders the garden. The lady has disappeared around a clutch of tall palms planted tightly with fan-leafed bushes and short, braided hibiscus trees. She must be looking for the child; now, she turns and waits expectantly for my sisters, dropping into a respectful bow. My sister loudly orders her out, and I flush with embarrassment. Mayati should be more graceful!

I walk over to a bench of polished granite. As I sit down, I hear rustling in the garden behind me. I turn, and to my astonishment, I find a little boy in hiding. At sight of me his eyes widen and he goes stone still, like a statue. He stands under the trees, the blinking sunlight flashing on his copper brown skin. He can't be three years old yet, his ears aren't pierced and his hair isn't shaved into a prince's side lock, but he's not far from it. His hair curls into soft black coils like Father's does, swirling over big baby cheeks. His eyes are so dark their irises disappear into infinite black pools, the same midnight black of Father's eyes. He has a half a pomegranate in each hand. His mouth and chin are stained red from greedily biting the sweet seeds straight out of the fruit. I've never spent any time at all with Father's other wives or children, but at once I'm sure I've seen this boy before. I almost feel like I know him.

"Tutankhaten!"

A whisper of a smile creeps across the boy's face, and I smile back. He walks towards me, towards the woman calling him, looking up at me the whole time. As he passes, he stops and hands me one half of his fruit. Before I can thank him, he's gone, running away through the flowers just as quick as his little legs allow, his curls streaming behind him. As he takes the woman's hand, he casts one last look at me over his shoulder before they vanish into the palace.

"Ankhesenpaaten! What are you doing?"

Mayati and Meketaten are suddenly beside me, and scowling terribly. My oldest sister snatches the pomegranate away. She throws it into the garden mulch and I cry out in protest. "It was mine!"

I hate how sharp her face looks when she bends down, sticking her hennaed finger at me. "Don't take anything from him! He is our rival."

Our rival? I do not understand her. "But why should I be mean? My nurse says that I should be kind to Father's other children!" Surely, being the children of the Great Royal Wife doesn't mean that we can't have any friends!

"You know nothing!" Mayati accuses me. I grimace as my sister stalks away from the garden, her pleasure obviously robbed by Tutankhaten's presence and my stupidity. And if Meketaten leaves, there will be no swimming for me. But I want to know more about Tutankhaten!

Meketaten takes my arm softly and explains, "You're just a baby, you don't know any better. Tutankhaten's mother Beketaten

5

was our mother's greatest rival, and royally blooded too. She came to Amarna when she was fourteen, when I was just a little girl like you. She was breathtakingly beautiful, not like you but still gorgeous, and Father was quite mad to have her."

Well, that makes sense: that little boy was as pretty as a jewel. "So what happened? If he is a royal prince, why would I be rude to him? Should we not bow before him? Was that his mother the princess?"

Meketaten looks about, to be sure that we are alone. "Listen to me, little sister. Mother hated Beketaten; she was sure Father's new wife wanted to steal her title. None of his other wives had a chance, but Beketaten was flawless, and born to it. But then, a little before her pregnancy was announced, she did something terrible, so terrible!"

I gasp. "What? Tell me! Was she naughty? Was she disobedient?"

"Worse. I remember it clearly. We were in the audience room, and Father had just revealed that Aten would become the only god of Egypt. And Beketaten-I don't know how she dared, she must have had blood of fire-she told Father to his face that it was *wrong* to forbid the people their false gods!"

"She was a heretic!" I cry, and my sister pinches my arm for saying this so loud. That is very, very bad, the worst thing anyone could be! Poor Father, to have such an unfaithful wife!

"She turned on Mother, too, and called her an ambitious upstart, a grasping commoner, and other foul things not worth repeating. Father could bear no more of it. He was so angry; he grabbed Beketaten by her throat and dragged her from the audience chamber with his own hands. I remember Grandmother begging for her life, and Mother said he should behead Beketaten, royal blood or not. But she was pregnant, and she went down on her knees and begged forgiveness, she begged for the life of her child, and she had it; yet Father would never trust her again. She gave him Tutankhaten and died with childbed fever four days later, and that was the end of Beketaten."

"Oh!" I cry. I cannot help looking over my shoulder, to where the pretty boy stood moments ago. From all my sister's patient but confusing words, I gather but one thing. "He has no mother? Prince Tutankhaten has no mother?"

"Worse than that, Ankhesenpaaten. She is dead, but he will always be tainted by her heresy. Mother says he must never be trusted; she says our enemies pray for him to become king. His fool of a mother made her outburst before half the court, so that all of Amarna heard of her heresy."

"And what of Father? What does he think?"

Now Meketaten shrugs. "What can he think? Tutankhaten is his first born and only worthy son, but he has promised Mother that *her* son shall rule Egypt one day. Father sees to Tutankhaten's dignity, because he is divinely born, even if Beketaten was a wicked little traitor. No servant can look at him, they must prostrate themselves before him like they would Father, and the little prince has everything he could ever want or need. But Father only visits him once or twice a month; he cannot be around the prince for long without being reminded of Beketaten's cruel treachery."

I flinch at this thought. I am always left behind, yet I can't imagine being completely alone, with no one around me but servants who can't look in my eyes, and all the toys in the world but no one to play with.

Meketaten's eyes flicker in warning. "Don't think of it, Ankhesenpaaten. Mother has fought very hard to make sure her daughters have a higher station than the prince. It would be best if you ignored him entirely, until… until his future is determined, and Mother says it's all right."

I bite my lips. I certainly don't want to be ungrateful to my mother! But I can't help pitying the dark little boy with the long black curls. Surely, he shouldn't be blamed for his mother's wrong heartedness! Surely, her evil ways will not pass to him, as if his royal blood was cursed!

"We won't speak of this anymore," Meketaten declares. "I'll take you back to your nurse then make sure Mayati isn't very angry with you."

Chapter Two

Year Eleven

I do not see Tutankhaten again after that chance meeting in the garden. I know he lives in our house, though. Father's highest, most favored wives are stashed in palaces about the city, but with Beketaten dead and Tutankhaten having such a mighty claim to the throne, Mother likes him where she can see him. He must live on the far side of our mansion, near the bridge that connects to the Great Palace where Father does all his work. But Meketaten hasn't missed a moment to warn me away from him, and my nurse Tia rarely lets me be alone.

Anyway, tonight I have something else to be excited for: my first royal banquet. I bathe and dress to the roar of drums as they roll through the hallways, all the way from across the bridge. My heart dances with them, and I tap my toes as my nurse dresses me in a grown up pleated gown and little gold sandals. I have a new bracelet of red beads, with a very good and grown up gold clasp, and Tia has braided all my long black hair over one shoulder and clipped on gold barrettes. She even dabs a bit of glossy red paint on my lips-just a bit-and smiles when she holds up my mirror. I smile as well, to see how shiny my full lips are, and I try to imagine what I'll look like as a grown-up woman. My eyes are very big, a pale shade of brown that's full of gold and green and rimmed with thick black lashes, and my nose is delicate and very straight. It is a pleasing face, a fine face, just like everyone tells me. But still, I am a tiny girl. Mayati calls me a dwarf, actually; I wish I were tall and blossoming with curves like her.

Mayati and Meketaten wait outside my room. Mayati wears a stunning gown of deep blue, and even I know that the dye is imported indigo and very costly. It is very nearly sheer, too, and she looks every bit the woman already. Meketaten is always beautiful, in her soft way. Her dress is a very pale coral and it suits her lighter coloring. I think we look quite lovely all together; and when we pass the guards with their crossed spears, and walk through the tall gilded doors into the great hall, everybody applauds us.

My family sits at a high table before us, raised up above everyone on a granite dais. Father and Mother sit regally in their matching thrones, both with great gold collars about their necks. Father's eyes crinkle with his great, laughing smile, and Mother lays her hand on his arm affectionately. Happiest of all: my grandmother has come! She is not well now, everyone can see, but once she was a mighty woman who sat at my grandfather's side, ruling Egypt for many years. In her dignity, she wears no wig, but proudly displays her long henna dyed curls under a golden diadem. I adore her. My mother can be overbearing and frightening at times, especially if she thinks I've disobeyed her tight restrictions; but Grandmother always has a gentle smile and kind word for me, and she likes to ask me about my singing and my studies. To her, I'm more than just a fancy and fragile doll.

The court doesn't pay attention long after we are announced. There are far more exciting things: dancers wearing silver bells on their belts and musicians sitting on their shins throughout our great hall, playing their lutes and their lyres. The drums rumble lively, their flutes trill magically. They sit interspersed in groups around the massive lotus style columns.

The noblemen sit at the front of the room, arranged in low backed chairs before low tables stocked with wine and honey cakes, and every good thing that they could desire. Their women congregate a bit further behind the men, laughing raucously from their stools and low couches. Some of the women have placed little scent cones on their braided wigs, and the heat of the open flames melts the waxy cone so that the perfumed oils within are slowly released. The hall is filled by the most amazing smell of cinnamon, almond, orange oil, and myrrh.

As soon as we are sitting beside Mother, servants pile our gold plates high with duck and boiled greens and bread, and there is a tasty fruit sauce to dip our meat in. It is an amazing party, just as I imagined it would be.

Only, Grandmother does not look so merry. She is to Father's left, and hemmed in on the other side by her younger brother Vizier Ay, who has no royal blood at all and serves my father. Grandmother is always impeccably mannered, but her smile is shallow and her eyes stare away into the distance, as if she really wanted to be somewhere else. Probably with her husband, I should think. It wouldn't be very nice to be a widow, and her husband the old Pharaoh is nearly seven years dead. For four years before that, Grandfather ruled and Father sat to his left, and Grandmother was the first woman in the land.

"Is my dearest mother displeased?" Father asks, for he sees it too.

"No, son, I am a weary old woman; you should not trouble yourself on my account. Let me again offer you my congratulations, Pharaoh of Egypt. You have achieved the unbelievable." Her tone is muted as she says this; she sounds exhausted, as if she had just run, and lost, a great race.

"My king has achieved a great and undying victory, Mother," my own mother says, raising her cup as well. Grandmother tilts her head in a deferential bow.

Father says, "I thank you, Mother. But truly, Aten's victory is a victory for all. The people will understand what is required of them, now that there will be no more confusing falsehoods spread about by unqualified men. And you can sleep at night, my mother, without fear of unrest keeping you awake."

I bite my lips, wishing that I could understand what has happened. Does Father mean that he has defeated our enemies?

Poor Grandmother, who is tired and old and missing her dead husband! She is trying very graciously to be pleasing, and to be grateful to Father, who has obviously made our family safe again, and taught us all the right way to pray.

When the banquet is over, and I am drowsy and full of sweets, I ask my sister Mayati, "Have the heretics really lost?"

Mayati is glowing with excitement, breathless when she tells me, "The old High Priest from Thebes is finally dead. The soldiers found him in Nubia, of all places! Now the nomarchs from every district have declared for Aten at last. They will come to Amarna next year, to swear their loyalty in person! It is over. Father has won, and the true god is now the only god in Egypt."

Chapter Three

Year Twelve

It is so unfair, so completely unfair! In just months, Father will hold an enormous, triumphant celebration. Everyone who matters in Egypt will come to worship and swear for Aten, there will be ceremonies and banquets and feasting in the streets, and ambassadors from around the world will come with tribute. Of course, there must be entertainment for all these guests, and Mother wants us to perform a song and a dance. But I can't dance-I haven't even been taught-and so I'm going to be in the back with my baby sister, playing little ivory clappers.

I really don't care about the dance, but I thought perhaps I could sing the song myself. Why should my sisters get to sing *and* dance, while I sit on my shins and clap like a baby the whole time? My music tutor tells me that I'm so lovely everyone will be looking at me anyway, and my eyes fill up with tears. I don't want to be simply looked at, banished to the background like a painting or a statue! It really isn't nice to be gawked at all the time, never noticed for anything but for how I decorate more important people!

After our lessons, the tutor is so busy fawning over my older sisters that I get the reckless idea to simply leave. She won't notice, no one will. I back out of the room silently, and then I hurry through the cavernous hallway, crying, hardly caring where I go as long as it's away from my sisters and their eager plans for the dance.

But my tears slow as I realize-all at once-that I am totally alone. There are no guards in this hall, no nurses or sisters. I hold my breath, creeping along in silence. I am in the part of the palace where the royal tutors practice and study. The nobly born sons of Father's most loyal subjects learn here. I have taken reading and writing classes with Senqed just after them and seen them playing in the courtyards, tall and rowdy and nearly foreign to my eyes. Mother would not want me roaming freely around outsiders, especially rough young nobles!

"Are you all right?"

I nearly leap out of my calfskin sandals. A boy is behind me, and I thought I was alone. When I turn, I gasp in shock. "Prince Tutankhaten!"

He offers the most half-hearted bow I've ever seen; nothing more than the bob of his head, a token gesture of deference to my mother's station. His eyes are dancing; does he mean to laugh at me? "I am fine," I say quickly, wiping my eyes with as much dignity as possible. I take a quick look at him; he is nearly as tall as me now, and his hair is shaved into a thick, shiny black side lock. He wears a fine beaded collar around his neck, and gold cuffs on his bronze arms. He seems much older now, much changed, but again, I feel a deep sense of recognition when I look into his black eyes.

He motions back towards the library, where the royal tutor Senqed sends us to find scrolls for study. "You came past crying. Are you sure?"

My heart thumps chaotically. My sisters have warned me away from him. They have called him a usurper in the making, a boy tainted by heresy, a boy who could challenge Mayati's royal inheritance. But I'm too curious about him to turn away. I still remember his smile, and his gift of a pomegranate, and the terrible truth of his loneliness.

"I... I wanted to sing for the ambassadors, but Mayati

14

and Meketaten will." When I tell the prince, who never sings or dances for anyone and is hidden away as if he might be stolen... or steal something himself... it sounds quite foolish. It's only a song.

"It's nothing," I say quickly.

"You're a good singer," he says.

"Well, yes, I am better than *them*, anyway, but- How do you know that?"

"Oh... I'm always waiting for fat old Senqed, who takes too long to check my work. I was bored one day, I walked about. I saw you."

"You saw me? Not Mayati, or someone else?"

"It was you. I know you. You wore a green dress and pink flowers in your hair. There were six harps behind you."

"You watched," I realize.

Tutankhaten shrugs. "I did. Your voice is pretty."

I smile softly, looking down so he doesn't see how pleased this makes me. "Were you watching me today?"

"No," he says shortly. "I was looking for a text."

"Oh," I say, flushing red as roses. "Did you find it?"

"Not yet," he tells me. He has a strong way of speaking, the tone of a boy already accustomed to commanding those around him. But there is a deep shyness behind it all. I feel it. He says, "I thought... maybe you would help me."

"Me! I can try." Whoever asks me for help? I am the one to be helped, to be carried and fussed over, and kept back from anything remotely dangerous. A thrill of excitement rushes through me, the excitement of being singled out for something, of being needed.

"I want to borrow *The Annals of Tuthmosis III*. Do you know it?"

I look at him curiously. "Senqed gives me instructions to study. You know: how to live, how to behave." I walk past him, into the cavernous library, where from floor to ceiling there are scrolls of great wisdom.

"It is my own selection, not Senqed's."

I blink in surprise, wondering why such a young boy, who

ought to be out playing in the sun, would be skulking about in a dark library, seeking the stories of our revered ancestors. I know if I were him, I would want to spend my days running free. But Tutankhaten stands quietly beside me as I pull his scrolls down from the low shelf. It was easy enough to find them. They are all sorted alphabetically by author, but also by subject as well. Surely, spending so much time in the library, as the prince seems to, he would know that?

"Here you are: the story of The Battle of Meggido."

"Thank you," he says, with quiet pleasure. The sound of boys' laughter in the hallway draws our eyes to the door.

"I should go," I realize. But I don't want to leave. I want to know why he cares about Meggido, and why he wants to pass a bright summer day reading about a battle where even the winners are many years dead.

Of course, I do leave him, I must. But when I see that no one even noticed that I was gone, I wish I had stayed behind. Mayati and Meketaten are in the baths, spreading masks on their pretty faces and lying in steam. My plump nursemaid thinks I stayed overlong at music, and from this she decides to ask hopefully, "You were not given the singing lead...?"

I roll my eyes, and she begins to unbraid my hair for my own midday bath. "Meketaten has some of it, and Mayati the best part, the one I can do perfectly."

"Hmm. I imagine it is because she's newly become a woman, and it is a special time for her. You will have your own special days."

She combs my thick black hair carefully, smoothing the pretty crimp left by the braids. I watch her reflection in my silver hand mirror. I want very much to ask her about Tutankhaten, but then I will have to tell her that I wandered alone, and I think that's much better as a secret for now. And then, just as I'm biting back my words, Mayati comes to my door.

"Mother's gone away to have the baby," she says. She's run here straight from the bath, with wet hair and damp skin. "You must remember her in your devotions."

Mayati wants me to pray that it's a boy. I was just a little girl the last time Mother moved to her beautiful sandstone pavilion, with clinging vines and a big, beautiful pool in the middle. She will rest in relative peace before having her sixth baby, and pray Aten, it'll be a healthy boy. I know that a wife's main duty is to give her husband a living son, which Mother hasn't been able to do once in twelve years. Father has not named an heir yet; nor even indicated an apparent heir. He is waiting for his Great Royal Wife to deliver a son; he has promised that her son will sit on the throne of Egypt. It will please Aten, too, he says. Mother *must* have a boy.

So I forget the song, and my curiosities about Tutankhaten, and I pray dutifully for Mother to have a son. Since Mayati is a woman, she attends Mother, as does Lady Teye and my youthful aunt Lady Mutnojme, Mother's little sister, who lives in Ay's villa and almost never comes to court. Mother is surrounded by her kinswomen and the prayers of her people. But somehow everything goes wrong, and she has a girl. Even worse, she bleeds so much that she can't ever have a baby again. It's awful, but Mother and Father don't speak of it. They seem to hold their breath, as if the midwives' words were some awful curse that could be empowered through its mention. All attention is turned to Father's great celebration at the end of this summer. The world is coming to my father's feet with respect and awe, allegiance and tribute; and there are a million things to do for the glory of Egypt, Aten, and our house.

Chapter Four

For weeks before Father's Triumph, there is nothing but bustling and hammering as our subjects ready Amarna. They set up the courtyards for the ceremonies where the nomarchs will make obeisance to Father and Aten. They whitewash all the buildings, buff the limestone and granite walkways, and plant exotic flowers in every garden bed. They clear the streets of peasants to make way for great Nubian princes and Asian ambassadors. Barges stacked high with amphorae of wine compete for space beside the thousands of jugs of beer that will be given to every citizen, every day of the festival.

As the palace fills day by day with chests of bronze deben to gift the people with, and the halls with anxious, hurried officials, Mother sends for her oldest daughters-Mayati, Meketaten, and me.

I am the last to arrive, as ever. My nurse walks me through the halls and into mother's sweeping, airy antechamber, where the sunlight streams down in floods from the high, latticed windows. Along the wall there is a mural of Mother and Father together; they stand in a garden offering incense to Aten, who in turn blesses them with his life-giving touch. I know every last flower-mostly red and blue-because of the endless days that I spent walking with a basket on my head, back and forth, back and forth under my mother's watchful eye, until I could do it prettily. It would not do to stumble or limp, she said, and this is what I did while Mayati and Meketaten danced.

They are just beyond the open doors. Amber incense hangs in the air like thick, lazy fog. My mother stands in the center in a gauzy white gown, her hand held delicately in the air, as if indicating something. Her skin is the color of honey; her body is full of sweeping curves under the cloud-thin gown. Her lotion is full of gold dust, and so she seems to glow. Today, she wears severe make-up, thick green on her eyes, also sparkling with gold, and heavy black kohl lining her hazel eyes. She wears a wig of steeply angled black braids, touching the nape of her neck in the back and sweeping down to her chin in the front. But it is what she says that truly interests me.

"Things have... changed a bit, darling," she says, piling my sister's loose black curls atop her head with long ivory pins. Mayati has lovely, glossy hair; mine is thick, unruly until Tia tames it, spilling down my back in tight black ringlets that make my eyes seem very light. "You will be thirteen soon, well of an age for a husband and children."

"So why does Father not arrange it, then?"

"Because he is a young king, and young kings are ever reluctant to name their heirs. And none so much as your father, who has had a tumultuous reign already, as well as a father who he was... anxious to move away from. But you are his firstborn, his heiress. Prince Smenkhare will be a good match for you; you are brilliant, and he is pleasant, and easily diverted. When your father and I finally do cross over, you will be the true ruler of Egypt. That will please your Father. That is his true heart's desire."

I step into Mother's private sitting room, my eyes wide. I've never heard these things spoken of, at least not by my mother! So, she will make Mayati a Pharaoh's Wife, and that Pharaoh will be Smenkhare, father's half-brother. A melodious little laugh echoes from Mother's throat, and she smiles at me. "Come, little one. Your sister is thinking of marriage."

I cross the room and sit on my shins beside Meketaten, taking care to straighten my best pleated robe. Mother nods her head slightly, in approval. But their talk slides easily from Pharaohs to wedding gowns, Mayati wanting peach or pale green, and a diadem and matching jewelry set of gold and amber.

"Carnelian is better for a bride," Mother says, "Carnelian for passion, or green stones, for fertility. Or turquoise, because- Because it is a symbol of beauty and desire." Mother seemed to have bitten her own words back, as if she would have described the sky blue stone another way. "And so a white gown, or one of cream with thread of gold, would be better for those bold stones."

"What about amethyst?" I ask eagerly. "Amethyst is a good stone for a bride, isn't it?" I don't know why I say it, but in my heart, I have a sudden vision of a long, winding rope of purple. I can even feel it cold against my skin. I can't explain it, but I hear only one word, as if Aten whispered it to me. *Beloved.* I know somehow, as sure as I know my own name, that my husband will give me this amethyst. But who will he be?

Mayati laughs-a short, shrill and mocking noise-and asks me, "What would you know of brides?"

I feel my cheeks grow hot, but Mother's warm voice rides over my sister. "I am certain Ankhesenpaaten will know a great deal someday, my dear firstborn. Perhaps more than you might like."

Chastened, my sister sits back, her wide cat-like eyes appraising me in a new way. My mother's words should please me, but they only sound strange, forbidding, like a warning. I've never thought much about getting married, even though I've always known I would have to have a husband one day. But I wonder again, who will it be? Mayati will marry a Pharaoh, but who will marry me? And how will I like him? He could not be as magnificent as Father, so that will always be a disappointment. My father commands, but surely my husband must be bound to obey. Perhaps he will have to obey me!

I linger behind after my sisters trot off together. I know my nurse sits in the antechamber waiting, but I stand beside the door and watch my mother as she lays an elaborate collar of gold flower beads over her ebony vanity. She checks her face in the mirror, pushing at her cheeks to test the firmness of her skin. For a moment, I see sadness all over her, but then, in the reflection of polished silver, her eyes meet mine. "What is it, little one?"

"Mother, who will my husband be?"

She laughs softly. "That is some six years away, my darling. You'll not marry till you're at least twelve, so be patient."

I shift my weight nervously. I really want to know. After all, I will spend much more of my life as a wife than a daughter. I will spend much more time with this person than with my mother and father. This man, whoever he is, shall make me a mother.

Mother sighs, turning to me. "Ankhesenpaaten… you're a strikingly lovely girl. Perhaps it would be better if you were… less so. I fear..." She pinches her lips shut, denying me anymore of her cryptic words.

I don't understand; all of my life, she's told me that my beauty was a blessing, with a power of its own. Now it saddens her? *Frightens* her? "What do you mean?" I ask, stepping forward. There seems to be something wrong now, something concerning my future that pains her.

Mother comes to me, she bends her knees to reach my face, and then she smiles. But it is a hollow smile, I can tell. "I cannot tell you who you will marry. First, daughter, we must see what happens with your sister. Then… things will become clearer. But you must always love your sister, and not be jealous of her. And you must always take what good you can of your life, no matter what you are bid to do."

She doesn't want to tell me who she'll pick for me! Or maybe she can't; could it be that she really doesn't know, has never thought about it? Then why should she be sad about it? And why should I be jealous of Mayati? Will my station be so much lower than hers? Will she order me about, even when I'm a married woman?

"I assure you, little one, you will be well cared for. You will always be a princess, and you will never know want."

Well, that's a relief, I suppose. I thought maybe she might marry me to one of Father's servants. The way she acts, I thought maybe she was even embarrassed by the match Father has in mind for me! She kisses my cheeks and smooths my little beaded collar. "I must oversee the preparations, Ankhesenpaaten. You must go with your nurse now."

Mother's strange behavior only grows more so over the next few days. I note it in the way she holds Father's lean brown arm as they watch the gold canopy hung over a temporary wooden dais; she clings to it, instead of sailing along beside him. She seems to have lost him, even though he is right there at her side, like a caught fish slipping through her hands to escape.

Surprisingly, Mayati comes up behind me on the grand balcony. She follows my eyes, murmuring, "They don't share a bed anymore. She has shunned her king. I think she is afraid to die in childbirth, but she should look to her husband and lord. She should fear his displeasure more than anything else!"

"What do you mean?" It is strange to hear her speak this way of Mother. Her words are jarring, off-tone, just like Mother and Father in the courtyard below.

"Look!" Mayati draws her breath as a chariot rolls to a stop in the courtyard. A woman with a heavy braided wig steps down. Her dress is made of blue and green beads, and impossibly tight. She can take but very little steps as she comes forward to bow before Father, but incredibly, she can get herself down to the ground not only gracefully but gorgeously, never mind the tight dress. "Lady Kiya, a King's Wife. She has her own palace, but I cannot believe she comes here. He must have asked her to. Lady Kiya would love to see Mother-and all of us-bundled off in disgrace and donkey carts."

My father breaks away from Mother. I cannot see his face, but he gets so close to the woman when she rises that he seems to want to step through her. He must smell her breath, so close, and, offended for my mother I hope it stinks of garlic and onions. Lady Kiya laughs, but it is drowned by the air. She bows her head to my mother then, and takes Father's hand, kneeling low again as he holds her.

I whirl around to my sister. "What's happening? Why is Father acting so... so oddly?"

Mayati purses her lips. "He is Pharaoh; he may do as he pleases. It is Mother who has lost him. That's why she wants me to-" Mayati catches herself. She never tells me secrets, but I know this one already.

"To marry Smenkhare," I finish. He is much older than us; he's in his early twenties, and he has a wife already, but that has never mattered to anyone. She isn't even highly born, just pretty. I guess he's all right, but he seems weak, and he always laughs too hard when Father is witty. I wouldn't want him for a husband. He reminds me of one those little birds that hover over hippopotamuses, picking nits from their hides.

Mayati nods, and I wonder if she knows what I'm thinking. She's watching in that funny way again, the way she did when Mother defended me with her oddly chilling words. *She may know more than you like.*

"I must marry him before it's too late," Mayati finally murmurs, looking darkly on the scene below us. Across the courtyard, a porter drops a crate of faience plates and cups, all clattering to the ground with the high ringing sound of shattering glass.

I turn away as Father gives a loud shout to the man's overseer. "Before what is too late?"

She makes a sound of impatience in her throat and declares, "Before some woman steals Mother's title, her place, and we are all forgotten! He could have many more children, Ankhesenpaaten, many more. Who's to stop him from giving one of *them* the crown, if not Mother? She is not a born princess, you know. And speaking of that, there is always Prince Tutankhaten, with his rich royal blood, and spoiled rotten on top. What will *he* become, and what will he do to us if we're not protected?"

"He doesn't seem spoiled, Mayati," I say, forgetting whatever it is she cares about for a moment, as I think of the dark little prince. "Just… himself. He works hard at his studies, and spoiled implies that he doesn't deserve his gifts and talents. I am sure he does."

"You've seen him again? Alone?" she asks, her voice quick and sharp. Only now, she seems more interested in gathering information from me than yelling at me. Either way, I find myself shaking my head. If I don't speak it, is it still a lie?

"Hmm," my sister murmurs. She turns back to the courtyard, where my mother once more walks along with Father. She opens her mouth to speak to him, but Mayati and I watch her words die on the wind, as Father's deep dark eyes roam restlessly.

When Father returns, my three sisters run to him. He opens his great arms wide, waiting for me before snatching us all into a tight embrace. He praises us and asks after our schooling, and then he tells us he will open his treasury so that we each may wear new jewels for the celebration. "I have a rope of pearls in mind for you, my beauty," he tells Mayati. "Pearls from the Red Sea, a hundred of them, each bigger than the tip of my thumb. You shall be the first and finest young lady in the world."

"And what for me, *Abi*, what for me?" Meketaten asks.

"For my little gazelle, I have in mind a collar of Baltic Amber, more ancient than anything you have ever learned of in your studies. It once adorned the neck of a golden idol of Hathor, but now it shall be yours, for you are a real flesh and blood goddess."

When Father turns his eyes on me, I am too shy to ask, but my little sister who is still a baby cries out for her gift. Father offers her a radiant smile and says, "Why, I have your gift right here, little Nefer!" And just like a benevolent god, Father produces a shining gold bracelet from his voluminous pleated robe. It is just small enough to clasp about Nefer's little wrist, and as he sets the pin, Father tells us that this, too, was once wasted on an idol. He has melted all the idols down into talents, and taken all their jewels, and there is no one left to protest this since the High Priest of Amun was killed in Nubia. It is really the right thing, to take such pretty jewels from heretical temples and bring them safely to Father's treasury!

"Ankhesenpaaten," Father says, and I straighten up eagerly. "For you, there will be a collar of silver and turquoise." He smiles richly and says, "Yes, the turquoise is for you, my fairest little lady. I thought perhaps I would bring it now, but then I realized that such a grown girl as yourself would rather have her jewels delivered from the treasury master, as your sisters will. Can you wait?"

"I can, Father," I say brightly. I am often shy before Father's majesty; and never boldly piping up for a gift or word of praise like my sisters do. But now I flush with pleasure that he has seen *me*, that he knows I am a big girl with patience and gratitude.

And then he is gone, he has much to do, and we girls never can claim too much of Pharaoh's time. No matter what has happened with Mother, Father is brimming with joy, tall with the pride of his victory. It isn't just a victory for Father, but something much grander than that! Aten himself has granted Father's vision success. Aten himself has reached down and blessed Father with a brilliant achievement, unlike anything a Pharaoh has ever done or will do again. Father has turned the world about until it matched his designs, and he must have been very excited and nervous doing it; but now he has won and the whole world is coming to his shining new city to claim allegiance to the brilliant new god of Egypt.

Chapter Five

And then, finally, the first morning of the Triumph is here. We are woken before dawn, bathed, and dressed in the finest white linen. Our new jewels blink in the light of great oil lamps as we are put in our places behind Mother and Father and the High Priest Meri-Re, whose assistants choke the cavernous stone hall with sweet clouds of frankincense and myrrh.

The hallways close around us, and we are in a massive tunnel of stone that bends and magnifies the pounding drums right into our hearts. The crowd down on the Royal Road is chanting Father's name, and from the sound of it, hundreds of thousands of people have descended on Amarna. Mother has warned us again and again: this is the most important moment of Father's life. *Everything* must go perfectly. The people must see what glory comes to them when they bow their heads to Aten and Father!

We turn onto the bridge, towards the bright morning sun and the Window of Appearances. And what a sight! Truly, the entire world has packed between the palaces and temples of our shining new city! There are Egyptians from across the length of our land, but also Nubians as well, beautiful ebony-skinned men in red and white kilts, who have brought chests of gold and ivory and spices in tribute. There are Asians, with their colorful heavy robes and long curling beards. My father has even bravely invited the Hittites, wild northern men who are nothing but barbarians. It is whispered, fearfully, that their strange iron swords can smash a warrior's shield-or his heaviest of bodily bones-in a single stroke. But Father is not afraid of these hostiles, and so they have come with their hardy steppe horses for us, all to honor Father and Aten. The trumpets sound pure, high notes, and the people, Egyptians and Nubians and Asians and even Hittites, go silent and fall on hands and knees with their faces pressed to the ground in prostration.

As if it were not enough excitement, to see the petty rulers of every village coming on their knees to Father and swearing to love Aten above any false idol! As if it were not enough, to see all the great courtiers of Amarna arrayed like birds of paradise in all their finery! No! Now, as I prepare to enter the great banquet hall for what promises to be the grandest feast ever, Mayati pulls me to the side and exclaims, "You will never believe it! *Tutankhaten* is in the hall, and sitting to Father's left! He is introducing him to the entire world as the Prince of Egypt!"

"What can it mean?" Meketaten gasps.

"I told you: Mother will lose her place, and we will go with her! Look, he puts a heretic's son beside him, where I ought to sit! Can there be any other explanation? Father knows he cannot have a son from her, and he is testing the people's response to his heretic son!"

"What is Mother doing?" I ask, reminding myself that that is the most important thing, Mother's feelings, not that the curious prince will dine with us!

"What can she do? She is smiling and welcoming the praise of the noblemen, but anyone from Amarna knows what a bad turn this is for her! They all know she had a sixth daughter, and with servants' gossip, they might know the full truth!"

The hall is tightly packed and rolling with conversations that take three blasts of a trumpet to deaden. We are quickly announced, and loudly applauded. At father's side, the black eyes of the prince slide sideways. He wears a gorgeous pleated robe and a gold and carnelian broad collar. His black side lock is braided with golden beads. When we sit to Mother's right, Tutankhaten gives us all a dark smile, and Mayati forgets her own manners to glare at him.

And how beautifully he behaves, while Mayati steams! How elegantly he eats and drinks and washes his bronze fingers in the silver bowl of rose water, as if he had been sitting and practicing court manners every day of his life. For all I know he has, alone, curious boy! And when it is over, at least for the children, he makes a courteous and stylish bow, and everyone grins and applauds his precociousness. Mayati is careful to note this for her sisters, with a subtle widening of her eyes. *See? Look at him! He flaunts himself.* I wonder for a moment if she is right. Could our entire lives be altered because Mother can have no son?

Tutankhaten leaves before we do, going off with Maia his nurse. I want nothing more than to catch sight of him. We cross the sycamore gardens under the moonlight, and as the roaring banquet fades away, I hear only the swishing of our linen gowns and the small pattering of our sandals. Close to the bridge, where his room must be, I think I see a heavy cedar door sliding closed, but nothing more.

On the next day it is just us girls again, and Mother and Father together and beautiful. We process through the city in ceremonial chariots, standing stiff like statues under the hard sun. Our white sheaths have thread of gold stitched throughout the linen, reflecting the brilliant sun, Aten's face to the world. We are glorious, I know it. Father could never replace us! He was only proud of Tutankhaten, and why shouldn't he be? The Babylonians do not know Tutankhaten's mother was a heretic, the men from Byblos do not know his mother was a heretic!

The entire world has come, and now watches us process. They've come jubilantly, in all their beautifully odd costumes, ranging in fabric from purple wool to bright red cowhide to deep green felt encrusted with pearls. And of course, Egyptians;

I cannot tell them apart, the people of Amarna and the guests from the heretical districts, but none of that matters anymore. They all swear their love and loyalty to Aten now.

And then, the crowd surges forward. They are pushed up into the line of soldiers by another group of armed men. Something is happening in the background, along the processional route yet tucked in the shadows of the narrow cross street. Father and Mother-a pair of hawks-tilt their heads ever so slightly to examine the commotion. When I squint, I can just make out the figure of a foreign man taken away, roughly, his strange and heavy wool sleeves flapping around his flailing arms.

No one else along the route has noticed. Mother and Father do not seem to care, either. When we trot into the palace courtyard and stable boys collect our chariots, Mother straightens her immaculate golden gown and offers a radiant smile. Father reaches out his strong, gold bound arm and draws the Vizier Ay to his side.

"Everything is going very well, Your Majesty. Now, there will be boating on the river, and the men of worth will watch your horse master Lord Rameses and his chariot racing."

"And the oxen?" Father asks expectantly, as we sweep briskly along.

"Roasting in every quarter of the city. Bread and beer have already arrived. Music is everywhere, and I have just personally listened to a roomful of Asian ambassadors praising Amarna as the finest city in the world. They especially admire the Central City, with its wide avenues and beautiful squares."

"They have not appreciated the entire layout? Of course not; the Asian princes have sent me witty and personable lords, not astronomers."

"They shall know soon, Your Majesty." A few more paces, and Ay declares, "The mayors of Memphis and the other prominent cities shall present Your Majesties-" he smiles dashingly at my mother, "-with gifts of commemoration at this afternoon's feast."

Father laughs knowingly. "And what about old Mayor Ptahmose? He does not dare remain in Thebes…"

Ay grins. "He does not dare come, either. He reports to being stuck in Abydos with a flux."

"How disappointingly unoriginal," Father complains, and he and his vizier laugh again.

Mother looks once to Mayati. "Come along," Mayati tells us, Meketaten and me and little Nefer, who was scared half to death of her chariot and still shaking. We must go and dress again.

The great hall last night was nothing; tonight, the noise is deafening and the guests spill into the gardens. My mother has placed Smenkhare next to Mayati, and the prince doesn't miss his opportunity to speak with the First Daughter. Grandmother is, as ever, full of muted dignity and quiet thoughts; yet quick with a kindly smile for me. And, again, Tutankhaten is here. I could get used to him, I think, if he did not drive Mother and Mayati both so mad. It is brutally obvious, and Mother must not realize that in her flashy gown of netted gold beads, lapis studded cap crown, and heavy bright golden earrings, she looks like a beacon of broiling animosity. But Tutankhaten never says or does anything unpleasant. He's charmed Grandmother already; that is obvious. I've never seen her so pleased to sit at a banquet, and she's looking right at him. I don't think she cares at all if Mother is upset, and that's new too.

The babies are brought out, my two smallest sisters. Mayati should hold the baby up so the people can see her, but she is so stupidly wrapped into her conversation with Prince Smenkhare that she doesn't even remember. Mother-ever alert-motions to Meketaten, who quickly takes our baby sister and does her duty.

My younger sisters' reception also means that it is near time for us to leave as well. Tutankhaten is off first, gone away with his pretty nurse. Meketaten wants to take the babies back herself, and so she does. Mayati rushes to her chambers quickly,

31

her face flushed and happy. And I am left to walk along alone, my nurse thinking I am with my sisters.

I walk leisurely to the bridge. At the window, I stop to look over Amarna. The twilight is purple, the first stars are out. Everywhere, there is rolling music and singing and laughing. The air is tangy with herbs and sizzling beef, and underneath that the sweetness of a thousand blooming flowers. The massive garrisoned walls of the palace enclosure run along the river side, and across the Royal Road, the Great Temple of Aten is an enormous stone sentinel of soft white in the dimming violet light. I smile into the night, into my city, alive with one enormous celebration. And then I turn back to the hall, remembering my nurse, and I walk just slowly enough to savor the light and the scents.

There, in the darkness beyond the great doors of the King's House, a shadow stands against a flaming lamp. He doesn't stand then: he moves, slowly forward, pressed so close to the wall that I can't be truly sure he isn't more than a trick of the light. I swallow, and push forward, wishing I were not so dreadfully alone.

Suddenly, recognition. I rush on, as quickly as I can with my tight sheath and tiny, dainty steps. "Tutankhaten!"

He turns at once, and I swear his hands and his back push right against the wall as if he's been caught stealing. His eyes go wide like I'm a terrible apparition, and I realize I've scared him half to death! "I'm sorry!" I laugh, hand to my heart. "I was frightened, I did not know who or what you were! I'm so glad to see it's you!" I've coaxed a nervous smile from him, and so I ask, "What are you doing here, alone?"

Tutankhaten's still startled. He looks both ways, and truly I wish my own eyes were so black and could slide with such ethereal mystery. If Tutankhaten were a girl, he would be more beautiful than any of us with those dark and darting eyes.

Finally, he sighs; resignation of some sort. Just what was he doing here? "I am waiting," he says inexplicably.

"Where is Lady Maia?"

He shrugs in frustration. "Gone and coming back, some time."

"Why should she leave you here?"

"Shouldn't you get to your *own* nurse?" he counters, defiantly raising his eyebrows, his eyes flashing with temper.

I flush, and then I wonder if he really is trying to steal my home as Mayati thinks! "She is *my* servant, I am not hers," I attempt, at once ashamed to speak so about Tia.

He sighs again, and worries his lip between his bright white teeth. "Who else is coming?"

"I don't know. I am last for now."

Tutankhaten looks me up and down. "All right. I don't want to wait anymore. Will you help me?"

Again, he asks me for help. But this is something more serious than a scroll, I can tell by the anxious tightness in his shoulders.

The dark little prince grimaces. He looks down at his left foot, and following his eyes I see it's really very swollen in his gold-trimmed sandal. "I can't really walk right now. I sent Maia for a crutch, but I don't want to wait anymore. Help me go home."

Chapter Six

At first, I'm so shocked that I don't know what to say. To see the mysterious, brilliant young prince hiding away like this, because of some injury, is quite confusing. And then, ridiculously-and oh, so hopefully-I think, *would we make a pair, he and I? Is this Aten's sign, that he is the friend I've prayed so hard for?*

"I *said*, don't tell anyone. I don't think your mother knows." The way he says *your mother* is almost like he spits it. Of course; he's a perceptive boy, and he must know that he'd have more of Father if it didn't make Mother so mad. And Beketaten called our mother *commoner*. Perhaps he really does think he ought to be Crown Prince.

But I really don't care. A smile flushes my face. "No, I won't tell a soul. You can trust me."

Tutankhaten sighs, and I see that he's quite upset. So I say, "Listen-you must know about me, right?"

He narrows his eyes, but his voice is soft now. His eyes seem endlessly dark, the eyes of a creature estranged from the ordinary world. "I know... I know what I see for myself."

I twitch the linen of my gauzy white robe up, and tilt my little right foot. "Broken the day I was born. So I know what it is to be hurt, even if I was a baby when it happened. Mother forbids me everything fun because of it. I won't tell anyone you hurt yourself," I promise him, even though I can't imagine

35

why my mother would grudge him for that. I can't imagine why he is so desperate for secrecy. I wonder how he did it, my mind racing through different scenarios: he was wrestling, running, diving off the harbor wall into the river. When I look at Tutankhaten, I get the feeling he would do all of these things, and more. He is like a firebrand, just waiting to touch the coals.

His eyes sparkle in the moonlight, just like the first stars of night came into them. "Is that why you don't dance like your sisters?"

I flush. "Yes. I can't do anything they can, and Mayati makes sure I remember it. And Mother never lets me go anywhere, she treats me like I'll break. Again, I guess. Tia-my nurse-does whatever she says. I hate it."

Tutankhaten stands up then, coming beside me. He smells clean and sweet, like mint and cardamom. "I need to-" He lifts his arm and carefully drapes it over my shoulders. "Like this."

I don't know why, but my hand reaches up and holds his as if it were pulled. The other I slide about his slim waist. I expect him to lean hard on me, but he barely touches me at all. Still, I can feel the strength of him, like one of Father's imported lion cubs whose young tawny bodies are full of force and spring.

"How did you hurt your foot?" I ask. I turn my face up as a warm, sweet wind rushes along the bridge. Before us, the King's House lays open, the sycamores swaying and shaking their leaves. There's a flight of stairs leading down to the courtyard, and I wonder how we'll best negotiate it.

Tutankhaten doesn't answer me. "It's nothing," he says dismissively. And then, "I guess they don't let you ride the horses, do they?"

"Oh, no, not really. I have a little mare, but she's very old and slow, and I don't get to ride her much. But I love her... I love the stables, and all the horses."

"I like the stable best, too," Tutankhaten agrees. He goes on to tell me that Lord Rameses gives him his lessons five days a week, and that he loves the desert horses bred by the Bedu tribesmen far to the east. But then he tells me he loves all the animals, especially his six dogs. He talks about animals the way I do; he knows that they're not just creatures but individuals, each one different from the next. Another thing we have in common! Oh, could he be mine, really mine, as Mayati has Meketaten? He wouldn't make fun of me for wanting to catch the little green lizards in the garden, or for swimming with fresh braids in my hair. And he certainly wouldn't make fun of me for not being able to run, when he's injured himself, for as long as it lasts! But I hope for his sake it's nothing serious.

Oh, I like Prince Tutankhaten; he seems to like me, too. As his guard comes down, his smile widens, and it's just the brilliant sort of smile I knew he'd have. When I talk, he fixes his fathomless eyes on me; he just soaks up everything I have to say, like my every little word matters. It feels so wonderful! Best of all, Tutankhaten doesn't treat me like my sisters and mother do, or like my father does. He doesn't talk to me like I'm a delicate doll or an annoyance, nor the most beautiful girl in the world, expected to adorn and stay nearly silent. I can't explain it any other way than this: he speaks to the person inside me, who no one else can see. We're halfway down the stairs before I realize it, taking them as easily as we'd stroll through the garden.

His bedroom is on the far side of the King's House; the rooms of our most intimate servants are nearby. His nurse Maia is shocked to see us together. She is a gorgeous woman too, but one whose features are set off, beautiful and strange at once in the dancing lamplight. She frowns, and puts her arms out to Tutankhaten, but he turns to me and smiles. "Thank you, Ankhesenpaaten. You shall not-" he purses his lips, and softens his voice. "I trust you, not to tell."

"Never," I swear. "I'll never tell your secrets."

I can barely pull myself away from Tutankhaten. In the darkness, I can see that his chambers-larger than mine, after all, but not as large as Mayati's-are full of shelves and scrolls, and neatly stacked boxes. How I would like to know their secrets! But not tonight. Tonight, I leave him at his gilded door, the gold on his neck and wrists glowing warmly in the firelight. The light streaks across the dark courtyard, and doesn't disappear until I've stepped back into the portico before my own door. He watched for me, to be sure that I made it safely home.

Tutankhaten, Tutankhaten! I'm a thousand miles from sleep for thinking of him, and the blossoming feeling that we're meant to be true friends. But I climb dutifully into bed, and Tia gives me warmed milk with cinnamon. Her gently lined eyes dance perceptively. "What is it, my little lady? You are steaming over something."

I bite my lips nervously. Mother's never truly told me not to play with Tutankhaten; how could she, without being disrespectful to Father? But Mayati will be furious if she finds out… if we really do become friends. Oh, I hope he wants to! I can't help myself. "Tia? Do you know anything about Prince Tutankhaten?"

"Prince Tutankhaten?" Tia asks in surprise. "Was he at the banquet?"

"He was, Tia, tell me about him!"

"Well… he is a clever boy, I hear, always at his studies. He can be quite demanding sometimes, but that's no surprise, with how he's brought up, as a young god."

I cannot give his secret away, not even to Tia. But I do wonder how he hurt himself. So I ask her, "Is he… does he like to run and wrestle, with the other boys?"

Tia clucks her tongue softly. "He is Pharaoh's son, child. He may not run wild with the young lords. But I believe he is learning to drive his own chariot, earlier than I have ever seen it done."

Did he fall from his chariot? How terrible! It is a rough sport, but of course he would want to master it. After all, Father is a hunter, and so are all of his courtiers. And then I see it so clearly in my heart that it could be right before me: Tutankhaten, galloping too fast in his chariot, laughing as the wind whips his side lock about. Yes, I think he would love it, rough sport or not.

"You should sleep now," Tia says, lifting up my sheets. She arranges the fine curtain around my bed and backs away, leaving me to listen to the music drifting on the warm night air.

I never really sleep. I just fade away, imagining the lights and musicians in the great hall. I see the great, worldly men in all their dazzling jewels, and Father and Mother presiding over it all in golden splendor. I imagine they are laughing, toasting their beautiful victory, reveling in their triumph.

And then, I hear my door opening, and there are voices in my room. I sit up at once, and I realize the music has stopped. "Is the party over?"

Mayati, veiled by the curtain, sounds utterly terrorized. "Get up and bring what things you can grab quickly; we are going to Father's chambers. Tia is packing your clothes."

"Where are the guests?" I ask, very tired and very confused. I push the curtains back, and my sister's face is positively grey with fear.

"They are going back to their homes or barges, or their apartments in the Great Palace. Musicians are in the courtyard to entertain them as they leave. Hurry now, there really isn't any time left." Her voice holds steady as she pulls me physically from my bed. She throws a robe over my shoulders and snatches the few things she thinks I might want: a box of small jewels and a silver mirror, my ivory comb, a glass bottle of lavender perfume. Without any word at all, she brings me deep into Father's apartments; through his small throne room, where the sharp faced Vizier Ay stands at attention, past his antechamber, and to his private rooms. Mother and Father do not even notice us; they are huddled to one side of his Aswan granite desk in furious conference.

"What is going on, Mayati? Have we offended our parents?" I ask, horrified.

"What? No, sister-" she grabs my hands. I am stricken when

I see tears in her eyes. "Sister, Ankhesenpaaten, someone has brought plague to our city!"

When the plague was in Babylon, Senqed told me last year, one in three people died. They had raging fevers, hot enough to make them crazed, but that isn't the worst. On their bodies, on their necks and in their armpits, putrid black swellings disfigured them. No one would tend the dying. No one would care for the dead. This cannot be the same thing that has come here? This is Amarna; such a horrible sickness cannot come here! I could not die in such a disgusting and painful way! I could not die at six years old! I am stone still and mute with terror at the thought.

Mayati and I will stay here, in Father's chambers, and nobody has said how long we will stay here for. Meketaten is not with us, either. She is staying with our little sisters in the nursery, and the really fearsome thing is why: *The little girls were not overmuch at the festival, Nefertiti. And only Meketaten touched any of them. Let them stay together; their chances will be better.*

We none of us have any sleep; no one even thinks of preparing for it. Mayati and I go to Father's bed, but we sit apart and alert, waiting for any news. I think Mayati is afraid to breathe near me now. Am I infected? How would anyone know?

I suppose the fever would come on first, or perhaps a sore throat. Dear Aten, is my throat sore now? I push my hand to my head to feel if I am burning. It is no use: the night breezes are not blowing, and suddenly the entire chamber seems brutally hot. Blessed Aten, we could all have it! Tutankhaten! Will he be safe across the courtyard, so close to the servants? Oh! I bow my head and whisper a long prayer to the god, begging him to protect all of us.

My father's words cut into my prayer. "No, Nefertiti. We do not want them all here. The stench would be unbearable, the water would be fouled. They must leave tomorrow, when they learn of it."

Mother counters him, "There would be trouble, with all the people leaving at once. There would be chaos, and death, and damage. And they will carry the illness with them everywhere they go."

"They shall not rot here!" Father yells, and I shrink into myself, shaking with fear. People, rotting. I cannot think of it.

"You mustn't let them go, my lord. It will mean a nightmare for Egypt. I beg you: send your soldiers out to lock down the city!"

"Leave it, woman!" Father says, smacking his desk. The golden *merkhet* hung by line from a stand swings softly. Mother retreats unhappily. I sit in shock at his words, contemplating a gruesome reality. It cannot be real, here in my home of soft breezes and sweet music. What good is being Pharaoh's child at all if I can still die so terribly? I cannot think of death. I have never seen it, not really. The only times I have heard death spoken of, my father has been happy. We say we shall cross over to a beautiful world. My father will join with Aten as he pleases, to travel the sky, and we shall live in a lush riverside paradise. This is because we are the children of the god. But we cannot anger Father, for he holds the keys of immortality. He can damn a man physically and spiritually, killing his body and his soul both. He has done it, from his throne room, with but a wave of his hand; and the condemned was taken out, beheaded, and his body execrated and burned. Surely, with such a power over life and death and immortality, Father can keep us alive! So there, I think. I cannot die, not forever, not really anyway.

But then, why are we quarantined? I try to understand it, but I can't. I lie back on my father's bed, watching him and Mother whisper harshly to each other. Mother is terrified, plainly. No matter who survives, something awful will happen just outside our house.

In the second to last hour of the night, a little more than an hour and a half before sunrise, the Asians and the Hittites run off together, to make their way north. A Nubian prince, returning from the ambassador to Kush's party, is quick to spot them and make his inquiries. The harbor is choked with traffic at sunrise; by then, every Egyptian knows that death is breathing heavily on Amarna. Vizier Ay, the only one with cold enough blood to pass Father's orders with infection likely everywhere, brings us this news, and worse. In the first hour of this new day, there is a stampede at our docks, and the Mayor of Abydos loses a son among a hundred other trampled victims.

By nightfall, there is silence in the city. It is the silence of death, I think. Never before did I notice all the noise around me, living here in the King's House. The footfalls of servants, heavy doors pounding shut, laughter from the gardens: all are gone. Solitary birds sing outside on the rooftop, but even they are subdued, as if they, too, hold their breath in terror.

But it is nothing to what comes next. Once the city is emptied of all who live elsewhere, excepting those dead Hittites who likely brought this devastation to Amarna, the citizens get on with their dying. The plague spreads virulently in the poorest quarters. The pestilence cripples the commerce harbor, and Mother reminds Vizier Ay quietly to draw the chains across the palace harbor, if he has not yet done so. Each day brings new reports, a hundred dead in the night, three hundred. It is as if an angry god took a sickle to us, slashing us down like stalks of wheat at harvest. But how could this happen, when we have just given Aten such glory? How can this happen, when we are the god's own children? *We* will not die! We cannot catch plague! We are only locked in the four rooms of Father's majestic apartments for... because-

Mayati cuts into my thoughts. She tells me that the dead are now so many they must be burned, with no chance for an afterlife at all, and I descend into panicked tears. Mother, high strung and wretched, slaps Mayati across both cheeks but cannot comfort me. Dear Aten, we will die! Aten, god of my father, *how* can this be? We were just rejoicing in our victory! I dare not ask my father this, but within the hour Mayati voices my fears. Father, wearing a hole into the floor with his caged pacing, stops short and says, "Maybe we will die. Maybe we will not. More likely, we will live and our city will die. Someone has done this thing to us; it is not Aten's doing. Someone meant to destroy Amarna, at the height of my glory!"

We lean back on our shins, and Father continues in his brooding. He wants the city searched. He wants an investigation. He wants to punish someone for this horror, but he is trapped away by the quarantine he himself ordered. He can do nothing. He can hear screams and miserable wailing from the street far below, but he cannot rush out to put order to any of it. Father is burning himself up with helpless rage, and his family before him is still with terror.

Our meals are delivered only to the door. Mother retrieves them herself, four times a day. She will see none of the servants, none of the kitchen staff. Our help leaves all our food at the door. They leave water as well, and Mother bids us to bathe unsatisfyingly from buckets. They leave two jugs of strong date palm wine also, and blocks of opium resins; Father cannot lay himself down for sleep without it. His glory is in ashes, and that is a terrible thing for a proud man. It has gotten worse in Amarna. Mayati says that stable boys have died. The plague is behind our walls now.

For one week, for two weeks, there is only silence. I want to ask who has fallen sick, but my parents' eyes are odd, and they frighten me. Finally, Father tells us that he knows a bit about plague. We do not know why it comes (but he is sure it is not the doing of an angry Aten) or who it strikes, but once it is in a city it will swirl about, claiming its victims with a vengeance. Until, he says, suddenly, it will stop. Presumably it has taken all who are meant to succumb, or are so weak that they succumb,

43

and it moves on or vanishes entirely. "You see, my darlings, we none of us are sick at all. My blood is not weak. We shall live, my beauties, and together we shall rebuild. We shall rise from the ashes like the Phoenix of legend, and be greater than ever before."

He holds Mayati and me in his arms, and he speaks over our heads to Mother: "I shall not be defeated by this, Nefertiti. The Hittites sent their infected here, I am sure of it. It is not Aten's doing that thousands die in Amarna, when Aten is finally victorious. It is humiliating and surely all will blame me for it, for a while, but we shall find ways to heal and divert those who survive. We shall endure, as our images carved into the eternal cliffs shall endure."

Mother nods reassuringly, but then she shakes her head. "Oh..." she moans softly, "But your enemies will survive also. We know that this is not Aten's doing; but they *will* ascribe it to their forbidden god. Those who seek power will surely rally the simple people into a religious fervor, and they will attack, in droves of hundreds or thousands. This is just the crisis they have prayed for, just the thing to give hope and power to the conquered!"

Mayati gasps, and we both look up in fear to Father. The heretics will return? When they have been hammered down so fiercely? They will attack us?

Father's chin lifts in defiance. His voice is cold, smooth as gold. "Let them test me. If they have not lost enough of their kin to the axe and the deserts and the mines! If they have not tasted enough of my fury, let them come for more! They have no wealth now, no leaders and no hope. If they wish to martyr themselves, then I am pleased to grant them their righteous death!"

Such talk is frightening. I do not like to think of blood and killing, not even when it is done to our enemies. I lay my head against my father's broad chest. His strong hand cups my head softly, he smoothes my tight curls down. His voice is as rich and smooth as honey, but somehow it makes his bloody words all the more terrifying. Can he so easily take life?

44

"My lord," Mother says, her voice cool. She can see my wide eyes.

"Come," he says, directing all of us. "We shall pray here, together, right now."

Then, suddenly, it does stop, just as Father said. There is shouting in the hallways. A servant runs along, banging on the outer doors. His muffled cry is easily and eagerly understood. "There are no new sick! There are no new sick men today!"

Mother covers her little gasp with her hand. Her eyes fall brightly on Father.

Mayati demands, "It is over? Can we go out now? Can we *bathe?*"

"Not yet, ladies," he commands us. "Not for another two days."

But then, my heart breaks. I hardly hear Vizier Ay, but his lips move so slowly from his ashen face that there is no mistake: my sisters are dead. Tutankhaten is alive, but Meketaten, and my youngest sisters, all took the plague and died in the nursery. All their nurses, all their servants, all but three scullery maids in the outer chambers are dead. It is an entire wing of death in our home. It is like the plague blew a fine and fatal breath along one full side of the King's House, with four of my sisters trapped inside.

My mother cries from her guts. She sinks to the floor, one hand to her heart and one over her belly. She wails her misery, her body rocks from it. After a long spell, she turns her tear soaked face up to my father, and there is only one question in her pleading eyes: *How?*

The entire room rings with the words that no one will speak: is this Aten's judgment on us? Or perhaps... could it be the punishment of the old, forbidden gods? Father swallows, and the knot in his throat hammers up and down with it. I can see him breathing, heavy and still. His eyes shut, and he turns his face from her. He puts his hand on Vizier Ay's narrow shoulder. "I shall see it, then," he says with cold, stony courage. "Take me to my daughters."

Chapter Seven

Year Thirteen

Everything is different now. For the first few weeks, Mother kept Mayati and me at her side. Actually, we attended her more than she clung to us. She lay in bed, and we brought her tea and sang her songs, hoping that she would say anything at all. She seemed dead too, like so many of her babies. We thought she might like to go to the Great Temple, to take her trouble to Aten. But when Mayati offered to ready a private litter for her, Mother's heart broke on her face, and she rolled away from us. "No, no..." she said, her voice sick. I didn't understand it, but Mayati's lips pinched together in a thin line.

"We shall go," Mayati said to Mother's back. "We shall give thanks for our lives, and pray for Father."

Mother's shoulders fell in a great exhale, but she did not forbid us.

Father is another matter. When my four sisters died, it was as if Father took a great step back from all of us. He's not mean, but he speaks to us more like... more like he was just our king, not our father at all. Perhaps somewhere inside his heart, he is afraid he might lose us anyway, so he ought to harden to us now. I don't know why I think that: Father has never shown an ounce of fear in his life. And he is still a giant in his court, defying our cruel fate with fierce determination. But we are no longer a family, at least not as we were; it's like our parents think that Mayati and I died with our sisters. Every morning I leave flowers for Aten hoping he will heal us, and for my sisters in the next world.

Mayati watches this anxiously, her teeth nipping her thumbnail, her eyes darting around like some animal on the hunt. She does not pray for family, she prays that Father won't dump us off. "He could send us to another palace... He could move another woman into Mother's chambers, and start a new family. He might think we're accursed, you know. He would want to be rid of us."

"Why must it always be *that* with you?" I ask, exhausted from it all. "Father is not thinking about a new family! He's just lost the one he favored most-four of his six daughters by his chief wife."

"You don't know what you're talking about."

"Yes, of course," I say angrily.

"No-" Mayati sighs, tilting her head so her long braids swing over her shoulder. She looks very much like Mother, with the sculpted line of her jaw and her intelligent eyes. "What I mean is, you are too young. You weren't alive when Father commanded Beketaten to his side. You see only Father, the king who gives you sweets and praise. But there is much more to him, things you're too young to understand. You must trust me. Our mother has long held a favored place in his heart. After all, she was the first to embrace Aten, and Father is weak for her beauty. But Father cannot bear tragedy. There is no place for it in his world. Our sisters' deaths will become our Mother's problem, and Father will extract himself and start again. He is young, he is blessed, and his eye is easily taken... It is natural. Everything depends on the girl he chooses-if she is ambitious..." Mayati bites her lip.

Her words are upsetting. Father is Pharaoh, not heartless.

He could not be as careless as that, not with us! But still, I ask, "What... what do you think will happen to us?"

Mayati shakes her head. "I cannot know. But I'll fight to keep what I-what *we*-have. If he gives another woman the title of Great Royal Wife, then any children she has will be solid candidates for the throne as well. And she'll ever be trying to diminish us in his sight."

"Unless you marry Smenkhare, as Mother wants. Then he'll be the next Pharaoh, right? Right?"

But my sister does not answer me, so I say, "Do you *want* to marry him, Mayati?"

She nods her head, lowering her eyes. "Sometimes. He's handsome, and... well, he says pretty things to me. And he would let me rule. But if he isn't going to be Pharaoh, then what would be the point?"

Now that Mayati and I are alone, I *must* attend the banquets, every one of them. It is not enough to be seven years old, either. Now I have to wear very grown up gowns, in a rainbow of colors, and very heavy jewels. My sister's amber collar-Hathor's amber collar-is mine too. Tia brushes glossy red ocher cream on my lips and lines my eyes dark with kohl, and then she hands me my silver mirror. "You see how pretty you are?" she asks me, a smile on her plump, kind face.

It is really true; with the kohl, my eyes are wide, and the swirl of green and gold and pale brown seems to glow behind the thick rimming of black. The shiny red color makes the wide bow of my mouth stand out, and my honey bronze skin shines in the firelight. I press a shy finger to my lips, and I smile. I am not as vain as Mayati, always with her face in her mirror, but I can't deny that I have been blessed with something to be grateful for. Aten was generous with me. But then I see Meketaten's collar around my neck, and I feel guilty that I'm alive and she is gone, shut away in a dark tomb. "I want to wear the silver," I say. "The silver and turquoise that Father gave me." Maybe he will see it, and remember that happy day.

Maybe he will come and talk to me again the way he used to, if he remembers. Tia clasps the ornately worked necklace around my throat, and sets a *seshed* circlet with hanging silver beads over my hundreds of straight, skinny black braids.

When I first enter the hall, I feel a wash of relief: Mother is just taking her place at the table, and she has put off her pale mourning robes for a deep blue gown. But then, my sister grips my fingers and I see that she was right! There is some *girl* beside Father, a timorous, trembly-looking creature with big brown eyes. I recognize her as the High Priest Meri-Re's baby daughter; she is really very young, younger than Mayati. And she is not *nearly* the beauty Mother is!

The girl bows her head with stiff courtesy as we come up the dais. I can't imagine how he could look at her and not Mother. I can't believe that Mother's eyes only widen for a moment, before she, too, makes a stylish bow to Father. He doesn't seem to think anything's the matter, because he grins at her boyishly and raises his golden chalice in greeting. "You were right," I whisper to Mayati.

"Of course I was right," she hisses back. "This little fool-" she throws a nasty look to the young lady beside Father, rejecting the girl's attempt at courtesy, "-won't last long. But there will be others: dangerous women, not just awestruck children. It was like this when I was small."

Father's new bride sits stiffly at our table, too terrified to smile as waves of courtiers wish her well in her new life. Father turns from his general's conversation every so often, so that that she can refill his chalice with deep purple wine. I think Mayati is right, though: he pays her very little attention. What could she possibly say to Pharaoh, this common young girl?

And then, surprisingly, Tutankhaten is announced. I must not turn to him. I really can't, not with Mayati at my elbow instantly, fury steaming off of her. Only when he walks up the dais, and bows to my father and mother respectfully, do I dare glance up from under the silver beads dangling from my *seshed* circlet. He meets my eyes instantly. There is a hidden smile of greeting on his lips, nothing anyone else would note.

Though young, he knows very well the world he walks in. Tutankhaten looks incredibly regal with a golden diadem on his head and thick gold cuffs about his arms; he is proud, and it shows in every motion he makes. I approve immensely. And he is obviously healed.

Now the crowds of guests go back to their seats, and servants carry archery targets into the middle of the room. Servants shuffle onto the dais, half bent over. They give Tutankhaten a small bow and a quiver of ivory tipped arrows, and the herald announces that Tutankhaten, Prince of Egypt, will shoot for the pleasure of Pharaoh and his guests. Mayati-already feeling disadvantaged by another woman in her mother's chair-catches her breath. Everyone applauds, and I snap my head back to the prince to see if he will please them or faint from all the expectant eyes. He has rarely seen the court, and now he looks down, out at the waiting lords. Some are drunk, with ruddy faces and laughter in their eyes; some quite obviously look away, at the flower adorned girls serving the wine, or their half-eaten plates. Tutankhaten plucks an arrow, and slowly sets it to his bow.

"Go on, boy!" Father calls, his voice slurry with drink. "Do not be a coward!"

Tutankhaten's body tightens noticeably, and I cringe in sympathy. Why should Father yell that? He never speaks that way to me! It seems that is the very thing to say to *spoil* Tutankhaten's concentration!

But then, quicker than anyone can see, Tutankhaten makes his shot. The arrow buries itself just outside the center. And then another arrow, and another, five in all, in rapid succession, clustered in the middle of the target like a constellation. The men break into startled applause, and some laugh warmly. As Tutankhaten turns to bow for Father, his chin is very high, and there's a dark gleam of satisfaction in his eyes. Father breaks into laughter, and he stands and extends his arm to Tutankhaten. "Come, sit by my side."

Father says something very quiet, very quick to the girl at his side, go or get or something of the sort. She stands and hurriedly backs away, into the sunset of gilded red and orange curtains behind us. Tutankhaten walks slowly, cautiously down the dais, his eyes taking everything and everyone in. He must note the tightness in my mother's smile, Mayati's burning stare, the hawkish interest of Vizier Ay. He seems so small before them all, the long braid of his side lock curling over the shoulder of his white tunic, his narrow wrists covered in gold. I wonder if he is afraid as he sits in the girl's chair, and is presented with a cup of unwatered wine. His lips touch it, but his throat doesn't move.

"He's good at archery," I murmur to my sister, hoping that she'll ease off him a bit. He knows about his mother, he knows that Father's enemies would look to make him king, and therefore he cannot be. He should be our friend, our ally, especially if my sister's predictions are true.

"Isn't he," Mayati muses, cold and unyielding. I know she would have preferred that he failed, and it makes me sad.

Another servant comes running down the far side of the hall, and I look expectantly to Tutankhaten; but this man rushes straight past the prince and brings a scroll to Father. With a flick of his wrist, Father cuts the seal. He peruses the message quickly, and then murmurs to young General Horemhab over Tutankhaten's head.

When he speaks to all the men around him, Vizier Ay and Horemhab, Meri-Re and the architect Paranefer who is planning a new temple, he says, "They have taken the bait. Our enemies have stepped out of the desert and into our sight, and now we shall destroy them."

Chapter Eight

In the silence of bright mid-day, when most all the court is sleeping or bathing in the wilting heat, Mayati comes to my room. She beckons me to follow her again. She has painted swirling vines and flowers onto her hands with henna, and now she presses an intricately patterned finger to her lips. "Come quietly, never mind your sandals."

My eyes widen at her request, and I jump out of bed. It was like this with the plague, just like this, Mayati beckoning me from my bed with urgent whispers. I think of the anonymous acts of violence now occurring outside Thebes: Pharaoh's warehouses torched, garrisons overrun in the dead of night by peasants with black paint on their faces. Could we be under attack now?

Out in the hallway, there is nothing but soft silence. A servant polishing the hallway's wide bronze lamps drops into a bow, and we go on, towards Mother's chambers. Mayati pushes me back before we round the corner. Within moments, one of Mother's maids comes out, and Mayati pushes one of her little silver rings into the girl's hands. The servant has left Mother's outer door open, and now my sister wants to enter uninvited!

"You are mad!" I shake my head quickly.

"Shh!" Mayati grabs my hand and together, we slide through the opening, into the darkness of Mother's empty presence chamber. I cannot really be doing this! If anyone comes out, Mayati will bolt, and I'll be caught. Perhaps that's why she's brought me! Now, we've sidled up beside the inner doors, and Mother's voice is strong beyond them.

"It was never something I considered before," she is saying. "How many nobly raised women would?"

"Do you not think I would have told you of this sooner, if I thought you could be helped? My lady, it is simply not foolproof, and I would not have your life on my hands."

Mayati flushes with excitement, and I am quite terrified, wondering what Mother could mean to do. Her life? Mother's *life?*

Mother's hard sigh is audible. "Nani, I was a fool to think… I did not know him as well as I thought. If I lose my husband's love and favor, then what is my life worth?"

"You have had many great misfortunes lately, this is true. But the herbs do not always prevent conception. The magic is strong, but there are stronger in this world. If you were to conceive, and bear a child, you will die. You must accept your fate, Your Majesty. Look to your children; they will need your protection now."

"This is not my fate! This is *his*, and I shouldn't suffer it. I never meant for this to happen… I never meant to deny the goddesses! I didn't know he would go so far! You must beseech them not to punish me so! I will offer to them when I can-"

My sister makes a little choking sob, and then she clamps her hand over her mouth. I don't understand… Goddesses? Mother couldn't believe in any goddesses, not immortal ones! We believe in Aten alone, as Father taught us! And what can she mean, punishment?

The older woman's voice is quiet, almost reproachful. "You are your own goddess now, my lady. You have made it so. What need would you have for the old-fashioned guides of women?" My mother remains silent, and the old midwife says, "Accept your fate, wife of Pharaoh. You still have mortal flesh, and no mortal can defy their fate."

"No, Nani! I order you to bring your potion!" Mother's imperious voice cracks, and wavers. "I cannot lose it all…"

When Nani still does not respond, Mother declares, "You will not defy *me*, witch woman! You will bring me the herbs to prevent conception, and if I conceive you will care for that as well. And you will have a bracelet of gold, and we will never speak of this again."

Mayati turns on her heel and scurries out, and I clench my fist not to scream as she leaves me alone. But no one catches me as I make my escape. My sister stands breathless into the sycamore garden, her hand on her chest. "She is false, she is false!" Mayati whispers. She looks at me, and for the first time in her life, there are true tears in her eyes. "How is that possible? They built this city together, for Aten! They built it all, for Aten, and he raised her up to Great Royal Wife, in Aten's name!"

"She is like... like our enemies?" I ask, puzzled. I was born in Amarna, when the whole city was under construction. I know nothing of old gods and goddesses, other than my father's talk of heretics and crooked priests. I cannot believe that when Mother was a little girl, she was taught to pray to this *Amun*, rather than to Aten. And as for goddesses... Father only speaks of us, not these celestial ones Nani and Mother hiss about!

"I can't believe it..." my sister says, distraught.

I hate the sadness in her pretty face, so I speak of something else. "What does Mother mean, potions and herbs?"

"So she doesn't get pregnant," Mayati says, her voice growing scornful. "She's going to trick him, try to play the wife again, after she stupidly turned him away. I don't see how it will work, and... At least the Seer's daughter is a true believer, who wasn't corrupted by the earlier times, before the truth came to Egypt." She looks down at me and warns in a hiss, "Say nothing, to anyone. Not even your nurse. Can you do that?"

I nod, stung by her sudden change towards me. It's never true sisterhood with her; she always turns on me, always grows cold or mean.

A sudden sound, and we turn our heads at once. The ancient

midwife is coming through the courtyard, leaving the King's House. She wears a blue merchant's shawl over her white robe, even in the heat, even in the Great Palace. Her hair is nearly white, yet a thick mass of braids. She wears little paint on her eyes, but the gaze from her brown face is respectably and beautifully profound. She looks steadily at us, as she walks to the steps leading from our house to the bridge. I think she knows we know, and she will hurry back to Mother and tell her that her daughters are little spies. But she looks away from us, and nimbly climbs the stairs.

Mayati spins about quickly, her gown swirling about her ankles as she goes back to her apartments to sulk and plot.

But then, as I am about to go to my own chamber, I hear my name called lightly, as if it were carried on the wind. My sister's door slides shut, and I turn. Prince Tutankhaten stands in the portico outside his door, watching me.

I go to him at once. "Where are you off to?" I ask boldly, noting his athletic attire. He is wearing a short kilt and no shirt, and his only ornament is a pair of gold arm cuffs, miniature versions of Father's. I look down and note that in his sandals, his left foot is tightly bound up, in a protective manner I have only ever seen wrestlers use before one of the court's gambling matches. I narrow my eyes and ask, "You are not better?"

He laughs and says, "First answer: I'm going to train. I must practice galloping."

"In the chariot?" I ask, astonished that he would drive two frothing beasts at such a pace. He is just my height, and I am a small girl!

Tutankhaten grins and his dark eyes gleam brilliantly. "No, on horseback. I ride *and* drive. I must be ready for the winter. Father will have me blooded in my first hunt if I can handle my chariot and my horses well enough by then. He has promised, and given me four horses of my own. Triumph is the best of them."

"And your… your injury? Did you break your foot?" It doesn't look that way to me, but why is he all wrapped up, so many months later?

He shakes his head smoothly, making the pure gold beads capping the braids in his side lock click together. "It's not broken, Ankhesenpaaten. I just... I have pain, sometimes. It can get pretty bad, and I don't like to walk when it does. That's what you saw before... well, last year. My physician-Lord Pentju-says it won't ever get any better, so I have to work twice as hard when I'm well."

I don't understand. He suffers, like I saw last year, all the time? "How did it happen?"

Tutankhaten shrugs his shoulders easily. "I don't know. It's just always been that way. It doesn't hurt now, but Pentju's convinced I need to do *this*," He indicates the binding, and rolls his eyes. I grin, thinking, *so you do listen to somebody.* "Anyway, I don't care. If it doesn't hurt, I don't even think about it."

"You are still lucky," I say quietly. "You can still do whatever you want. You can race horses and learn to hunt."

His head tilts slightly, and his eyes narrow in pleasure. "Yes, I am lucky."

"And are you still studying Meggido?"

He laughs again, as if he was pleased that I had remembered. How could I forget such a strange thing? "I still study battles, on my own time. Senqed is burying me with geometry now. And then I must learn all the rites for the Great Temple, and Akkadian as well, when I'm not charting the stars in the sky."

"How busy you must be!" By now, we are walking along together. It's happened naturally, without my noticing it. I like this proud boy, who unlike Mayati seems to wear no mask before me. I have never met anyone like him, and I admire him already. "And obviously, you must practice archery as well..."

Tutankhaten grins. "I saw you watching me."

"You were not nervous at all, to shoot before Father and all the court!"

Tutankhaten shakes his head. "No, truly I was. Especially-" He bites his lip, just like I do, and I swear I can hear his thoughts: *especially after Father got on me, called me coward before everyone.*

Then his glittering black eyes meet mine and he says, "But I saw you watching me, and I knew I had a friend, and so I wasn't afraid at all anymore. And I shot better for it."

I flush with delight. "When can I see you, Tutankhaten? Will you be at the banquet tonight?"

"No," he says. He takes the steps carefully, and then stops, with one hand on the door to the bridge. "But I'm usually in the library after my morning lessons. Come whenever you can get away."

"I will," I promise him happily.

"I can't be late." Tutankhaten offers me that radiant smile again. "Goodbye, Ankhesenpaaten. I'll look out for you in the library."

"What have you been up to?" Tia asks me, scurrying behind me as I come through my door. "You must take your bath, quickly now! Your lady mother has sent over new jewels that she bids you wear tonight. Did you forget you were to go to the banquet?"

"I was speaking with Tutankhaten," I announce, testing her.

She makes a little *tsk* noise. "Your mother wouldn't approve of that!" Tia holds out her hand to take my stripped gown, and she wraps me in a lightweight robe.

"I don't care, Tia! I've lost almost all my family, and I like the prince. *You* said he was a clever boy, and he is! You always encourage me to take more interest in my schooling, and I'll bet Tutankhaten knows more than Mayati! I'm going to meet him in the library some time, and you just can't tell my mother!"

Tia raises her eyebrows, leading me to grab her arms and cry, "Oh, you can't, Tia, please! There's no harm in it! Let me have him, Tia!" I'm astonished to feel big, fat tears rolling down my cheeks. I want to be friends with Tutankhaten more than anything. He is mine, I know it; he is the one I prayed to Aten for so many times. We barely know each other, but he's my best friend already. And I know he feels the same way. And now, with my other sisters dead and gone, and Mayati crazy about her inheritance…

"Hurry up, child," Tia says softly, conceding without speaking of it. "You don't want to be anything less than perfectly prepared for tonight."

Chapter Nine

Father's sandals smack loudly over the walkway of the Great Temple. His lords and their wives and children have all come to worship together, while we, the remainder of the royal family, worship in the privacy of the inner chambers. Now we walk together, after prayer, and Father sees his headmen. He speaks quite frankly before Mayati and me these days, as if we were no longer children at all but courtiers, private courtiers whom only Father may speak to.

"He is a *dangerous* bastard," Father clarifies soundly. "Already, he has a hidden network of devotees, who think he is divinely sent by Amun to challenge me. They are of wretched station and desperate, I am sure. They have no more formidable weapons than their stealth and their zealotry."

"Many of his followers will be known to the common people, Your Majesty, and the common people can be bought." This is General Horemhab. No one mentions that he would know best about commoners because he is the lowest of a commoner, the lowest born man at court I am sure. He is a broad faced and massive man, coarsely built, but full of rakish confidence. He has climbed to dizzying heights under my father, who admires men bold enough to change their condition, so long as they are beneficial to his laws. First, Horemhab brought those soldiers loyal to Amun to submission and paid them off to build Amarna. Then, he whipped up a great force of men to protect the city. He went off to Nubia to pacify the Ayukati, and now he will hunt heretics, all as Father pleases. He is younger than Father but not by much, and never did two more different men walk together through this world.

Father agrees, but adds, "You must employ the whip with the bribe, General. Your soldiers will find some men to make examples of... for heretical speech, inciting, and obstruction. Make it memorable, and be sure to put rumors into the streets of Thebes that one was killed for *not* informing on his brother. And, as you said, we shall make it no secret that we bring gifts for all those who come forth with information that leads to justice."

"And The Slave, Your Majesty?" Horemhab asks. The Slave is what he is called in Amarna, but he has whipped up a religious fury around Thebes by calling himself Amun's Slave. We know nothing about this rebel but that he is a poor man, a basely born bastard from a line of whores. But somewhere in that messy, ambiguous blood there is a trace of an old dead Prophet of Amun, as rumor tells it, and this has given our shadowy menace something of credibility among the peasants of the south.

"Let it only be known that I shall hunt him until he is ashes at my feet, and anyone who can lead me to him will be considered lordly in my sight."

Horemhab bows at his dismissal. He swirls his cloak behind him as if he is so very important, his wide shoulders swaying as he stalks away.

"What a fool this slave is," Mother purrs, stepping beside Father. "He shall be dead and forgotten inside a month."

"I don't doubt it," Father says, almost merrily. "I almost prefer a princely enemy, Nefertiti."

She laughs musically, and draws the architect Paranefer into their conversation gracefully. "I drove out to see your new temple, my lord, and it is coming along magnificently. Your Majesty's choice of red granite on the pylon is especially stunning. Tell his Majesty, Paranefer; the entranceway will be completed soon, won't it?"

"Indeed," Father's favored architect says, his voice of silk as always. "I had ample time to fit Your Majesty's alterations with the plans, and now we shall see completion of the first phase within two weeks. I daresay it will be Your Majesty's most beautiful project yet." Paranefer is years younger than Father, but he is of ancient breeding and he knows far better than to discuss the reason *why* he had so much time: the shipments of granite were threatened by this Slave's activities. Such precious cargo, floated on the current all the way north from Aswan and worthless if cracked in any way, could not be lightly risked when one in twenty ships are fired or sabotaged in the southern ports.

Father is pleased with his temple's success, so pleased that he makes a rare concession. "It will be *our* most beautiful project yet, Paranefer. A jewel to crown seven years of masterpieces!" He is even so pleased that he slips his arm about Mother's waist and walks her along like he is a proud new husband.

"Mother's taken the herbs," I whisper to Mayati once we are back in our hall.

My sister doesn't seem very impressed. "The danger is still there. But maybe... maybe she can keep our place, and make me a Great Royal Wife after her. I will never bow to some baby, some other woman's child. I swear it, by Aten himself."

I watch her dart off to the baths, and I shrug my shoulders. I am fortunate to be a third-well, now a second-daughter, who need not care about inheritance. I need not think of it for another moment, actually. I must meet my singing tutor, and so I turn away from the fleeting glimpse of floating linen robes that is my sister.

Chapter Ten

It will be ten days at least before I can sneak away to visit Tutankhaten. Father is courting Libyan chiefs and desert warlords from the southwest, all in an effort to secure mercenary soldiers. He feasts his guests with exotic, expensive meats dressed in thick, succulent gravies and richly spiced marinades. Vegetables in creamy, garlicky sauces sit beside confections of giant ostrich eggs; cakes are packed full of dates and dried fruits and drizzled with honey-butter. We girls must be on hand to delight the dignitaries, day and night. His boring little wife isn't with us ever, and I'm glad; Mother is back in her rightful place. We drink the finest wines of Egypt, complimented by tall earthen jugs of specialty wines from far off Cyprus and Crete. Father, the grand, golden host of it all, compliments me with his insistence that I drink a cup of golden Cypriot wine, unwatered (because watering would be an insult to the wine); it's warm and delicious and dizzying.

When Grandmother makes a late appearance at a banquet, I'm stunned to see how thin she is. But she holds herself tall, and her silver diadem flashes from her hennaed hair. She walks gracefully up the dais, and bows as easily and prettily as a fifteen year old. Immediately, she turns to Father. "Son... I hear many rumors, even in my sickbed. Is it true that you will make more war on fellow Egyptians?"

Father smiles winsomely, but there is something sharp to

it all, like a lion's smile as he stalks the desert mountains. He sweeps his hand elegantly down the table, towards the lower ends, where his foreign guests sit devouring a rich-gravied roast. "It seems that way, Mother."

Disdain pinches Grandmother's lips together as she looks at the foreigners.

"It is not *my* doing," Father says, shaking his head. "My enemies plot against me, so I will have them removed. You look much better today, Mother. I hope your health continues to improve."

His blessings for good health don't reach his eyes; in fact, he almost looks like he is threatening his own mother. For the first time in my life, I see something inside my father that I had never recognized before. It is something beyond simple ruthlessness, something much more deadly, something ugly. Perhaps the plague brought it out, or perhaps it was always there. I don't know, but by Aten, for the first time in my life the sight of my father-the look on his face, the forward, aggressive tilt of his body-chills my blood. His enemies must fear him terribly.

Grandmother says, "I thank you, dear Son, but I am now past caring if I remain long in this world. My place is made in the next, and I do not fear the journey."

For some reason, Father is displeased. He sits back in his chair, brooding over her words. *My place is made... I do not fear the journey.* Those words, so simple, yet so heavy with courage and serenity, seem to ring around my heart. Grandmother stands calm and proud, skinnier than a girl but hard as stone, until Father waves his hand. "Sit, Mother," he says shortly, and perhaps I'm not the only one who finds his curt treatment of the noble lady bitter to my eyes.

And then, a few days later, while my nurse is off finding me fresh fruit, a messenger comes to say that my singing tutor is ill. I dismiss the messenger at once, barely holding back my smile. I feel terrible as Tia comes in, her thick legs moving slowly and her face full of love, but I don't tell her a thing. I am not treated as a little girl anymore, so why should I tell my nurse everything like a little girl would? After my breakfast, I head straight for the library.

Tutankhaten looks up when I enter, as if he were expecting me. A wide smile appears on his dark face. He doesn't rise to greet me-which tells me in that moment what he thinks about his station in life-but indicates to the chair beside him with a little nod. I curl into the chair excitedly, and ask, "What is all this?" Before me are countless opened scrolls, full of graphs and angles and annotations that are really quite beyond me.

"The sky," he says plainly, as if it were the most obvious thing in the world. "These," he says, with a motion of his elegant hand that directs me to a chart, "are the thirty-six decans. They tell time, rising forty minutes apart. We can tell anything concerning time or direction with the stars. Pharaoh has planned his city by them, and by the sun's path across the sky."

"I'm not taught astronomy," I murmur enviously.

"I'll bet you know Kochab," Tutankhaten says encouragingly.

"The North Star."

"Well, if you know Kochab, and you measure him and another star with a *merkhet*, then you can find your position or tell the time as you need to. It's useful not only for building sacred temples, but in case you must navigate the desert or even the sea. I could show you," Tutankhaten offers. "You ought to know."

"In case I must lead men across the desert?" I ask with a giggle.

Tutankhaten grins and says, "In case you build temples, too, and you want them placed correctly, and you want to know it is right without asking a priest."

I don't think I would build a temple, but that really doesn't matter. I want to know.

Next, he produces an ivory *merkhet*, a fancy version of a student's tool, and then we are quite occupied with foolishly measuring points about the room and making angles between them. I have never cared more for math, and when Tutankhaten sets his pointer on a bald scribe's head as if it were a shining star, I burst into loud, disruptive laughter.

"Mother would say I've forgotten myself," I tell him in a forced whisper. "I hope the librarians and scribes won't speak to her about this."

He shakes his head quickly, a small, confident gesture. "They say *nothing* about me or what I do. But maybe next time we should go for a swim instead. This is supposed to be a quiet place."

"Ooh, could we? Even just in the lotus pool?"

Tutankhaten bites his lip slowly, debating himself. "Sometimes... in the early evening..." he looks about, to satisfy himself that no one of any real importance is in earshot, "the sacred lake in Pharaoh's private chapel is deserted. All the attendants are feasting in the great hall." And then: "Oh. But *you* have to go to the banquets all the time. Why?"

"I don't know," I tell him truthfully. "I wish I didn't. No one talks to me at all, except Mayati. And I'm always tired with my tutors in the day, because I am up so late. But do you really swim there?" The sacred lake is supposed to be rejuvenating, purifying. The only ones allowed are Father and Mother, even Mayati and me are barred. I could laugh to think of little Tutankhaten, sneaking in for a twilight swim while everyone is roistering in the hall without him. It is very wrong, but still, I smile in delight at the thought.

"Maybe you won't go to the feasting one night," he suggests. "Maybe you'll have a headache. The water is warm and the air gets cool. It's perfect."

"I don't know. I can't imagine... We could get in trouble."

Tutankhaten smiles enchantingly. "It's worth it. And the priests who maintain the chapel always drink too much wine. They wouldn't see us if they *were* there."

Chapter Eleven

And then, at the end of the summer, there are no more banquets for me to attend. The Asians and Libyans have gone home, promising to send mercenaries to Father's border forts for their assignments. The days are still parching and hot, but the flood waters are gone. In their wake, a heavy layer of silt and mud stains the fields across the river; it scents the air with a fine, damp, earthy mist. All of the canals and artificial ponds are full of sparkling, nourishing water, reflecting in their depths a cloudless turquoise sky. The buildings and walls of the city are bright with new whitewash, the city has been scrubbed top to bottom, and now the peasants are waiting to plant the blackened fields.

For once, the days and nights are almost quiet, and my hours are briefly my own. We still feed a respectable crowd of dignitaries and notables, but I need not be there in all my finery. And that is how I find myself naked, halfway into the water, eyes closed, my curls held clumsily atop my head. My eyes are shut in fear, but I am laughing.

"Come *on* if you're coming!"

"I don't know-"

"You only cheat yourself," Tutankhaten warns. And then he is gone, swimming through the dark blue water just like a lean bronze fish.

I look about the high white walls of the beloved chapel.

There are tamarisk trees growing around the perimeter of the small, rectangular lake. They are nearly black in the deepening indigo of nightfall. Torches line the pool, glowing orange in the water and throwing the grey silhouettes of the trees on the towering walls. And here I stand, skinny as a reed, wavering in waist deep water. It's so warm, lapping around my belly. The air is cooling, as the desert night settles into the river valley. I take a deep breath and sink into Pharaoh's sacred lake.

When I come up, breathless, refreshed, Tutankhaten is treading water before me. "Catch me!" he cries, diving away. I race him across the pool. We laugh and splash, we float and open our eyes underwater, trying to make out each other's dim outlines. And then we sit on the steps, with the warm water up to our chests, and he tells me, "The chapel attendants will be back soon. They never stay out too late, since they must prepare for worship at sunrise. The other morning, the junior priest was hungover, and he spilled the sacred oil." I look at Tutankhaten and blink in surprise. I'd had no idea that he worshiped Aten with Father, alone at sunrise, while we girls lounged in our beds! He splashes a tiny bit of water on my exposed, bent knee. "I'm glad you wanted to come."

"So am I," I say honestly. "Thank you."

"I think I should teach you to ride a horse; really ride, that is," Tutankhaten tells me, quite seriously. If I didn't know how old he was-a year and a half younger than me-I could never tell. He could be five or fifteen as it pleases him, as if time has no hold on him. Tutankhaten can do anything he wants, I am sure.

But this is still Father's house, and I am still forbidden many things because of being delicate. "I doubt I'd be allowed. I doubt Lord Rameses would even bridle a horse for me without Father's say so. Besides, I could be hurt."

Tutankhaten raises his neat black eyebrows. "Then we'll bridle one horse, and you can sit behind me, and we'll canter together. You will love it; it's like rocking on the river to seat a cantering horse. And with me you'll be safe."

"Tutankhaten... it would be disobedient." I shake my head. "I long to, really, but I can't."

I think he will frown, but he just smiles that warm smile. "Whatever you like."

It must be so strange and wonderful to be him... the only one he need obey is Pharaoh. Lord Rameses would not deny *him* a horse! Tutankhaten asks me urgently, "But you'll swim again, won't you? You'll come back and see me?"

I nod, splashing the water with my fingertips.

His eyes sparkle with delight. He climbs out of the water, quick as a kingfisher, and winds his kilt around his skinny body. He slides his golden cuffs back onto his wrists and looks down at me. "I'd like that, Ankhesenpaaten. We must be the best of friends, now and always."

Chapter Twelve

At midwinter, when the days are growing cooler, excitement boils in the sycamore grove. It is our own excitement, mine and Tutankhaten's. He has proven himself, and now he will hunt with Father and his dearest friends.

Yesterday morning, Tutankhaten brought me to check on his horses and run his red hounds about the arena. He has trained them well, and softly. They listened for his sharp, quiet words, and he shouted far less than the Horse Master, Lord Rameses, who supervises all the beasts and bellows for his hounds just to sit. Tutankhaten badly wants a hawk. We lingered about when they were brought out in their hoods, and the great men going off to hunt were warm with him, approving of his interest. Tutankhaten ordered the servants to let him offer a bird its chunk of flesh at the creature's meal time. And then he showed me his chariot, in the back of the enormous royal stables. Tutankhaten told me they will cross the river and go into the Western Desert, and test the steadiness of the prince's bow on ostriches as fast as horses.

"You can shoot while you're moving?" I asked him, impressed.

"Oh-you must have a driver when you want to shoot seriously." Tutankhaten told me, as he leaned easily on the beautiful cedar fencing. "I can ride with no hands, and I want to drive with the reins around my hips to see if I can do it.

Father likes it when I try… But if you *really* mean to shoot, you can't be bothered to steer yourself."

"That's better, isn't it? To have a driver?"

To my surprise, he made a little face. "It's much worse. I had to practice just that for a while, keeping my balance with someone else steering. For me, it's better to be in charge, to know first in my heart that I will turn this way or that. But I can do it now, and I want to make my first kill."

Now, it is early morning, and the servants carry several trunks out from Tutankhaten's bedroom. Tutankhaten's clothes for the trip must be loaded onto the barge. They will sleep in the desert for a week, with the scorpions and snakes and jackals. I can't imagine it, but he is thrilled.

"They'll be loading the horses onto the barges now," Tutankhaten says eagerly. He turns to me. "I have to do it, you know. I *have* to see my own arrows in the bird."

"If your shot moving is as good as your shot standing, I am sure you will," I say softly.

"I know…" His eyes are wide with anticipation. "At practice, yes, but out *there*?" Tutankhaten motions to the west. "I *must* do it."

I see him off, assuring him that he will be brilliant. He squeezes his shoulders to his ears and pinches his eyes shut. It is so very important that he is successful here. It would have been everything for Father, too, and for any prince, to be a hunter and an athlete, even a warrior if needed. Tutankhaten is small in his kilt and robe, but by the end of a week, he will have made his first kill in a difficult and fast paced sport.

But as much as it is for Tutankhaten, his first hunting trip will be quite boring for me, I am certain. I'm growing accustomed to seeing him in the library, pouring through all the scrolls Father has collected. And though I long to join him at his sport, but I fear disobeying my parents, it's still fun to watch him ride his horses. Tutankhaten shows me how to make a horse curvette and rear up, or canter pretty loops down the sandy course. His seat on his horse is ridiculously steady, naturally, as if his body were just a pendulum swinging easily with his horse's motion.

I decide to go back to my nurse, because there will be no one to talk to. Father is gone, Mother will handle any petitioners or problems that arise, and Mayati has been an enigma lately. My nurse spends the midday hours braiding my thick curls tight over my head to cascade down one shoulder, and then, restless from all that sitting, I go off to walk in the gardens.

I adore the rose garden. Roses were imported by a Pharaoh many years ago, and they are grown all over the palace grounds. But only the rose garden is flushed full of this exotic, deliciously fragrant flower.

Yet I see that I am not alone. My sister is behind an ebony trellis... with Prince Smenkhare.

Right away I think I ought to leave, but I can't. My feet have grown roots. Mayati has never looked so... so *girlish*, so lovely; it is incredible, like she's another person entirely with him. Her cheeks are flushed like the roses, her words are high and breathy. I can't hear what they say, but Smenkhare is murmuring something close to her ear, and it draws a sweet laugh from Mayati. And then she pulls back, shaking her head. I can hear her say, "No... my father would have your head."

"But he knows we are meant to be together, everyone knows," Smenkhare says. He steps closer, his voice silky as he claims, "*Aten* knows we are meant to be together, and soon you will be my wife."

This catches her, and before my eyes, he lays his hand on my sister's cheek. His whisper carries on the warm, rose scented wind. "It's only a kiss..."

My heart quickens; she tilts her face up, and lets him put his mouth on hers. Why should she do that? And why should he want to taste her, like she was some sweet fruit? I can see my sister sigh, and for a moment I think, *how pretty they are together.* I've not seen Father and Mother kiss this way since... oh, for years.

But then, I don't like it. Mayati is different, not herself, and it isn't nice anymore. It's like… like she's given him her mighty strength. She doesn't let anyone touch her, or tell her what to do, but here this man has gotten his hands around her, Pharaoh's firstborn, and it weakens her. What if he only wants power? What if he is not as Mother thinks, content to drink wine on the side, watching others take all the glory for themselves?

I don't want this prince, this son of my grandfather's lesser wife, to see me watching him coax my sister into giving up whatever it is he seeks from her. I back up the steps and disappear into the portico, into the shadows.

Chapter Thirteen

The men come in from their hunting party in high spirits. They've made many kills, and the giant dead birds-blessedly relieved of their long, ugly necks and heads-are given over to servants. There will be meat, and fine leather, and beautiful plumes for fans and ornamentation. Tutankhaten descends the barge a star, at the proud Pharaoh's side, his face glowing with high emotion. I clap my hands together and I wish I could run down the stone quay and hug him before everyone. I know he has done it!

But then, a servant in white robes does run down the quay, his back bent in the shuffling approach one must take before Pharaoh. Father good naturedly indicates that he should rise and offer his message. When he does, Father's face transforms as if rare storm clouds raced south to blast the sun.

"They have killed themselves," Father swears, marching along so quickly that we struggle to keep up. He doesn't even take a moment to bathe or change from his hunting clothes before issuing his orders. "Dispatch more soldiers, Horemhab. Clean out the village; end it. And this time, you yourself will go, at the head of my mercenaries. Then, go on to Thebes. Set martial law on the city. I want curfews, summary executions for any disturbance of my peace. And put that damned Mayor Ptahmose under house arrest!"

"Your Majesty," Vizier Ay says quickly, his bow still slung

over his shoulder, "We've had no intelligence that suggests the mayor has anything to do with this."

"I care not! He is a plotter, an instigator!" Father barks. He shakes his head at Ay's stupidity. "One man making trouble, I can understand, but it is impossible that the peasants would stir themselves up this way! There will be treacherous lords and fat purses behind this, mark it."

The heavily muscled, pale-eyed general clears his throat. "Your Majesty, I must beg your forgiveness."

"Oh? Continue."

"Your Majesty, as you said, this is certainly a wider conspiracy than we first believed. I must implore you to let me send a captain to deal with the south. My place is at your side, Divinity, overseeing what will certainly become a larger operation."

"You think this will spread? You think this is a threat to me, here in Amarna? You think other cities will join with Thebes, perhaps even the northern cities?"

I gasp softy. This has always been the worst fear: that the people, the masses of common people, would incredibly rise together to defy their sovereign, their lord, their god on earth. If such a thing were to happen, there would be no mercenary army in the world to save us!

Horemhab bows his head. "I believe that it has gone beyond one peasant ringleader. It is beyond one city. I believe Your Majesty does right to turn suspicion on what strong men remain in Thebes, and to restrict the mayor's activities. It will be for his protection, of course. But again, I must beg you: do not send me from you now, with such a storm brewing!"

At my side, Tutankhaten, staring at Horemhab's broad back, furrows his brows.

"Then send your man, Horemhab. Have you someone in mind?"

"I would honor the Grand Vizier's son with this mission. The young man has become a skillful leader of men, and he has a fist of granite. He would not flinch from the task."

"No, why should he?" Father asks quickly, as if this task

did not involve the extermination of an entire Egyptian village, and that done with foreign axe men. I cringe at my own graphic thought.

But then, Vizier Ay interjects, "Nakhtmin is not ready for such responsibility. He is but sixteen years old, willful and at times careless. Such a task must be entrusted to a dependable older man."

"You speak against your own son's abilities?" Father asks incredulously.

Ay lowers his head reverently. "My first duty is to Pharaoh, Your Majesty, even above the advancement of my own family. It would be a spectacular honor for my son, but alas, I do not think him quite prepared. I would be neglecting my duty to Your Majesty to second the good general's proposal."

"Very well. I shall send General May into the south, and Horemhab, you will prepare plans to deal with any wider disturbance. And Vizier Ay, you shall continue to head my spy service and issue bribes to informants. Treasurer Panhesy knows to accommodate your needs."

At the Great Palace, the grown men sweep away from us. Tutankhaten's achievement has been eclipsed by the new threat to our house, but all he says is, "Didn't you think that was strange?"

"Strange? I don't know. I thought they had accepted Father's law, Aten's law. Now it seems we're back where we were before the plague. Worse, maybe."

Tutankhaten's black eyes narrow. "No: I mean Father's servants. Neither of them wanted to punish the heretics."

"Well, Horemhab is working with Father to secure the city, and you heard Ay: his son's too green."

"No…" Tutankhaten breathes, thinking hard. He stares down the corridor after the men and says, "No, they didn't want it. They didn't want to attack the village, or let their kin do it, or anything. They want old General May to do it."

"Nothing is as it seems here," I say, not for the first time.

"No," he says, frowning. "It's really not."

With the renewed threat of rebellion and heresy, Father and Mother are a team once again. Of course, he never takes private meals with all of us anymore, and I am quite sure I never hear him coming down the corridor to Mother's apartments at night. But that isn't so very important, is it? Not when his new little wife-nor thankfully, his more dangerous older wives-no longer sits at the high table on feast nights. Even with the danger, I grin watching my parents ride out in one chariot together, going to the Great Temple or to confer with General May. Lord Ay and his wife, Lady Teye, are also ever present in our lives. Ay is a cold man, almost reptilian. The idea that men who want us dead are rising from the shadows all across the land barely raises his pulse, I'm sure. Mayati tells me that he has spies all over Egypt, a giant network that sits over the land like a dark spider. He is tenacious in Father's service, but a great friend of Mother's as well, and he seems to be devoted to his wife. That is unusual in such a wealthy man.

Lady Teye is older than my mother, by some ten or more years, and a force in her own right. She is my mother's most intimate chamber lady, which gives her a great deal of power over any courtier seeking favor from the Great Royal Wife. She is also my mother's aunt through marriage, though she dare not tout it all about the court. My mother would pretend that she was royally born, just like Beketaten, actually, which was why Beketaten, the real thing, caused Mother so much grief. My haughty mother certainly wouldn't appreciate any mothering from the common Lady Teye. Not that Teye seems very motherly! She has a son, Nakhtmin, who she couldn't be bothered to raise at court. She sent him off to live with relations as soon as her confinement was over, and he grew up to be a soldier. Teye's just like her husband, a cold fish, except in one thing: her devotion to Lord Ay. Teye's father was not a court man, he was a mining superviser in Akhmim, and when the thirteen year old Teye was brought to marry Ay, twice her age, she experienced such a vault in status and lifestyle that she is devoted to Ay the way Mayati is devoted to Aten. We none of us doubt that she tells everything that happens in Mother's chambers to Lord Ay, but she keeps meticulous order in our household, and Mother never gives her secrets away anyhow. And Teye can be counted on to give impartial, clever advice, so Mother relies on her conversation. Ten years ago, Father conferred a rare honor on Teye: he made her a Person of Gold, entitled not only to wear the flesh of the gods, but to a greater portion of annual income from his treasury and honors close to what must be paid a princess. Quite a leap indeed, for a miner's daughter!

On the night I finally hear Father and Mother laughing together once again, Mayati comes to my room in darkness, stepping gingerly past my slumbering nurse, bending before my bed to snatch up my sandals. She pulls back the curtains around my bed, her face appearing like the moon out of clouds. She beckons me with her finger, and I huff and put my pillow over my face; but then I get up and follow her. She has no Meketaten now, it's only us, and so again I go along with her, not knowing where my devious sister will lead.

The air is chilled, but full of the sweet scent of night blooming jasmine. Mayati leads me along under the stars, all the way to the lotus pool. We pass a young guard-a bright eyed Nubian youth-who falls aside at my sister's sweet smile. Only when we pass through the lamp-lit hallway does she murmur, "I think Mother will speak to Father about my marriage tonight. She is with Lady Teye now, preparing."

So we will spy on them all: Pharaoh, the Great Royal Wife, and the high flying Lady Teye! "And will you leave me again?" I demand, determined not to go a step further.

Mayati widens her eyes. "No! Sister, *please*! This is everything to me... I don't want to be alone."

I think of my sister in the rose garden, laughing as Smenkhare whispered in her ear. For some reason, he makes her happy in a way I've never seen. "Swear you won't leave me," I say, setting my condition.

She sighs impatiently. "Yes, yes! I swear. Come on."

Sure enough, Mother and Lady Teye are in the garden, as graceful as herons leaning towards each other. They sit at a light table and drink wine from detailed alabaster cups, their face illuminated by glowing lamps. The pungent odor of myrrh swirls through the air. They discuss Prince Smenkhare, his pleasing countenance and manners, the docile temperament of his lady mother.

Mayati holds her breath, waiting for any mention of Father's approach. "Teye will leave first," she determines. She smiles as Mother recounts some of Smenkhare's memorable poems, and I wonder if he writes any about my sister. I wonder if my own husband will write poems for me, if he will cherish me and always be sweet. Will he make my cheeks glow and my eyes brighten, as Smenkhare does for Mayati?

Incredibly, Mother's thoughts seem to echo my own, for she says to Teye, "My little one asked about marriage not too long ago."

"What did you tell her?" Teye asks. Her eyes look frank and hard in the moonlight, and by the tone of her voice, she seems to know something about it. Perhaps the name of my own husband will be revealed! I look to Mayati eagerly, and she grins slightly, for once sharing my excitement.

"How could I tell her anything? And now, with the others gone… She is not like Mayati, Teye. She does not desire power, at least not as far as I can tell. Ankhesenpaaten would have been better off a lord's daughter; she would make a merry adored first wife for some handsome young nobleman."

"Better off than *what*?" I gulp, looking to my sister.

She makes a little hiss, pinching my arm.

"The princess Ankhesenpaaten is a shy child," Teye says in a low, murmuring voice. "But she will not need much other than her looks to attract the favor of a king. She will do well enough for herself, even if she does not pursue it."

I give a little gasp and grab my sister's hand. The favor of a king? What can she mean? I look at Mayati, because Teye can only mean that I am to marry Pharaoh, just like my elder sister. Mayati's jaw has dropped, and she glares at Mother in open distress.

"My little one is blessed with rare beauty, but she is not physically strong. You remember, the midwife broke her foot… It broke my heart to see her as a baby, with her little cast. And she was such a tiny baby…"

"Don't worry, Your Majesty. The prince will be happy to have her, and treat her well. I should think any man would be smitten, and care for her generously."

I can hardly believe this. I cry, silently, because I don't want to marry Smenkhare. I don't like him, he's cloyingly sweet, he laughs too loud, he's old… And I don't want to rival my sister! What life would that be, when Mayati has already tormented me for all my childhood? How could we share a *husband*? And how could my mother be speaking this way about me? Telling Teye that I am not strong? My cheeks burn with anger.

When Teye leaves, she goes through the door opposite to us, her white robes like a trail of smoke behind her. Mother-thoughtless, heartless Mother!-sits up tall and waits for Father to join her.

From the start, it does not go well for her. Father seems irritated at the night-time interruption, tamping his staff of office on the ground like he's crushing bugs with it. Mother has no choice now but to press on, and I hold my breath so hard I get dizzy. She talks about the future, about the fight for Aten's glory, and about the tragedy that fell on our house. She adds, "And now, with the uprisings, our loyal citizens have a great desire for reassurance, that… that should anything happen, the succession would be peaceful and smooth."

"You want me to announce my heir, Nefertiti?" Father's eyes narrow to dark slits, and he says, cruelly, "I am not satisfied that there will be no more worthy children to choose from. Can you be sure?"

"No, my lord…" Mother says, eating the insult with a gracefully bowed head. "And of course, you need not announce anything. But give the people something to hope for, some sign that a loyal couple waits in the wings behind us!"

"Speak your peace, woman. I grow restless."

Mother says quickly, "Mayati is loyal, to you, to Aten. Of all your children, she is most devoted to the god, and she would not hesitate to lay her life down to defend Aten's law. Marry her to Prince Smenkhare, who has royal blood but is not in the direct line. He is loyal as well, but also soft; our brilliant daughter would guide the marriage."

Father is silent for so long that I think he hasn't heard her. He sits back in his chair, his eyes on his chief wife for some time before he says, "You speak true of the princess. I know well-and pride in-her commitment to the Great God. Meri-Re informs me of how often she lays offerings at the alters, and how she directs the youngest courtiers on matters of worship. She is most worthy."

Mayati catches her own breath, but I drop my eyes to the floor. My life has suddenly become measured, dated.

"And that is why I will not give her away to such a man. My half-brother!" Father now laughs, his eyes and teeth flashing in the firelight. "That insipid weakling-is this the best you can do, Nefertiti? I am disappointed in you!" Yes, tell her! Suddenly I can breathe again.

Now, his voice goes low, almost threateningly so. "I have no intention of giving up what is mine so easily! And not to my father's low-born son, of all men! *My* son, *my* blood, shall follow me as Pharaoh-there can be no other way!"

"Tutankhaten?" Mother demands, forgetting her carefully chosen words and submissive posture. My sister sucks her breath. She might become Tutankhaten's wife! I would not wish it on him. But then... would I marry him as well? I find myself pleased with this thought. He would be a kind husband, someone to laugh with, someone I could love.

Father's smile is leonine in the darkness. "And why not? He is mine, and he is pure. But perhaps, I shall have another worthy son, a son from a woman of true faith. I am just thirty; do you think me an old man already?"

"So you will break your promise!" Mother accuses shrilly. "You will bypass your daughter... who is worthier than all others... for some other woman's-some woman's-" She chokes back a word that was certainly ugly. "Let me remind you, husband, that it is *my* image that watches over the city of Amarna, and the land of Egypt! It was my heart-my design-that poured into the Great Temple, when we raised it stone by stone! The people will not forget as easily as their king!"

My father leaps over the table so fast, so violently, that Mayati and I both jump back. He grabs her face in his hands as if he would kiss her, but I can see the awful force in his arms as he presses his palms into my mother's cheeks. "Do not speak treacherous words, beloved wife. What is done can easily be undone, what is raised up can easily be brought crashing down."

She doesn't dare talk back. Mother's wide eyes hold Father in a furious gaze, and then, finally, she says in a voice as clear and crisp as winter wind. "Forgive me, my lord."

"Smenkhare shall never be king in Amarna, Nefertiti. I would not give my city-or either of those two *goddesses*-to that man! Put it from your mind, woman! Do the duty I have entrusted you with, and no other, or you shall find yourself in a dark place indeed."

When I return to my room-my sister walking far ahead of me, glaring back at me as if I had betrayed her already, stolen her husband as Mother will one day force me to-Tia is awake. I fall into her arms and tell her everything, soaking her soft robe with my tears. "You are more a mother to me!" I declare. "How *could* she? How could Father allow it?"

To my horror, she doesn't rail against this fate as I thought she would. "They do it because to marry you and your sister to opposing men-neither one of your father's line-would be to sow the seeds of war. Both of your husbands would have a strong claim to the throne, and they would plot against each other. They would tear the court, and your father's house, apart. Your father might have been angry tonight, he might have taunted your mother, but even the viziers agree that Mayati is most likely to inherit. You must be a king's wife, or else your husband will seek to make himself king through you."

"Oh, Tia, how can I do it? What will become of me? Mayati will rule my life forever! Better I had never been born!"

She pats my back softly and murmurs, "There, there, child… It need not be as bad as all that. As a princess, you will have your own palace, and your own life. You need not endure your sister forever."

It isn't much of a hope, but it is something. No husband would want warring women in his home, even a home he visits occasionally. But who will my husband be? "It won't be Smenkhare… but who? If Smenkhare isn't worthy in Father's eyes, and father does not want to let Tutankhaten inherit because of his mother, then who will it be?"

Chapter Fourteen

The next morning, I decide that I must speak with Mayati. If this thing comes to pass, then she will be a Great Royal Wife, and we need not be enemies. I plan to tell her that I will only want a palace of my own, and a private life. A new servant opens her door and says that my sister is still in her bath. Looking past the girl, I see that there are three new servant girls in Mayati's two room chambers, taking instruction from one of my mother's old head maids.

"Excuse us, your highness."

Footsteps and voices behind me; I step aside and watch in wonder as porters approach the door, bearing boxes stamped with my father's treasury seal. Gifts for Mayati, large jewels by the look of it. I sigh, and return to my room for another hour.

When I come back, the flurry of activity has only intensified. Mayati stands on a stool as her servant pins and folds her into an elaborate cream and gold gown. Two women hold a full length mirror of polished silver before her. My sister stares at herself with a detached gaze, her fingers resting along the line of her neck, as if she were feeling her pulse for a sign of life. When I can see myself behind her in the mirror-small and bronze, in a tight white sheath and braids, my gold and hazel eyes bright with good intentions-Mayati murmurs, "What do you want?" She does not even meet my eyes in the mirror, she continues on looking at herself, the most interesting sight for her.

"I want to talk to you about last night. No matter what Father said, I'm sure he'll make you his heiress, and… and that means what Mother planned for us will happen. I want to say that it needn't matter, if we must share a husband. I want us to remain-to be-sisters, always. There need not be anything bad between us."

For a moment, my sister's dark eyes turn liquid, as if she would weep. I can't be sure I even saw it, for when she turns her head to me, she is as hard as stone again. "None of that will happen now. I am not to be Father's heiress."

"Oh… he was just angry, Mayati! He has no son who can inherit the throne, not yet, and he will have to train someone soon!"

"No," she says shortly, waving her servants away. Mayati steps down from the stool and comes before me. She holds herself as aloof as a goddess, cloaking herself in dignity. "I will not be his heiress. My son will be his heir, my son will be Pharaoh. I am a married woman now. Father has made me his wife."

What?" I step back from Mayati like she's infected. "What?" She has displaced *Mother*, our mother! I shake my head fiercely as she begins to speak, to assign blame, to tell me that it was all his doing. "Mother's going to *kill* you!" I shout, furious. "She has every right! You are the biggest traitor in Egypt! You are… oh, how awful!"

When she grabs my shoulders I cringe, as if her touch would burn me. "Shut your mouth!" she cries wildly. The servants scatter like mice, and we are alone in her gaudy coral and gold bedroom. A gilded solar disk hangs prominently on her wall, its rays extending down over her vanity. "You call me traitor? Mother is the worse traitor, or did you forget her petitioning the old dead goddesses? It doesn't matter anyway-there's nothing she can do, it is the will of Pharaoh."

"Mayati!" I cry, bereft. I search my heart for something to say, something to reach her, to call some sanity back into my wildly spinning life. "What about Smenkhare? You love him!"

She swallows, shaking her head tightly. "He is... he is nothing. He can be nothing. This is something greater, this is for Aten."

"No," I breathe furiously. "I don't believe it! You've done wrong, you've both done something very wrong! You will break Mother's heart. Her own daughter! It is terrible, you must see that! How *could* he? How could you?"

Mayati spins away from me, hiding her face. She pulls the lid off one of her new gifts, and lifts out a heavy golden necklace. I think it looks like a yoke, like a heavy slave's collar ready for the chain. This must be a nightmare, a terrible nightmare. I will wake up any minute. And then, I hear her words, muffled, as if drifting in a poisonous fog. "Take care what you say, little sister. Everyone says you have the face of a goddess. If he could not give me away, do you think he will let you leave this place? Our fates are intertwined, did you forget? It is only a matter of when."

I'm in my bed, and I can't remember how I got there. I only know that a royal physician came and gave me a strong, noxious tasting drink that seemed to blur time, stretching and pulling at it like dough. I can remember a banquet, my sister taking a seat beside my father, my mother rising sharply and leaving the table with Lady Teye and her entourage.

Suddenly, it is morning. Pale pink light fills my small room, throwing long shadows over the painted marsh on my wall. I couldn't sleep again if I tried. I want to leave this place.

Tutankhaten is always up before the sun, and so I hurry to him before his tutor can. I doubt he can make any sense of this mess, but I clutch his arms and recount every last bit. The words are almost too terrible to speak. "I am alone," I whisper, crying. "I have no family now. There's no future for me!"

"No, you have me! You'll always have me. We'll always be friends, no matter what, I swear on Aten himself."

"Tutankhaten, I can't imagine it!" My throat is tight at the thought. "It can't happen. I won't do it. I swear I won't! I can't believe..." Oh, I don't even understand it fully. But if I think too much on it, I will vomit on the floor. I put my hands over my belly, afraid it will happen anyway.

Tutankhaten watches me with a fathomless stare. What does he make of it? He doesn't tell me. His fingers brush over his writing box, and then he sets it down. "I'm not going to my tutor today," he declares. "I'm going to take you riding. I always feel better after I ride."

"Riding? I can't-" I cut myself off. These are my parents' rules, but what loyalty do they show me? Mother would have given me to a man that makes my skin crawl, and Father... it turns out he is no father at all.

Tutankhaten holds out his hand, as if he's read my thoughts. "Forget them. You can't stop them anyway, right? Let's have some fun. I promise you'll forget everything once you feel the wind in your hair."

He orders his horse, Triumph, a graceful bay gelding with a powerful chest. A stable boy brings the horse out and Tutankhaten uses a red granite block to swing onto the tasseled blanket strapped to its back. He slides forward, and holds his arm out to me. I'm surprised at the strength in those skinny arms as Tutankhaten helps me climb on behind him. I look down warily; the view is much different than from the back of my old little mare, the ground is much farther away.

"Put your arms around me," Tutankhaten says, and I straighten my gown around my knees and wrap my arms around his slim waist. The horse's walk is much faster than my mare's lazy amble, its steps longer. Our hips roll and sway with the easy four beat gait. Tutankhaten lets the horse stretch as Lord Rameses teaches us, and then he says, "Are you ready? We're going to trot."

"I don't know how. Don't let me fall, Tutankhaten!" I am

suddenly terrified that I am not strong enough to hold on! What have I done?

"Don't think of falling, silly!" he laughs, looking halfway over his shoulder with a wide grin. "Triumph is comfortable, and I'm in charge. You needn't do anything but relax and hold on. Let your legs hang, let your hips be soft."

"Soft?"

"Soft, easy. Just go with it. You'll see."

He nudges his horse with his heels, and Triumph picks up his pace. It's a steady, floating two-beat gait. My curls brush off my face and play in the wind, my long gown sails along. I laugh, nervous and delighted.

"Just wait," he says. "It gets much better."

"Tutankhaten!"

Father's voice bellows across the sandy arena, harsh and angry. I look over my shoulder and gasp in horror. Father and Mother are together, Father in the foreground, his face black and his hands on his hips; Mother behind him, glaring angrily yet grasping her hands in fear. How did they know?

Tutankhaten exhales heavily. His shoulders slump as he realizes that we're caught. He breaks the horse down to a walk. "It's my fault. I'll tell him I made you come with me."

"No–" I begin, but the sight of my father drains my courage. I dig my fingers into Tutankhaten's waist and press my cheek against his back. He'll be whipped, I know it. But Father would not whip his daughter. "No, let me take the blame," I say quietly.

Tutankhaten shakes his head. "I can't do that."

We ride up to Father, who snatches the reins under Triumph's chin. His eyes are murderous on Tutankhaten, and Mother rushes forward as if I were ready to fall. "Help her–"

Before she reaches my side, I swing my leg over and slide down to the ground. The drop is longer than I expected and I stumble back, just like the fragile little doll she thinks me. I flush and straighten myself.

"How dare you endanger my daughter this way?" Mother

shouts, startling Triumph. Tutankhaten cannot steady him, with Father clutching the reins.

"Get down!" Father barks, and Tutankhaten dismounts at once. He stands before Father, his back straight and his head bowed. "Answer the Great Royal Wife!"

"I did not endanger her, madam," Tutankhaten says clearly. "I would never harm the princess. I can control my horse. I would not have put her on otherwise."

"Arrogant boy!" Mother snaps. She wheels on Father. "Well? He has defied you!"

"It wasn't his fault!" I cry, but it's no use. Father is outraged, and Mother goads him the way she once would have, before the plague.

"You think to disobey me?" he demands. Tutankhaten remains silent. "To take Ankhesenpaaten on your horse, when she has been commanded against it? You think you're strong enough to protect her, little boy? Let's see how good you truly are, when you're on something with spirit!" Father turns back to the stable boy, whose hand is pressed against the ugly fresh bruise on his cheek. "Bring out my stallion. Bring out Aten's Fury, and give him the light bit."

As Triumph is led away, Father clamps his hand down on my shoulder. "You disappoint me, Ankhesenpaaten. But I know this was not your doing. Now you'll see why you should not trust yourself to a boy's care."

He's going to hurt Tutankhaten! He's going to put him on a horse that's years beyond his ability, a stud stallion, a horse Father himself rarely rides! Tutankhaten stands absolutely still, holding his chin high but keeping his eyes on the sand at his feet. He holds his breath rather than let his chest heave with fear. The great red horse is brought out, and already he's dancing around, mocking the weak grip of the stable boy. He is a snorting, pawing beast who must be held at the mounting block by two men.

"Go on, mount up! You are confident enough to take my princess out, show us how you handle this horse!"

Tutankhaten bows his head again. "Yes, sir."

He approaches the horse slowly, and the horse seems to size him up as well. Fury lets out a great snort, as if he were challenging Tutankhaten. I cannot look. I cannot look away. Tutankhaten runs his palms along the horse's high-arched neck, its heavily muscled shoulder. "Easy..." he murmurs.

His jaw is set tight with determination when he steps onto the block, and I say a quick prayer for him. I try not to think of Father's heavy hand on my shoulder, and my sister's marriage.

Tutankhaten swings lightly onto Fury's back, but the horse isn't having any of it from the beginning. He won't walk; he prances sideways as Tutankhaten eases him forward. The horse throws his head high in the air, chomping on his bit and tossing his red mane about. Tutankhaten sits proudly through it all, the only sign of his fear in the pinch of his shoulder blades. And then, he asks Fury to trot.

The horse bolts. He doesn't just run-which Tutankhaten could handle-he puts his head down between his knees and bucks, twisting his powerful body as it leaps into the air. I scream as the red stallion charges across the arena, doing everything he can to unseat the small boy on his back. Tutankhaten sits as long as he can, clinging to the horse's mane first and then his neck; but finally, Fury approaches the corner of the arena, spins, and throws a powerful, end-game buck. Tutankhaten flies through the air and lands with a dull thud on his back. He doesn't move.

I pull out of Father's grasp to go to him, but Father snatches my arm and holds me still, ignoring my tears. "It's for you that he's learned this lesson, my fairest! Watch it, remember it."

Thank Aten, he stirs. Tutankhaten had the wind knocked out of him, but he finally coughs and sits up, seemingly unharmed. He spits sand from his mouth, and after another stunned moment, pushes himself up and brushes off his kilt.

Father's loud, triumphant laugh echoes through the arena. "It seems you've a few things to learn yet, Tutankhaten! Come. We'll go back to the palace."

Tutankhaten's face is flushed with anger, his eyes burn, but

Father doesn't notice. I watch him as long as I can, as Father pulls me along towards his waiting chariot.

And then, Tutankhaten doesn't follow. Incredibly, he goes to Fury, who having thrown his rider is now content to linger by the stable's entrance, sniffing the air for his honeyed grain. I stop completely, and when Father turns to scold me, he makes a little noise of astonishment. Tutankhaten grabs the horse's tangled reins and leads him along to the block.

"Oh, *Abi*, stop him!" I cry, looking up at Father, whose eyes are narrowed, a ghostly, knowing smile barely pulling up his lips.

"No, no, Ankhesenpaaten. Let the prince test his heart, if he's bold enough. It's good for him." Father lets go of me, and I hurry to the rail.

If I didn't know better, I'd say the horse was plain astonished to have to face the challenge once again, after having had such a one-sided victory. He blows his nostrils out and stamps his feet, and when Tutankhaten swings onto his back, the horse lifts them off the ground, threatening to rear up. I clench my fists, pushing my knuckles into the cedar fence so hard it hurts. *Don't let him fall again!*

In the same corner where he was thrown, Tutankhaten digs his heels into Fury's belly, and the great horse leaps forward and tries to tuck his head again. I dig my nails into the wood and lean forward, terrified.

But Tutankhaten has a trick. He sits up as straight as he can, and he draws one rein up so hard that his fist is near his chin. The horse-used to the rider jerking back-can't clamp on the bit and deaden his mouth, and he can't pull the reins through Tutankhaten's hands. He can only spin in his circle, but Tutankhaten can sit that easily, his calves flexed hard as he pushes the horse to keep it running. Now Father's laughter is soft, chuckling, proud. "You see, Nefertiti? You see what a fine son I have? I can hardly stay angry with him."

Tutankhaten doesn't fall again. Eventually, he lets Fury widen his circle, and the horse melts into a canter so graceful, so fluid, that there is no doubt this is a horse meant for a king. His head arches proudly and his red tail streams behind him, and Tutankhaten has never looked finer in his life. Then Tutankhaten rewards Fury, taking him off the circle and letting him into a flat gallop around the arena. He leans forward as the horse stretches out, his strong legs braced around Fury's body; he strokes the horse on his neck as they run. Aten himself would want a horse so fast! When he sits up, Fury slows to a canter, and then down to a brisk trot. Tutankhaten comes right out the gate and trots up to us, the horse snorting and blowing, the prince's eyes defiant and fierce. He does not wait for a smiling, laughing Father to speak. He haughtily proclaims, "I'm going to hitch him to my chariot!"

"Oh, are you?" Father asks, allowing Tutankhaten's pride and anger, amused by it. "We'll see, young man. We'll see. For now, you'll walk him until he's cool yourself, brush him, and put him away. And don't let me hear you've made a servant do it."

Chapter Fifteen

Amarna stands sparkling white in the sun on a fair harvest day. The river beside the Great Palace reflects the brilliant blue of the sky, and the breeze carries the mingled scent of incense and blooming flowers. But down at the harbor, there is nothing but short tempers and fear. The transports of grain and produce-pomegranates, melons, geese, cattle and the like-from several important districts have been late for some days. Worse, no one has word of the barges, no city reports sheltering them. Father hopes they were delayed in the country, but he sends Lord Ay scurrying about, looking for more sinister reasons.

Father is growing tired, I can tell. There has never been a king in all our family's history who was continuously at war with his own people, and it is wearing on Father as if each one year of his reign carried the weight of five. He is ill-tempered, edgy, and suspicious of his closest friends. Mayati says he often counts the men who have wronged him and still live, or makes lists of the lords who have prominent relatives in Thebes. She says he smokes opium every night, and sometimes starts drinking his wine in the morning. She is pregnant now. He will break ground on her palace when the river floods; it is to be annexed to the Great Palace as well, and he's given her two other sanctuaries about the city.

Mother watches from her gilded throne with hard shining eyes. If I were her, I would throw my wine in his face and lock myself away from him, but she is a Great Royal Wife and wants to remain one, and will endure any shame to keep her crown. So she isn't rude in any way, but neither does she converse with him about the rebels, or the late tax barges, or anything else she once would have helped him with. Instead, she charms the court around her, collecting circles of laughing officials. She tells amusing anecdotes and is the exact opposite of Father, who sits drumming his fingers and washing his throat with wine.

I hate it here. Was this palace ever full of laughter and light? Did I ever have a father and mother, who shone like gold in the sun, who loved us completely? I know the plague did it. Father-the one I knew and loved-shines through less and less, so that it might be weeks or months without a sight of him. The man in his place turns on his friends and family alike, testing loyalty and punishing any hesitation, any fear. And he finds it everywhere. He had a man-a friend-dragged out of the court by Nubian guards, after tricking him with swirling, shadowy words into admitting that he still communicates with his mother, a cousin of the mayor of Thebes. Father accused those remaining in Thebes of defiance, of holding grand feasts unofficially dedicated to idols. The unfortunate man stupidly told Father that there were food shortages in that city, and that it was not safe for women to go about by night, or even by day in some areas. His own mother feared to go to the market.

Father took this for sympathy. The lady should have come to Amarna! Did Father not promise to build homes and supply farmland for all who followed him, and Aten? Did he not raise a shining city laid out to the path of sun and stars, swollen fat with the prosperity of all Egypt? Had he ever asked for anything more than friendship, and obedience? I don't know what happened to the courtier. I can't forget the sound of his screams, echoing through the cavernous stone hall as he pled for mercy. I cannot understand how Father sat down to his meal after this, tearing into his red and bloody steak with his golden knife, as a man he often entertained in private company was likely taken off to death merely for worrying over his old mother's safety.

And through all of this, in the back of my heart, in a place I hardly dare to look, are Mayati's hideous words. Sometimes my mother hugs me to her for a while, and I feel her shoulders shaking. But then, she straightens up and turns away from me, setting her jaw in stone. She never talks to me anymore. It's as if she's given us both up to him already, without even a pretense of resistance. He is Pharaoh; he is to be obeyed. How could she do it?

And then, on a bright summer day full of the shouting and trumpeting as thousands of foreign troops and Amarna conscripts prepare to be deployed against our enemies, Grandmother arrives from her palace at the north of the city. Oh, I wish I could run to her, stay with her, leave this dark place behind!

Father is not there to greet her; he is resting, trying to recover from the madness he oversees and the heavy toll his drinking and smoking is taking on his health. Our enemies commandeered many of our tax ships, which bring us our food, likely with the help of local authorities. By all signs, there is a force of three thousand fighters in the desert, appearing like a sandstorm to strike Father's bands of mercenary soldiers, and then dissolving into the cliffs as quickly as they came. A true believer himself, I know that Father must weigh the courage of one who fights for faith-and food and family-against one who fights for pay. I no longer wonder why they do not accept Aten, why they do not feel his presence when they pray as I do. It really doesn't matter. As soon as one district is pacified, sabotage and defiance spring up in another. The south of Egypt is in uproar, especially after Father raised the taxes yet again last year, even though the flood was weak. Father must attend the rebellion above all other things, and it exhausts him.

Surprisingly, Mother and Grandmother spend a whole hour strolling through the gardens. Grandmother-slim, frail, slow-has taken Mother's arm, but it seems that Mother is the one who leans for support. The two women take a seat in the shade of a sycamore, and I strain to hear what they speak of from the balcony overhead.

"That's a new sight," Tutankhaten says coming up behind me.

"It would be nice, if it didn't have to come about like… like this."

"Your mother is very sad," Tutankhaten agrees.

"She isn't alone," I say quietly.

"I'm sure Grandmother will want to see us. Why don't we pick her fresh flowers while we wait?

I wanted to watch, to listen, to grasp at any word that might make me understand what's happening to us. But as I take Tutankhaten's arm and walk away, I know I am glad to turn my back on everything. "Oh, Tutankhaten," I say, as we stream through the alternating shadow and sunlight of the portico, "Let's run away! Let's go be normal people."

"What-raise goats and chickens together?" He laughs wryly. "It couldn't be. We aren't like them; we're not even truly mortal." He brings me along into a pillared garden, where jasmine spills down the walls and a little granite-lined pool teams with fat, yellow fish. As I flounce down in a field of boldly colored lilies, Tutankhaten says mischievously, "We could go to Punt, I guess. We could sell ourselves as acrobats."

I can't help laughing, even through the tears that fall over my cheeks. Acrobats indeed! "I'm afraid I wouldn't give a very good show."

"We'd be great. I'd do flips and juggle swords. You could be the beautiful lady twirling and throwing fire. We'd stun the crowd." Tutankhaten plucks a handful of deep pink blossoms and puts them into my hands.

And then, our grandmother's voice: "Beautiful children," she breathes, shaking her head, staring at Tutankhaten and me waist-deep in flowers. She notes the tears in my eyes and the smile on my face, the hasty bouquet in my hands. Tutankhaten gathers another and pushes himself up. He presents himself, and the flowers, with a stylish bow. "My lady grandmother, these are for you."

"I treasure them, dearest child. Let me see you."

Tutankhaten always stands as straight as a young palm, but now he draws himself up to show the respect he has for her, and for himself. Grandmother-like me-is quite small, and she needn't bend down very far to gaze into the prince's black eyes. "I can see your mother in you..." Grandmother murmurs wistfully. "That proud princess, Beketaten... She left to give you her strength, and so she is with you still. She should have ruled Egypt; this sorrow would not so long be upon us! You must listen for her voice in your heart, Prince of Egypt. When the blessed day comes, if you seek her, she will guide you."

She walks forward, followed by a very confused Tutankhaten. The treason seems to pour from Grandmother's lips, as the flood rushes in once a levee has crumbled. Her words are disturbing and strange; yet compelled by the might and purity in my grandmother's still gorgeous face, I bow low, holding myself for endless moments.

"Rise, my granddaughter."

I look up, surprised to see that her usually pallid cheeks are ruddy and lush with color and life. She arranges my long, skinny braids carefully over my shoulders and says, "You are such a lovely girl, Ankhesenpaaten. Not only for your beauty, of which all the land speaks of so often, but for your gentle heart. There are women around you who will tell you it is weakness. They will tell you a woman must be heartless and cunning to rule, but it is not so! It was for love and honor that I devoted my life to your grandfather, and to this once blessed land. Love and honor, and nothing for myself! That is what's required from a Great Royal Wife, above anything. And I lived long and well at Pharaoh's side." She looks up to the sky suddenly, crying out, "Better that the Lord of the Underworld would have called me with my husband, so many years ago. I would have been spared this mockery of my son's!"

Tutankhaten and I exchange a nervous glance. Old grandmother has lost her wits!

"Oh, poor innocent children... You believe only what you've been told, and it is not my place to deliver you from it. But know this: what you see is only a cruel shadow of what was, before my ravenous son tore apart this land. He should have replaced the priests and stopped there, but he has indulged his own desire and called it the will of a Sun God! This house will fall to dust, unless my son recovers his soul. I have come to beg it of him, but I fear I have left it too long."

Tutankhaten instinctively steps closer to me, as Grandmother's lament echoes through the courtyard garden.

"Yes, yes... There is my hope: a chance of a future for us, and this land..." She takes our hands, one in each of hers, and joins them together. Tutankhaten and I lace our fingers obediently, and Grandmother lays her hands over both of ours. "You are a holy pair. You can feel it in your hearts. You must protect each other, survive whatever is to come, and rise through it. The gods have created you together, one for the other. But be careful-"

A high pitched scream cuts her voice off. And then, the terrible call. "They've attacked Pharaoh!"

I forget everything and rush to his room, swept along by the awful fear that my father is dead. Oh, let my *abi* live! Tutankhaten hasn't let go of my hand; he holds it firmly as he brings me through the crush of soldiers and officials. Vizier Ay cuts past us as he darts towards the king's chambers.

"Move!" Tutankhaten finally shouts, frustrated to no end by the bodies in his usually clear path. With one hand out, he pushes the backs of those who are accustomed to bowing before him.

When the last heads clear away, I see my Father in his open chested chamber robe, standing tall beyond his gilded doorway. He's surrounded by Ay, Horemhab, and a handful of elite Nubian guards. He is alive, unharmed! We walk straight into his antechamber, and I want to rush into his arms. But I cannot. Almost immediately, my sister bursts in crying, hurrying to him; Father's molten, broiling stare stops her cold beside Tutankhaten and me. He speaks only to Ay and Horemhab, his voice a jagged hiss as he rattles off instructions for locking down the palace.

Only then do I look about the room; I immediately grab Tutankhaten's arm in horror. A young man-really just a boy only a few years older than us-lies dead on the floor. One of Father's golden diadems, complete with a flowing white and gold *nemes* cloth, is on his head, as if he had snuck in and tried it on. But more shocking still, his arms and legs are twisted and seized into his body, as if he had died wrapping himself into knots. Thick blood drips like syrup through his clenched teeth. I turn to Tutankhaten without caring who sees; he puts his arm around my back in comfort. His eyes are fixed on the poor boy, before they flicker to Father, full of awful, crushing understanding. This agonizing death was meant for our all-mighty Father!

Once the soldiers-and their general-are gone, Father kneels down before the dead servant boy. His lips curl in disgust as he reaches for his diadem and head cloth, but Vizier Ay interrupts him. "Allow me, Your Majesty."

Father stays his hand, clenching his fingers into a huge, hard bronze fist. Ay-with a minimum of contact-gently slides the diadem off, and holds it up to the wide saucer of flame beside him. After only a moment's examination, he says, "Ah... See here. They have made small incisions into the metal, and likely coated it in some venom. When the roughened gold scratched against his head, he was finished." Ay gazes in wonder at my father. "This one came close, Your Majesty. Someone close has betrayed you."

My father stands slowly. He gives one final look at the dead servant on the floor, before motioning for two soldiers to take him away. I peer on him once more as he's carried roughly off; he was a pretty boy, with a rosebud mouth and a sweeping of kohl around his eyes. But the warmth of life is gone from his soft cheeks. Though my father has executed hundreds, this boy is the first dead person I've ever seen.

Father growls, "My enemies are in Amarna now, Lord Ay."

Ay only nods. Of course they are in Amarna; they are in our own house!

Father stops pacing before the wide, high window. He stands in the flooding sunlight, his palms spread open as if in prayer. His voice is as quiet as a whisper, but somehow so strong it carries through the room. "So be it, then. Let them come with all they have. I am ready. I've been ready all my life."

Chapter Sixteen

Our city is plunged into a nightmare. Doors are kicked in under darkness, and by day men-and even women-are dragged from their homes to the depths of the palace dungeons. Our palace is locked down, which means no more sailing, and no more hunting trips for Tutankhaten. Men begin to disappear from the court, and no one dares to ask where they have gone. Father stalks his halls in silence, while Vizier Ay, the Minister of Justice, works night and day to discover the threats to Father's life. Mother stands at Ay's side, issuing orders while her husband broods in his rage, seeing a threat in every whisper and shadow.

They do not find the poisoner, but they *do* find that most of the common people in our city-Aten's own holy city-have houses full of shrines to the forbidden gods. The blood runs thick in the central square of Amarna; the headsman of Amarna makes his fortune as the city holds its breath in fear. I lie awake in terror at the thought, touching my neck, wondering what it might mean to die with such quick brutality. I wish my mother would come and hold me and make me understand, but that won't ever happen again, I don't think.

During all of this, my sister is taken to her confinement in Mother's own birth pavilion. Her screams could easily wake the dead entombed in the eastern cliffs. I linger in the garden outside the pavilion, watching from a safe distance as Father paces like a caged lion. If Mayati has a son, the succession is ensured. Aten's reign will go on, and we will win this fight. But if she has a daughter, or if she loses the baby, then we will be no better off than we were.

My sister's cries stop abruptly, followed by the shrill screams of a newborn baby. Father stands stone still, turning into one of his statues, holding his hands out in hope. When the ancient, unwilling midwife Nani appears on the portico, there is a gleam of laughter in her eyes.

"Well? What is it?" Father demands urgently.

Nani smothers her delight and bends her crooked back. "A daughter, Majesty. A healthy, hardy daughter."

Father curls his lips in anger, disappointment, disgust. "Treacherous," he breathes. He does not go in to see my sister. Her dream of being his Great Royal Wife is dashed, and Father stalks off without another word.

"Something is happening," Tutankhaten breathes, bright eyed outside my chamber door. "Hurry."

We walk along together to the bridge over the Royal Road, staring down to the Great Temple, where all the chariots of the court wait in a jumble. We can smell the incense rising from the open air sanctuary, enough to proclaim that a great ceremony is taking place. But it is no ceremony that we have been invited to. "What could it be? Another marriage? A new Great Royal Wife?" My sister is still in her confinement, and she has failed Father, so it cannot be her!

Tutankhaten pushes himself up into the window of appearances, sitting in this sacred place where Father shares his presence with the people. But no one looks up to see his dark son perched on the lime-washed sandstone, letting his long legs dangle over the road. "Lord Ay is coming out," Tutankhaten reports. "And now, your mother- *What?*"

"What is it? Tutankhaten, what is it?"

Tutankhaten looks down on me, his eyes burning. "What does she have on her head? What *is* that?"

He slides over, and I peer out onto the road. Sure enough my mother stands before the Great Temple, surrounded by prostrating courtiers. A tall blue crown graces her head, and in the morning light I can see a double *uraeus* blinking in the sun. Now Father comes, taking her hand. There is applause, and more bowing, and I shake my head in confusion. "I don't understand," I say.

"I'll tell you!" Tutankhaten exclaims, jumping down from the window. "He has made her Co-Regent, that's what! Look: she wears a new crown and Pharaoh's emblem on her brow. There is nothing that conniving woman won't do to deny me my rights!"

"My mother's become a *king*?" I whisper in disbelief.

Tutankhaten stands before me, hot with anger. "No one needs to tell *me*. I can see it plain as day. They are scrambling to hold power, just like Grandmother always said. And now, when it is so *obvious* that Aten will not give him a son to take my place, he decides instead to bump your mother to Co-Regent! Well, I will not bow to her as my king! I will bow to no common-born woman as my Pharaoh, nor any common born man!"

I've never seen his anger so clearly, anger at what my mother has done to him, anger at his lost status of heir apparent. Surely, he was born to be king, but everyone-including Father-has conspired to keep it away from him, all because of what his mother said one careless day. She made an enemy of Father, and worse, of Mother, long before Tutankhaten was born. "You wouldn't want it, Tutankhaten," I say quickly, to diffuse his anger. "However would you clean up this mess they've made? We'll be lucky to keep this throne. Come," I say, holding out my hand. "It's warm enough to swim. Let them fret and scheme to hold power. We're lucky we'll never have a thing to do with it."

Later that day, as we walk back laughing from the lotus pool, my mother sweeps down on us. Indeed, she has been made Father's Co-Regent. There is a look of hard triumph in her eyes, and she purses her lips in pleasure as Tutankhaten manages to hide his sudden leap of anger and betrayal.

"I have dreadful news," she says, which wasn't what I was expecting at all. "You grandmother is dead."

"Grandmother!" I cry, clutching Tutankhaten's hand. "How? Was it her illness?"

"No," my mother says, with all the coldness of a woman who could watch her daughter bedded by her husband, yet still take the man's hand as he made her his co-ruler. "She took poison. Her servants found her. A terrible-and preventable-tragedy. But she always said she wanted to be with her husband, the old king. Now she has gone to him. The court will enter mourning, so be sure to dress appropriately." Mother gives the two of us a long, hard look. "You are too much together. Everywhere I turn, Ankhesenpaaten, you are with this boy. You have no future together, surely you know that?"

I bow my head, refusing to foreswear Tutankhaten, unable to be openly defiant. Mother can say what she likes, but she is no mother to me, and no mother to Mayati. Poor Grandmother! The new Co-Regent of Egypt says nothing more. She floats around us, her long white cloak billowing in the breeze.

Chapter Seventeen

Summer, Year Sixteen

And then, on a bright summer morning, I become a woman. I clutch my blanket to my chest for a long while, wishing I could will this away. And then I think, why should I not?

I climb out of bed and quickly bundle the sheets in my arms. When Tia arrives with my breakfast, I thrust them at her. "Burn them."

"My lady?"

I swing my robe on, and sit at my ebony vanity, snatching at my mirror. "I said burn them. Or throw them in the river, I don't care." I stare on my reflection, sure that I see nothing there of the change that's happened in the middle of the night.

"You cannot think to hide this, princess," Tia says softly, coming to my side. "It would be improper, unnatural. You are a woman now."

"Do it!" I shout, startling myself. I close my eyes, blinking back the rushing surge of swirling, hissing fears.

I know now that I never want to marry. I don't want any crying babies, and I certainly don't want to face the terrors of childbirth! And I don't-not for all the gold in Egypt-want to be a wife to my *father*! I realize with fright that my heart is pounding far too hard. I look up at Tia, losing my breath.

Tia drops the incriminating bundle and rushes to my side. Her firm, business-like hand is on my back; she murmurs comfort. When I can speak again, after a long drink of water, I say, "It feels like... like my execution's been planned, and the date's just moved up. Oh, Tia, how can I escape this?"

After a long, mournful silence, Tia finally asks, "Did you hope to marry another?"

Her dangerous question wasn't what I expected. "Of course not," I tell her, looking away. "I know I could never have a husband of my choice."

My stout old nurse shakes her head softly. "Poor child," she says, and I know then that she can do nothing to help me.

Tutankhaten awaits me in the courtyard, and so I hurry through my bathing and dressing. He always rises before the sun; his targets will already be set up, his chairs and cushions and flock of servants ready to attend his ease. He's teaching me to shoot, as he taught me to read the stars, and speak both Akkadian and formal Nubian. Since the attempt on Father's life, our city's been run like a military camp and we are guarded as treasure. We cannot go abroad, or enter certain parts of the Great Palace. Even Tutankhaten's ventures to the royal stables-just a few buildings down the Royal Road-require such elaborate security measures and planning that he can rarely ride or drive. But when Father said that his hawk, given to him shortly after his success on Aten's Fury, must be raised by Lord Rameses, Tutankhaten dug in his heels and explained with confident reason that letting another man raise his hunting bird would be akin to giving the hawk away, and he could not properly hunt with another man's bird. Now the young, golden-brown hawk lives in his antechamber, much to Lady Maia's horror. We do what we can to keep some happiness in our lives, even with burly foreign guards hovering over us like attack dogs.

Father is merciless these days, more than ever before. He keeps a granite hand around Amarna's throat. His policemen line the streets, ever ready to arrest or beat anyone who hints at treachery. They search homes and market stalls for goddess figurines and scarab amulets, enforcing Father's command that there be no idol worship in Aten's sacred city, unless it is of statues or drawings of us. Father must be the supreme master, demanding ownership of the bodies, souls, and even the prayers of his people. Even so, insulting graffiti disfigures the city's shining walls at sunrise, and the scent of rebellion is potent in the air. I cannot imagine how he'll put an end to this; will he kill every last Egyptian, in order to remain their king? Was he always this way? I can't ever remember Father being so ruthless, so cruel. Was I just a baby, too blind to see him for what he was? Or has this throne, this golden burden, rotted him from the inside out?

When I come upon Tutankhaten, he tells me immediately, "They've caught the rebel Lord Pentuwer, and discovered all his plans to attack the garrison of Nubian soldiers." This year, he has finally grown taller than me. His princely side lock is long now, sweeping in black beaded braids past his collarbone. When unbound, it hangs down in a ripple of obsidian waves, as long as Mayati's hair. Though he is younger than me, his black eyes are made hard and deep by his education, and the countless dangers we have faced from the first day of the plague up until this very day. He constantly concerns himself with Father's troubles. "This has never happened before," Tutankhaten says, always referring back to his studies. "No king has battled with his own people over their private devotions. How can that fight ever be won?"

And then, he will stop, leave it alone. He knows his mother was beaten for voicing her own beliefs, and he is as cautious as he must be on such a deadly matter. Our Father kills people for praying to any god but Aten, and that is just the way it is.

But I have no time for this today. I grab his hand, the one without the bow, and lead him past servants and guards, back between the fluted sandstone columns. I lean over and whisper the hateful words in his ear, guarding my secret from everyone else. "I am a woman." I close my eyes and hover against him for a long moment, not wanting to face my own words.

Tutankhaten cries softly, *"Now? Just today? Just like that?"*

"That's how it happens," I say, resigned. "But I'm not telling. I don't look any different."

His pretty face fixes in a frown. He, too, thinks I am being improper. But all he says is, "Won't your servants gossip?"

"I have to try!" I hiss, gripping his bare shoulders. "And he has a new wife, the mayor of Amarna's daughter. Maybe he doesn't need me. Maybe if I stay away from him, and stay a little girl, he'll look past me. Everyone always used to!"

"No one can look past you," Tutankhaten says sadly. He closes his eyes. "But... but come, let's finish what we started. I've fixed the tension in my bow, like you wanted."

And so we go back into the garden. Tutankhaten-in his short kilt and leather arm guard-takes a strong stance before the target, his body all full of precise angles. His arm, doubled back at the elbow, releases an ivory tipped arrow and it flies for home, for the center of the target. A group of my father's retainers passes along the portico beyond, their robes swirling around them, their gaudy sandals and staffs smacking the ground. Tutankhaten's eyes follow them, until he turns to me. "Since it's easier to draw, you'll have to pull back a bit more to reach your mark. The tighter the bowstring is, the more powerful the bow. It has to have good snap. But let's wait a moment, so we don't shoot one of those viziers."

His dry humor makes me smile. I can forget my own trouble for just a moment, and try to hit this target. Tutankhaten puts the gilded bow into my hands, and then straps the leather guard to my left forearm to protect me from the stinging string. We shoot the first arrow together, his hand guiding mine back to my jaw. It meets its brother on the bull's eye. "You're ridiculously good," I tell him, looking over my shoulder.

"I know," Tutankhaten says simply. He walks away and sits, leaning into the cushions. "Show me what you've learned," he says, and so I do, shooting three bull's eyes out of seven shots, thinking how very unfair it is that he is a boy.

That night, I go to a banquet when all custom says I should be in my bedroom, taking restful advantage of the five or so days of the woman's time. And I go the next night, and the next, and nothing happens at all. I hide it very well, I think. Maybe the laundresses will note more linen leaving their care than returning, but that's all. And the next month, the same thing. The summer rides along this way, and really, Father is far too drunk by evening to notice anyway.

His court is diminished; men have been dismissed, some arrested. Others remain in their villas, making excuses. They prefer to deal with Mother, seeking her for petitions when Father is conferenced with his generals, demanding they raise more foreign troops. But by the end of the sixteenth summer of Father's reign, the Asians melt away from our court. They have their own wars now; the Hittites are stirring in the north once more, like the bears that slumber long winters in grey northern caves and wake with ravenous hunger. They barge into the kingdom of Mitanni in the east, and in the west they sack the port of Byblos and drive the mayor into exile. We do not assist them-how could we? Father wouldn't dare raise Egyptian soldiers. Their pleas for aid fall on deaf ears, and so now they have no soldiers to sell us. We wait for another attack in our home; an assassin, poison, anything. We wait for word that there is an army marching against us, and all we have for soldiers are our few foreigners, and the scarcer hard men from Middle Egypt that Father can trust. We are surrounded, and all because Father insists that Egypt must pray as he commands when the priesthoods he hated are long smashed.

But summer ends quietly, thanks be to Aten. Mayati comes from her new palace to visit me on a cool day, bringing her pretty daughter along. The baby girl-named for my sister-toddles about and says a few words, and surprisingly Mayati carries her baby herself rather than letting a nurse mind her.

But when Mayati offers to let me hold her, I balk. "I don't know how," I protest, which is complete nonsense with all the baby sisters I once had. I offer my little niece date candy, but I cannot touch her.

Mayati doesn't push. Instead, she tells me, "Father's going to bless the fields in a few days. He wants you there with him."

"Me? Not Mother, not you?" My voice pinches in my throat. That is a woman's job, a royal, married woman, enacting a fertility rite. It is a terrible omen.

"Of course I'm going," she says sharply. "Why would I not? But he wants you to come along as well."

I blink the horror out of my eyes. Mayati stares at me, not bothering to hide her malicious jealousy. She hates me, as if I wouldn't run from this if I could! Oh, this is just awful! "I don't- I don't think I should," I say, shaking my head. "You're better for it."

My sister raises her eyebrows provocatively. "Will you tell His Majesty that? Shall I bring him your refusal? He sent me, you know. After everything, he sent *me* to fetch *you*."

I drop my gaze, chastened. "No, Mayati. I will come."

The days pass with dizzying speed; it's as if there's a lion rushing on my heels, tripping me, able to take me down at any moment but delaying the kill for his own reasons. The panic in my throat and heart keeps me from sleeping and eating, on edge at every moment. Father sends heavy gold to my door, to wear at the ceremony. Father's messenger comes, saying we will depart at sunrise on the following day. Father's guard appears just as I have finished dressing, to bring me down to the royal barge. And like a calf to slaughter, I go along, thinking, this is it. Childhood ends. I shall be a wife, a mother; I shall shame my own mother, and become my last sister's hated rival. I dig my nails into my palms. We mount the stairs and leave the King's House.

It happens so quickly. I join them on the barge, and Father extends his hand to me. I sit as a statue at his side, all of us in silence on the fair winter morning. The barge cuts across the river, to the blackened banks beyond. My sandals sink into fertile soil. Aten's priests burn incense, and from a distance, behind a line of soldiers, the farmers watch in curious awe. For the first time in my life, I realize that there were other ceremonies before this one; to which god? Who blessed the soil, and brought wheat forth from seed? The farmers know, but I do not. Do they think of Him, that other, as they listen to Father calling Aten to witness? Do they wish that it were the other, the old god, whoever he was, putting the life into their fields?

They do not sacrifice blood and life, but oil and water. Father sews a small patch of land himself, muddying his hands with soil. He then pours the purified water onto the yielding black earth. Our gauzy white robes billow in the northerly wind, our hems staining with flood-silt and mud sucking over our feet. Father, the tallest man around, raises his arms high to the Aten above. He speaks of Aten ordering a time for all things; he speaks of harvest, of death; he speaks of the dark magic-out of our sight but known and ordained by Aten-that draws life out of seed once more. He propitiates Aten, and calls on his heavenly father to bring a bounty for his beautiful children.

I lower my eyes in shame, then, certain that Aten has heard all my traitorous thoughts. Why should I not believe in Aten, in my father's reformation? Am I really so disloyal, as he accuses everyone else of being? Father startles me out of my guilty thoughts, calling my name. I look up and he beckons me to his side, and I go, my feet sucking in the mud. As Mayati glares on, Father pours the waters of blessing over my brow. It is warm, even in the chilled breeze. Father hands me sweet oil. "Bless the earth, child of Aten," he instructs.

I pour the libations onto the fresh earth, watching the oil pool into shining pockets of mud. Father nods in approval. He completes the ritual, and now, all work can begin. The crops will be sewn in neat rows, and Aten will draw life out from each grain of seed and nurture it with his beneficent rays. Our prosperity will spring again from the ground, from the dark womb of the earth. This is the greatest of mysteries; it's the truth right before my eyes. I contemplate the power of the god for a moment; surely, whatever men call him, the god of life is beautiful and strong.

Chapter Eighteen

When we return to the palace, Father murmurs something to Mayati that makes her eyes burn hatefully. As I knew she would, my sister approaches me. "Bathe, dress well, and join us for the mid-day meal. He means to honor you with a seat at his side."

"Mayati…" I swallow hard, watching my father's snapping robe as he disappears down the hallway. "It isn't happening today, is it?"

"How should I know?" she snaps. "But you haven't fooled anyone. We can all see you've grown, even if you still claim childhood."

I take a breath for courage, and close my eyes. I can still feel the rush of warm water over my face; I can still smell the fresh, damp earth in the air. All will be well. All must be well. When it happens, as I am sure it will, it will be but another ceremony, another mystery. That is all. Though every part of me rebels from this, I must be brave. I stay my trembling hands and tell my sister, in the most grown-up voice I can find, "I shall be pleased to join you both."

I enter the banquet hall in a pale gown, my father's golden collars heavy on my neck. The first person I see is not Father, but Mother, who seems to hold her own court a ways down the table. She studies me with hard eyes, until my cheeks burn and my stomach tightens.

"Princess," Father says, his voice carrying the warmth of nighttime. I take my seat on his other side, slowly, making all care to be graceful and decorous.

I had expected Father to speak with me; he said a prayer over the dirt, I should think taking a wife would be a much more sacred ceremony. I had expected a solemn, serene meal, where we might discuss and contemplate the mysteries of creation. Instead, there is a wild party around the high tables. Father, drunk, laughs loud and shouts down his table, insisting that all eat and drink merrily to show their gratitude. His drummers play a heavy, lively beat. Father draws dancing girls around us, each one rivaling to catch Pharaoh's eye even as they dance together in ways that frighten me. My father approves greatly of it all.

But at the very same time, the tables on the floor are in near silence. The men's words are as nervous and quick as mice. The most powerful men in Amarna do not care for the young gymnasts kicking their legs over their heads, and I'm sure they're not marveling over the caliber of the wine. Father stays alert to this as well, and with every cup of wine his eyes go harder.

He stands abruptly. The throne-heavy as only solid gold could be-scrapes the dais as the force of him throws it back. The dancers fall away, the music stops, and Father shouts, "What are you women cowering at?"

Forty pairs of eyes turn up to him, but not a man speaks. In the room, Lord Rameses, the viziers, General Horemhab who tonight is not at the high table, but in furious conference with the returned General May; and many more. Down our table beside Lord Ay, Mother raises her eyebrows in disbelief.

"Well? Speak! Vizier Ankheti!"

Lord Akheti stands up, patting his heavy belly nervously. He bows and says, "Majesty, we discuss the Nubian mercenaries lost in the desert. Many feel they defected, and that others will soon follow."

I look to at the hundred or so palace guard in the hall-all from Nubia. They do an excellent job of not hearing a thing, and remain like stone in their crisp uniforms. Does Ankheti really mean that our soldiers are deserting us? If the Asians no longer send men, and the Nubians dissolve back into the southlands, then who will protect us?

Father drains his cup and sets it down carefully. He caresses the curves of the gilded chalice with one long finger, and then he grabs the cup and throws it crashing to the floor. "Did ever a more ungrateful, traitorous council slurp like pigs from a king's cup?"

Ankheti stands in frozen horror. I think maybe Father will have him dragged away, like he did to the poor man who worried for his mother.

"How is the wine, Ankheti? Do you recognize the taste? Have you enjoyed it before?"

The man, meticulous in his dress and grooming, flushes at his king's harsh attention. He bows his head abashedly-why?-and says, "I do recognize it, Lord of Life."

"Indeed-it is from the cellar at Karnak! I gave you fifteen amphorae, of this very vintage!" He looks about the room, calling, "You may call me the butcher of Karnak-as the peasants in Thebes do-but hear this: you have all torn from the carcass! And when they come for me, they come for *you* fools. So quit huddling like girls, and think of how you shall help me destroy them!"

A hissing murmur rolls through the room at the king's craven words, but no one can see where it comes from. Father swings about seeking the source, in vain. I look at my sister: furious, haughty. I look to my mother, and she is still, her eyes cast down to the table. Lord Ay murmurs something to his wife; I think I see dread in his narrow, slanted eyes. The beauty of the morning ceremony slips away. My fear is actually a cold rush, freezing me from my fingertips to my belly. My father is not stable, and everyone can see it.

Father threatens them all; he promises them that his enemies are theirs, but if any man wants to slip away into the night, like those Nubian cowards, then they are welcome to it. But they had best run very far, for he, Father, will hunt them like the dogs they are, if the treacherous Egyptian peasants don't kill them first.

He stalks up the dais again, but he has no intention of staying in this company. He snatches up his staff of office, and then he turns to me. I do not know the man before me, but he grabs my arm and pulls me right out of my seat. I look to Mayati in horror, and she turns her face. Everyone turns their faces. My father pulls me along behind him so fast that I trip and stumble out of the hall. I shake in panic, my knees weak.

It is a nightmare that gets worse by the moment. He is terrifying, cold, foul tempered; I cannot walk so willingly now, I cannot go along in gracious obedience as I was told to do, and so he pulls me to his chambers. He yanks my gown away, tosses me down on his great feathered bed. He crushes me with his heavy body, running his hands roughly over me. The sudden pain is shocking, nauseating, like claws in my stomach, like my insides burning me alive. I scream for him to stop. Blinded by pain and fear, I scream for my father to help me. He shouts in astonished anger. He smothers my mouth with his enormous hand, and this is how I am made my father's wife.

Chapter Nineteen

"Sit still," Mayati says again, holding the thick needle to my cheek. "And *don't* hold your breath."

I swallow as the hot needle pierces and pops through my ear, not even daring to flinch at the sting. My sister holds linen smeared with a minty ointment to my ear. "Is it bleeding a lot?" I ask, sickened by the thought of my split blood.

"Not much. When Mother pierced your ears when you were a baby, you bled a lot, and you screamed too. Now the other," she says, wagging her finger. I turn my chin and brace myself for another bite, cringing a little more from the memory of the first. "Not so bad, see?" Mayati murmurs softly. "There. All done with the hard part."

She fits another, smaller hoop earring in each of the second piercings. When I look in the mirror, the heavy gold in my ears gives the impression of a sun encircling a moon.

"It's pretty," Mayati tells me, offering a rare smile.

I take another look, and then set her golden *ankh* mirror down. I thank her, but my quiet voice doesn't show much gratitude. My sister offers me wine, but it's too strong, it tastes nasty. She sees my face and gives me a sly smile. She retrieves a delicate bottle of blue glass, and pulls the long stopper out. To my complete surprise, my sister puts the stopper between her lips, puckering them over the dark, thick liquid. "Poppy syrup," she says. "Here. You can have this one, if you like."

By the time we dine, I can hardly keep my eyes open. No one really notices anyway. My sister is again my rival, dazzling in her fine clothes. My mother... I don't look at her, but I can see her gathering her ladies around her and a good number of the men as well. And him: I don't look towards that awful throne. It's easier this way, not to hear him, not to see him, as if he were dead. I hate him, but I am terrified to let him know it. I hate the heavy paint on my face. I hate the heavy headdress over the braids that took six hours put into my hair. I hate my throbbing ears, and everything they hear. I want to go back to my room, but it's not really mine either anymore, it's *his.* I feel like I'm dying, but I mustn't show it, I mustn't sob here and I can't leave, and no one cares...

"Sit up," Mayati hisses, cutting into my daze. "You look like a stunned animal."

"I am stunned," I breathe. "I... I don't want to be here. I don't want to be *this.*"

She laughs, as if I've said something ridiculous. "Everyone down there would trade with you in a heartbeat. Sit up, so Pharaoh doesn't think something's wrong with you."

"He wouldn't notice, no matter what was wrong," I say mutinously. But I realize, then, that she doesn't want to get in trouble for giving me opium. Mayati's not talking to me for my sake at all.

Two weeks later, Mayati yanks the curtains open around my bed, letting the daylight in. I don't want to get up.

"Come on!" she says, smacking my cheeks lightly. "Honestly, if I had known you'd do so much..."

"I don't want to-" I murmur, letting my eyes flutter shut again, trying to find that warm, safe place, the place of no pain.

"Suit yourself. Your prince is about to get caned though. I thought you'd want to see."

"What?" I push myself up, instantly dizzy from the effort and the strong drink.

"I told you he was rotten like his mother, and now everyone knows it."

"Mayati, tell me what happened!"

She notes the quick rise of my fear, and the way I suddenly came to life. Has *she* ever cared about anyone so much? I have to know how much trouble Tutankhaten will be in!

"Pharaoh had him before the court, and asked him if he could shoot blindfolded yet. He could have shown off again-we all know how much he enjoys it-but instead... I really couldn't believe it... He told Pharaoh that he, Tutankhaten, was not a monkey to do tricks! He said, 'We are not your pets, Your Majesty,' and then sat there with his little chin in the air and his eyes burning with defiance. He's insolent, just like his mother was. Now he will be beaten in the courtyard, and we can watch if you hurry."

I climb out of bed and tie the sash on my thick robe tighter, but then I lurch and reach out to my sister. "Are you going to be sick?"

"I don't know. I feel terrible, Mayati. But let's go." I can't just lie here, knowing that Tutankhaten's going to be beaten!

We step into the cool courtyard just as Father comes down the stairs, his steps loose from drunkenness. A hard-eyed Tutankhaten walks in silence before him, defiant with courage. I try to smile at him, to just show him that I'm with him.

"Move along!" Father barks.

No one can punish the royal prince, so Father must beat Tutankhaten himself. His servant trots out with a thick wooden switch, and Father orders Tutankhaten to put his hands on one of the whispering sycamores. I want to scream in protest, but I have no voice before my father.

The cane makes a cracking noise against Tutankhaten's slim bronze back. He gasps audibly at its fiery bite; but Prince Tutankhaten grits his teeth and muffles his cries. Hot, indignant tears fall over his cheeks. I can feel each strike burning and tearing on my own back. Ten times, Father lashes Tutankhaten, and then he stays the cane in the air and demands, "Have you had enough?"

I close my eyes, because I know Tutankhaten; he won't admit to the pain. He can't say such a thing-yes, I'm beaten, you win. It's impossible for him. There is silence, and then cane cracks again, and again.

I only breathe again when he throws the cane to the ground. He glares at Tutankhaten, and then me before I can duck my head. I cringe at the sight of my father's eyes. Unbelievably, Father shakes his head and abandons us, stalking off without a word. I don't dare thank Aten for this mercy; Aten is *his*, him.

When he's gone, I go to Tutankhaten. He clutches the curling bark of the tree with tight, trembling fingers.

"Is it bad?" he asks, clenching his jaw, whispering so he won't scream.

"I don't think you'll scar," I say, the best I can offer. I take his arms, but Tutankhaten doesn't want to let go of the tree.

"Come on," I say, pulling his hands away.

His fingers lace mine tightly. "I miss you."

It hurts so much I can't even tell him I miss him back. The only sound I can make is a little cry of anguish. There's nothing we can do about it anyway, but I wish more than anything it could be last summer. I wish we could run away and go swimming; I wish we could be free. I wish I was not married, painted like a doll and dying in my heart.

We walk to his large apartments together. Inside, Maia's hands cover her cheeks in horror. She looks at me accusingly, and I realize she blames me for this, and that my very presence here will bring more trouble. Tutankhaten stretches out across his bed. He closes his eyes as his nurse rubs cooling ointment over his back. I don't belong here anymore, not if I want Tutankhaten to be safe. With an aching heart, I go back to the land of death. I hear his cry of alarm and sorrow behind me-*No! Stay, please!* I hear Maia tell him to let me go, to think of his future. She's right. Tutankhaten still has one, and I don't want to ruin it for him.

Chapter Twenty

Summer, Year Seventeen

I jolt awake in the night, knowing intuitively that it is time. "Nani!" I call softly.

The old midwife turns around on her stool, roused from her half-sleep. "What is it, child?"

I nod at her. "I think it is happening."

"About time, isn't it?" she asks, coming to life. Nani has been a blessing during this awful pregnancy. Father summoned her early on, after I fainted dead to the floor in his presence. He thought it was the child he made on me making me weak and sick, never realizing that it was terror and panic at the sight of him that stole my breath and my consciousness. Even I knew that. The old midwife came out of her retirement for me, and she understood everything. She saved me, too, at least for a while; unimaginably fearless, old Nani did what no one else dared. She told the king that the child would be injured if he kept on coming to my bed, and so by the time I was four months pregnant, I finally had peace. I didn't tell her that it was too late, that I was already ruined, that my hands will never stop shaking and the nightmares are just as bad even without my father's painful and frightening nighttime visits.

But tonight I can only think of one thing: getting this creature out of me without dying in the process.

"I'll call for hot water," Nani says, and I nod, eager to get this over.

Though four babies have been born to my house since I was a little girl, and I really should know better, I'm quite surprised at how boring it all is. Twice an hour, my belly tightens and turns, a dull ache that spreads through my back. There's little to be done. I drink a hearty broth, and take Nani's teas and potions for strength, and then I sit back in my bed and study the list of Asian city-states, and their rulers and customs, that Tutankhaten gave me. Ugarit, Tunip, Jaffe, Jerusalem, Moab... The lands of the violent, chaotic god Ba'al. I let the far-away places and names fill my heart, so that I don't look at my tiny hips under my swollen belly and faint for fear.

But I can't ignore it for long. "Ooh, Nani, this one is worse!" I cry, pushing my hands into my back and gritting my teeth to the consuming pain.

The wise woman chuckles. "Thought it would be easy, did you? It'll get a whole lot worse than that before this child is born."

"You think I'll have a boy?" I ask, once the contraction vanishes again, as if it never came at all.

"Do you want a boy now?" she asks me carefully, and I purse my lips together. The seer knows the truth of it: I don't want either. My eyes brim with tears, and Nani pats my leg reassuringly. "Never mind all that. You think of something that makes you happy, little lady, to keep up your courage."

"I just want it out, Nani!" Out, away, in a nursery far from sight! I want nothing to do with this child. It can go to a nurse, and I will go back to my room and crawl into my bed, and lie in the darkness alone.

"This baby wants out, and we shall help it along. Now up, out of that bed! You must walk about, right through the pain."

And so, another absurd indignity: I walk circles in my room like a donkey on a track while the midwife's apprentice and assistants join to watch. As the night wears on, the pain grows worse, wrenching actually, and I beg Nani to let me sit. "Please! Just a moment, I cannot breathe, Nani!"

She motions to the bed, taking the opportunity to check my progress. I've learned to endure this as well, a woman pushing around and examining things. I dare not take a breath or open my eyes or even consider feeling my own body. "Not even close," she declares. "Up again, princess."

I walk only halfway around when a blinding, tearing pain lashes me. I scream and throw my weight onto the apprentice, who leads me gently on by my elbow. But then, dampness rushes down my thighs and onto the floor, and it is not just the waters that welcome the baby, but thick red blood. The younger women's faces screw up in fear, and my sobbing turns frantic. I'm quickly brought back to the bed, and urged to be strong, but not for the first time I think that I am far too young to be here, far too small.

The light of dawn shines in as I'm battered by wave after wave of relentless, ripping pains. I can hardly breathe or think, and the women's voices hang in the air, disembodied and surreal: "She is fighting it," they say. I wind up on the birthing stool without knowing how I got there, and I cannot hold the ropes to keep my battling body upright. There is no strength in my hands at all, no strength in my heart. *It would be good to let go*, a traitorous voice in my heart whispers. *It would be quiet there, on the other side; no Father.*

The sound of a commotion pulls me back into the world. I turn my head weakly towards the door as Nani's firm, but unintelligible voice issues some command. She is refusing someone admittance, and in my delirium I call out for my mother, sure she is here to give me courage.

Nani is at my side again. She presses a wet, cut flower, a pink lotus just opened up to greet the sun, into my shaking hands. "The prince is outside, child. He demanded to be let into this place, but I told him this was women's business. He says he'll wait for you, and your little one."

I am lucid for a moment, at this. I bite down on my screams, thinking that Tutankhaten loves me, and maybe it is worse to hear one you love dying than to be dying yourself. The lush pink of the flower soothes my exhausted eyes. I fall into the sight, noting absently how the droplets of water blink like stars on the petals.

Nani tells me I must stop pushing, and it's all I want to do. They say the baby is trapped, and I cannot understand them. They mean it will die? I will die? I can't be concerned anymore. If I die, this will all end, the agony in my belly and my back and between my thighs will float away, and it will all be quiet.

I am lying in my bed now, and Nani is forcing me to hear her, when all I want is sleep. "You must give me consent, your highness. Do you understand? We've no time to summon the king. You must choose, right now."

"Go away," I moan, taxed to my limit.

"Listen to me!" This woman is grabbing my face, making me see her, and really she ought not to do that. I am royally born; she should not be touching me. I hate to be touched… "If we do nothing, the child will die, and so will you! But if you let us pull the child from you, then perhaps the child will die, but you will live. Princess!"

I turn my head away without hearing her. They are clucking together now, these women, like hens in the kitchen courtyards. Suddenly a murderous scream tears through the pavilion; I recognize it dimly as my own. There is violent pain between my legs, and it is far too much to bear. I give way, finally falling into the welcoming darkness.

Chapter Twenty One

When I wake up in my own bed, I don't expect to see a live baby in Tia's arms. I try to sit up, until I feel how sore I am, like I've been gored by a bull. But sure enough, there is a swaddled infant hidden in blanket, tiny in Tia's tender clutch. Could it be possible?

"A girl," Tia says quietly, wiping her eyes. "Sick. The royal physician is certain she will pass away soon."

So, a girl, and doomed from the beginning. I look up fearfully. "Did you tell him?"

Tia nods. "A messenger was sent, yesterday. You slept the whole day through." She curls her lips in anger and adds, "He has not come yet, nor even sent a word."

"Oh, but that's so much better!" I tell her, pained even from speech. If Father were truly enraged, I would have been shaken from my bed. Maybe it's over now. Maybe I can drift into obscurity, as all the other wives have done. He is finished with me.

I settle back into bed, numb and sickened. When Tia asks me if I want my daughter, I cannot bear it. I close my eyes and turn my head, ignoring her. Nani comes in not much later. "He's still outside," she tells Tia, thinking me asleep.

I open my eyes and gasp, "Who?" Not Father!

"Awake, then," Nani says with a thin smile of gratitude. "You've made it. Now if we can keep the fever away, you shall survive this ill-done business."

129

"Who is *outside*?" I cry, desperate.

"The prince, your highness. Your prince. He's waited this whole time, since you were brought back from the pavilion. Let me bring him for you."

"No-" I begin, pinching my eyes shut. Now the pink lotus flower in a vase beside my bed-all budded up from missing the sun-makes sense. I remember: he picked it for me in the middle of yesterday's ordeal.

The doors open, and Tutankhaten steps in, his eyes rimmed with purple circles like bruises. He throws his arms around me. He lost his mother in childbirth; he thought he would lose me that way as well. But then he asks me, "Why is she still holding your daughter?"

I say very softly, "She will die."

"I know, Nani told me..." His eyes fill with tears, the tears I can't cry. He asks incredulously, "Have you not seen her yet?"

I bite my lips, and Tutankhaten shakes his head, bewildered. He springs up from the bed and goes to Tia with open arms. She cannot gainsay Tutankhaten, and so he brings the small but threatening bundle back to my bed.

"No!" I cry, turning my face away. I don't want to see her! She is Father's, she's even going straight to Aten. I don't want to see her!

"Ankhesenpaaten, you *must*," he says, quiet and urgent.

"No, I can't, I can't! Why are you doing this?"

"Because it is right," he whispers. "Because you are a mother now, no matter what," he says, sitting carefully, cradling my baby. "Look at her," he murmurs, afraid to speak above a breathy whisper. "Please, you must. She only has you."

"No."

"Shh, listen... She wants you. She needs you, and you need to hold her before she goes home." He admits softly, "I hope my mother held me before she went."

The first tear slides over my cheek. I sit up with Nani's help, and I know he's right when I see Nani nodding her head. There, in Tutankhaten's slim bronze arms, is my own child. He smiles softly, wistfully, as he pulls the blanket back from her sleeping face.

I draw my breath, because it's so terribly sad to see her. My baby is perfect, tiny, but perfect from her hummingbird-feather lashes around her almond eyes, to her little pink lips. "She is beautiful, like you," Tutankhaten says, touching the baby's plump honey toned cheek with his finger. My daughter stirs towards him, turns her little rosebud mouth to his finger. We both look expectantly to Nani; is this some sign that she'll live?

Nani's eyes cast down. "They all do that, awake or asleep."

By the time Tutankhaten puts her in my arms, I know I want her. Oh, more than anything I want her! She is everything I am, but she knows nothing of sorrow. She's as fresh and pure as the sunrise, and she is mine. We hold her for hours, Tutankhaten and I, amazed, in love. But by the first stars of night, my little girl's breath grows raspy, shallow, and then it stops all together. My one day baby, my fleeting sunshine child. Nani takes her away, murmuring words over the blessed dead, and I fall to sobs in Tutankhaten's arms. He clutches me, his own tears wet on my cheeks; he sings one of Maia's often hummed songs in a soft, sweet voice:

My love is across the river,
And the flood rages between us.
A crocodile waits on the sandbanks,
But I am not afraid.
I will swim to reach her,
I will cross the river to my love.

My father sends me two golden bracelets for my daughter, but denies me the joy of his presence. Tutankhaten throws them across the room, away from us, as if they were filled with poison like the diadem. He pulls the curtains tight around my bed, and brushes his fingers through my tangled hair as we lie in the darkness. Stunned by sorrow and lulled by the one who would never betray me, I mourn my daughter in silence.

Chapter Twenty Two

Winter, Year Seventeen

"Ankhesenpaaten, wake up…"

I open my eyes to a bright morning, with Tutankhaten at my side as he has been every morning for two months. But instantly, I hear something awful, the most agonized wailing of women that I've ever heard, even worse than when the plague came. "What is it?" I ask, stony dread deep in my belly.

"I don't know," Tutankhaten says, standing up.

A loud howl echoes in the hall once more, and I cry, "Where is Tia? Shouldn't she have our breakfast by now? I hope nothing's happened to her!"

"I'm going to see," Tutankhaten decides quietly. I realize it could be any one of a thousand evils: assassins broken into the palace, rebels marching on Amarna, my father executing a servant for spilling his morning wine.

As he opens the door, a gaggle of servants run through the hall, some wailing, some merely rushing to spread gossip. I'm reminded instantly of the day someone tried to poison my father, killing that pretty boy instead. "Wait!" I cry, climbing out of bed. The floor has never felt so cold on my feet. My legs still quiver, all these weeks later. I clutch his arm tightly, shaking my head. "It could be unsafe!"

133

"I know. Stay here-I'll come back for you. It's probably nothing serious."

I shake my head so hard my waist-skimming braids snap together. "Please don't leave me!"

He pinches his lips in disapproval, but we step out into the hall together. The courtyard is teeming with soldiers and servants all over again. Some women wail kneeling on the ground, tossing handfuls of mulch and garden dirt onto their gowns and faces. It is the sound of death; death has returned to our mansion yet again. I cling to Tutankhaten as we make our slow way through the misery; it centers around my father's enormous gilded doors.

Next to my father's door, Vizier Ay, the royal physician, and the captain of the guard stand with their heads together, whispering. Ay holds my mother's arm; her other hand covers her heart in shock. Mayati pushes her way through the crowd and falls to her knees, a great keening sob echoing from her lips.

I understand everything in one shocking, staggering moment: he is dead. My father the king, the god, my cruel husband, is dead.

Chapter Twenty Three

My mother is holding both of my hands tenderly, and suddenly, flashing behind my eyes, I see myself dragging my fingernails down her painted face.

I gulp, shocked at myself, frightened that I could imagine such a thing. I set myself hard on listening to her.

"He died of drink, Ankhesenpaaten. He drank himself to death, he smoked himself to death. It is shameful, and we'll not speak of it again."

My tearful sister steps forward and demands, "Who will be king? The palace is already surrounded by mourners and frightened peasants. What will you tell them?"

"Your father named me his Co-Regent, daughter, just for this reason. I will rule Egypt now."

"You! Alone! But you are a woman!"

"There is precedent," Mother declares, rising from her chair. She strides across her room and thrusts open the doors to her private garden, letting in a wave of pale gold sunlight. She basks in it for a long moment, and I swear I see a hidden smile working her lips and cheeks. "Pharaoh Hatshepsut was a woman, and she ruled for over twenty years. The aristocracy will follow me. In truth, they have been following me for more than two years."

She returns to us, standing before her oldest daughter. Mayati's eyes are hawkish. Her sharp chin is thrusted forward, making her full lips dominate her face in an enormous pout. The cut of her face is just the same as Father's, and I think how very much his creature she is. Mother smiles at her fiercest child and says, "Today we shall proclaim the beginning of my reign, and Meri-Re shall anoint you as my heiress. What need have we for men, who only muddle things up with their emotions and desires? I will be Pharaoh, and you, my dear eldest daughter, will be Pharaoh when I die."

I can't be sure what I'm hearing-women, ruling my father's nation? But it isn't his anymore; he's gone to join Aten in the heavens, and we are left alone to carry his burden.

Mayati bows her head to Mother, speaking of her honor. And I bow my head as well; I am free now. I am free, I can hardly imagine it! My father has left his palace in a shroud, and I should mourn, but I can't. His death has ended my nightmare.

My mother's fingers shock me. She strokes my face lightly, and I quiver at the touch. I hate her; she has freed me, but so late that it hardly matters at all! Her false affection repulses me. It's all I can do not to slap her hand.

"Nani says you are well recovered, for what you've endured." Mother's voice infuses with smothered anger. For me, for Father? Who can tell?

But well recovered? I shake in my sleep, torn apart by evil dreams. I ache for my daughter. The walk through my house was exhausting, and most days I have to fight to eat. Were it not for Tutankhaten, I would have no desire for life. Well recovered! I tremble with anger at her stupid and cruel deduction.

"It wasn't my fault, Ankhesenpaaten. I could not stand against him, not without causing you greater harm. I wept and worried for you every single day."

Liar! She worried only about her crown. I stare down at her carnelian beaded sandals, so that I don't have to see her awfully beautiful face, made so ugly by ambition.

"We shall all move to Mayati's palace, across the Royal Road."

"My palace!" Mayati protests, shaking her head.

"Yes, we shall take residence in the Annex Palace. We will have a new beginning there. Porters will come for what things you wish to bring this afternoon." I feel her hardened eyes on me, and she adds, "And Ankhesenpaaten, the young prince will remain behind, here in the King's House. He shall never share your chambers again; you are no child, and it is improper. You may tell him, as I surely will myself, that if he keeps to his studies and his youthful pleasures, if he conforms to my laws, then he will be safe as my devoted servant. And if not..." She lets her words dangle innocently into the air, but I know only too well what she means.

"Her *servant*?" Tutankhaten asks incredulously. "She-a commoner by blood-calls me *servant*?"

"She's going to be Pharaoh," I say, staring blankly at the pile of jewels lined up on my bed. All were given to me by Father, and I would not willingly feel their heavy cold weight on my neck and wrists. Even so, I tell Tia to pack them all, and then I sigh and sink my head in my hands. "I can't believe it. I am a widow."

Tutankhaten touches my shoulder, and I lean against him. "Do you grieve for him?" he asks me softly.

I shake my head tightly. No, never. Did he grieve for me? Again, never. "Do you?"

Tutankhaten shrugs his shoulders, averting his eyes. Yes, then. But he says, "I don't know what to think. I... He's my father, and you're my heart, my best friend. My *only* friend. I hate him for what he did to you, but still, he is my father. Was my father, I mean."

I bite my lips. "I would not take your love for him. I wouldn't ask it of you."

"I know," he says, kissing my cheek lightly. "You're not that way. But those two... I'll spend my life looking over my shoulder, waiting for one of them to decide I'm a threat. Did you think the people sounded happy when she announced that she would be their *Pharaoh*?"

"They didn't sound like anything."

Tutankhaten nods, his long side lock sweeping his slim chest. "They were silent. Exactly."

Later, we creep hand in hand towards the balcony above Mayati's elaborate sunken garden.

Her palace-Mother's now-is an elaborate, gaudy place full of the latest styles in art and architecture. Mother sits with her small council among sprays of purple and blue flowers, and silver-green leaves that shake in the winter wind. All the most powerful men are present, dining on freshly butchered ox with roasted onions and garlic. Ay, Horemhab, Meri-Re, Paranefer, and Panhesy join Mother, Mayati, and Teye. Prince Smenkhare is there as well, though I can't imagine he'll have much to add to their discussion. Lord Ay sits beside Mother, as if he had taken Father's place. His voice carries over the others as he laments the state of our land.

"The local leaders have more authority than we do," he claims. "How will we call up men to repair the levees and labor in the mines? Nothing can be built, tolls are not collected, and with each moment our hold on power crumbles away. There is precious little time to take decisive action, Your Majesty. This family came rushing out of the south centuries ago, taking its power by the sword and spear and axe. It can happen again, if we do not restore the monarchy."

"We must kill them!" Mayati bursts, a fiery figure in a bold orange gown and collar of golden flower petals. She has not yet changed into her mourning robes. "We can't delay another moment; we must make one last war against our enemies, a war to end all wars!"

The silence of shock falls over the party below us, and Tutankhaten and I exchange a nervous glance. Doesn't Mayati know that we have no soldiers, other than the few thousand in the elite palace guard and a handful of Amarna lords in their expensive chariots?

"My daughter is shaken with grief," Mother says coldly, glaring at Mayati.

The heavily built general sets aside his second skewer of meat and onions. "Who will make war for you, your highness? I have but a few companies of chariot officers, and no professional infantry. Shall we conscript peasants and command them to fight their neighbors, their brothers? They would sooner march on you, my lady."

I cannot believe he is so bold! Father is not gone a full day, and this peasant challenges his First Daughter, his widow! I expect her to slash at him, but my sister's passion rises without any violence. "But they will not relent," Mayati declares, leaning forward with a witty tone and a fire in her eyes. "Our enemies will never embrace our laws! There is nothing more dangerous than attacking an enemy and leaving him alive, able to recover and bite back! How goes that saying, about the stinging ant?"

Beside me, Tutankhaten grins and says, "If you strike an ant be sure to smash him, or he will surely sting back at the palm that struck him."

Horemhab laughs-he *laughs!*-and begins to explain that we have no warriors with which to strike, but Mother cuts him off and says, "We need not have enemies, my daughter. They do not fight us for any reason but our own provocation. And as for embracing our laws, there is only one which they reject, one which has been the source of all sorrow for these past eight years."

Beside me, Tutankhaten draws in his breath. He squeezes my hand tightly, because the unthinkable is happening right before our eyes.

"You cannot mean it!" Mayati cries, standing up. She looks to the High Priest Meri-Re, who modestly looks to his supper, avoiding her eyes.

"We must unite our land once more, daughter. I like it no better than you, but your father is gone, and I will not deplete this land, or our treasury, to march us to our doom! Now, sit, and keep still." Mother looks around the table and says, "Forgive her, my lords. My daughter is passionate, and a pious devotee of the Great God Aten, but she has much to learn about ruling a nation; she has much to learn about her own land and people! She must learn to listen, so that she might learn to lead."

But my sister is not a child, nor will she be bridled. "Mother? Lord Ay? Lady Teye? Do you mean that you will undo all that Father spent his life to make? You, his closest companions! Do you not fear his retribution? Do you not fear the wrath of Aten?"

It is Lord Ay who answers, and how! He actually lays his hand over my mother's, in a gesture that smacks of command. And he says, in that coldly serpentine voice of his, "We did not fear the wrath of Amun, child, nor that of Osiris, Lord of Death, and his companion in decay Anubis, when we did your father's bidding and sacked the Temple of Karnak. And if he had lived on, perhaps we would not be here, hanging to life and power with splintering fingernails. Perhaps Aten in heaven need not concern himself with the flesh and blood of Egypt, but if you seek to rule, you must learn to! If you wish to live, then you will hear your mother when she tells you: the day of Aten's lonely rule is over. If we do not make peace, and pay homage once more to the ancient gods of this land, then we will be devoured by the mob."

In the edgy, thoughtful silence that follows the vizier's grim prediction, Prince Smenkhare finally speaks. His eyes linger on my sister for the first moment of his speech, but then he looks around the table, wielding his attractive Tuthmosid smile. "Why must we do this drastic thing now? All has been quiet since the death of Pentuwer. The last harvest was plentiful enough, and there are other lands where we might seek soldiers. The Greeks, for example. Do they not fight for pay and plunder across the islands of the northern sea?"

"Pirates in rotten animal hides!" Lord Paranefer exclaims, horrified. "You would invite such bestial creatures to our shores?"

"If it meant preserving what we have made here," Smenkhare says in his smooth voice. He looks slyly to my sister once again, with warmth in his eyes. Her thick lips part and she breathes heavily. I can see plainly that she's relieved to have someone take up her part.

"Bah!" Horemhab says, sucking down his wine. "Pirates or not, they are the fiercest of fighters. But even such war-loving men could not face the fury of Egyptian warriors, were they to unite under a pretender to the throne! No, we must remove the cause of war, as Her Majesty so wisely instructs. You can stay safe in Amarna with your musicians and your perfumed boys, dear prince; Her Majesty must become a king for all her people, and she must not flinch to do what's needed to save this land."

"You dare speak so to me, Horemhab, Son of Nobody? Without my father and my brother, you'd be eating day old fish in that village of shit you called a home!"

Horemhab's hand flies to his side-though he is of course unarmed.

"Peace!" Lord Ay shouts, smacking the table with his palm. The others thankfully heed the senior official, muffling their anxious cries. "Now, have we not had enough? Do we want more of this? Revolt, sabotage, mobs taking the streets and holding the countryside against the crown's soldiers! Who can do any business? What man might venture out to trade, when the roads are held by brigands? Shall we exchange our security, the good lives we have made for our families, merely to enforce a spiritual point over an unwilling people? My sister, the Great Royal Wife Tiy, wife of Pharaoh Amunhotep himself, knew this day was coming. Who here among us did not cringe when our lord, Pharaoh Akhenaten, determined that the ancient gods would be abandoned, and worship of only *his* patron god enforced as law?"

"Aten spoke to him!" Mayati hisses, shaking her head furiously. She glares at him hatefully and says, "Aten told him that He would not tolerate the worship of any other! And *you*, Lord Ay, were foremost in bringing Aten's Supremacy to pass!"

"I obeyed my lord, your highness," Ay clarifies. "That was,

and is, my duty. But I advised him as I advised your mother: abandoning the old ones would cause ruin to this land, and to your family. Perhaps not while your father reigned, for he was a mighty god; but we here are, for the most part, mortal. We must do what we can. Now, her Majesty has determined to reach out to an honorable and trustworthy man of good birth, our Lord Paranefer's older brother, Lord Maya of Thebes. Together, we might secure a peace that allows us to retain our places, and by grace, our heads!"

My sister cuts her eyes, lifting her chin as if to remind the vizier of her position. Smenkhare shakes his head, burying himself in his wine.

Lord Meri-Re takes his turn to speak, his soft words hardly reaching the balcony and our astonished ears. "Lord Ay, can we trust this Maya? He was a priest of Amun who refused to renounce his faith, and was only pardoned for his connections. Then he hid in Palestine for two years, before returning-not to Amarna, to the king who granted him mercy-but to *Thebes*! Forgive me, Lord Paranefer, he is your brother, but I must admit I am alarmed that we would deal with such a man. How do we know he won't betray us to our enemies?"

"My brother is the most loyal of men, venerable Lord Seer. It was his loyalty to his god that cost him his place at court; but even though he would not renounce Amun, neither did he betray his king."

Ay nods his head, confiding, "It was Lord Maya who sent Pharaoh Akhenaten intelligence on the movements of the renegades. He is known throughout the land as a man of respect and honor. If we are to recover our power, not just in Amarna but throughout Egypt, Lord Maya is the ideal man to help us along the way."

After another moment of rumbling speeches, Mother rises from her place. "Good lords, Prince, dearest daughter, you have come here today because you care about your futures, and the future of Egypt. Some of you are afraid that we will betray the work of our lives by honoring the other gods once more; allow me to put you at ease. It was never meant to go so far! We none of us meant to offend or betray the gods of our fathers, and we have suffered greatly these past years."

Ay and Teye nod their heads in unison.

Mother rests her long, elegant fingers on the table and closes her eyes, as if a great sorrow oppressed her. I cannot know if she mourns Father; perhaps once, she would have, but how now, after what he did to her, and to us? "My husband... My husband... He was but a youth when Aten first spoke to him, and called him to his great and immortal destiny. But the truth is ours was not a mission to rid Egypt of her beloved gods and goddesses. The truth is the priests of Amun had become gluttonous; saving, of course, those like Lord Maya who were content to do the god's work, and the will of Pharaoh. We set out to free Egypt-and, let us not lie, liberate ourselves-from the oppression of those who sought a power greater than that which nature had given them. It was never Amun, nor Ptah nor Osiris, who offended, but the corpulent priesthoods who had dared trespass on Pharaoh's divine authority. And we succeeded; how we succeeded! Perhaps it was that taste of victory which whetted my husband's appetite for supreme control. Through Aten, my husband became the sole god of Egypt. So great was his vision and power that he unbound thousands of years of deeply woven tradition, and nestled himself in the middle of it. We who are constrained by mortal flesh and time will never hear the echoes of my husband's mighty roar; yet we can perceive that echo it shall, into eternity."

Mother closes her eyes, and allows herself a small, sad smile. A long moment passes, and I sink back onto my shins. I want her to be quiet. I don't want to hear anything like this. I don't want to remember the brilliance of a man who became a monster.

"Don't," Tutankhaten murmurs softly, squeezing my hand.

I nod, biting my lips. Mother goes on, finally, and speaking good sense too. She says, "Yet truly, my lords, we have made war where peace and good example ought to have served better. These past eight years have proven that not even a god-king can command the conscience of his people. We have seen that the great gods of Egypt have not died or gone away-in fact, we can see examples of their vengeance with the turn of each season! We have endured plague, war, the loss of allies and territories to barbarian armies, poor floods and worse harvests... Can anyone doubt that we are in a perilous place, clinging, as Lord Ay said, by our very fingernails to life and prosperity? Blinded by my husband's brilliance, we have neglected those old ones who blessed our home in the first days, and they have shown us their wrath! We can no longer remain blind and deaf; we cannot ignore our duties any longer. The time has come to restore this land to her glory, so that we may once again know the peace of the gods. I beseech you all to stand with me in this monumental task."

Mother has them. The men, Lady Teye, all but Mayati seem to agree. Smenkhare sighs and drinks his wine, as if he cannot argue with her wisdom. Much like us, he doesn't know any other gods, either. He learned of Aten as a little boy, when Father taught him because Grandfather was far too sick to bother with yet another child. But he's been here, watching like us these past few years. He's seen our world fall apart. We all know what we face, deep down, even those of us who rarely see the inside of a Pharaoh's council.

"I can't believe it," Tutankhaten murmurs, leaning forward to peer down on everyone as they are dismissed. He looks back at me, stunned. My mother, the new Pharaoh, is making policy that which his mother was beaten for saying. Tutankhaten laughs softly in disbelief.

But just then, that clever warrior Horemhab squints up at the carved stone balcony. He sees us, peering through the thick green fronds of the potted plants. Just as quickly, he turns politely to hear a private word from the taciturn treasurer Panhesy. Tutankhaten tugs my arm. "He saw us. Let's go."

We do not know this palace, but we slip around corridors and through muraled hallways to get away as quickly as we can. "You think he will tell?" I finally ask, near to swooning with panic.

Tutankhaten shakes his head. "No." He leans back against the wall and takes a deep breath, and then he smiles. "They are going to bring back the old gods."

"But were they not false?" I ask finally, mostly because I'm angry that everything I've ever learned is obviously a lie. I do not even know the truth about the gods! What *can* I know?

"I don't think so, Ankhesenpaaten. I think the priests were bad, but they are all gone now. I think it's just like your mother said; she and Father went too far."

"I hate this," I say, on the edge of tears again.

"Things will get better, you'll see," he says, slinging his arm around my shoulders. I flinch slightly, drawing my shoulders up and digging my nails into my palms. But his smile is so reassuring, so caring, that I lay my head on his shoulder, very tentatively. I can still remember when it was comforting to be held, loved, though it seems so very long ago.

"So you will pray to these gods?" I murmur, resigning to it.

Tutankhaten narrows his dark eyes thoughfully. "Well, really what's important is letting the common folk pray as they please, to their patron gods. But I think I shall certainly learn more about them. After all, these are the gods who gave our family power and divinity, and are as old as the river. But the most important thing for Egypt, and for your mother, is to make peace, and bringing back the old gods is the way to do it."

Chapter Twenty Four

I lie in bed in darkness that night. My new blanket, a pretty and delicate quilt with embroidered stars, is bunched up in my fists and clutched like a shield. Outside, the palace guard changes shifts with little more sound than their marching feet. A cold wind blows down the hall outside my door, probably from the showy third story balcony my sister designed to crown this wing. I only wonder if our enemies might be able to grapple over the side and swarm us.

But things will be better now, that's what Tutankhaten said. One day, we might not live in fear of enemies, outsiders. And we'll only have to give up all we know to do it. I twist in the sheets, ever chasing a cool and comfortable place. It is far too quiet now. There must be a nest of bats in a crack of this new palace façade, I hear them chirping and flapping past the latticed windows.

A door closes, a soft thump, somewhere outside my room. I pull the blankets up to my chin; I am shaking, horribly, but it won't stop. I stare at my hands as if they were some strange creature, unattached and beyond my control.

Tia has left a delicate alabaster decanter of wine for me, for this very reason. I climb out of bed stealthily, as if there were a sleeping lion in my bedroom that I dare not wake. I drink two cups of wine back to back, and wipe my mouth commonly with the back of my hand. The wine warms my belly, and I hope it will dull my sharp fear as well.

I wish more than anything that Tutankhaten was here.

The wine sends me to sleep eventually, but terribly I am jarred awake not much later. My violent nightmare breaks up like mist all around me, washed away by my tears. I do not risk sleep after this. In the long hours of blackness, I sit in my bed, my blankets like a tent around me, and I force myself to think of nothing but my own shallow breathing. Nevertheless, thoughts creep in. As the night wanes, and out of the solid blackness come forms of shadow and grey, my daughter's face haunts me and breaks my heart with guilt and longing. I push my many pillows and cushions up behind me; I lie back, propped up as I was when I took the helpless bundle from Tutankhaten's arms. She was so light that even now, with my empty arms aching, I can trick myself into feeling her tiny body anyway.

In the morning, the world breaks up again. Tia rushes into my room as I comb my hair, her face awash with tears. A grimace covers my own face, and I don't even want to ask.

"Your mother- Her Majesty-" Tia shuts her eyes. "Oh, child, they've killed her!"

I scream, but she begs me to quiet. There is more. "It was your sister. Your sister's killed your mother, and made Smenkhare the Pharaoh."

Mayati presides over a full court of Amarna's finest lords. She stands tall in a gown of gold cloth and a gold *shebyu* collar around her neck, and proclaims that she will pick up her father's great mission, she will take the glory of Aten unto herself, she will beat any rebels back and scorch their fields black. She kisses Smenkhare full on the mouth before she settles to her dinner, leaving little doubt of her intentions. Because the court is now fronted by Smenkhare's favored companions, hearty cheers ring out; but beyond the highest tables, there is appalled silence.

I look between them, horrified. He put her up to it, that's plain enough. Smenkhare climbs so quickly into my father's chair you'd think he's had his eye on it for years. Horemhab spoke true about him, and everyone at that council seems to know it. But now Horemhab must watch his back and mind what he eats. He skulks around the perimeter of the court, wondering when the new Pharaoh will attack.

Smenkhare dives gleefully into Father's private treasury. Though we are in mourning-double mourning-he orders up new barges, gold threaded garments, and jewels aplenty. When my sister balks, he pets her and praises her, and speaks of Aten. He is so false! Mayati can't see it, though. My sister hid away her first love somewhere deep in her belly when she stepped to Father's side. Now he is hers, Egypt is hers, and she spends much of her time on her knees in the Great Temple. Once I hear her say that she's avenged Father, and I shudder to think what she might mean. Have I truly been bred by murderers? My home, as it turns out, is no home at all, but a snake pit.

And then, Vizier Ay confronts them, coming out of his private mourning to feast with the new monarchs. Smenkhare makes a great fuss over him, and I turn away so he can't see the judgment in my eyes. Even as a Pharaoh, he still fawns over the strongman in the room. But my sister, at least, hasn't forgotten her anger. She looks at him coldly, her leonine eyes peering over Smenkhare's shoulder. I don't think they can get rid of Ay, not even if they wanted to. The veteran official oversees such a multitude of functions that the nation might just collapse if he stepped away from the reins; and clearly, Ay knows it.

He smiles politely. "Your Majesties, I have a few matters of business which need your attention. For one thing, we must hire men to collect the taxes. As discussed the other day, we're painfully short of soldiers. It might make a complete collection difficult, if not impossible."

Smenkhare's eyes go blank. "Do what you feel is best," he says.

Lord Ay bows his head, and Mayati scowls. Smenkhare's just given him a free hand to collect the wealth of Egypt as he pleases! She quickly adds, "We shall review all your plans first. Don't think we shall so easily forget your cowardly advice on the day my blessed father left this world!"

"Ah-Yes, about that... Lord Maya will answer your late mother's summons, I'm sure. He might be on the river in mere days, headed for this city."

"What?" Mayati shrieks. "But that... But she had not yet sent for him! It's impossible!"

Lord Ay spreads his hands, as if in helpless apology. "Majesty, she *did* send for him, that very day. Anyway, if you wish to send him back, be prepared for uprisings at tax time, especially in the south. But don't worry, if we're frugal, if we scrimp on feasting and needless expenses, your treasury might provide enough to keep Amarna fed for, oh, some six or seven years. Is that not right, Lord Panhesy?"

Panhesy looks up, a careful mask of indifference on his face, and says, "Indeed, my lord."

Smenkhare looks ill, and Mayati reclines back into her chair to sulk over her wine. "It can't be that bad," she mutters, shaking her head.

"My dear," Ay returns, "What do you think vexed your poor father so? This war drove him to his tomb before the first bit silver crept into his hair. Pursue it at all of our peril."

Four weeks later, for the first time in years, a barge bearing a nobleman from the city of Thebes slips into Amarna's royal harbor. Mayati paces her large balcony like a caged animal, wearing the soles of her gilded sandals to onionskins. "How can they expect me to be such a traitor?" she demands, somewhere between tears and fury.

Because you killed your own mother? I think this, of

course. I can never say it. "What has Lord Ay advised?" I ask carefully.

Mayati stops pacing. She sets her hands on her hips before me and spits, "Oh, he thinks we must hear the man out. He said at the very least, we must *seem* to be receptive to his suggestions. As if I don't know what he will say! Allow heresy; fund it, even!"

"And your husband?"

She closes her eyes and says, "Smenkhare thinks it's best if he meets the man alone. He says that if we must deceive Maya and all of Thebes, in order to pull in the year's taxes, then I had better remain behind. He says my love for Aten burns in my eyes, and Lord Maya would have to be a blind man not to see it."

"And you trust him to speak for you? He is only king through marriage…" It seems surprising that my fierce sister should allow Smenkhare this great power.

"Oh-He… he'll be loyal to me, and to Father."

Father… My father called Smenkhare an insipid weakling, for all he's strutted about giving orders these past few weeks. He would not let Smenkhare meet Maya alone, I'm sure of it.

"Yes…" Mayati muses, looking towards the harbor, towards the strange standards and emblems of the district of Thebes. "We'll trick this Lord Maya, and pull all our taxes in, and then we'll arrest him for heresy."

"Arrest him? But he's come on royal invitation, he's come for a parley!"

My sister curls her lips and sneers, "He is a heretic, a traitor! Father should have punished him years ago, when he refused to renounce Amun! I don't care what Lord Ay says, I don't care what anyone says! I am the Great Royal Wife and Smenkhare is Pharaoh, and we shall rule as we please!"

Down on the quay, Vizier Ay greets the man from Thebes, sweeping his arm out to escort the former priest of Amun into Aten's city. I lean over the brightly painted wall and swirl my wine thoughtfully. My sister is fierce; she is a lioness, a killer, her father's daughter through and through. And I fear that she is making a great mistake, one that could cost us everything.

That night, my sister and I enter the great hall arm in arm. We both wear the pale blue robes of mourning, as Father and Mother are still in the embalmer's care. It was hard enough to procure the blue dye, made from indigo that grows far to the north. Indigo, the deep purple dye from shellfish, and Baltic amber are all scarce now with the Hittites wilding in the northlands. Many of our former vassals no longer send tribute to us, but to the Hittite king.

My sister flushes with fury when she sees the new man sitting at a place of honor beside Lord Ay and Lord Paranefer. But I think the man has a kindly face, the face of a man who prefers peace to bloodshed. He is not nearly as handsome or silky as Paranefer, his younger brother. Years of hardship must have taken their toll on the man he once was. Heavy bags hang under his deep-set eyes, and his linen is not of the fine quality which we in Amarna enjoy. Even so, he wears a courteous, amicable smile as he makes polite talk with the other lords. His eyes shine with a keen intelligence, and I wonder what he's done with his time since his priesthood was abandoned and he exiled from court.

We reach the dais, and Smenkhare extends both his hands. Mayati releases me to receive her husband's embrace, and the new Pharaoh takes one of her hands. I bow and pass him by-but as I do, his broad hand comes to rest on my back. I stamp my feet immediately, and look to my sister.

"The loveliest women in Egypt!" Smenkhare declares in a warm, loose voice. "Here, there is a place for each of you at my side." Smenkhare swats one of his male companions out of the chair to his left, as Mayati takes the empty chair to his right.

Mayati looks to me, her eyes hot with shock. There are a thousand things said in that moment. There is everything-our childhood fights, being quarantined together during the plague, the rivals we were forced to become; and Mother's unnatural death. We stand before the whole court, not even breathing. She doesn't nod her head, but it's in her eyes. She will stand my friend, she will fight him. She doesn't want me with him any more than I want to marry him!

The banquet is served. Ox and roasted gazelle and duck, early vegetables simmered in oily sauce. I know well how to make a little show of eating, and I know how to put a wall between myself and the court, too. But my eyes are on the creature to my left, sitting like a characture in my father's seat. My sister charms him, but he can't seem to read the sudden spark in her face. He has insulted her, after she quite literally gave him the world. Smenkhare's spell is broken, and I pity him if my sister seeks her murderous vengeance!

When the feast is over, I let him leave well before me. Vizier Ay is next out, with his wife. I look to Mayati and ask, "Will you speak with him?"

"I'll do what I can, sister. You do what you can, too."

Not understanding fully, I motion two guards to escort me home, which isn't an uncommon thing for any of us. These two were among those my father put on me years before. We walk through the garden path adjoining our new home with the great palace. Behind me, the bridge over the Royal Road looms heavy in the twilight. Mayati wanted her own walls built thick and high, and the torch lit garden promenade is half sheltered between those walls and a long portico. Flames lick out of polished saucers, casting deep shadows onto the bold patterned murals. It is a beautiful palace, vivid with color and curtains as sheer as smoke. But I must leave it soon, and I don't know where I'll go. I can't stay here, waiting for Smenkhare to pounce. I can't go back to the King's House... I think I would die to sleep there again.

The two guards on the door open the doors, and I walk into a long gallery of pillars that cast heavy shadows in the light of tall, roaring lamps.

And then, terribly, Smenkhare is there. He lingers in the dark gallery, dwarfed by the enormous stone lotus flowers, half-hidden in the shadows. *Courage,* I think, walking on with my two soldiers.

But he is to be Pharaoh. He steps towards me, waves at them. "I shall keep you safe, Princess," he says gallantly, bowing a little. My soldiers are dismissed that easily. I want to look away, but one does not look away from a snake about to strike. I can only stand still, and wait.

"Come and walk with me, Princess."

My heart rushes in my ears as my whole being rebels. I am not a doll to be thrown around by whoever wears the cobra on his brow! "No, I won't," I say. I stand tall for the first time in many years.

"Are you afraid of me?" he asks, in a voice to coax honey from rocks, a cloying smile on his lips. "You must know I would never harm you. I think we will be good friends."

Someone should walk through this hall soon, I'm sure. There are dozens of servants who sleep in the palace, and officials who need to do a bit of late business before retiring. The foremost of the court have apartments in the Great Palace for just this purpose. I resist the urge to look about, but I hope more than anything that someone comes now. "I have somewhere to go," I say, hoping that maybe he'll let me pass.

"Then let me take you there! I would be the luckiest man alive, to walk with the greatest beauty of all."

Words escape me, and in that moment, he steps forward. He's telling me how flawless I am; he says I'm exquisite, living art. He is amazed by me. He cannot eat or sleep for thinking of me. I back up, and he pushes on, and somehow we're up against a column and he has his hand around my little neck, tilting my face to his. I shake my head, and he leers, and it's so dreadful! I feel the hard stone column against my back, he's pushed me against it, and I can't breathe-

"Your Majesty!

The voice is hard, urgent. Smenkhare closes his eyes before he looks over his shoulder. "What!"

He takes his hand off my shoulder, the other off my neck,

and turns around. I hold my breath as Ay says, "Your wife is looking for you."

"My *what*? Old man, what do you want?"

Ay doesn't flinch. "She says it's urgent, Your Majesty. Perhaps she has good news."

This stops him. I know what Ay means: he hints that my sister carries a child, an heir. Nothing would make Smenkhare's reign more legitimate. He looks back at me and murmurs, "Another time, my little beauty."

Smenkhare hurries off; I fall against the pillar, my hand to my chest as I gasp. Terrified I will faint, I look to Lord Ay. He asks me if he should summon someone, a physician, and my cheeks burn with humiliation. I shake my head, and then I force myself to breathe, I force myself to speak. "No- No, you may leave me. I... I am grateful, sir."

Lord Ay bows gallantly. "I am at your service, princess."

And then I am alone, and I feel myself slipping into panic again. The columns are oppressive. The stone against my hands is cold and there is menace in every shadow.

I turn around, hand still on my heart. I pass through the halls as quickly as I can, into the cool night air. Everything seems better out here. The guards at the door are oblivious to what happened beyond in Mayati's palace, and I've caught them at ease, enjoying the soft twilight breezes. I hurry through the flower-lined promenade that joins Mayati's palace with the Great Palace.

The Great Palace is dark, but I can hear the music and the courtiers finishing their dinner and wine within the hall. But there is no one in the hall that cares for me; I go on, to the place I loathe, because the only person I trust lives there now alone.

The King's House is lit up just the same as it always was, but the air is full of emptiness. Tutankhaten is in the courtyard, in the firelight, with the proud, alert Lady Ten Bows on his arm. The sycamores around him dance in shadow against the walls; the sky blackens and gives way to the stars. They both hear me coming from the top of the stairs; Tutankhaten smiles and I could burst into tears.

I come down the stairs and stand before him, going as silent as a stone. I can't speak the humiliating words. I am nothing but a doll to everyone, a doll to be passed about from one king to the next, and it's so terrible because they can do just what they want with me and all I can do is say *yes, my lord, I am honored*, and pinch my eyes shut, and die from the pain and shame.

"I have to leave that place," I murmur. I cast my eyes down, unable to look at my best friend because I'm afraid that Tutankhaten, who knows me so well, will see things in my eyes that he shouldn't. Then I catch sight of an enormous blue lizard laid out dead at Tutankhaten's feet. "The Agama?" I ask him, looking up. "You finally captured an Agama?"

"Lady Ten Bows caught it down the Royal Road, but I gave her meat for it instead. He's too pretty to be eaten." He shrugs it off, more concerned about me. "Come back here with me if you don't want to live with her. I have things to show you, herbs and powders... I've taken an interest in the more subtle tools of Anubis. It seems we must know them, and how to guard against them."

I blink, forever memorizing the way his mouth looked as it murmured a forbidden, mysterious name so easily. "You can guard against poison?" I whisper, terrified to be heard.

"Yes, but- What happened? What did she do to you? You look terrified."

I knew it, I knew he would see. "It's not Mayati," I say, and then I admit it. "Smenkhare wants me for his wife. Maybe tonight."

He draws his breath. "No!"

Now I do cry, because it's so awful.

"This will *not* happen again," Tutankhaten hisses, turning to his hawk. He tosses his arm lightly, and the lovely, powerful creature launches off, tucking up her golden talons as her great wings stretch out. She goes home, flying through his open door. He looks back at me. "What are you willing to do?"

"Anything!" I say, desperate. "I want to hide, until I can go away to my own palace. I can live in Kiya's palace; she's dead. Or maybe the palace at the north end of the city. Mayati will help me, she'll let me go, but I can't stay here tonight. Not if I mean to escape him."

Tutankhaten nods his head. He looks up to the stars and closes his eyes, as if in deep prayer. "All right," he breathes, meeting my eyes. "You once wanted to run away with me. Will you come with me now?"

Chapter Twenty-Five

A kiss for Maia's cheek, and a cloak for each of us, and we are gone. Tutankhaten also bundles up a bag of simply-bound papyrus books, copies of his precious scrolls. Maia takes the new box holding his poisonous substances, a knowing look in her eyes. As we step again into the night, I wonder how he came to possess such objects. "Where will we go?" I breathe, pulling up my skirts to ascend the stairs.

"Better not to say just yet," he responds, leading me into the bridge. He is cautious, checking each hall before we enter it, peering around corners before taking them. I stiffen as we pass the occasional checkpoint of guards. All let us pass, and all will tell Smenkhare which way we went.

Tutankhaten brings me down a long dark tunnel, a place I've never been before. He pulls his hood over his head and cuts around a trick wall, and then through a set of small, heavy bronze doors. Then suddenly, we are outside on the Royal Road, against the high outer walls.

Two chariots leave through the courtyard exit, and I tighten my fingers on his. He looks back for a moment, long enough to see and dismiss my concern. Just lords, returning home from the feast. Tutankhaten and I go on, to the Royal Stables.

There are always men on duty here. Grooms to watch the horses, soldiers to watch everything; they, too, let us pass and note our passing. Tutankhaten stops before Triumph's stall.

He hands me his leather and canvas satchel, and pulls open the trunk beside the door. A bridal, blanket, and cinch are carefully laid out inside, in leather and deep blue cloth with gold trim. Inside the stall, he murmurs softly to his horse. When they emerge, I see he has another bag tied to the blanket. It must have been hidden, somehow, within the stall.

Outside the stables, I climb up behind Tutankhaten and we ride off into the night. The wind in my face is cold and terrifying. I am running away from the palace, from a Pharaoh who wants to make me his second wife, and from everything I've ever known. Now I've brought Tutankhaten into it, twining his fate with my own. But were we ever separate? I can't remember a time that he did not laugh at my pleasure, or when I didn't cry for his sorrows.

When we're far enough from the palace, he nudges his horse into a smooth canter. At first I'm afraid, but when my hood pushes back and my curls whip in the wind, I forget everything and take a deep breath, tasting this freedom. I wish that we were leaving it all behind, galloping away from court and to our own fate. We ride out of the heart of the city, and into the desirable southern district where so many nobles keep grand villas. I've come here only during formal processions, but I know Lady Mutnojme, my mother's young sister, lives a quiet life here away from the dangers of court. Will he take me to her house? Lord Ay's house?

Tutankhaten pulls Triumph up before my grandmother's walled estate. I wiggle back so that he can slip down and open the enormous bronze gate. All is dark beyond; the place was deserted after Grandmother took her life years ago. He bars the gate from behind with the heavy bronze pole, and I help him climb back up onto the horse. We canter again, with only the moon and stars to light our way down the avenue of tamarisk trees. He intends us to make our stand here, under Grandmother's roof, the two of us alone against a king.

The estate is dark, deserted, but there is oil in the moonlit stable enough to spark a torch. Inside the great pillared house, there is a bit more oil and wicks for lamps. Sheets cover the furniture, and the wall paintings which delighted my grandmother in life are obscured by shadows. Tutankhaten stands in the dim light, hands on his hips. "It is better this way," he decides. "We must not light the house up."

When we find the inner courtyard, Tutankhaten snaps dry branches off overgrown orchard trees and quickly gets a fire going on the stone in the middle of Grandmother's neglected garden. We gather up all the sheets we can find, and because there is no proper mattress ready, we retire beside his campfire under the stars. We need not secure ourselves into the highest room, because there is no way we could resist Smenkhare with force should he come. We can only hope to hide.

I sit before the fire, my arms wrapped around my legs. Tutankhaten throws another branch on, sending bright orange sparks upwards into the blue-black sky. He settles beside me with a jug of wine. "It's old," he says, "but good. Dry red."

"Your favorite," I recognize.

"Yes, but I rarely drink it full like this. Maia likes it when I water my wine. But I think I will get drunk for the first time tonight." He laughs softly, even with his heart beating in his throat after our flight from the palace.

I take a long drink straight from the earthen jug. The delicately spiced vintage drips over my lips, and I pucker them clean. "It seems that's the only way," I say, trying not to let my tears fall.

"Don't say that, not ever. You're no coward, to hide in a bottle."

I look down shyly, my hair streaming over my cheeks like a veil. "The things he said to me!" I bite my lips immediately. These are secrets, shameful secrets, never to be shared, even if their poison rots me away.

I close my eyes, and I hear the cracking of another thick, dead branch, the protesting thud when it hits the camp fire with all of Tutankhaten's anger. Now I've disgusted him, too.

"Ankhesenpaaten…?" He takes my curls in his hand, and he sets them delicately behind my shoulder. "Don't cry. Don't ever cry again."

I sniff, and nod, but I really can't help it.

"If you could have anything in the world, what would it be?"

This makes me laugh a little, and peer out at Tutankhaten from the corners of my eyes. "You mean, like a new gown? A palace? I don't care about any of that. Of course, I *must* find somewhere to live now, away from that... from His *Majesty*."

Tutankhaten does not laugh. His black eyes glow and dance in the firelight, as solemn and serious as a man three times his age. "No, I do not mean simple things that can be bought. I mean, what would you wish your life to be, if it were in your hands?"

"Oh... *Oh*," I murmur, shaking my head. "Nothing like this. Look what she did to my mother!" I need not say who, she's sitting in my mother's throne. "And my mother, she was no innocent. The other wives lived in fear of her. Who knows what she did... The plague took my other sisters, but even after, Mayati saw me-sees me-as nothing but a rival. Even now, she only takes my part because she is jealous and betrayed! And..." I pinch my lips. I dare not even mention him, Father, or what I became to him.

"You want a home," he says quietly, and I nod, and I cry all over again.

"Where people love each other. Where they care, and don't spend their days scheming on each other, hurting each other. But instead I must hide from Smenkhare. And how long do you think it will last? He wants to marry me. He won't be put off forever, Tutankhaten!"

"Ankhesenpaaten," he says, his young voice hard, "I swore to myself- I swore I'd never let this happen to you again. I won't let him marry you."

"What do you mean?" I ask, alarmed by the severity of his voice. "What could you do?"

Tutankhaten looks plainly at me. "I want the life you speak of, a quiet and happy life, a good life of trust and love. I want to spend every day with you, I want to ride and sail with you. I want you to feel safe. I would give my own life to make it so, and I know just how to do it." Tutankhaten takes my hands and murmurs urgently, "Marry me, Ankhesenpaaten. Tonight. Be *my* wife, so that for anyone else to claim you would be a crime and an insult to me. That half-blood Smenkhare cannot treat *me* so shamefully. He would have to kill me first, and he can't kill me without risking the wrath of the people and debasing himself."

I gape at him, speechless. I did not hear him. Marriage? Tutankhaten wants marriage, with *me*?

"I know," he says quietly. "You say you don't like to be married, that you never want to be married again. But couldn't you also say that you just didn't like to be married to *him*? Couldn't you be happy with me, as you are right now? Don't I make you happy?"

"Tutankhaten..." I stumble, helpless, "there is more to marriage than riding horses together! Surely you know this."

He looks back to the fire. "I don't want *that*."

"But you will!" I cry. "You will turn into a man in a year or so, and then you'll be like every other man: nasty. You'll want to do nasty things, just like they all do!"

"I want to make you happy," he tells me softly, looking back up at me with big, dark eyes. "I want what you want: a home, a real home. And I can give it to you, right now." Only now does he produce the big bag that he tied to his horse. He opens it up before me; gold winks out of the darkness, piles of gold gleaming in the firelight. "It is enough to live on our own, in a place of our own choosing. No court, no schemes, just a house and a garden, and a barge to sail the river. If we live simply, this will hold us until I'm old enough find work as a scholar or a hunter. I will invest in the trade caravans, the market, and the mines like the other lords, and make a great estate for you. I can do it. I can support you, in the style you require. I swear I'll give you anything you want, and I'll keep you safe."

I'm touched by his earnest plans. "You would *work* for a living?" I ask, surprised. "You are a royal prince!"

"I would work. I'd want you to have the best of everything." He tilts his head in entreat, letting his long black side lock

163

swing off his chest. "So… Can I call you my wife? You have been my best friend since the beginning of my life; I want to end my life with you at my side. I want to make you happy again."

My breath catches. Dissembling, I gulp the wine, which does nothing to quench my dry mouth and only makes me dizzier. I ran from one marriage, and straight into the offer of another! But this-marriage with Tutankhaten-is something else entirely. Still… he doesn't know what it would mean! I must stall, delay. "How would it be legal? How would we… make it real?"

He bows his head and murmurs, "All that is required is our intention to join together, and for you to cross my threshold. And… and a kiss, to show the gods that we've become one."

"The gods," I repeat. Now we will marry before the old, forbidden gods?

"Yes, Ankhesenpaaten," he says most seriously. "I am bred by Aten himself, or at least his spirit possessing my father when he visited my mother. But that does not obliterate all that I am. My mother was born to Amun. One of my ancestors was a goddess, a woman-king named for Hathor. The sire of my line is named for Thoth. The world is full of spirits and magic, and if you are to be my wife, you must know I venerate *all* that is holy, by whatever name it is given."

I lower my gaze, frightened of all this talk of gods. I have had enough of gods and their work.

Tutankhaten goes on, admitting softly, "You know I've always loved you. Grandmother knew… she told me-" He bites his lower lip again, anxious. "She told me you were made for me, made to be my wife. She says the gods cut one breath in half and created both our souls with it. In that way, we've been married for all our lives. We would be happy together, as we always were."

"Grandmother said that?" I ask softly, remembering the last time I saw her. Tutankhaten and I were picking flowers, just before that poor servant boy died from a poisoned diadem.

"All the time," he says, waiting for me to answer him.

"And you wouldn't- you wouldn't be like other men? I mean, you would love me always? I don't want to lose *you*, too-" I bite my lips, refusing to say any more about that. I never want another man I love to betray me, to tear me to pieces, to shame me to dust. I never want to fear and hate someone I love again, as if they had up and turned into a hissing demon before I could even blink my eyes.

"I am nothing like other men," he tells me adamantly. "And of course I will always love you. I always *have* loved you."

I nod quickly. "All right. I'll do it."

Tutankhaten stands quickly, but remembers to help me up as well. We face each other. My hands are warm in his. A soft breeze stirs the leaves of the garden, tickling my face with my hair. The hum of insects is like a minstrel, and the stars overhead are our guests, our witnesses. I look down at the ground, at my gilded sandals peeking from my pale blue gown. I can't speak for terror, for the chaotic, dizzying thumping in my chest. Tutankhaten squeezes my hands lightly; I look up into his black eyes, and they seem so honest. Even now, though, I can't trust. But drunk on wine and fear, I run into my second marriage at age twelve.

"It will be just as you want, I promise," Tutankhaten tells me, his voice quiet under the endless, star-studded sky. "You'll never regret being my wife."

I nod, hoping this is true.

He leads me into the shadows of the portico. "Step over the threshold with me," he says.

We cross into the house together, as I cling to his hand for life itself. Tutankhaten whispers "May the gods bless our life together."

"May the gods bless us," I murmur, copying him without caring who I pray to.

Then, Tutankhaten turns to me. I duck my head shyly, and then I close my eyes, and turn my face up for my new husband's kiss. Tutankhaten, my husband!

I can feel the warmth of him before I feel his kiss. He takes my curls in his hands, and I can feel their light tremble. He always smells so sweet, minty breath, skin that gives off a fine smell of cardamom and honey, touched with morning frankincense. His mouth presses against mine awkwardly, quickly. In that brief moment, I notice-detached, as if it were not me feeling, but being told-that his lips are soft and yielding.

"There," he whispers. I open my eyes, glad that it is over. It was not bad, not at all; but he won't understand why such a gentle touch could make me so... so dizzy with fear. Tutankhaten's eyes are shy, but he is proud as he takes my shaking hands again. "It is done. We are husband and wife now, and no *Smenkhare* will split us apart."

Chapter Twenty-Six

I wake up with the bright sun beating on my face and my head aching from wine. For a moment, I'm confused. I've slept wound up in sheets beside the smoldering remains of a campfire. A tangled, unkempt garden surrounds me, and I am alone. It is so unlike my ordered and luxurious life that I think I dream.

And then I remember everything: Smenkhare trying to trap me in the gallery, my frantic flight from the palace. Tutankhaten... Tutankhaten, my husband! I gulp in fear and cover my face, hearing nothing but the swirling, pumping blood in my ears. *What have I done?*

"There are men on the road," Tutankhaten's voice drifts through the portico. He steps into the garden, carrying a large block of hard cheese in his arms. "From the cellar. This and some wine are all that's left. But these trees are full of fruit. There are oranges and figs growing throughout this estate, and I think Grandmother grew pomegranates as well. It's a perfect time for pomegranates. Would you gather some for our breakfast?" He falls silent, gazing on me, a soft smile playing on his face.

I blush, biting my lips. Then I grow anxious. "What... what do you mean, men on the road? Are they looking for us?"

Tutankhaten nods. "I think so. But they kept going. Still, it can't be long before someone thinks to look here. And we can't last long on fruit. I thought to go down to the river and catch some fish, but I've no idea how to clean and cook it." He grimaces and adds, "I suppose I must learn it all now."

"Do you want to go back?" I ask, horrified. In the night, with the wine in our bellies, he seemed so sure of his plan, so sure we could make a life together away from court. But now the sun shines on reality: we are fugitives, hiding out in an abandoned mansion with no food and no way to acquire any, at least not without being discovered. We've been served hand and foot our whole lives, and neither of us knows the first thing about ordering a house or caring for ourselves. "Do you regret... this?"

"No!" Tutankhaten assures me, coming to my side. "Never! Listen... We'll have to face them, if we mean to live our honest life, the good life we want. I hope you were right about your sister. She's hated me forever, but I hope she'll take our part in this for your sake. I would give up any claim to the throne, I swear it, just to have her let us live together, in peace."

"You would give up your claim to the throne?" I ask in astonishment. "But... but you have always felt that being Pharaoh was *your* right, over anyone else!"

"Sure," he murmurs. "For you." Then he looks away, towards the orchards. "Gather some fruit for our breakfast, and then we'll eat and look over the rooms so we can make a proper bed tonight. I'm going to get water from the well and turn Triumph out into the paddock."

He hands me the block of white cheese, and motions to the fig trees. I set myself to the simple task of gathering food for our table, concentrating on this alone, and refusing to wonder how many quiet breakfasts we'll be allowed, or what tomorrow will bring.

In the afternoon, as I stand before Grandmother's enormous kitchen table, looking over the fruit, onions, and hard early melons that I pulled from her badly neglected fields,

Tutankhaten shouts down the stairs. "They're here! They're just outside the gates!"

I rush up the stairs, dizzy from panic. Tutankhaten clutches my hand and we hurry to the rooftop. I clamp my hand over my shriek as I see the soldiers at the gate and the dust settling around three chariots. "Tutankhaten, what will we do? Pharaoh's going to kill us! His guards will drag us back!"

"No, no they won't. They're going to let us keep this house, and we're going to be loyal subjects of your sister and her foolish husband."

"How can you think that? How can you be so brave?"

Tutankhaten turns to me, bursting with nerve and confidence. "The gods will protect us," he promises quickly, the battle before us making him breathless. "Aten will protect us, and so will Grandmother. I want you to hide in our bedroom, and only come out when you hear me call to you." He grins like a little lion, eager for his first hunt. "Courage," he says, nodding his head. "It's now or never, to get that life you wanted."

He goes off, and I should too, but I can't pull myself away. I can hear the shouting of men as they try the gate and find it barred. In moments, Tutankhaten rides down the long path, Triumph carrying him at a brisk trot. He sits tall and proud, the reins loose and one hand casually on his hip. Down the narrow road, the polished bronze spearheads of the soldiers wink in the sun. My fingernails dig into my palms as Tutankhaten approaches the armed men: a slim weaponless boy on a horse, riding out to face my uncle's soldiers.

He slides down and unbars the gate, but no men come rushing in. And then, the strangest sight of all: the soldiers, whatever lords are in the chariots, all of them to a man fall to their knees before Tutankhaten. Still, I hold my breath. Perhaps they cannot truss him up and bring him back to the palace; he is holy, of holy birth and blood. They simply can't touch him until Pharaoh gives the final order.

They rise, and Tutankhaten vaults back onto his horse. They all come down the dusty manor road, Tutankhaten riding beside a man in a chariot. As they get closer, I make out the tall, wiry frame of the Grand Vizier Ay. Why would he come to arrest us? He is not in favor with Smenkhare! His face reveals nothing. Finally, I tear myself away from the rooftop. But before I get to Grandmother's bedroom, Tutankhaten's voice rings through the house, calling my name.

My hands tremble as I pull open the heavy front doors. My chest tightens in fear; Ay's face is grim, Tutankhaten's eyes burn bright. I walk slowly down the steps, going to my doom. He jumps down from the horse and runs to me. "Ankhesenpaaten, they've been killed!"

"What?" He makes no sense!

Vizier Ay steps down from his chariot and bows deeply before me. "I... I am so sorry, your highness. Your sister, Pharaoh, and her daughter... all were killed at their breakfast. They are dead, Princess. We were forced to kill Lord Panhesy, who attempted to flee the palace after committing his terrible crime. He conspired with a chamber maid in your sister's service, also dead now. Prince Tutankhaten must come back and take up his father's crown."

"No, no!" I shriek. The world swings around me and grows dark around the edges. The darkness closes in on the light, my lungs scream for breath. I hear Tutankhaten cry out to Ay, and then the world goes black.

By the time we reach the palace, I am crushed by fear. I can think of nothing, as if my heart finally shut down. I can't think of Tutankhaten taking the throne, that murderous, corrupting throne. I can't think of my sister, who died just as she stood my friend for first time in our lives, or her innocent toddler who, like my own daughter, had no part in any of this but still lost her life. I can't remember the horrors I have lived at my father's hands, nor the rebellion and plague that tore my perfect home apart. I can do nothing but shake and stare.

Tutankhaten brings me to my bed. Tia makes me a strong drink of wine and opium, and Tutankhaten returns with Pentju, his physician, who makes an effort to examine without touching me when he finds that I revolt in terror at a man's hands on my body.

Finally, he has Tutankhaten take my pulse, instructing him to hold my wrist and count the beats. The doctor peers into my eyes and notes my shallow, rapid breathing. "She is in shock, Your Majesty," Pentju says quietly.

"I've given her a draught," Tia offers, hovering over me.

"That is well, but what she-The Great Royal Wife?" He looks at Tutankhaten, who nods. "What Her Majesty needs is restful sleep, gentle company, and security."

The Great Royal Wife... I look at Tutankhaten in disbelief. That is my mother's title. How could I have my mother's title? I don't want it! And Tutankhaten should not wish to be Pharaoh, after what it did to Father! Mute with horror, I can't even scream.

He sits gently on my bed, tucking the covers over me. "I'm going to take care of you now, Ankhesenpaaten, remember? You're my wife."

"No," I whisper, shaking my head. "No, don't be Pharaoh! It is too much! It broke *Father*," I say softly, finally speaking of him.

But Tutankhaten has been exalted already. Just days ago, he might have argued with me about why he should, why he's fit for it, but now all he does is kiss my cheek and murmur, "Hush. Everything will be well. Rest, Ankhesenpaaten, please. You must get better."

PART TWO

1333 BC-1325 BC

Chapter One

For the next few days, I could shatter like fine alabaster. Tutankhaten won't talk about anything troubling at my bedside. He tells me about his horses and his dogs, and Lady Ten Bows, and how he plans to host his first hunting expedition before it grows too warm. But when he tells me this last bit, on the third day, I can tell that something's bothering him. I scoot up in my throne of pillows and lay my hand over his.

"I don't know them as I should," he admits quietly. "They've clapped at my shooting and praised me in the field or the arena, and of course I listen to everything I can make myself privy to. But I can't..." he swallows, looking at me with pained eyes.

"You are afraid," I breathe, recognizing it.

"No," he says quickly, but then he sighs and says, "A little. Some were in this court when my *mother* was born. I know I must be a god, but even gods need to learn and grow wise."

"You will learn," I tell him. I smile softly, smoothing the new red gem gilding his finger, with his new seal painstakingly engraved on the surface. "I am sure, because it's all you've ever done: studied and practiced, and done better than anyone else."

"But Ankhesenpaaten," he whispers, "It is one thing to practice mathematics in study, but another to actually build a temple. And surely, on the hunt one mistake can kill a man.

I cannot *practice* now. I must *be* king. And there are men who want to snatch it from me, I feel it already."

You wanted this, I think. To be Pharaoh is to be blessed, but to live and breathe and eat every day knowing that the basest of men covet your crown, your wife, your throne. And then, there are intrigues and calamities, treasuries to balance, taxes to levy, infrastructure to maintain... I want to remind him that all I ever wanted was a manor house, and fields to get lost in. I want to tell him how deadly scared I am, not only that men will attack him from the outside, but the constant pressure and ultimate power might rot him from the soul out. But that would be sour, and would only add to his burden. So I say instead, "There are great kings in your blood, some who claimed their throne not so much older than you. Yes, you'll snatch wisdom as you go, but you'll master it like you master anything."

He smiles a little, hanging his head back, cracking his neck. He's always held his stress in his shoulders, and the only thing that relaxes him is to ride or drive or shoot, or study.

"What are you reading?" I ask softly.

"Medical texts," he says, grinning with his eyes closed. "How the body is made, how it is hurt, how it's fixed."

"That sounds disgusting," I say.

"Yes," he says cheerfully, sounding like a boy again. "It's obscene."

The state barge rocks gently in the low, glistening river. Tutankhaten escorts me up the stairs to the palatial high deck, and right away, a sweet river breeze brushes over me. I notice immediately that the royal barge carries musicians again, for the first time in at least three years. The canopy sparkles gold in the sun, and the wide dais has been filled with large cushions beside a low, gilded chair. Tutankhaten has thought for my comfort. We take our places, Ay and Lady Teye in low seats beside us, fan bearers on either side of the king and servants ready to provide refreshment. The trumpets call, a low drum begins to beat for the oarsmen, and we cast off from the quay.

I feel strange and frightened, and I long to return in hiding to my chambers. But Tutankhaten is bright, clear eyed, and at ease with his gold-cuffed ankles crossed on a footstool before him. He's been accustomed to fan bearers and full prostration his whole life, and so the ceremony and obedience surrounding a Pharaoh doesn't dazzle him a bit.

I recline onto my arm, leaning close to him as Ay opens the discussion with pleasantries about the fair day, and the improved mood in the city. "Our agents in the city tell us that most men believed Your Majesty to be the rightful heir, and though they lament the loss of Pharaoh Smenkhare and his Great Royal Wife, they are relieved and hopeful at Your Majesty's ascension. They pray Your Majesty will bring better times to Egypt."

"I will," Tutankhaten says simply. "And you may tell Lord Maya that he can present himself in the audience chamber tomorrow, to discuss the necessary arrangements for restoring the traditional faith." With that light statement, Tutankhaten announces his intention to restore the old faith.

"I am glad to hear it, Your Majesty," Lord Ay says, touching his heart. He looks at both of us, and suddenly I think of how he saved me from Smenkhare, how he knows that I almost fainted, and I flush with embarrassment. I turn my head, and Lady Teye is staring at me. She offers me a little bow, a little smile, but it doesn't reach her eyes. Is she bored? Does she think me a child, and Tutankhaten a child, and does she mind very much serving royals she thinks of as children? Presumably, she thinks she will order my apartments as she did my mother's, but I don't want it. She would talk of nothing but my mother, whom she adored. Everything I want her to do would be compared to the way my mother would have had it, and perhaps this woman-old enough to be my grandmother and a Person of Gold since I was in swaddling-would even presume to instruct me. If I am to be Great Royal Wife, I must figure out my own way of doing things, and I'll certainly not have my traitorous mother shoved in my face at every turn.

"What of my coronation, Lord Ay?" Tutankhaten's eager voice cuts through my thoughts, and I slide a bit closer to him.

"Your Majesty must bury your father first, and your uncle. And truly, it is best if we wait a bit longer after that as well."

"Wait?" Tutankhaten asks in surprise, turning sharp attention to Lord Ay. "With all that's gone on? Shouldn't I be anointed and take the ancient crowns immediately?"

Ay and Teye exchange a quick look. Ay bows his head and asks, "Your Majesty, who would crown you? Lord Meri-Re, the Chief Seer of Aten?" The Grand Vizier's tone proclaims all he feels about this plan.

Tutankhaten sits back. "Meri-Re wants to crown me. You think I ought to wait until I have made a High Priest of Amun?"

"Yes, Your Majesty. Amun and Ptah must give you your crowns. You will only be legitimate to all of your people if it is done just so."

"And Lord Maya is the key to all this?"

"In a way, Your Majesty. He was chosen to speak from many concerned noblemen. Of course, none of these were ever engaged in any rebellion."

Tutankhaten is quiet for a long time. Surely, he is wondering how Ay could ever know that, since the people we must deal with are certainly Amun worshippers or Ptah worshippers; my father said that everyone outside Amarna was a heretic and a traitor in their hearts. But when Tutankhaten speaks, surprisingly he says, "Lord Ay, while we do all this, I want to plan a hunt in the Western Desert for next week. A great, roaring thing, full of chariots and dogs."

Ay laughs softly, nodding his head. "It is surely overdue, Your Majesty. I'm sure Lord Rameses would be delighted to organize it with you."

Tutankhaten smiles winsomely. "I will make a great hunt for us, better than any before. Oh- One more thing, Lord Ay:

I've not yet received my father's Book of Days. It was not left in his chambers, and I'm sure Smenkhare didn't assign it for burial, he hasn't the right to it."

Lord Ay makes a little face of wonder. "Did you speak with the head steward of the King's House?"

"I did… he could not locate it. And it is not in my new chambers, either."

"Perhaps Pharaoh Smenkhare took it elsewhere. I shall have a look about the Annex Palace, the chambers he used as an office, and attempt to locate it."

Tutankhaten admits softly, "I truly hope you can find it, Lord Ay. My father's private words would be of much comfort to me now."

"But of course, Your Majesty," Lord Ay says, watching his young new lord very closely.

That night, Tutankhaten sends for me. We haven't had a chance to speak since we left the barge, but finally he is returned from a routine day of council, ritual, and the heaviest tutoring he's ever known. I bring his orange blossom tea myself, finding him on the wide balcony. I try not to imagine my mother and Smenkhare in their turn pacing here, staring out at a failing Amarna under a heavy white moon.

Tutankhaten is ensconced in cushions and pillows under a night sky bejeweled with stars. Two small saucers of flame on ebony stands dance and gutter beside him; the salt added to the oil keeps the lamps from smoking. Nestled into the cushions are five enormous books, each wrapped in dark-dyed linen cloth. I swallow to dampen my parched throat. "Are those… what you wanted?" I cannot begrudge him his desire to hear his father's voice once more, but I dislike it greatly.

Tutankhaten nods, taking one heavy volume in his hands and smoothing his palms over the cloth. Just as I narrow my eyes warily, as if he were caressing a scorpion, he looks up to me and explains, "Everyone he dealt with as king is studied between these covers. Through these pages, I can know the men I must rule."

So that is what it's all about! I kneel beside him, lowering the gold tray and pouring hot tea. After serving him, I settle next to him and ask, "You can know each of these men simply through this... this great diary?"

"Oh yes! It's incredible... the actions of hundreds of important men are recorded over seventeen years, in a thorough study of their evolution." Tutankhaten grins. "Father made sure to learn as much as he could about their desires and their weaknesses, their sympathies, their piety... And it's all right here. What do you think of that?"

"I think it's a most powerful tool. Tell me something, about someone."

Delighted, Tutankhaten says, "Hmm. Well, Lord Ay doesn't really care which god he prays to, so long as that god pays in gold. But he is utterly loyal, and what he truly desires is to be deified, the way some people speak of Pentju's father, Amunhotep son of Hapu. This is why he works so tirelessly in Pharaoh's service, and has such a care for his public image."

I laugh at Ay's astonishing desire. "Deified! Well, he has served god-kings for so long, perhaps he fancies himself part of the family. Do you have a study of everyone's hearts?"

"I don't know. I've only had time to look through the first book. But I've found enough about this Lord Maya to know that he was in constant communication with Amarna, giving details on rebellious factions in Thebes and men who spoke against the crown. He was spared his life to do so. His young brother Paranefer... he's an esteemed temple architect now, but he came to Amarna as a willing hostage at eighteen, to ensure Maya's continued cooperation and gratitude."

"And who was Lord Maya, exactly?"

Tutankhaten's eyes dance in the firelight. "The Second Prophet of Amun. The first, the High Priest, was run through as a fugitive in Nubia. Lord Maya was spared, but at a price: his little brother, and his service as Father's ears in Thebes."

I pout in thought. "But... he is a spy, then! How can anything he says be trusted? How can a spy-who must have earned the ire of the Amun worshippers-be effective in healing the divisions in our land?"

"Because no one but Father, me, you, and the few elite officials in the land know the truth of it; to the rest, he is a man who sacrificed his wealth and turned down a place in Amarna's court to stand on his principles. He is highly respected, a man of honor, a former priest of Amun educated at Grandfather's court. And now Maya is here to offer his guidance and support, and his powerful connections. We will take all he has to give, and save this country."

"And the rebels?" Even Maya could be a rebel, in secret. How would we ever know?

Tutankhaten leans close to me, speaking in a breath that delicately brushes my face, "They are *all* rebels, I think. Every man who stayed in Thebes or Memphis, that's what Father said. So I shall have to be a lord of rebels, Ankhesenpaaten, or no lord at all."

Chapter Two

Though Tutankhaten has turned to the worship of Egypt's ancient gods, when the time comes for my father and mother's funeral, he commands that the service shall be done entirely as Father wanted it, without any mention of Osiris or Amun. Young men sing the hymns my father wrote himself, and Meri-Re prays over their elaborate gold coffins, commending their souls to Aten's eternal care. Tutankhaten acts as chief mourner, walking the entire way behind the pallbearers and sledges; but I am carried in a private litter, so that no one might see my tears. The joyous words of Father's psalms, speaking of jubilee and eternal life, remind me of the man of sunshine who once illuminated our home with brilliance and beauty. These memories-of him lifting me into the air and calling me his most beautiful child, him telling me stories as I fell asleep with my head in his lap-are what torture me, leaping into my more comfortable hatred like nasty fish heads popping out of the still water.

Through the gauzy curtains, I watch Meri-Re perform Aten's rituals over my father's coffin. I hear a low moan as a bull is slaughtered, and a sickening wet splash as his blood rushes from his throat into the bowl held by Meri-Re's assistant. The sung hymns and spoken prayers blend together inaudibly, and I am glad for it.

After my father's rights are finished, Meri-Re turns his

attention to Mother's shining coffin. I can't watch this. I turn my face to the wooden paneling behind me and cry for the loss of her, which happened years ago, when she decided to care more for her own legacy than for me. Is she satisfied, in whatever place her soul has ascended to? She will be known as a Pharaoh for all eternity, she will join Father and Aten to circle the world. I wonder if she notes that her only living daughter does not pour oil on the golden brow of her coffin, nor stand by to see her funeral sledge dragged into the rocky caverns beneath the cliffs. I doubt it very much indeed.

When it's over, Tutankhaten takes my hand and escorts me to a feast that is supposed to honor my parents. But our court is hardly in mourning; they are breathless with new hope and eager to retain a position in Tutankhaten's new, traditionalist government. Tutankhaten's face is flushed with satisfaction that he has taken his proper place, even as he mourns his father.

But there are still cries of rebellion in several districts, and Horemhab seeks Tutankhaten out almost immediately, finding us in the audience chamber. High on the granite dais, in a chair I never thought to sit in, we watch as our noblemen enter in state and bow their faces to the floor as if we were gods indeed. Tutankhaten doesn't even blink. But he does sit up a bit when he sees Horemhab burst through the doors. The man's legs must be the size of tree trunks, I am sure. In his short kilt and netted tunic, with his flowing white cloak, Horemhab is the embodiment of physical prowess and strength. The man makes his prostration again and again as he approaches the dais, the row of viziers presided over by Ay, the fan-bearers with their glistening gold fans mounted with thick white ostrich plumes, the honor guards with their long, flashing axes, and above it all, our royal selves.

"You may speak," Ay grants, for Pharaoh is removed, remote, ethereal.

"My king," he begins humbly, "I have come to make report on the present uprisings in districts to the northwest and south. I beg Divinity's leave to punish the rebels in His name."

"This is a matter that must be considered carefully," Ay observes.

"We grant it," Tutankhaten says suddenly, and his Lord Vizier and many others turn to their youthful god-king with surprise. In their silence, he goes on. "We have made declarations and laws that are most beneficial to the peoples of this land. Those who rebel are traitorous fools, and if they wish to do violence in our domain, they shall meet violence."

It is only later, when we walk about the lush summer garden, bathed in golden afternoon light, that Horemhab and Ay join us to discuss the meat of the matter.

"We should not enrage the people, Your Majesty," Ay says, his voice pinched with caution. "They do not trust you yet. We have no ready troops but those of foreign extraction, and foreigners have killed too many Egyptians on Pharaoh's orders in years past. This could ignite more fires, rather than extinguishing the present ones."

Tutankhaten walks along with me, his eyes on the blossoms glowing in the early sunset. He seems inattentive, but I notice that his face bears the alert, calculating look he wears at study. I stroll slowly at his side, my arm in his, quite assaulted by the sweet and musky scents on the thick, hot flood time air.

"With Your Majesty's leave, I would train Egyptians. There are enough of Your Majesty's father's veterans about, along with their sons and kin. I could ready a company by the third month of Inundation, loyal Egyptians to punish their king's enemies," Horemhab explains.

"It would be dangerous, Your Majesty," Ay warns again, against the plan. "If you commit yourself now, you will be committing yourself for a year or more of fighting, I am certain. And your new Treasurer, Lord Maya, is concerned that this growing conflict will have a negative effect on the taxation this year. Your Majesty is on perilous ground."

Tutankhaten looks over the high garden wall to the brilliant sky over the setting sun. I think I am the only one that can hear the hum of excitement in his voice as he says, "All the more reason to squash this rebellion now, my good lord. General

Horemhab, you have my blessing. I desire constant reports, as you prepare for the date of your departure, and steady dispatches concerning this action."

Lord Ay, who obviously disdains Horemhab for his low birth, purses his thin lips but does not gainsay his new king. The decision is Tutankhaten's now.

Horemhab says, "Your Majesty, I must say: these men in the northwest, at least, do not appear to be religiously motivated. The people are pleased with Your Majesty's decrees, and desire peace. There are malcontents, of course, but my intelligence suggests that they are stirred up by a series of opportunistic agitators holding no true moral objective. I will make war on the force as a whole, but I shall also seek these men. Once they are eliminated, the supporters are sure to scatter."

"Excellent, Horemhab," Tutankhaten says warmly.

It seems that Father's youngest, most common general is coming into great favor. He always brings his reports to Tutankhaten at nighttime, his uniform polished, his bearing immaculate. When Tutankhaten shows real emotion with the man, his eyes shining with true laughter as Horemhab relates a humorous tale from a Nubian battlefield, I worry that he might like the military too much. At night I find him laid out across his great bed, pouring over the battle stories of Pharaoh Ahmose, our indirect ancestor, who cast out the hated Asian occupiers several hundred years ago.We go out to the balcony Mother called her own for one night and stand under the stars, gazing down the Royal Road.

"Do you think you can beat them?" I ask Tutankhaten nervously, meaning these new insurgents.

"I won't stop until I beat them," he says plainly, breathing in the night. "I plan to advance Horemhab to the rank of Overseer of the Army to do so. And even Ay's brought his soldier son Nakhtmin to court, though he did not want to use force against the rebels. He thinks Nakhtmin, who has been running security for our southern gold mining operations, might have something to offer to our effort."

"What could Ay's son offer to Horemhab's military

expeditions?" I ask, knowing that old Ay never speaks of his own youth as a soldier and long ago cast off his soldier's uniform for a safer and more profitable life at court. How different could his son be, even though he is in the military?

Tutankhaten shakes his head. "Nakhtmin is nothing like his father. He is a true soldier, you'll see. I like him already."

I make a small murmur, not telling Tutankhaten that I've heard nasty rumors about the captain with the open laugh and long, streaming braids: he is a reckless seducer, never married and with a score of broken-hearted maidens and furious fathers behind him. But if he is a good officer, and he can put down the rebels with Horemhab, his faults will be overlooked in Tutankhaten's court.

Tutankhaten smiles brilliantly at me. His confidence is contagious, and I take his hands in mine as we stand beneath the stars. "You will be a great king," I predict.

His eyes flash with pleasure, and I cannot help but smile back at him. He has everything he ever wanted now, and on this warm night, gazing into his dark, excited face, I feel his confidence seeping into my fearful little heart. Perhaps the bad times are ending, and I will know happiness once again.

In the morning, after prayer and the audience chamber and a session with his council, Tutankhaten flees his tutor Senqed and takes sanctuary in the stables. While I stand daintily in my gilded sandals, stroking the muzzle of my old, fat mare, Tutankhaten leaves me for the stallions' quarters, where the stalls are wide and the walls and gates are thick. I cannot believe it when he comes past me leading Fury. The red horse shines like a bronze sword, his nostrils flaring and snorting, his dark eyes flashing. He wears a halter of braided leather and silver, no bridal, no blanket. Curious, I follow at a safe distance behind. Tutankhaten lets Fury into the arena and then leans up against the fence. The horse blinks at his freedom for just a moment before he bolts, galloping and leaping and twisting through the arena like a yearling colt.

We stand together for a while, watching the horse run in a warm silence that has no need or use for words; then he leaves me and enters the arena with the stallion. I gaze on, breathless as he holds his arms out and somehow makes the horse stand still, stomping, his red mane streaming in the hot wind. I can hardly believe it when Tutankhaten runs at the animal, but I can believe it less when the stallion seems to run with him, passing the slim young king quickly. It's almost as if they are playing, burning off the same high temper and spirit. I lean on my hands on the fence and watch as if bewitched, wondering what sort of king such a wild, brave boy might make.

And then, as Horemhab seems to be with us ever more and more, something happens that shakes the general, and I can hardly believe it.

He stands before the throne one morning, advocating the hiring of a troop of Greek pirates. As Tutankhaten gazes on in rapt wonder-and Lord Ay watches with pursed lips-Horemhab describes the Greek *phalanx*, a wall of shields and spears that horses hate to charge. He says it will change the style of warfare one day, but for now the querulous Greeks have not the men or unity or wealth to affect world affairs. But, Horemhab declares, fighting them when they duck beneath their shields is like trying to shoot a giant tortoise, and we would do well to have such a weapon at our disposal.

As Tutankhaten gives his assent, requesting that they come to demonstrate their skills, I look about the room impatiently. I am shocked when I see what could be my mother's face looking at me from across the audience chamber. Of course I realize right away that it is Lady Mutnojme, Mother's little sister, but still I cannot speak when Lady Teye presents her at the foot of our dais.

"Auntie," Tutankhaten offers most generously, being that she is his auntie through marriage to me alone. But he felt my hesitation, and he covered my hand with his on the arm of my throne, and now he says, "You are most welcome at my court."

She looks so much like my mother, but her face is longer

and her gaze is unsharpened by calculation and constant royal intrigue. I remember her kindness; she used to braid ribbons into my hair and paint me pictures when Ay allowed her at court. She is a beautiful young woman, and when she comes up from her obeisance, General Horemhab locks his gaze with hers, and incredibly, the fearless hardened warrior loses his breath quite visibly. Ay scowls at the impropriety and Teye ignores it pointedly, but the Lady Mutnojme cannot look away. Teye quite pulls her, and she does not drop her gaze from the general's as she backs away from our thrones. When she is gone, the flustered general cannot seem to recover himself. I am sure he will ask Ay for permission to marry her, meeting whatever demands the wily old vizier sets.

I cannot help but shudder for Mutnojme. Horemhab is a brute, and he should not have been giving her such a nasty expression, as if she were some object to be possessed at any cost. But I would have ignored his bald rudeness, at best; my lady aunt seemed transfixed by it. And though I am not afraid anymore, not even with the rebellions and our shaky hold on power, when I retreat to my room that night I shut my servants out of my large private chamber, and cry in quiet misery into my pillows.

Chapter Three

Tutankhaten has been running about the palace for days, learning his new duties as Pharaoh and reveling in his new freedom to ride and drive when he pleases. The pace he keeps is grueling, and so I am not surprised a bit when I am summoned to his chambers only to find him sitting on his bed, his jaw clenched in pain and his eyes burning with frustration. The little old physician Pentju brings him a tea and then sets himself to wrapping up the offending left foot. Tutankhaten chokes it down in an open throated gulp and then looks at me in misery. "What shall I do now?" he breathes, his voice bound up with pain. "I must return to the audience chamber, I have the new soldiers to look over before they depart for the rebellious districts, I have a thousand things to do and I shall not appear before my people like- like *this!*"

"Divinity must take some time for his religious lessons," Pentju advises. "And he has been neglecting his tutor, I believe. Shall I summon Master Senqed to attend on you here?"

"Do what you like," Tutankhaten grumbles dismissively, and then he looks to me. "I still have to process before the people tomorrow. Do you know that men have come from all the close districts, bringing their families for a chance to see us? I will not disappoint them."

I open my mouth to advise against it, because it will be worse than painful for him to stand in a chariot for hours on

191

end as we process in a winding pattern through the city center. But the simmering frustration in his eyes stops me, and instead I sit down on the bed and take his tight hand in my own.

I keep him company after Pentju has gone to fetch Senqed, rubbing his shoulders as he looks over Lord Ay's suggestions for which men to grant Charters of Immunity, that coveted prize that absolves a great lord from paying his taxes. It seems that Lord Ay is making all of Tutankhaten's appointments, too, and I wonder if the day will ever come when Tutankhaten regrets that. But for now, young as he is, what else can he do? He has the Book of Days to study the characters of the men, but little practical knowledge.

Tutankhaten looks up at me, grinning wryly. "We shall make Lord Paranefer the High Priest of Amun at Karnak."

"Tutankhaten!" I cry, giggling at the thought. "Can you do that? Won't the Amun worshippers be offended? He was Father's closest friend, who designed this city!"

"He was Father's *hostage* for years, don't forget. But yes, I can do it, and I will. Lord Ay says they shall not have their temple with all its wealth *and* their chosen prophet to lead them to insubordination and mischief. Paranefer is excited to oversee the rebuilding efforts, and he will delight in the beauty and wealth of the place once it is running again. And Ankhesenpaaten, remember: *we* are Amun worshippers now."

"Oh, yes," I say easily. I wonder that Tutankhaten will give so much wealth back to the temples-all told, one third of our yearly income-but he and the wily Grand Vizier must have plenty of schemes in waiting to keep the true power and profit of the temples in our hands.

The next day, I am with him when Lord Ay arrives, announcing that it is time to process for the people. Lord Ay notes the bandaging around Tutankhaten's foot but says nothing about it, and I wonder how much he knows of my lord's affliction. My mother, if she knew, would have told it all. "Your chariot awaits, Your Majesty," Ay says, sweeping a bow.

Tutankhaten waves a servant over, and has the youth unbind his foot. He casts his dark eyes up at the Lord Grand Vizier. "I shall not drive," he states. "Tell Lord Rameses to put the white and gold blanket and bridal on Aten's Fury. I will ride through my city today."

Ay gasps in shock. "Your Majesty, that is not prudent! That horse is a stud stallion! He must have a hard hand to curb him!"

"And so he shall today," Tutankhaten retorts. "I have done it already, did you not know?"

Ay isn't a bit reassured. "The crowds will be loud, frightening! The beast will run!"

"No," Tutankhaten says, his voice heavy with command. He waves his chin in dismissal. "He is a war horse by blood. He fears nothing; he is only eager for diversion. Ready him."

Tutankhaten's instincts were right: he looks incredible and majestic riding Fury down the avenues of central Amarna. The horse defiantly dances on the road, snorting and rocking back on his hind legs. It's absolutely glorious, and the people eat it up. The men are impressed and proud; my father performed no such feats for them! The women, I think, clutch a little fear in their hearts at the sight of such a slim boy on such a powerful, rebellious creature. They must think of their own sons. By the time we turn off the Royal Road word has spread, and the newly marriageable maidens of Amarna shriek their approval and throw flowers into the street. Trampled by the horse, the flowers release a heady, sweet fragrance in a cloud around us.

But suddenly, icy fingers stroke my neck. The sight of Tutankhaten's slim back leaning and tilting with Fury's motion, the beautiful white cloak snapping in the breeze, the powerful red horse carrying him through a surging crowd become menacing, evil visions. There is some unseen terror here, dark whispers like *djinni* laughter, just behind the bright day. I grip the railing of my ceremonial chariot, suddenly compelled to run to him, to catch him before he falls.

But then, looking again, I can see-ever so slightly-the gilded heels of Tutankhaten's sandals nudging and prodding my father's stallion into his wild display. *He knows what he's doing; he always knows what he's doing.*

The frightening spell is gone as quick as it came. I gulp the air, seeing nothing before me now but a people exultant in their revelry. I know what's happening in the street: he's done it for me a hundred times in the last year. Tutankhaten has allowed them to forget fear for a moment, to know only pride and joy. In a rare breach of royal protocol, my driver asks softly, "Are you well, Your Majesty?"

"Perfectly," I breathe back, without turning my head.

We return to the Great Palace, and Tutankhaten wheels his horse around into a terrifying rear. Lord Ay gasps as he pulls up beside me, only to laugh as Tutankhaten drops the horse down and pats his neck affectionately. "Your Majesty won the crowd," he says, giving a little bow of appreciation from his flower pelted, gilded chariot. "I did not expect this."

"I wish everything were so easy!" Tutankhaten laughs. He slides down-I don't think anyone notices the extra care he takes-and hands the horse off to an impressed Lord Rameses. "Give him melon, Master Rameses, rind and all. He did an exemplary job."

Lord Rameses grins and pats the big horse. "I'd say he remembers Your Majesty's pulley rein and tiny circles, and didn't want another go of it."

"He's my horse now," Tutankhaten says, brushing Fury's pure red muzzle with his palm. The horse wiggles his lip into the young Pharaoh's hand, as if he were agreeing.

Chapter Four

The people of Amarna may adore Tutankhaten already, but even so rebellion spreads throughout the land. Like Father did before him, Tutankhaten keeps Horemhab close even when the soldiers are sent out to deal with the insurgents. But as Lord Ay predicted, the use of force only encourages more resistance. They do not trust the promise of Tutankhaten's reforms, and all throughout the south they say they will not allow Akhenaten's pure-blood son grind them to dust as Akhenaten destroyed their fathers.

This upsets him more than the actual rebellion, I think. Tutankhaten is already in a sour temper, bearing his weight on his staff of office as the bones in his foot ache and throb and refuse to heal. Before he should, Tutankhaten grits his teeth against the pain and orders his chariot readied, and spends an entire morning running against the wind, with Aten's Fury hitched up to a matching red gelding. Lord Ay, whose wisdom has been proven a shade greater than Horemhab's joins me by the fence and says, "He must come in now. There is a matter of great import to discuss."

As the chariot careens through the arena with alarming speed, I look up at the old vizier and say softly, "I cannot call him in. Can you?"

Lord Ay purses his thin lips. He must wait until the king has tired of his sport. By the time Tutankhaten hands his horses over to the stable boys, I am covered in dust and eager for a mid-day bath. As the Great Royal Wife, even to a boy far removed from caring about my body, I endure a long routine of beautification. In my steaming bathroom, my servants scrub me with a polishing mixture of Dead Sea salt, lemon juice, and olive oil. Once rinsed, I lie on a granite bench while they paint honeyed wax over my skin and then rip it away with linen strips, so that no offensive hair grows anywhere save on my head and my sculpted eyebrows. They use rose oil to make my long black ringlets shine like obsidian, filling the bathroom with the most delicious scent. By the time they rub rose and almond scented cream into my skin, a new servant enters to tell me, "Pharaoh sends for you, Majesty. He says it is most urgent."

I hurry into a dark blue gown. In Tutankhaten's chambers, I am surprised to see his council waiting in the antechamber, the gilded doors of the private chamber shut in their faces. Lord Ay and Lord Maya are hissing in a furious whispered discussion, while the viziers stand about in nervous silence. By their expression I can tell that Tutankhaten's temper has broken over their heads. Only Horemhab seems in decent spirits, toying absently with the golden *merkhet* that once graced my father's desk. Though he is on the king's council, he does not seem to share confidence with any of them. He gives me a polite smile as I walk delicately past them.

The butler Ipay opens the doors, and I quickly join Tutankhaten on his bed. Pentju sits nearby in a gold-detailed chair, his wizened hands folded neatly in his lap.

"Oh, Ankhesenpaaten!" my young husband cries softly, "You will not believe what they have asked me to do!"

"What?" I take his hands, and they are burning hot.

"You know I must be coroneted by Paranefer and the new High Priest of Ptah, but they want it done in Memphis. And they say to soothe the people, I should change my name! My *name*! I shall not do it. Not for a bunch of old ninnies, jumping at their shadows! How *dare* they? My name is sacred!"

Taken by surprise, I do not know what to say. It is an

outrageous demand, to be sure. But almost before the words leave Tutankhaten's lips, I find myself intrigued. And Memphis! I know right away that I wish to leave this place behind, and start anew with Tutankhaten in a place where my father's image doesn't cast such a heavy shadow. "What do they wish you to change it to?" I ask carefully.

"Something to praise Amun, to show how dedicated I am to restoring the old ways. But I need not change my name to restore the old ones! I won't do it!"

Sitting beside him, I can feel the heat of his anger effusing from his skin. I must find something to say to calm him; we need those old ninnies, as he calls them, who hover just beyond the door. Has he forgotten that his reign is hardly secure yet?

But Pentju speaks first. "Your Majesty, you will not survive if you are crowned in Amarna, rather than the traditional city for Pharaoh's coronation. And it is not so much this council that needs appeasement but the people in the street. It is the Egyptian in the field who will be most touched by this gesture, and who will follow you in turn no matter what the great lords do."

Tutankhaten frowns. "I shall not fear them, Pentju. I saw how at the feast to honor the ascension of my father's *akhu* to the next world, they cared nothing for him, only for securing a place in the new court. They followed him here to make their fortunes, and they desert his laws instantly when there will be profit in the priesthoods once again. I shall not fear them, and I shall not do their bidding. They would make me, you know. I- I have changed too much already, maybe... I do believe in Aten, Pentju. With all my heart. Do not forget that."

I bite my lips, torn between the sense of duty and belief I was raised to, and my own desperate need to be free. It is impossible for me to think of the dangers of this new, transitioning court, or of the frightening masses of mobs throughout this country, demanding fairness and faith and a Pharaoh who brings them prosperity. I can only think that I can't go on this way. I can't live in this place. It has been long enough since he died, since my daughter died, since I became

197

dead to my mother like all my sisters gone in the plague, and yet I cannot escape the oppression of memory. But this is my misery alone. Tutankhaten is my closest friend, my own self, really; even still, how could he truly understand that I can't breathe here in my father's world? Beside me his anger has turned to insecurity. He who has sought forbidden wisdom of the old ones for years now is questioning his loyalty to Aten, and worse, to Father. I close my eyes, refusing to do what my mother or Mayati so obviously would: play on his sense of duty to Egypt to get my will done.

But Pentju doesn't hesitate. "You made a commitment for the well-being of your people, Your Majesty. And you know that there are other gods in this world. You have felt them. You have offered to them, in secret, for some time now."

Tutankhaten claims my hand off my lap. His fingers have a slight tremble, until he tightens them on mine. "Yes, I know."

Pentju's voice is hushed, reverent. "He had his reasons, my young lord, but it should not have been done as it was."

"Yes," Tutankhaten repeats. And then he looks up at his physician and teacher, and his dark eyes cut with a ferocity shocking for his age. "But they shall wait for my answer. You may tell them so, all of them. Lord Ay as well."

Tutankhaten leaves his council in wonder over the next week. He takes his chariot out to the flat expanse of desert pressing against the eastern cliffs, where Horemhab trains five hundred new recruits for Tutankhaten's security force. He returns for dinner smelling of leather and horseflesh, with at least a little peace in his eyes. He says nothing at all about his council's proposal, even when Ay tells him, "Changing your name to revere Amun will do more to end these little rebellions than any militia Horemhab could ever raise."

Tutankhaten eats his steak in silence, musing over the staff dancers stomping and sparring on the floor of the great hall. It doesn't matter what Ay says about Horemhab; Tutankhaten is hot for the military in a way that startles me. I had always assumed his interest in warfare was intellectual only. He could not mean to fight! Surely, his riding and driving is enough sport for him, especially with his unpredictable pain!

During this time, old Nani comes to crave my permanent dismissal. "I am an old woman, Your Majesty. I wish to go to my daughter's home in the north and drink wine and sit in the sun until my days in this world are finished."

Tears fill my eyes, so much that I turn away. I don't know why I cry, I never see the old wise-woman anyway, and I certainly have no use for her services. Maybe it was her kindness; she was the only one, save Tutankhaten, who showed even a glimmer of anger towards Father for what he did to me. I press my fingers to the hollow of my throat and steady myself. "Of course," I tell her. "Of course you may go home." *May Aten bless you*, I think, the customary good-bye that sticks in my throat.

The old crone's eyes are bright with a smile. "You are looking much better these days, Your Majesty. There are those who say your prince was always supposed to be king. And you will rule well together. These uprisings will end once the people know of Pharaoh's goodness."

"I want to leave Amarna," I confess to this woman who has seen me sick with fear of Father and half dead in childbirth. "I have to leave this place. I cannot breathe here. I cannot sleep."

Nani nods her head astutely. "And His Majesty?"

I shrug miserably. "It is his home, the only home he's ever known. I think he feels like he is losing too much, too fast. His father, the worship he was raised to, even his name. He knows it is the right thing to do, yet he is but a boy."

"You must tell him what you told me, madam. Perhaps your desire for a new home will give him the strength to leave Amarna."

"Do you think we must go as well?" I ask, trusting Nani's wisdom over any learned man at court.

Nani purses her dark, full lips together. Her old woman's voice is severe when she says, "I think your crowns depend on it."

As Tia sets a pretty bejeweled royal diadem over my loose curls, Tutankhaten arrives at my door, fresh from the Temple and sweet with holy oil. For the first time in days, a bright, excited smile dances on his lips. I rise and cross the gallery of my chamber. "My lord," I say, dropping a little bow. "What has happened?"

"The Greeks are here! Horemhab's arranged for a demonstration of their unique fighting style in the city square."

"Shall we see them now?" I ask, pleased that he is in better spirits.

Tutankhaten grins and offers me his arm. We take a chariot into the city center, where our courtiers and the more prosperous men of the city gather in the shadow of the treasury offices. I cannot help noticing my father's frighteningly exaggerated stone visage glaring down on us, stretched by elongating shadows in the creamy morning light. Heralds blast their trumpets and everyone shuffles down into prostration as Tutankhaten and I take our places in a shaded pavilion.

The Greeks are men with odd ruddy or olive complexions and short wool garments too thick for the Egyptian sun. Some of them have hair the color of spun gold, some have red hair, and all of them wear heavy helmets with animal parts on them, the horns of bulls or high crests of horsehair.Excited, I slip my fingers through Tutankhaten's, and he grins at me. "Horemhab says horses won't charge their *phalanx*.I'll bet Fury would, though."

The Greek commander-a thick, middle aged man with nasty war scars and flowing golden hair-hails us in his heavy foreign tongue, and so they begin. There is a great clashing of shields as two solid blocks of men clash. Each man is pressed shoulder to shoulder with his neighbor making two bristling, opposing walls of spears.It is indeed a strange style of fighting, and I can see how a horse might be reluctant to charge such a wall of men and weapons. Certainly, when they duck beneath their shields like a giant, prickly tortoise, a charioteer's arrows would be useless. And the men are vicious, even in mock combat. Tutankhaten is entranced, blood flies, and the crowd roars with glee.

But then, an odd shouting rises along the far side of the square, followed by cries and hisses. The Greek commander calls for a halt and every man among them tightens their grasp on their spears.

"What is it?" Tutankhaten demands, sitting tall.

A peasant man pushes up the line, pawing at indignant merchants in their fine linen robes. "He will use them against us!" the man shouts, pointing incredibly to the royal pavilion, to Tutankhaten. "He will use these foreign dogs to kill us, like his father did!"

In the shocked silence, Tutankhaten licks his lips and clenches his fingers around the lion heads on his throne. My own heart quickens; I look for any sign that the crowd will go along with him and surge over us like a scorching, blinding *khamsin* wind.

In the pavilion beneath us, Horemhab turns to a brace of powerful Nubian guards. "Arrest him," he says, disgusted.

"No!" Tutankhaten shouts, turning in his throne. "It's what he wants, to prove his point! Have the police step into their ranks, but let that man go free."

"Tutankhaten…" I breathe, frightened. Should he not be taken away, punished?

My young husband turns to me, his gaze all dark fire. "Trust me! He is sacrificing himself to make his point. Father spoke to me of such men. When I have him dragged off to the dungeons for speaking his fears they will say he spoke truly."

I pinch my lips until they pale, and sit back in my gilded throne. And sure enough, as a row of armed police step forward but leave the man free to shout and wail, the crowd-eager for more of the fight-begins to hoot and jeer the heckler away. I look at Tutankhaten, and he nods slightly, but he is angry nonetheless. "I will show them," he tells me quietly. "I will be my own man. I will be a king for all the people, and I will bring glory to this land once more."

I nod, admiring his fearless determination. But I doubt very much that we will ever be free of Father's shadow, even if we run all the way to Memphis.

At sunset, after Tia and my new maids finish braiding my hair, I slip into a gauzy white robe and go to Tutankhaten's chambers. Ipay tells me that he is on the balcony making private offerings.

I walk through the narrow, guarded corridor and out onto the balcony. Tutankhaten is at the far end, on his knees with his arms slightly outstretched and his palms up in prayer. He is facing the west, the sunset. Now twilight, oil lamps flicker around him. He burns the heady, sweet *kyphi* incense used at sunset ceremonies. It was Father's favorite incense.

Not wanting to intrude in Tutankhaten's prayer, I wait in the shadows of the cool stone doorway. He finishes his prayer, holds up more of the incense and then places it in the wide golden burner. When he comes to me, his eyes shine as if he had wept.

"What is it?" I ask. I would take him in my arms, but I sense that his dignity would be offended. Tutankhaten doesn't easily own up to those emotions Father considered weak, such as pain or fear or sadness.

"Today… that man…" he shakes his head. "My council says it only demonstrates the need for a name change, and for us to remove to Memphis as soon as possible."

"Oh, Tutankhaten, please let us do it!" I cry. "I don't want to be here anymore. I can't stand it, to always have *him* staring down on me, to have every place we go haunted by his presence! You can still worship Aten if you please, but we can have a fresh start, away from all this-"

He frowns for a moment, and I fear he will disagree with me. Can his pride be so offended by his council's request? But he only reaches out and touches my braids softly, and then he looks down to his gilded sandals and nods. "It must be done," he says quietly. "I think… I fear they will believe they can twist me about as they please, but I will show them they shall not! And still, I know it's the right thing to do."

I cry for relief, flinging myself into his arms with abandon. Usually I despise such intimate affection, but once his surprise is gone, and his arms wind around my back to hold me close, I cry on his shoulder. "I want to change my name too, Tutankhaten. I want to be reborn to this new life, with you. As if it never happened."

He doesn't need to ask what I am referring to, but still his sigh is heavy. There is something more to his suffering tonight, and these past few days, and I dare not consider it. "Please," I whisper. "Please."

"It shall be done," he tells me, his youthful voice as weighted as a tired old man's.

In the morning we ascend the great dais in the largest audience chamber in Amarna, and to the thunderous applause of the court, Tutankhaten proclaims that he shall take the name of Tutankhamun, the Living Image of Amun, and I shall be Ankhesenamun, Great Royal Wife. The honorary of King's Daughter is stripped from my titles, as if my father had never existed at all. And even though we walk in his palace, under images of him smiting his enemies with a heavy hand, I am as light as a newborn child. I lace my fingers with Tutankhaten's as we leave our court behind, striding out into the portico where a hard, fresh breeze rocks my heavy gold earrings until they swing like pendulums. "I can hardly believe it!" I gasp in delight. "We will go to Memphis!"

"The duck hunting is supposed to be good in the marshes," he muses quietly.

"Oh, Tutankhaten," I say, though I am anxious to use our new names, "you cannot think they forced you to it! You'll see, this is really for the best."

He looks at me, his eyes all dark fire. "No one will force me to anything again. I have begun this restoration as I was bid, but soon I will reveal my own plans for Egypt."

Though I was not alive then, my father must have spoken words just like this when he became king, and they ring chilly in the warm morning sun. I try to keep my voice light. "What plans?"

"I shall raise a great army," he tells me, a smile finally dancing at the corners of his full, well-formed mouth. "We shall take back the territories Father lost in the north, and secure the south as well. Egypt's enemies will tremble before my army!"

I am not surprised at all. Tutankhaten is drawn to warfare like a moth to the flame. The first day I ever spoke to him he was seeking out stories of the great battles of our ancestors. "Ay will be irritated that Horemhab will gain such power. You know he considers him little better than a peasant, for all he's done for this family. Ay won't like him leading a massive national army."

Tutankhaten turns to me sharply. "Horemhab will be my Overseer, Ankhesenpaaten, but I will lead my army, as our ancestors did, as is proper."

Mute with sudden horror, I dig my nails into his arm. "Tutankhaten- no-"

"You think I cannot?" he demands, his face burning the way it did when Father questioned his ability, and his affliction. "No one will be a better warrior than me! Already I put our subjects' sons to shame, and I've been driving for but five years. And there are grown men who can't shoot like me, you know it!"

"I don't want to lose you," I whisper, nauseated at the thought of Tutankhaten injured on the field of battle.

"You won't! I'm Pharaoh, not some spearman with one shield!"

There is no speaking sense to him! Just last night, after dinner, he was soaking a swollen, aching foot. Now he will sword fight, spear fight, and train for marches, as well as learn war craft? "Horemhab will teach you?" I ask, clutching his hand as if I could ever hold him back.

His temper cools, and he says, "Yes, but it will be years before I can actually go to war. I have to win support, obviously, increase my income, and raise an army on top of learning how to fight and lead men. But that's my dream: to regain our empire, and keep our borders and foreign commerce safe. And when I've made Egypt into a glorious empire once more, and painted temple walls with the tales of my victories, everyone will forget the bad times, and they will know that I am the one who was always meant to rule."

Chapter Five

We glide on the shrinking river, an endless convoy of barges bearing not only all the goods we bring, but a large chunk of the court and all their families and goods as well. Entire barges are given way to roped baskets and trunks, or animals to kill and cook as we lay over for the night, or laughing servant girls sharing watered wine, enjoying their vacation. Horemhab's palace guard-finally fleshed out with true Egyptians, from Middle Egypt-leads and follows with their flotillas. The convoy moves around us as we sit on the deck of the royal barge, watching our country slip past. There are ancient cities surrounded by groves of palms, and mud-brick villages piling at the edge of the black land. Every field is baked dry at the end of the harvest, and we can see our own transport barges bobbing in the harbors, and sometimes our tax-collectors descending on a village or family granary.

The people stop their work and come down to the banks and watch our passing barges, standing silent under the blue sky. They look like herds of skittish gazelle, ready to run one way or the next. With each day we get farther from Amarna, the scourge of neglect and poverty grows. The city buildings crumble and the peasants are thin, the demand in their faces frightening. In my rush to run from Amarna, I had forgotten what we were sailing into: a land my father deemed hostile, a place that had to be controlled with a granite fist and washed regularly with tears and blood. Tutankhamun-as I am learning to call him now-watches all of this with a silent stare. Our laughter and games of *senet* fall away by the fourth day, and I can't help but hold his hand in fear.

And then, Memphis rises, and the shining pyramids around her. The city spills chaotically out of her famous white walls, with stark brown blocks of mud-brick apartments pushing up to the very base. The entire place is a maze of alleys and claustrophobic corridors crowding with the poorest people I have ever seen. Nearly grown children stand naked on the banks, washing their only garment on a river bank choked with reed rafts. A fine stench of fish and filth and smoke creeps into the air. And then, it is abruptly gone. The gleaming eastern wall rises out of the river to our left, and the scent of incense streams from the approaching harbor.

We dock at the long royal quay. Awaiting us is a tall, broad-shouldered old man in gauzy linen and a wide broad collar, shaded by a servant and surrounded by fans, and twenty of the city elders. Behind them is a fleet of waiting chariots, and a road into a dark city that seems to have swallowed up the sun.

Tutankhamun turns to me, the vulture and cobra winking in his diadem. "Now or never," he murmurs, nodding his head once. I want to snatch at his arm, but I mustn't. I am so terrified I don't think my legs will work, but when Tutankhamun picks up his gilded staff and holds his hand out to me, I force myself up, gazing on Memphis with wary eyes.

The rich-looking man bows to Pharaoh, mimicked by all his fellows. He rises and presses his fat, ringed hands together in pleasure. "I am Lord Intef, Your Majesty, your humble servant and Mayor of Memphis. On this most proud and joyous day, it is my great honor to escort Your Majesty to your palace."

The shadows fall as we enter Memphis. The tall walls, taller government buildings, and labyrinth of apartment buildings must keep all but midday light out of most windows. Far down the road, a palace rises above the city, and I can only hope that my own quarters will be high enough to provide light and fresh air.

Here, too, people line the roads, but they are a different sort. These are clean-dressed and smiling, many of them comely women and children who throw posies of flowers into the street. But there are enough men wearing the same leather netting over their kilts to tell me that security is high, and this is no spontaneous show of love.

In the chariot beside us, Mayor Intef proclaims, "There is no city safer than Memphis! I myself personally fund five thousand police to keep order. You can see it yourself, Your Majesty-there is no shouting, no disorder, no trash in your city streets! Criminals fear the justice of Mayor Intef!"

Tutankhamun says nothing. Raised in the shining city of Amarna, his critical eye roams over every ugly and unordered thing in Memphis. And then, sharply, as if a line were drawn, lovely stone townhouses take over for the mud-brick apartments and cloth-roofed market stalls. The gardens are gorgeous, some hanging to maximize space in the tight city. A great square opens up, full of towering statues and lines of obelisks. Mayor Intef boasts that these are Grandfather's statues, and many of the obelisks were placed by our most ancient ancestors.

Within three days' time, it is easy to see that Intef is the strong man in this corner of Lower Egypt. In the grand gilded hall of our Memphis palace, it is Intef who truly commands. Even if only for a moment, each man in the hall shakes his hand and murmurs a few words. The man Tutankhaten named High Priest of Ptah, a Memphis lord with ties to Amarna, fawns over Intef as if the mayor held keys to eternal paradise.

"Mayor Intef is accustomed to holding his own court," Lord Ay observes coolly. "Though the viziers travelled about the land, no one in Egypt has seen Pharaoh outside of Amarna in over ten years. There will be one hundred lords like him, acting like rulers of petty kingdoms, but hardly any with such power as the Mayor of Memphis. His profits from the harbor alone-the bottleneck that channels all the river's many branches into one-are gargantuan. The only man who might rival him is

Djarmuti, out of the far north east of Egypt, where the land routes to Memphis and the Red Sea ports must turn south. He is kin to Rameses, and about thirty other chariot officers who hold important posts in the land. If we are to promote anyone without causing a shift in power, it must be Intef over Djarmuti."

"Why?" Tutankhamun asks, turning curious eyes on his Grand Vizier.

"A king must not favor any one of the mighty clans too much above the others. The woman Pharaoh took power by promoting the family of the old High Priest of Amun, unleashing all the events that tore this country apart. Intef is a lonely operator, and not a military man: a much safer bet. Forgive me, Your Majesty, but it was only through great strategy and might that the renegade priest's head wound up on a stick, rather than your blessed father's."

Tutankhamun hisses through his bright white teeth. He fixes his dark, astonished stare on Lord Ay, angered by the vizier's hideous, coarse words. "Mind your tongue!"

The wiry old man makes a gesture of apology. "I beg your pardon, Lord, but it is the absolute truth. Better Your Majesty knows it, for your father knew it-in all its bloody detail-each and every day he drew breath."

Tutankhamun is gone with his tutor Senqed, leaving me to preside over the massive block of the Memphis palace enclosure. I've barely seen my servants to ordering my countless cedar trunks, I am lost in my enormous wardrobe chamber, and I haven't seen outside this wing, but I am the mistress of this house. I grip Tia's arm-fearing that I might faint-and stare in horror over the many officials who run my household, and the innumerable servants standing behind them for my inspection. It isn't very regal, the way my lips and throat go dry at the thought of ordering them all.

"I can't do it," I whisper later, as Tia shakes one of my linen gowns out of a woven reed basket. My own things are not yet unpacked; how can I master a palace if I can't put order to my own chambers? Perhaps I should have taken Teye's assistance; perhaps I should summon her now. I'm sure she's offended that I haven't...

"Of course you can, my little lady. It would be overwhelming for anyone, let alone a young woman who has been away from her lessons for some time. Why don't you send for Lady Mutnojme? She's had the running of Lord Ay's estate for several years, with Lady Teye living at court. She can teach you, I'd imagine."

I brighten at this. Of course! Mutnojme is skilled, but more, she has nothing to do with court. She wasn't there to watch us all fall apart, and so I won't have to think of it around her. And she is merry, too. I want so much to be merry! So I send a royal scribe off to Ay's new townhouse, to fetch my aunt. She comes that very afternoon, wearing an easy smile and a beautiful rope of polished malachite beads around her neck. "I need your help," I say, forgetting the polite things I ought to say first.

"Anything," she says, making a little graceful bow. I almost tell her that she need not bow to me, that I wish she wouldn't, but I bite my lips. She is my subject like any other. "How can I help Your Majesty?"

"This palace... I don't know what to do here, to put it in order."

She looks about the elegantly furnished antechamber, and to the three young maids separating bunches of dried lavender for my linen chests. We walk out to my balcony, which thankfully faces the northeast for the coolest river breezes. Far beneath us, the palace enclosure operates like a city within a city, hosting foreign dignitaries, viziers and ministers, and servants all. We have bakers, laundresses, chariot-drivers in their cabs, royal scribes to take transcriptions, accountants to pay out the wages... And I must oversee them to be sure my household stewards aren't thieving or wasting, to keep good order. I must make and keep a home worthy of a Pharaoh.

My aunt turns to me, the green beads in her long wig

clicking musically. "Would you require me to live here, with you?"

"Well, you couldn't go back to Amarna..."

She laughs softly and says, "I don't want to go back to Amarna. All the interesting people are here now. But it would be better for us if I had my own rooms in the palace."

"I want you to stay with me," I say suddenly, shocking myself at my outburst of truth, of the emotion I always try to hide. I look down before she sees my tears. "Of course you can have chambers in the palace."

"Then I would be glad to do it, Your Majesty. But I will marry soon, I think. It shouldn't matter, though. You'll be supervising everything yourself in a few weeks, I'm sure."

"General Horemhab?" I ask shyly, wondering how the thought of it doesn't have her sick with fear.

Mutnojme grins merrily and says, "He doesn't know it yet, but he's going to ask me to marry him."

I flush with shame, realizing that I'm the different one, not her. Like any woman, Mutnojme seeks marriage with a strong nobleman, and she'll want children soon as well. But Mutnojme is the sort of woman one can't stay too sad around. Her laughter is infectious, and so is her confidence. She teaches me all I must need to know about running a great estate, how to audit the ledgers and keep the servants in line, and it's far simpler than I thought once I get going. In a few short weeks, I no longer need her over my shoulder, checking my work. As I walk through my palace, commanding my servants and taking their obeisance, I feel like a Great Royal Wife in deed, not just name.

Mutnojme reminds me of other things, too. We call upon the finest dressmakers in the city and set a trend for long, hooded sleeves and loose gauzy downs that trail like smoke in the breeze. She spends hours braiding my long black curls into elaborate cascading plaits, fitted with gold beads and scented with rose oil. I am stunned when the daughters of the court begin to appear the same way-letting their hair down or wearing long wigs, and ordering up loose, dreamy robes in the thinnest linen they can afford.

"You have no finest feature," Mutnojme declares critically, holding a fine cosmetic brush above my face. I laugh, and she explains, "I mean, your face is equally striking, in any of its parts. Your eyes are lovely and strange, green and brown and gold all at once. I'm going to use gold dust and kohl to bring them out, and gloss your lips with a mix of cream and red ochre."

I close my eyes and feel the cold paint, the soft strokes of the brush. Mutnojme holds my round mirror up, a new mirror with Hathor's cow-eared face on the handle. I smile, because finally I am happy again. I know I am beautiful, I am Great Royal Wife; I am blessed. I have Tutankhamun for a husband and a palace under my command, our own palace, our own home. When I look up at Mutnojme, I have tears in my eyes. She is far too merry a woman for tears, and so she cries in mock-despair, "You will smear your kohl!"

I take a breath to steady myself, wondering if she can ever understand what this means to me. This is my home, this is my life, and I am glad for it at last.

Chapter Six

1333 BC
Second Month of Summer,
Year One Tutankhamun

On a sizzling summer day, Lord Paranefer, High Priest of Amun, Lord Hebnetjer, High Priest of Ptah, and my own little self purify and anoint Tutankhamun in the newly restored Temple of Amun. They shave his beautiful long side lock away and make him into a man with their hot knife, and only then do they place the archaic crowns of power on his small head.

Tutankhamun emerges from the temple stunned with pain and dazzled by the ancient rituals of power. I take his arm quickly, before he swoons and collapses. The thousands of people packing the streets erupt into wild, jubilant cheering. Tutankhamun looks down on them in wonder. Surely, these cannot be the same people who looked at us with such hostile, frightened eyes three months ago? "I have done it," he says, his voice breathy from shock. "They accept me."

I grin with pride, and walk him down to the waiting flower-adorned ceremonial chariot, pulled by two horses of such brilliant white coats they're blinding in the sun. Two young girls, virgin twins chosen to tend the sacred Apis Bull, garland

Pharaoh's snorting horses with fragrant wreaths. We ride back to the palace in triumph, through the roaring streets of Lower Egypt's most ancient city, toward the blinking electrum caps on the great pyramids that shine like stars in the western sky.

After his coronation, Tutankhamun jumps into the world of soldiery. He studies the arts of the scimitar and *khepesh* swords with Horemhab, the spear with Rameses, and spends long hours going bow for bow with Nakhtmin, racing through the deserts outside of Memphis in their chariots. General Horemhab spends hours teaching him of ancient battles, of the movements of divisions and companies and platoons. They sit on the balcony at night surrounded by fire, Lady Ten Bows preening on a golden perch behind her master and wide maps and scrolls before them, covered with little gold counters to represent companies of soldiers.

Tutankhamun is as good a student of warfare as he is of languages and theology. He impresses the general and Rameses, and all the servants who gather around the courtyards of Memphis to watch their lord and his general trample the gardens sword fighting. Truthfully, he looks very good, truly natural with his sword in his hand, as fearless and eager to fight as a young lion. When the city buzzes with excited rumors about Pharaoh becoming a warrior like his ancestors, Lord Ay asks Tutankhamun bluntly, "What does all this mean?"

Tutankhamun sets aside his steak knife and washes his fingers in rosewater. He dries them carefully, watching as his signet rings flash in the lamplight. When he looks at Lord Ay, it is with a dark, winsome smile, a smile to charm the hardest heart. "I have neglected my training for too long, Lord Ay. General Horemhab began studying sword fighting at eight. Do you think King Suppililiuma will fear me if I show no interest in martial arts?"

"Your Majesty is concerned about the Hittites," Ay realizes. "They have consolidated their power in the north of Asia, and they control Kadesh through Aitakama, but so far they have posed no outright threat to Egypt, and if we support the buffer state of Amurru then we need not fear the Hittites turning any farther south..."

"You are mad!" Tutankhamun announces haughtily, his voice high and shrill. "Why else would they seek to control Kadesh but to control the wide roads and plentiful grain of the Biqa Valley? That is Egyptian grain, those are Egyptian trade routes! Why else would they sew discord among our vassels, if not to weaken the region and ready it for the kill, thereby adding all of its timber and silver, copper and tin to the Hittite treasury? And strengthen deceitful Amurru? Once the Hittites control the wealth of Syria, the Amurru will step aside and let them march south, into Palestine, and perhaps even into Egypt! And what about Nubia? Your own son tells me that his gold transports-my transports-are regularly attacked, even robbed. Egypt will soon be a laughing stock in the world, and I will be shamed as well."

"We should not provoke them, Your Majesty. They are a warlike people, barbarous people... Especially when we have not yet secured *domestic* order!" Ay protests, his face grey.

"Lord Ay, I will follow your advise and secure this land. But Egypt and Hatti must have a reckoning soon, and I'd rather it be at a time of my choosing, not King Suppililiuma's! I will do this, Ay. I command it."

Lord Ay eats and drinks in silence for a long time, gazing at the shaking belts of the dancing girls as if he were simply enjoying the feast. But when he speaks again, he asks, "Do you desire a large army?"

Tutankhamun nods enthusiastically. "We should have four or five divisions, at least, ready to be led out at any time."

"And you wish to lead them yourself, one day."

"I do," Tutankhamun says proudly. "As my ancestors did. I wish to put the fear of Horus into my enemies, and heap piles of tribute before the god in Karnak."

Ay nods, absorbing this. "Well... then we must concentrate on efficiency in government, to be sure to keep Your Majesty's treasuries fat. No country can be great without a well-run bureaucracy. Have you given any thought to offering the vizier's post to Lord Intef? He already has his own police force, he presides over the *Kenbet* of this district, and he consistently posts high tax returns in the springtime. He will make the most of Lower Egypt, as he has done in Memphis."

"I wish Ankheti hadn't resigned," Tutankhamun says, drumming his fingers in irritation.

"We did speak of favoring Intef, Your Majesty; he is certainly qualified for the position."

"All right," Tutankhamun decides. "I'll make Intef the Vizier of Lower Egypt, because you say he is good for it, and I trust you in this. But you must trust me about the Hittites! I must defeat them one day."

Chapter Seven

Spring, Year One

In the early harvest time of Tutankhamun's first year, he invites the men he trains with on a duck hunting trip. We are both eager to row further downstream, to cross from our home of cliffs and desert into the wide marshlands of Lower Egypt. Mutnojme comes along as well, claiming the same reason when we both know she just wants to be with Horemhab.

The Delta is beautiful, a land of soothing green and blue. The thick forests of reeds line both banks, full of calling birds and bullfrogs and a thousand other creatures. Groves of palms and wild sycamores and acacia shade mud-brick houses, granaries, and barns. And then, for as far as the eye can see behind the marshes, the fertile fields spread out to the desert, crowned in gold with emmer wheat. The peasant farmers are thick in the fields with their donkeys and ox carts, striking down and piling up the mature stalks so the grain within can be beaten and trampled out.

Our small, flat bottomed barges navigate these shallow channels slowly. In places, we must be poled along. Rameses and Horemhab know the way well. They've promised Pharaoh a fine spot for duck hunting, where the birds are so thick in the brush that one might cast a wide net out and catch dozens.

The king and his noble companions will hunt with throwing sticks, and their hounds will track the fallen birds down; and if they are not dead from the stick or the fall from flight, then the hounds will shake them till their necks snap.

Rameses and his sturdy little son Seti order the houndsmen, and the dogs are brought on, their strong thin red bodies bursting with joy, whining and barking for love of the hunt. Mutnojme and I both warm with smiles for the five year old who imitates his father's bold, open stride with his tiny fists on his hips. Seti watches Tutankhamun as well, with careful but wide eyes, noting how all the men defer to one so much younger than his own father.

Tutankhamun gathers up his ebony sticks and gives me a little bow. "I'm off to hunt, my lady."

"I want plenty of duck for dinner," I tease. I can think of nothing more difficult than hitting a bird in mid-flight with a slim, hooked stick.

"You'll have it," Tutankhamun says with a grin, and he jumps down onto the muddy riverbank. He walks off with Nakhtmin, laughing. There is a small gulf of age between Pharaoh and Ay's son, but they are becoming close. Nakhtmin seems to have no mind for his own advancement, unless it's through the ranks of the army. He's an unwilling courtier but a consummate athlete, and that must be why Tutankhamun favors him.

Mutnojme and I walk a good distance back. Already, the hunters are spiriting off into the dense reeds, their red dogs winding almost invisible paths around them. The reeds grow taller by the moment, and suddenly, Mutnojme is gone, and then the servant bearing my sunshade is lost as well. I stop and look up, but I can't see the blue and gold tasseled parasol. I turn around again, the reeds crashing together as I push into them. "Mutnojme! Mutnojme!"

I listen, at first hearing nothing but the pounding of my own heart. But then, I hear something- Not my aunt, but a woman, a woman softly weeping. I sweep through the reeds, hurrying towards the sound. Incredibly, when I push the reeds aside I'm on the bank of one of the river's many channels. I must have gotten turned around somehow... And here before me, a woman with loose black waves and a topless white sheath kneels by the water, searching as if she's lost something, weeping as if that thing were her very heart.

"Can I help you?" I ask, stepping forward.

The woman turns on me preternaturally, so quickly, as if she is angry to be interrupted. Her face is beautiful and horrible, her eyes are endlessly blue, a blue like the very bottom of the river. Her anger is so violent it burns me up, but then she fixes her eyes on my face, on the royal diadem on my brow. She stretches her arms out to me, crying, "He is gone... He is gone from me, forever, and I cannot follow him..."

The chill that passes through me is enough to freeze my teeth. The horrible loss in the woman's face, the monstrous thing behind her beauty, the icy hiss of her words... I am stunned. I can feel my hands reaching behind me for the reeds, my fingers grabbing for them as if I were drowning.

"You need not run from *me*, Princess of Egypt! We are alike, you and me." Her warm smile, sudden, not reaching her tearful eyes, is somehow more terrifying than her wailing. She is a madwoman, deranged, really, but something horrifyingly more powerful than me. I back into the reeds, unable to turn but desperate to get away, even as she calls to me in an awful voice, "Take heed, sister! Take care, Bride of Horus! The Bride of Horus becomes the Bride of Osiris, all things in their time!"

Terrified, I leap back into the reeds, tumbling gracelessly through them, hearing nothing but the sound of their lashing. Is the woman chasing me? I cannot run with the poorly healed bones in my foot; she would catch me in a flash, like a crocodile snapping on a fish.

"Your Majesty!" Mutnojme cries, grabbing my shoulders as I stumble into her. "We were walking together, and then you were lost!"

"There's a woman!" I gasp, looking back through the wall of reeds. "A madwoman, crying on the riverbank and speaking nonsense! I thought she was hurt... She knew me, she looked to my diadem and shouted at me..."

"Where's this, madam?" one of my guards asks, stepping up with his spear in hand.

I point and say, "Along the water..."

Five men rush off, and I turn back to Mutnojme and shake my head. "She was terrible... So beautiful, but so terrible."

"The madwoman?" Mutnojme asks. "She was beautiful? How do you know she was mad?"

"Mad with grief," I say, my breathing slowing with my guards and my lady aunt beside me. "She was wailing, 'He is gone, he is gone'. It was so... so painfully sad. And she shouted at me!"

Mutnojme makes a gesture to ward away evil. "Let's hope they find her."

But the guards return, upset and empty-handed. "We'd better catch up to the main group, Your Majesty," the captain suggests warily. "We found no sign of her, not even a track in the mud. I don't like the feel of it."

There is a sudden rush of waterfowl from the marshes, and the dogs bark out a gleeful chorus. Out in the distance a dark, spinning object launches from the reeds. It's almost too fast to see, but the stick rings around the darting body of a thick, glossy duck. The bird's graceful flight cuts off instantly; robbed of motion, it tumbles to the ground, helpless before the onslaught of the dogs. I close my eyes and cringe at the violence. The baying of the red hounds echoes off the water, followed by the men's happy shouting. Pharaoh made a perfect throw.

"Come on, Your Majesty," Mutnojme says, looking behind me again as if the woman might follow us. "The hunters are just down the path."

Tutankhamun walks back with his hand in mine, and a brace of dead ducks slung over his shoulder like he was any ordinary youth. We take our little rafts back to the main river, and drink cool white wine on our barge while our servants prepare the fat birds for our feast. The men-relieved that Mutnojme and I are unharmed-laugh about the strange woman in the water, deciding she had lost her lover to another woman and was mad for unrequited passion. I sit beside Tutankhamun silent until now, my small hand still curled up in his. "No," I tell them, my voice like cold water thrown over a fire. "He didn't abandon her, he was dead. She was a widow. And she wasn't a peasant. She... she spoke to me... She didn't cower."

"Because she's insane," Horemhab declares, with a hearty laugh that would dispel any demon. "This only proves she was a crazy fishwife, wailing in the water."

"No." I shake my head. "She was no fishwife. She was something... She was powerful."

"Perhaps you saw Isis," Rameses suggests mysteriously.

Tutankhamun narrows his eyes. "Isis? The Goddess Isis?"

Rameses draws himself up, meeting each of our eyes. "In the old days, the gods and goddesses were told to appear to who they chose. They could appear as a man or a woman, or an animal even. Hence the old wisdom of being generous to the meanest looking travellers, and never taking any creature for granted. You, the Great Royal Wife, were separated from your group. You saw a woman weeping into the river, searching, as Isis searched for Osiris. She was no one we know, but powerful, and with strange eyes, and she spoke to you plainly, though you wear the uraeus on your brow. And then she disappeared, leaving no track or trace. Perhaps you saw the Goddess Isis."

Nakhtmin is the first to offer a nervous laugh. "You've had too much wine, Rameses!"

"I... I don't think so," I say quickly.

Tutankhamun, of course, is fascinated. "Did she say anything else?"

I turn to look at him, his dark, pretty face framed by a white *nemes* cloth and sparkling electrum diadem. "No... nothing. I told you, she was wailing for her husband. Well- She called me Bride of Horus, and the like, but of course she knew me for your wife."

"You saw Isis," he says softly, proudly, his lips stretching into that honey smile. "You've been honored."

I can't help it; his smile always warms my heart, and I gratefully forget the numbing fear I felt before the strange woman. I laugh, and lean against my best friend. Tutankhamun gladly drops his arm over my shoulders, squeezing gently. Maybe it really is a sign for us, a sign that we've brought the old gods back and done right by our people. Or perhaps my skittish little heart has gotten the best of me again, making a goddess out of a poor peasant on the riverbank. Either way, I am determined to be happy, to enjoy this day with Tutankhamun and Mutnojme and these loud, laughing soldiers we seem to have taken as friends.

They leave off talking about goddesses and crazy women and apparitions, and turn instead to the comical dilemma of Nakhtmin's betrothed, the High Priest of Ptah's eldest daughter.

"She's still at her mother's! I've never known a woman so... so determined to be chased. We're all but wed, I've given her a house and jewels and servants, and still she hides in her mother's skirts. I've been carrying that stupid lute all over court, trying to make up a song to please her, so that I can finally bring her home."

Everyone laughs. Nakhtmin is a famous womanizer, rich and good looking enough to have a pack of scandal following him. The idea of him strumming away beneath the balcony of his intended bride's townhouse, desperately pleading true love is ridiculous. This Lady Iset, whoever she is, must be putting him in his place for his terrible reputation! She must be making him earn her love through the chase. And he *is* chasing her, like a hound, too, but he is never quite fast enough. Nakhtmin quotes some of his verses, which are simply awful, and it makes the other officers crack jokes and plead for mercy. Mutnojme and Horemhab exchange a long, sweet stare, and anyone who notices pretends not to.

This is a happy crowd. No one talks of politics. No one reads each other's faces looking for secrets. Although I had never wanted to rule this fierce nation, Tutankhamun has made me a happy home, and for the first time in many months, I am able to completely relax at his side. A cool wind blows over our barge, and I close my eyes and feel it kiss my face. Tutankhamun's hand slides down my arm and finds my hand, and we lace our fingers together.

Chapter Eight

Summer Year Two

I think I've never been so happy in all my life. It is a different sort of happy, of course: there are pieces of me that are gone forever, and that can't change. But this summer has been a sweet one. Tutankhamun seems to want nothing as much as to see me smiling, and we sail every afternoon, gliding along the river with the sprawling, stately Saqqara necropolis glowing warmly under the sinking sun. He tells me how well things are going, how the great temples of the land are up and running, and covered with scaffolding and workmen. His second harvest was a great improvement, for the engineers he dispatched out of Amarna before we ever came to Memphis. It is a pleasure to see him learning the ins and outs of running this great land, the largest and most bountiful estate in the world. His military training adds to his confidence. His rigorous schedule of religious duties makes him humble, a thing I never thought kingly until I saw his dark face bowed to something greater than himself, in the quiet sanctuary of our palace chapel. I begin to think he can do this, that he can survive the mighty burden of his crown.

In the daytime, I have Mutnojme, and we sit in the gardens of Memphis and talk like sisters. She tells me about her life away from court, how she tended her orchards and hosted parties for the young ladies who lived nearby. She says she was utterly terrified by her sister and all the people who served her, but that going to Amarna was like a great festival in the early days, when it was a tent city under construction, and my parents even gave her two acrobatic dwarves from Punt as a gift. And then, she says that she was supposed to marry the seer Meri-Re.

"Why didn't you?" I ask, setting aside a large box of raw lapis lazuli stones. Tutankhamun is adamant that I look the part of his Great Royal Wife, and that I have all new jewels to replace the old ones I hate to touch.

"I was too young. That's what my uncle said. He told Meri-Re, and your father, who wanted the match, that they would have to wait until I was thirteen. But then, they just stopped talking to me about it, and it never came to anything. My uncle's too greedy."

"Lord Ay?" I ask, laughing, paying no attention to the fact that Lord Ay cared more for Mutnojme, not even his daughter, than my father cared for me. There was nothing I was too young for, no matter how terrifying. I murmur, "He is rich enough. Does he thirst for more? Is he so avaricious?"

"He is! Why do you think I was rarely allowed to court?"

I shake my head, I don't know. There could be a thousand reasons.

She smiles behind the blue wine glass and says, "To drive up the mystery, and therefore the amount he'd be offered for my bride price. My sister was called the most beautiful woman in the world, like you will now be called. Many men came to seek my hand, Lord Meri-Re among them, but my dear uncle will only let me go to the highest bidder."

"That's awful! Poor Horemhab will spend all his newfound wealth to have you!"

She laughs a rich, musical laugh and blushes crimson, and I know that she is very much in love, maybe the way my sister was in love with Smenkhare so long ago. I drum my fingers on the table, and then I lay one hand over the other to stop myself. "I wish you all happiness with him," I say, and I mean it.

But it goes wrong, completely wrong. I slip into her chambers one day, with a new green fabric threaded with gold to show her, and Lady Teye is already there.

"You must put it out of your mind, Mutnojme. That's all there is to it. He is not for you."

"But why not? What is wrong with him? He is a mighty general, high in Pharaoh's favor, and he loves me!"

"*Loves* you?" Teye spits, her voice like a poisonous asp. "I hope he does not love you. I hope you have done nothing to make him love you!"

"Of course not, Auntie! But-"

"Then there is no harm done. He has asked, your uncle has denied him, and now you will forget it. Honestly! You are as good as a princess, Mutnojme!"

"He is the new Overseer of Pharaoh's Army! He is one of Pharaoh's closest companions!"

"And he was born on a dirt floor, like an animal! He may have favor now, but he is not one of us, and he will not last."

"One of *us*? What *us*? We don't have any royal blood, Auntie! Grandfather was a chariot officer, like the hundreds Horemhab commands!"

"He was a chariot officer who had a sister in a royal harem, and whose daughter caught the eye of a king and became Great Royal Wife! Enough with this foolishness! The general has been told that there is another match in mind for you, and indeed there is. Don't think that because you've inherited a bit of gold, you can forget your duty! You will marry to benefit your family, as I did, as no less a woman than your royal mistress, the Great Royal Wife did! And you will keep your thoughts, and your hands, off that soldier, or you'll find yourself disgraced and disinherited."

I duck into the darkness of Mutnojme's wardrobing room, holding my breath until the studded cedar door shuts softly behind Teye. And then I go to Mutnojme, surprising her as she washes tears from her face. She looks up from the alabaster bowl of lavender water and gasps, "How much did you hear?"

"Enough," I say, shaking my head in sympathy. "I am sorry."

"It doesn't make a bit of sense," she says, wiping her fingers under her eyes to fix her make-up. "Horemhab is powerful, he'll only become *more* powerful as Pharaoh grows and goes off to war. He's not beneath me, and my uncle's not above an alliance with him."

"Your uncle doesn't like a strong military," I murmur. "He never has. He doesn't trust it. Maybe he thinks Horemhab would grow too powerful with you, too influential. It isn't personal, I'm sure. Lord Ay does nothing without calculating the cost, today, tomorrow, and ten years down the road."

"But he's old! He thinks this is old King Amunhotep's reign. He doesn't understand your husband. It doesn't matter if Ay doesn't want a mighty army. King Tutankhamun wants a mighty army. When Ay is retired-and really, how much longer can he work?-when my uncle retires, this country will be a true empire once more, and when that happens I'll be Horemhab's wife. I don't know who my uncle plans to sell me off to, but I promise you, I will not do it. They'll have to bundle me up like a slave and drag me away, and we all know they wouldn't dare!"

Chapter Nine

Winter, Year Two

By the gods, I think Mutnojme's sneaking off to play the wife to Horemhab. She disappears for hours in the morning, while her lordly uncle sits in the audience chamber and the soldiers roam the city in freedom. When I do find her again, sitting in the gardens and singing a little love song, there's a dizzy, dreamy look in her eyes.

I cannot- I cannot imagine what she'd do it for. I cannot imagine that big, brutish beast in bed with my delicate, graceful aunt. I cannot believe that she goes to him again and again, but I know she does, because I can almost smell him on her. I cannot believe she loves it, loves his touch as much as she loves him. I cannot believe he, that rough, overmuscled, peasant born soldier, has more tenderness in his heart for Mutnojme than I ever inspired in my own-

I won't think it, I can't. I won't wear the vulture and cobra on my brow and look at my lady and feel less than her, because she is beloved and I was nothing more than a toy to be broken and discarded.

But this isn't the worst of it, not at all. Lady Teye threatened Mutnojme with disgrace, and the loss of her fortune, if she continued on with the general. And that woman... she is like a hound, sniffing sniffing sniffing away, suspicious and squint eyed, roused by the obvious fact that her niece, who should be pining, is instead soaring, dancing through the palace as if the earth had no hold on her. It is the height of foolishness, and I am determined to tell her so, before she destroys herself just to please a man with no connection to her or authority over her.

But Tutankhamun finds me first. He is growing tall now, twelve years old and shooting up like sedge grass. He is lean and well cut from his soldiery, with a dark honey smile, and already the young maidens at court are on him like bees swarming a fragrant flower. Still, thank the gods, he cares far more for his hawk and his bows and his chariots than for all the giggling females around him; but I know the day will come, just like the flood comes each year, just like the sun rises high each day. He can deny it all he wants, but Tutankhamun is only a breath away from manhood, and I dread the change more than anything else on earth.

"Take a ride with me," he says, leaning forward on his staff and smiling gallantly.

"A ride? Where to?"

"Just around the arena. You look vexed. You need a little sun, a little wind, I know it."

I can't help but smile. "I do," I say, and he takes my small hand and tucks it in his arm gallantly.

"I think you ought to learn to drive your own chariot. It's long overdue."

"Me, drive?" I pull away. "I couldn't."

"Oh, no? What if I teach you?"

Tutankhamun stands before me, but it's my mother's face that I see, screwed up in worry. *You'll never keep your balance, and if you fall you might limp like you did as a little girl. How will you hold two galloping hunters, and keep your balance?*

"Come," Tutankhamun says, hand out, his smile charming, his dark eyes eager for adventure and speed. "Let me teach you. I won't let you get hurt, I promise."

"You'd better not," I warn, taking his hand warily.

So we walk down to the arena, and Tutankhamun calls for

his steadiest team, and incredibly, he gets me driving the two sleek chestnuts around at a stately walk. Under Tutankhamun's instruction, I put the horses through pretty turns and circles, until I am confident that they'll go where I want them to. "It doesn't seem like much, when I think of you dashing through the desert!" I call, laughing at myself. Even so, the feeling of guiding two powerful horses with my own small hands is thrilling.

"Walk before running," Tutankhamun says, leaning back against the rail, smiling with the hot sun beating on his bronze face.

I toss my hair and cry lightly, "As if you would let me run!"

"I would not hold you back, if you were properly taught," he says. "You want to go faster?"

"Yes!" I cry, shocking myself.

Tutankhamun tells me to turn back to the track, and before I know it he's called out for his horses to trot.

"It's the same thing!" He yells to me over the pounding hooves. "Remember your weight, start your turns earlier!"

I laugh aloud, terrified and thrilled as the wind lifts my curls off my shoulders. The corners come much faster now, and it takes several laps before my turns are smooth and round, but I do it, and I think I do it well. I proudly rein the team to a halt before him.

"It really never gets any harder than that out in the city," Tutankhamun tells me, laying his hand on the chariot rail. "A house could collapse beside these two, they won't flinch."

"When can I make them canter?" I demand, reluctant to let go of the braided leather reins.

Tutankhamun laughs and says, "You didn't want to try, and now you're ready to run?"

"You're a good teacher."

"And you're a Tuthmosid, who wants to fly on the wind. Your mother had you bound up like a poppet on a string, but you can't get away from your blood. But let's practice trotting more. When you can make the chariot travel in a serpentine, and make it pretty, then I'll teach you to fly."

"Show me how you do it," I press, eager to learn more.

"Climb down," Tutankhamun says, and he springs into the cab. As I stand in the center, my pretty gilded sandals sinking into the sand, Tutankhamun wheels the chariot to the wall at a brisk trot. I don't hear or see his command, but suddenly both horses strike out into a canter with matching left forelegs. Once Tutankhamun gets halfway around, they burst forward into a measured gallop. He whips around the arena and turns in the corner, charging down the diagonal. I hike my tight sheath and jump back, laughing as Tutankhamun flies past me. Gradually, he breaks his horses down again; the beasts are so powerful, so well-conditioned, that they hardly pant at all. He draws them up beside me and looks down as if it were nothing at all to race the wind.

"What does it feel like?" I ask, imagining my small hands curbing and holding two galloping horses.

"Better than walking or trotting," he teases, stepping down.

"So… So why don't you show me? Be my driver, and let me feel what it is to have the wind in my face."

"I think you should learn a little more, before all that."

My cheeks flush, and I look down. "You think I can't do it."

"No, Ankhesenamun. I think it is dangerous. It doesn't look that way because I've done it since an age I had no business doing it at. I wouldn't want to see you on the ground with a mouth full of sand. It's happened to me too many times. I promised I wouldn't let you get hurt."

"I won't, I won't!" I cry. "I trust you. You can hold me, and I won't fall, I swear. And if I do fall… well, at least it will be doing something I wanted to do, something I thought I could never do!"

Tutankhamun presses his lips together, sizing me up with those sharp black eyes. Finally, he nods and says, "All right, just once. *Once.*"

I step back into the chariot, my fingers gingerly touching the braided leather reins. I realize that Tutankhamun usually has gauntlets and gloves on when he means to seriously drive. At a gallop, or even a canter, the braided leather reins could tear my soft hands apart. Tutankhamun climbs up behind me and reaches through my arms, taking the reins in his bare fingers. His voice is warm in my ear. "Ready?"

With a tight grip on the rail before me, I say, "Let's go."

I thought I was steady, but when the horses surge forward I fall back against Tutankhamun's chest, terrified and completely disoriented. I cry his name in panic, but he only pushes them on, snapping the reins and calling another command. And then he says over my shoulder, "I've got you, don't worry. I'll never let you fall."

My heart pounds, I shriek against the wind, but I can't deny the pleasure of it. Tutankhamun gives a scream of joy, a hunter's cry of delight. We race around the track; the painted walls of the roofless arena flash by in a blur. I have no balance, but Tutankhamun is like a wall behind me, holding me steady as he shifts his weight through the corners.

And then, incredibly, I catch on, as if it were truly in my blood. My hips shift through the turns just like his. My fear flies off on the wind, and I forget that we're in the confines of the arena, imagining easily that we were racing through the open desert. And then, unbelievably, Tutankhamun murmurs, "Drive," and his fingers slide back to mine. I take the furious power of his two chargers in my hands. He makes a subtle motion with his fingers, curbing the horses without even breaking the smooth line of his wrist, arm and hand. Their beautiful necks pull into a high, proud arch, and suddenly their mouths feel light as feathers in my fingers.

I regret it when we slow down. I turn my head back to him. "We *were* flying!"

"Flying is fifteen chariots running down a pack of antelope," he says breezily. "But you did beautifully! You are a huntress born, I am sure."

I'm giddy with delight as we come to a stop. My blood

rushes, and I feel almost drunk from the speed, from the excitement pumping in my veins. Our laughter echoes off the high walls surrounding the stable, right up to the brilliant turquoise sky. I've never gone anywhere so fast in my life. "I want to do it again," I say, wishing we didn't have to let the horses rest.

"I know all about it," Tutankhamun tells me. "I feel free when I run against the wind. There is no court, and no care, just a rush of speed and the pounding of hooves."

I look up at him, at the warmth in his face, and for the first time in our lives I can feel his arms around me, not the grip of a child but the arms of my husband. His hands, still on the reins, quiver over mine. When he looks down at me, his eyes seem to flush with heat and darkness. I can sense his blossoming desire, as sure as anything in the world, and it makes me utterly sick and breathless with fear. I stiffen, and pray not to faint.

Tutankhamun jumps down and calls to the stable boy to take the horses. When I find the courage to turn, he's smiling at me, hand in the air to help me down. It's like nothing happened at all; could it all have been my imagination? My cheeks burn, scalded by more than the wind.

Tutankhamun's groom runs up with his voluminous white robe and gilded ebony staff. He swings his robe over his bare shoulders. He takes his staff in one hand, and the other, he holds out to me, a beautiful smile on his face. "Back to duty," Tutankhamun says cheerfully, lacing his fingers with mine just like the sweet boy I love always does.

When we return to the palace, Horemhab and Ay immediately tear Tutankhamun away from me. Mutnojme rushes to my side and declares, "The Libyans are attacking our western border. The Medjai are completely overrun. The mayors of the oases and western districts have sent messengers beseeching Pharaoh for help. Horemhab says something must be done. We shall not suffer foreigners depriving Egyptians of their property!"

I look sharply at my aunt. "Horemhab says?" This dangerous

nonsense is all over the palace, like a disease! Why should she throw herself at him, risking everything? Why should he allow it, seek it? And why, *why* should Tutankhamun fall face-first into the very same madness? I will lose him, I know it. I won't be able to look at him, I won't want to ride with him or sail or-

Mutnojme grabs my hands as if I was a girlfriend, not the Great Royal Wife at all, and she pulls me into the garden. "I've been with him," she whispers nervously. The silver beads in her short braids jingle as she turns her head about, looking for spies.

"I know," I tell her, squeezing her hands back. "I know, and your lady aunt will find out soon, if you don't stop it!"

"Oh, but I can't!" she cries softly, a blissful look on her face. "I love him, and I wouldn't take it back, not for anything. Not even if old Ay found out!"

I am stunned by her passion. She has the same hard brightness in her eyes that Tutankhamun wears returning from a desert hunt. I wrap my arms around my body, for suddenly I'm cold as ice.

"Your Majesty...?" Mutnojme says suddenly, the joy in her eyes yielding to concern. "What is wrong?"

"Nothing..." I breathe. The brilliantly colored blossoms and dark, shiny leaves of the hibiscus trees blur together as tears cloud my eyes.

"Your Majesty, why do you cry?"

"Because you are a fool!" I say angrily. "Any woman would envy your freedom, yet you throw it away, and for *what*? To let some nasty man have his way with you, rutting like a beast of the field?"

Her lips part in astonishment. I think she will defend herself, but horribly she asks me, "You are happy with Pharaoh, aren't you? He's so sweet on you... Has something happened? Has he been careless with you?"

I clench my jaw, horrified that she would ask this. She should not ask me this.

"He is a very young man, Your Majesty. Young men are

often clumsy for want of experience. My cook's daughter married a boy Pharaoh's age, and came running home to her mother in tears the next morning. But within a few days, they were singing love songs and picking baby names. Don't worry, little niece; he adores you. You'll work things out together."

"Tutankhamun's done nothing to me!" Really, this is too much! Mutnojme knows just what I am remembering, I can tell. Her eyes are full of pity, which is embarrassing enough. I am not to be pitied. She reaches out in a tender gesture and smoothes my long curls away from my teary cheeks. I turn away from her, because I think she can see everything in my face. She can see my shame, my bruised thighs, my blood splashed like spilt wine on a white linen sheet. "Mutnojme…" I hiss, almost inaudibly, "Do not speak of it."

Just then, Captain Nakhtmin rushes through the hall, his long braids flying behind him. He spots us in the garden and whoops wildly, "Pharaoh has declared war! We're going to war! We're going to fight the Libyans!"

Chapter Ten

We need not call up conscriptions for the Libyans. The *seheny* officers, two hundred now, a troop of Nubian bowmen, and the Greek infantry that Tutankhamun hired are enough to rally the Medjai on the border. It is agony for Tutankhamun to see them go off without him. He is still too young, too green a fighter, and he strains like a curbed colt watching Horemhab's barges full of rowdy, eager soldiers, rowing north with the current. Only Pentju and I know how much it means to him, to prove himself as a warrior. When they are gone, Tutankhamun spends long hours furiously matching swords with the older officers left behind, and roaring down on targets with his chariot and bow.

But he spends almost all the rest of his time with me, and fortunately, he seems himself still. I never see that hot look in his eyes again, and we are rarely ever apart. We target shoot in the courtyard gardens and send Lady Ten Bows off to hunt, watching in awe as the golden hawk mounts high on the wind. He takes me by the hand and we stroll through the gardens. Tutankhamun plucks up flowers, his smile pure honey. I duck my head, shy and quivering as he weaves them into my thick black curls, but nothing worse happens than that. One day, I find him waiting for me as I return from my mid-day bath, biting his lips to hold back a secret. "I have a surprise for you," he says, clutching at my hand and bringing me along in my sheer bathrobe, my skin still wet and shiny with sweet oil.

"Where are we going?" I ask, anxious because he's taking me down into the palace proper, where all business is done. My hair hangs to my waist in soaking ringlets; I pull it over my shoulder and attempt to tidy it, and think that this really isn't proper at all. I don't even have a bit of paint on my eyes.

"The throne room."

I give a little gasp, but when the guards push open the heavy gilded doors, the room is dark and empty. The throne on the dais is covered with a sheet. Tutankhamun puts me before it, climbing up the dais and taking a corner of the sheet in his hand. He looks back to me, his black eyes sparkling. "Close your eyes."

So I do, and I feel the breeze on my face when he draws the cloth away. "All right," he murmurs, coming to my side. "Look."

I open my eyes, and draw my breath immediately. "You've put me on your new throne!" I turn to Tutankhamun, who grins, though he's still worrying his lower lip, nipping it with his bright white teeth. "You have done me a great honor, Tutankhamun. I thank you, truly."

"Yes, but... It's really more than that. Look again, tell me what you see."

I turn back to the gleaming golden throne. On it, Tutankhamun sits easily in throne made of gems and glass inlay, and I stand before him, my hand touching his shoulder tenderly. Of course it is not the best of likenesses, but we look like twins on it, and I smile. I note immediately that he's been deliberately provocative, that he uses both of his names, that Aten blesses us as well as the protective gods Wadjet and Nekhbet. "You wear the crown of Mandulis, a sun god..." I gasp again, and say, "And I wear the crown of Isis." I swallow, looking into his eyes. "But she frightens me. Her mysteries frighten me. Osiris was murdered; it was a terrible thing-"

"She came to you," Tutankhamun interrupts quietly. "And she is the protector of Pharaoh as well. She was the sister and wife of the first Pharaoh, she loved him with her whole soul, and that love made him into the god of the Underworld, of death and rebirth and fertility. They were one, and the spirit of their son Horus fills every living king. You and me-" he cuts himself off, saying instead, "I think it is fitting. There's something else, too. A sign, a sign just for us. For you. Something that seemed a burden, but really makes us a pair. Something no one else will notice, or even understand. Maybe you'll be mad about it, but..."

I lean closer to the magnificent throne, and I cannot help the little gurgle of shocked laughter that escapes my lips. Under my sheer silver gown, I wear only one sandal, on my right foot, the foot that was injured when I was born. Beneath his silver kilt, planted squarely on a foot rest, Tutankhamun's feet have only one sandal, on his left foot, the foot that mysteriously aches at unpredictable times and grieves him sorely. "Tutankhamun!" I cry in astonishment. What king would do such a thing? What king would take something so personal, and stamp it into eternity this way?

"It's just like... just like the gods and their goddesses. It is a sign, to tell us that we fit together, we make a whole. Have you never thought of it?"

"Yes," I say, remembering it well. "When I was a little girl, and my sisters teased me and I was alone-" I break off, and then admit, barely above a whisper, "Yes, yes, I thought it. I think it still."

His lips part to speak, but then the door opens, and a royal scribe begs forgiveness. "Your Majesty, there is news from General Horemhab, and Lord Ay has summoned the council."

Tutankhamun had been holding his breath, and his exhale is hard. His smile is beautiful, and his fingers touch my wet curls softly. "You're my best friend," he says. "Forever. That is what I honor, with my new throne. All the rest... it's nothing to that."

I look to the throne again, because my eyes are full of tears. I don't want to love Tutankhamun as much as I do. When I think of the way he held me on his chariot... No, I really don't want to love him, but I don't think I can help it. Why can't things-and people-ever stay as they are?

Tutankhamun extends his hand. "Will you come with me?"

"Of course," I say, letting him take my hand. I cannot help but come when he calls. How many more days like this can we possibly have?

The news is incredible. Tutankhamun's first campaign was a complete victory, and General Horemhab is marching his soldiers back into Egypt with a thousand captives and enough plunder to please the gods. Tutankhamun closes his eyes and tilts his pretty face up to the sun, whispering soft words of thanks and praise. And then he goes off to make ablutions before he enters his temple, his immaculate robe swirling behind him.

Chapter Eleven

On the day of Horemhab's return, Tutankhamun and I sit in a shaded pavilion in our finest jewels, crowned as a god and a goddess. We are high above the High Priest of Ptah, who swirls his incense into the sky, and the viziers who stand clumped together just above the road. Horemhab parades scores and scores of captured Libyan raiders down the Royal Road, men chained together at the neck. Tutankhamun looks over them jealously. He spins the tall gold and ebony staff on its end, staring after the tall, proud chariot officers in their polished bronze and leather cuirasses. Tutankhamun's eyes brim with frustration, he frets like a mewed hawk that's dying to fly. He longs to share this victory with them, even as he is the king who made it possible. Tutankhamun stares on as Horemhab is showered with blossoms and praise, his body rigid under his heavy crown.

Later, while he stands impatiently before me so I can relieve him of his oppressive costume, he laments, "I should have gone with them! I can shoot as well as any man. Better!"

I smile softy and reach around his neck to unclasp his heavy collar. "You are Pharaoh, Tutankhamun. You ordered the battle, you financed it. It is as much your victory as Horemhab's."

Tutankhamun is unconvinced. "Only I missed all the action. And my people watch another man lead *my* soldiers to victory!

243

It will never happen again, I swear it. If the Hittites themselves attack tomorrow, I will fight them myself!"

I dip a soft cloth in water, and I gently wipe the black kohl from his eyes. "Tutankhamun," I whisper, "Your people have not been so happy in ten years, maybe more. You have given them their souls back, and now you give them their pride. You're going to raise the army you always wanted, and in time you shall command it. But today, for just this day, you must simply enjoy being a successful and adored young king."

Tutankhamun looks down at me. Slowly, his frustration burns away, and a smile begins in his eyes. And then, before I can think, before I understand it, he leans down and kisses me.

An astonished gasp escapes me as our lips touch, as I breathe his warm, sweet breath. Against my volition, my head instinctively tilts back to welcome him, and Tutankhamun tightens his arms around me, as if it were all some dance with the steps written into us too long ago to remember.

My eyes flicker open, and I see his great big bed behind us. All the warmth of Tutankhamun shatters around me, and in its broken mess, ugly, painful, choking fear rushes through me. I pull back only to have him follow, pressing on urgently, the way they all do. I scream in horror, "What are you doing? Stop! Stop it now!"

He stands bewildered, stunned as if I had slapped his face. *"Why?"*

Tutankhamun shakes his head and reaches out for me, and I stumble back, terrorized, dizzy, unable to breathe. "I love you," he says, utterly confused, utterly hungry for more. "I want to love you! I think of you all the time! Don't you think of me?"

"How *could* I?" I shriek. "You swore, you *swore* you would never do this!"

His lips fall open, like I've kicked him in his guts. "My lady," he says quietly, bowing stiffly. Tutankhamun retreats in silence, slipping from his chambers like a ghost.

"It isn't his fault," Tia tells me later, brushing my hair gently. I rarely have need of my old nurse anymore, but I knew no one else could understand but her. She explains, "His Majesty is a very young man, you know. And he is a lonely young man, who has had a difficult life already. You were his only friend and now you are his beautiful wife, and he adores you. It is natural, as he reaches manhood, that he would have strong feelings for you, and want to act on them."

"Tia, he promised," I cry, thinking back to Grandmother's house. He *did* promise he would never do this, I am sure of it. "He is a liar; he's just like all the rest!"

"Oh, my little lady..." she says sadly. I watch her shaking her head in my polished silver mirror. "He loves you very much, my lady. Perhaps he was impulsive, even clumsy, but he means you no harm. Can you not see it?"

"What does it matter what I see?" I demand. "I can see a good thing today, and tomorrow it can be rotten, just like that. You know it!"

Henutawy, a fifteen year old chamber maid with glass beads in her hair, presents herself in the doorway. "His Majesty is here, my lady."

"Tia!" I cry, whirling in my chair. "What can he want?"

"Shall I stay?" Tia asks me, looking every bit the stout matron in her severe Nubian wig.

I nod my head, and then I shake it in despair. I am a twice married woman, not a virgin on her wedding night. And Tutankhamun knows that Tia is semi-retired, and I hardly ever call her to attend me. I cannot ask her to chaperone Pharaoh when he visits his wife's chambers, no matter what will happen. I've insulted him enough already. "Oh..." I hide my face in my small hands. "Go, Tia."

Moments later, Tutankhamun appears in my doorway wearing a pale, sick grimace. "Do you hate me now?"

He is wretched. My immediate urge is to rush to him with comforting arms, but I am frozen, as cold as a stone statue at night, as cold as Hittite ice. "No," I murmur sadly, gazing at the floor beneath his gold-sandaled feet. "I couldn't hate you." And I can't. If he would just stop now, if he would never do *that* again...

I see his deep sigh of relief. "I wouldn't... I wouldn't ever hurt you."

This I cannot answer.

Tutankhamun frowns and looks away. "Can we just pretend it didn't happen? Just... go down to our banquet, laugh and drink wine? It's supposed to be a victory celebration. I made a mistake, a stupid, stupid mistake."

My cheeks burn up to hear the handsome young Pharaoh of Egypt describe his kiss as a mistake. "Let's go to the banquet," I say, nodding. Yes, go to the banquet, forget, make it like it never happened.

Tutankhamun sighs heavily, switching his eyes to me only to nod his head, before he looks away again. We walk along together, and when we reach the loud banquet hall, I take his arm as custom, doing my part to repair this... this accident. That must be all it was. A little mistake, no true harm done. But for the first time in our lives, Tutankhamun stiffens uncomfortably when I touch him.

Under the hot Giza sun, Tutankhamun tosses his robe away and glares at the other youth, Huy Tasheru. Huy is a high-born boy who is lauded as the future star of the chariot corps. His father Huy the Elder will soon become the Viceroy of Nubia. But now, Tutankhamun and Huy are about to fight.

Egyptian soldiers are made first to fight with their hands, and Horemhab has told us that this can be deadly. In a brutal way of culling the weakest soldiers, many are often severely injured or killed outright, because the commanders will let the fight go on as far as it must. But here, under the watchful gazes of Horemhab, Rameses, and Nakhtmin, the young charioteer balks, unable to raise his head let alone fight.

"Come on!" Tutankhamun yells angrily, standing in the middle of the yard.

"Go, boy!" General Horemhab bellows. "You heard your king!"

Huy grimaces, and moves half-heartedly into the circle. It will do the young Pharaoh no good to toss Huy onto his back like he was a gaming table, helpless and not the least bit threatening. Tutankhamun wants a fair fight, which he plainly cannot get. So as the youth advances on him, Tutankhamun kicks sand into his eyes and calls out, "You advance on your enemy like you woke up wanting a beating! Come *get* it!"

The boy is blinded by stinging hot sand, and Tutankhamun dances closer, hissing taunts, goading Huy out of his fear of striking his king. But he doesn't hit the boy, even as his insults grow more injurious by the word. Finally he says the right thing, and the snapped Huy rushes him.

Huy's as strong as can be. They grapple like rampant lions while I drum my fingers on my thigh nervously.

Tutankhamun finally sweeps the boy off his feet, but Huy pulls him down in kind and they roll across the sand, beating each other like two peasants on the docks. I look to Horemhab, thinking that maybe he shouldn't allow this. I certainly can't stop it. Tutankhamun strikes a fierce blow to Huy's belly, stealing his breath. Tutankhamun jumps up, wiping his bleeding mouth with the back of his hand, his eyes flashing at the sight of his blood. As soon as Huy stands, Tutankhamun beckons him on again. Huy rushes, and Tutankhamun does what he had been practicing, what he had wanted to do: he grabs his furious attacker by the neck, and uses everything in him to put the astonished young man flat on his back. Huy stays down, catching his breath, eyes up at the sky.

Horemhab claps twice to signal the end, as Rameses murmurs, "He's ready."

But he's not ready. In fact, Tutankhamun's limping off the field, yet no one else can see it. Pharaoh takes a sip of water from a leather soldier's water bag. Huy comes up to bow, but Pharaoh tosses the sack at him. "Good fight," Tutankhamun says amicably, and then he walks to Nakhtmin. "I think I will make him my *kedjen,* my driver. You want to go with the sword next?"

Nakhtmin keeps his hands clasped behind his back, standing square. He grins, nods his head. "Sure." I swallow, and clench my hand a little tighter.

They have fought before; they spar, not try to kill each other. I've often thought that fighting with either the hooked scimitar or the great *khepesh* was like a dance. Tutankhamun and Nakhtmin circle each other like warring hawks, each guarding their own circle while making attacks on each other. Their elegant gestures and lithe, muscular bodies shine with sweat. They look like polished carvings of heroic warriors, breathed into life. And all I hear is the crashing ring of their swords. When I'm finally at peace under the spell of their art, Nakhtmin rings a hard blow against Tutankhamun's sword. Tutankhamun throws it off, but then stumbles, and his ankle twists down to the ground.

Nakhtmin thinks he has struck a particularly fierce blow, and he rushes on. I shriek, "Nakhtmin, stop! Stop!"

"Your Majesty!" Nakhtmin says, dropping his sword to come to Tutankhamun's aid.

I can't hear what Tutankhamun says back, but his teeth are bared, and his eyes closed. Now everyone snaps to life, and the officers and all the servants rush on him. I grimace, thinking he will hate that, and then I stand and cut through everyone.

Tutankhamun's up, leaning on his sword and Nakhtmin's arm. I slip the sword away and slide under his arm, murmuring, "Is it broken?"

"Something is," he tells me through his teeth. "Just get me out of here."

When we make it to the loggia of the new Giza rest house, I sit Tutankhamun on the nearest bench. I dismiss all the servants and order Nakhtmin, "Find the Royal Physician, Lord Pentju." And then I look at Tutankhamun, and stroke his cheek softly.

He turns his eyes up at me, breathing a little harder

now that no one is here to see it. But he doesn't speak. He is determined to be a warrior, as he was determined to learn other languages and read the secrets of the sky. But in this one thing, Tutankhamun has a weakness. And so he thinks he must work twice as hard as the next man, and I am not to tell him the truth, that he is beating his body to death to become the fiercest warrior in Egypt. He sighs heavily between his clenched teeth and looks down, refusing to even murmur from the pain.

Pentju comes bustling in with his physician's bag. He takes one look at the swollen foot-which is turning a deep plum color around Tutankhamun's ankle-and produces potent poppy syrup before anything. As Tutankhamun's eyes cloud from the medicine, the physician pushes and prods, drawing an agonized but silent sneer from his royal patient. Finally, Pentju pronounces his verdict. "You have two broken bones. Two broken long bones in your foot."

Tutankhamun murmurs, "So, like you predicted."

Pentju bows his head, nodding. "Your ankle is broken as well, but you know that." He looks at Pharaoh in the way only he dares to and says, "And you felt it coming, I'll bet."

Tutankhamun looks away. "What, was I supposed to quit? Cry for my nurse? Tell me," he says, again looking down on his physician, "When can I train again? We will go to Nubia next year, after Opet."

"Tutankhamun!" I cry, astonished.

He runs his hand over his close cropped black hair, a gesture of irritation, and then turns challenging eyes on both of us. "Pentju?" he demands.

"Months, Your Majesty," Pentju says quietly. "But I warn you-"

"No, you curse me. Keep it to yourself," Tutankhamun snaps, and the doctor bandages his patient in silence.

Chapter Twelve

Summer, Year Three

When we finally sail for the holy city of Thebes, it could not be more different than the day two years ago when our barge first cruised along the banks of Memphis. Then, the people watched us in stony silence, and I could very nearly hear hissing in the air. Now they loudly cheer us along, lining the harbor to watch our golden sails crack open with the wind. I sit under an ebony and cloth of gold canopy, staring on as hundreds of people jump down into the swollen river to wave and shout us blessings.

I look over at Tutankhamun, who smiles pleasantly at me, then turns his gaze down as he sets up a *senet* board. The sharp broken bones in his foot have softened to mend, and thankfully, Tutankhamun is in much less pain. He won't take his wit-dulling medicine anymore, though he cannot endure walking or even standing for long, and of course abandoning potent medicine like that had him sick to his stomach for days. Still, the warmth is back in his bronze face, and he smiles despite his suffering. As ever, even depending on a carved cane, he bears himself with grace, and his dress is immaculate. Today he wears a bright white kilt, and leaves his robe open to show his fine bronze body. A blue and gold *nemes* cloth is draped carefully under his royal diadem. A heavy gold chain and medallion, inlaid with blue glass so brilliant it seems to glow, hangs around his neck. And his cane: it is nothing ordinary. A bound Nubian prisoner, his back painfully arched-or broken, depending-is the hand grip. Horemhab encourages him in this, laughing and boasting about what a run they'll make on the rebellious country. It makes me sick, yet Tutankhamun doesn't want to hear it. So, we become a house of held tongues for another reason.

"Are you anxious to see Thebes?" I ask, searching for anything to say, anything to break the polite silence between us.

Tutankhamun nods, eyes still on the board. "Wait until you see it. It is twice the size of Memphis, at least, and the temples of Karnak have forests of obelisques, all capped in my electrum. Karnak will still have scaffolding-I would have broken the treasury to do the Holy City all at once-but Luxor is nearly finished. Now it must be painted."

"Was it all so broken?" I ask quietly, imagining the damage my father's foreign soldiers must have wrought in the sacred precincts.

Tutankhamun gives me a sideways look. "Demolished," he murmurs. "Even the temples of the ancestors that had names with *Amun* in them were hacked out. I'll probably never get everything restored, even if I dedicated a lifetime to finding all the damage."

"Are you sure we should go?" I ask, growing nervous.

Tutankhamun smiles gently. "Of course we should go. Who do you think is building it all back?"

That night, Mutnojme helps me prepare for sleep. She plaits my long hair tightly; her hands are better than the servant woman's and in the morning my hair will curl perfectly for it. She's almost as good as Tia, who, with Maia, was officially retired down in Memphis before we left.

Mutnojme wears a gorgeous gown, a sheer but bold blue

diaphanous sheath. Her red lips are freshly painted, and her long lashes are newly shadowed in black. I watch her in my silver hand mirror, knowing what she plans to do as if I could see into her very heart. Finally, she murmurs, "I will be careful."

"You sleep in Teye's cabin. How can you get away?"

"She will be dining with Paranefer's wife tonight," Mutnojme says with a breathy smile.

"There will be soldiers everywhere, you know."

"And they will look the other way for their general," Mutnojme says with a gambler's confidence.

I stand up, remembering a dark violet shawl that I have, without any flashy gold piping or jewels. I grab it, and toss it at my stubborn aunt. "At least cover your head," I tell her.

I say nothing more. I don't know if she meets the general in his cabin, or somewhere on land, towards the palm-groved farm village we harbor near. I try not to think of their passion as I bed down in my private, lonely chamber. Tutankhamun lies just beside me, in his state cabin, with only a thin wall of wood between us. I could go to him if I wanted. It is late, but he is likely still reading by the glowing light of his alabaster lamps.

But instead I pull my blankets high and stare at the mahogany tester above me, at the swaths of silver-threaded netting cascading down to the floor. And like I do on so many nights, I put my fingers to my lips and remember the disastrous kiss that's thrown this terrible wall between us. I can still feel the rise of panic-from my belly to my chest to my throat-that made me scream and push Tutankhamun away. Yet more than this, I remember-why?-the warmth of his mouth, the gentle heat of his sweet breath, the rich, fragrant scent of his skin. I remember the way my head tipped back for him, the way my lips parted on their own, the way he so shyly tightened his arms around my back and pulled me against his slim chest. No one has ever touched me like that before. And I've never, ever, responded that way: like a lotus blossom opening to the sun.

But it doesn't matter, any of that. When I close my eyes,

evil memories dance in the darkness of my thoughts until I put my pillow over my face and scream them away. I want my friend to come to me, I want to bury my head against his chest and feel him protecting me again. I want the comfort of him, who I shared whispers and secrets with since I was a child. But Tutankhamun doesn't touch me now, not really. He takes my arm sometimes, when he's in pain, when we're before our courtiers; but in not talking about it, that kiss has sprouted roots and raised a wall between us, like I knew it would.

The knock on my door is so soft I think it is the barge bumping against some driftwood. When it comes again, I sit up and bite my lips. Perhaps my auntie has returned early from her illicit meeting. Perhaps she cannot get back onto her barge safely, and thinks to sleep here with me. She will see my tears. I pull my robe on, and pour water into the bowl of rose petals on my little vanity. Only after I bathe my face do I open the door, and there is Tutankhamun, his back turned and the moonlight glowing around him.

He turns at once, his face half-hidden in darkness. "I can't sleep," he says. "I'm sorry if I woke you, I'll go-"

"No! No, please... Will you take a glass of wine with me? I can't sleep either."

His lips part, but he doesn't speak. I open the door wider, and he comes. I pull out a cushioned chair and pour two glasses of spiced wine, and then I sit across from him and ask, "What keeps the King of Egypt awake?"

His lowers his eyes, staring at his bandaged foot.

"Are you in pain?" I ask him softly.

He nods tightly, but that isn't the matter either. "Ankhesenamun... Pentju told me something when I started fighting."

I nod, waiting.

Tutankhamun grimaces and says, "He says I'm going to break myself; that the bones in my foot are getting thinner and they will break, likely at just the wrong time. He says I won't be able to fight or hunt, or anything. I'll be done, useless, bound to the palace like a servant woman. Maybe I won't even be able to run in my *Sed* Festival."

I take his hand, horrified by what this will mean for him. He has been a hunter for most of his young life, it's his passion, and besides, he is determined to be a warrior. Though he has set out to become the finest in both arts, he will lose both if the old man is right. All I can think to do is hold his hand and ask, "How long have you known?"

"Six months," Tutankhamun admits.

"Before you started planning your Nubian campaign," I notice, refusing to shake my head in wonder.

"I have to keep going!" he cries softly. "I have to keep fighting. I will do it, I will have victory in Nubia and inscribe it on the Wall of Proclamation, and I'll win victory in Asia, too."

"But *why*?" I demand, unable to hold it back a moment longer. "Why, when you know you can be hurt? You are everything, you are Pharaoh! And you are everything to me, as well. Why risk that?"

He lowers his eyes, but I can see his anger easily. "I have no choice."

"You could be... you could be badly hurt," I breathe, horrified.

Tutankhamun shakes his head. "I could have been smothered in my sleep by your mother's servants when I was a baby. We all know she wanted it done! I could have taken the plague; I could have been assassinated by countless courtiers at countless times, or made the focus of a plot by Pharaoh's enemies. But I wasn't! I was destined to become Pharaoh, to lead the people of Egypt. And I will lead from the front, in the traditional way of our ancestors. But how can I lead, if I am not a true warrior?"

"You believe you must do this," I whisper, blinking back tears. I think it's ridiculous, but then I have never cared for ruling a nation. I wanted a private life, but my family tore itself apart like a pack of hyenas, and we are all that's left.

"I must do it if it breaks me to pieces, and then I must keep doing it. You understand me. And it won't be so bad after my training is over, trust me. You *do* support me, don't you? I need you by my side."

"Of course I'm by your side, Tutankhamun," I murmur. For the first time in weeks, he laces his fingers through mine. Yet rather than being comforted by this, and comforting in return, I feel the hard beat of his pulse, and it… it uncoils something in me. I lose my breath, thinking of what's unsaid between us.

Tutankhamun drops my hand as if it burned him. "I have to sleep," he says abruptly. He stands, and then smiles down on me. "I'm sure I can now. Thank you."

I open my mouth to speak, but what can I say? What do I even want to say? A lame *goodnight* comes out, and he nods, and shuts the door behind him. I put my hands in my face, hiding my burning cheeks.

Chapter Thirteen

Thebes is everything Tutankhamun said it would be, and a thousand times more. My father did not do the city justice in his descriptions. For as far as the eyes can see, blinding white stone canyons rise into the sky, and giant obelisks burn bright as the sun. Clouds of incense drift over the city from the hundreds of temples packed onto both banks of the river. Statues of my ancestors, five or ten times the height of a man, dominate with their serene and protective countenances. Every sacred complex is connected by proud limestone concourses, which border lush ornamental gardens and groves of sacred trees. In the west, tall desert mountains pierce the sky, as eternal and lasting as the kings who sleep beneath them. Thousands of people, tens of thousands, cheer our arrival, and both the river and the canal to our new home, Malkata Palace, are littered with tossed flowers. Truly, it's bizarre to be so adored, when only a few short years ago we had to hide in the palace for fear of our own people.

Malkata Palace, as big as a city entire, is on the west bank, nearby the track into the mountains. Along the way, the riverbank is dotted with temples dedicated to the Pharaohs of yesterday. My grandfather and my great-grandfather's temples are beautiful, surrounded with tall columns and covered in bright paintings. A warm glow from within invites the visitor to come and lay offerings, and take a moment of solitude before the *akhu* of the dead king. Lush gardens and thick fruit orchards surround the temples. Tutankhamun points down the river to a cleared over patch of land and says, "One day soon, I will begin my own temple there."

"The one you'll record your Nubian victory on," I force myself to say.

Tutankhamun looks sideways at me, and finally, a rich smile spreads across his face. "Yes. My victory, may the gods will it."

We glide down the wide canal, and pull into a harbor at the corner of an enormous lake. It shines blue and clear in the sun, a massive pool of water on the edge of the desert. "Grandfather dug this out," Tutankhamun says, peering down through the clear blue water into the depths below. "Men once stood at the bottom of this lake. Can you imagine it?"

"The whole thing? It was desert?" I marvel at the monumental task, surely as timely and expensive as building any temple. "What inspired him?"

"The courtiers say it was for love."

"Love?" I ask softly. "For the gods? His people?"

"For his Great Royal Wife. For Grandmother." Tutankhamun says, gazing across the expanse of shimmering blue water.

"I miss her," I say quietly, as our barge bumps up against the quay. "Of everyone who died, perhaps I miss my grandmother most. Grandmother, and Meketaten."

"They are with us now," Tutankhamun says, taking my hand. "And we must live for them as well."

We have almost no time to settle in. Before our trunks are even unpacked, we must attend the great marriage between Amun and Mut, the festival of Opet.

On the first morning of the festival, Tutankhamun stands in Malkata's courtyard, glaring at his elaborate gold trimmed litter as if it were a pack of mad, tangled hyenas. "I don't like it," he complains softly. "I'd rather ride my horse. I'd rather take a chariot."

"You mustn't ride a horse or take a chariot with a broken foot, Tutankhamun," I say. "Besides, Teye says it is traditional for us to be carried in open litter, and Amun's shrine will be carried on thirteen poles, as you ordered. You shall have seven, I six. You see?"

He sighs. "Yes. I see."

We are borne into Karnak on a barge festooned in flowers, and I finally get a closer look at this awe-inspiring labyrinth of temples and pillared sun-courts. It is truly a breathtaking sight. For three years, Tutankhamun has poured his treasury into the restoration and polishing of this ancient city. And how beautiful it is! Karnak is a city of the gods, with each avenue of whispering myrrh trees and guardian sphinxes bringing the faithful to another divine mansion.

We parade down the Avenue. The enormous shrine of Amun on its thirteen poles is hoisted reverently into the air by twenty six priests. Tutankhamun and I, in separate litters, are also carried along. Musicians follow, and acrobats, and the whole city comes out to sing and dance in the streets, and everyone wears garlands of flowers. Even the wide, silty river is crushed with boatfuls of drunken noblemen. And when we reach the Temple of Luxor, even more priests, and temple singers, greet us.

I know one girl already, I met her at a feast just last night: Lady Amenia, who is little Seti's cousin and one of the thousands of new appointments Tutankhamun has made with Ay from the noble families of the land. She is beautiful girl, with big sloe eyes the color of dark wine and long, graceful legs. I am sure her fine looks were not unconsidered when she was named a Chantress of Amun; her dark, plummy coloring makes a very pretty picture in her pure white robes.

After much ceremony, Amun is left with his divine wife. Tutankhamun and I return to our barge and row across the river.

The palace is gorgeous, and my quarters are immaculate. My antechamber is a pillared gallery with a black stone floor, my bedroom full of beautiful blue tiles. My grandmother's giant mahogany bed stands in the center of the room, draped with gauzy curtains and deep Tyrian purple cloth. Gold gleams on the furniture, some old, some newly ordered by Tutankhamun's chamberlains. A wide balcony hooks around the white washed palace walls, giving a sweeping view of both the desert mountains and the lakeside gardens.

For days, Tutankhamun and I roam the halls, staring in awe at images of our young grandfather smiting his enemies. But his reign was mostly a peaceful and prosperous one: our empire was tightly controlled, and wealth poured in from the corners of the world. In that spirit, Malkata is dedicated to beauty, and the sacred mysteries of birth, life, and death. It was a fitting home for a Pharaoh and his wife who were blessed with love, children, and a long and peaceful reign.

"Look," my young lord murmurs one day, crouching by a small gold and ebony chair in one of the store rooms. "Look, Ankhesenamun! It is *her.*"

I kneel at his side. Sure enough, on a small chair, I see the name of Tutankhamun's mother in raised relief. "She must have been a very young girl when this chair was made for her." The girl in the image before me is far smaller than me, wearing flowers in her hair.

"When I was small," he says quietly, "I hated her for leaving me."

"Surely she didn't want to die, Tutankhamun."

"I know. But I was a baby, and I thought she left me. I was alone for a long time, before I ever knew what it meant to have someone. I'll never know what I lost, or what I should have had."

"You have me, Tutankhamun. I will never leave you."

Tutankhamun sighs. He smiles sadly at me, and squeezes my arm. But he says nothing, and his glittering black eyes are full of unshared secrets.

Chapter Fourteen

Spring, Year Three

I follow the thumping, thwacking noise to a long, gallery style garden. Tutankhamun stands with his back to me, between the twisting branches of fig trees, shooting one arrow upon another in rapid succession.

"I think you've killed it!" I call playfully, passing though the grove. I am grateful to see him fully healed, no matter how temporary his physician thinks it is.

Tutankhamun lowers his bow, but does not turn around.

"I waited for you this morning," I tell him, sure that we were to share our breakfast as usual.

He sighs and closes his eyes.

"Tutankhamun? What is it?"

His eyes do not open, but his lips do, and nothing at all comes out.

"You are frightening me! Say something!" Have we been attacked? Is there plague? I run through all the possibilities, discounting nothing.

"I must tell you something that I would rather not," he finally says, eyes cast down. "And I was going to come to breakfast, but I thought I would shoot first, to clear my thoughts and figure out the words I need. I have not found them yet."

"How long have you been out here?" I ask quietly, feeling his grief over anything else.

His black eyes cast sideways to me. "Since just after the sunrise prayer."

We stand in silence, while I nervously shift in the finest, softest, prettiest ostrich leather sandals I've ever had, made from a bird Tutankhamun himself shot. "Just say it, whatever it is," I breathe.

Tutankhamun bursts out, "There's a girl-a woman, I mean-and she's going to have a baby in the summer, after I'm gone. My baby."

I waver, I rock on my heels. I didn't hear him right, I must be sure. "A woman is having *your* baby?"

He looks down, nodding his head.

I have to turn away from this, but then I am reminded: I can't turn my back on him, on Pharaoh. Biting my lips, I make a deep bow and say, "Congratulations. Please... I have to go."

He flinches, and I walk away, everything in me sinking to the limestone path under my sandals.

And then, I can't move. I must look over my shoulder to see Tutankhamun. He squats down against the fig tree, his bow on the ground before him, elbows on knees, his face in his hands. I hurry back to him, and fall to my knees. I wrap my arms around his neck like I used to do. I am crying, but I whisper to him, "I'm glad for you. I really am."

"No," he murmurs softly, muffled by his arms, my hair.

"Yes, I promise, it's all right..." It must be. I must make it so. Things are changed, but-

He looks up and says, "Nothing's all right. I want my wife, and she doesn't want me."

My throat's never been so dry. My pulse flutters in my neck. I close my eyes and say, "I want you forever, but I can't do that one thing. I really can't. You remember, don't you?"

"Yes," he says, a little hiss of a word. He takes a calming breath and says, "But this is me, not him, and I want you for my own."

"I *am* yours!" I protest.

He looks at me carefully and proclaims, "No you're not. You either hate me, or you're afraid of me. But I am yours, so much that I die without you."

He is so tragic that for a moment, I wonder if it's all a game to him. Surely, if he can learn to make love with his body in his harem, he can learn to make it with his words. And then I see the ache in his eyes and I know it is real, and I collapse down beside him, my gown flaring out around my legs. I look to him, and hot tears flood my eyes. "Why do you make me speak of this? Why should I have to remember it? I was so happy with you!"

"As what, children? You are my *wife*, my only wife who carries a title. I adore you. That girl-she wasn't anything! I didn't even remember her face until I was told about the baby. It's only you, Ankhesenamun. You are my goddess. You are my life. And you should never, *ever* be afraid of me. I don't want you to remember that horrible time! I want you to forget, I want to wash it away like it never was. You think you were happy these last years? You cannot imagine how happy I could make you. And I would make you the mother of a king."

His eyes are too hot, and I look down, away. His words are too bold, but some part of me hears him. I am stunned with disbelief, but I feel as if he is winding a spell around me with his gentle voice and pretty black gaze. I catch my breath and demand, "And if I was not happy? What if I hate it? What if I scream and tell you to go away?"

"Then I kiss your hand and leave you in peace. But you won't hate it. You'll come back to me, I know it."

I cry in shock, "You are even conceited when you whisper to a woman!"

"No, *hapepy*," he murmurs. "I am in love with you, and I know how to love you. There is something sacred between us, can't you feel it?"

The name he calls me makes my lips part. It means *beloved*, and there is a memory to it, one I can't quite place. "I don't know what I'm feeling," I say. "I want to be your wife, I want to be like other women, so much, but you just don't understand-"

He cuts me off by putting his hand on my cheek. I catch my breath, and he kisses me. I close my eyes at the sweetness of it, at the way he overwhelms me with this slightest touch. And just when I think he will kiss me again, he pulls back, leaving me breathless, hanging.

"Do you love me, Ankhesenamun?"

"Yes," I admit, dizzy. "But I feel like I'm falling. I... it's too fast."

"Then I'll wait for you to come to me," Tutankhamun decides, leaning back against the tree.

Chapter Fifteen

Summer Year Four

In the darkness of pre-dawn, I watch as Tutankhamun's priests and grooms dress him in ceremonial armor. After he is anointed with oil, they wind his short kilt around him, and hook a jeweled sash-made by the priestesses of Sekhmet-around his waist. Next comes the short shirt of leopard skin, and another sacred ornament, a broad collar with four alternating rows of gold and lapis lazuli. Tutankhamun clasps his gold and lapis arm cuffs on, and then covers his wrists in the same way. Ipay ties a diadem around his forehead, letting the long red bands hang down his back. His eyes flash when Ipay presents him with his black-hilted sword. Finally, Tutankhamun sets the imperial blue *khepresh* crown on his head. He turns to me, opening his arms for my opinion of the ancient costume.

"Like a conqueror," I say, nodding my head. "Like an Egyptian Emperor."

"Don't cry," he tells me.

"You weren't supposed to see," I tell him. "I don't want you to leave." I step up and slide my arms around his waist, putting my head against the same spot on his chest and shoulder that I always did. "I've never been without you and I don't want you

265

to be in danger, and I can't imagine not being able to talk to you every day, and know you're all right. Please be careful!"

Tutankhamun murmurs, "I'm going to make my name. Don't be afraid for me; be afraid for Egypt's enemies." Tutankhamun pulls back and tucks my hand under his arm, and we go out into the fragrant early morning. The first birds are singing in the lush gardens, but the torches still shine brightly in the grey half-light.

In the holy district of Karnak, priests line the path to the barge, chanting and burning their incense. The omens are good, the bull slaughtered without even a moan of protest. Tutankhamun's fresh cedar flagship awaits him at the front of his proud new fleet, gold pennants snapping in the wind. All the people are out in their finest, with ready handfuls of flowers to throw beneath Tutankhamun's feet.

He stands beside me at Amun's magnificent courtyard alter, holding a piece of wood coal to fire. The coal catches, sparking and smoking, and he sets into the cup of the golden incense burner. He picks out reddish chunks of myrrh and sets them on the coal with deliberate care. The thick, slightly salty scent is instantly released in thick plumes of smoke, swirling up to greet Amun. Tutankhamun adds sweet frankincense, and sets the top on the burner. We make our offerings, he and I. I perform my part, anointing him, and then I wait behind as Tutankhamun and the High Priest enter the Holy of Holies, the inner chamber.

When he returns, he kneels before me and bows for my blessing. His crowned head is bowed, and his white cloak floats gracefully off his shoulders, billowing on the clouds of sweet incense. He has never looked so glorious in all his life. And there is no fear in him.

Tutankhamun emerges from the temple into blinding sunlight, to roars of applause, cheering, calls of blessing and wishes for victory from his noblemen. He walks along through their feverish pride and approval, his smart white cloak swirling in the breeze. His page holds his golden ceremonial chariot, with Aten's Fury and his red gelding match stomping and snorting in the sun. He turns to me, the sun pouring over his shoulders, and I flush with pride that he is mine. "I will miss you every single moment," I tell him, reaching to straighten the lovely golden broach fastening his cloak. But those weak words and slight touch aren't nearly enough to express what I feel. Tutankhamun's in love with me, and everything in me wants to love him back, to be this beautiful young king's Great Royal Wife in truth. "Tutankhamun," I say boldly, even as I bite my lips. I look up at him and put my hands on his shoulders, and then I stand up on my toes and kiss his soft lips.

At once the world-Karnak, the roaring cheers of the crowd, even the war-fade into the background. Tutankhamun looks down at me with a warm, half-lidded gaze; then he closes his eyes and kisses me again, and his arms are tight around my back, holding me off the ground. When he finally sets me down, he whispers my name as if it were a prayer.

"Win your war," I tell him, holding his dark, pretty face in my hands. "Win," I say, my breath trembling, "and then come back to your true wife."

A wide, surprised smile illuminates his handsome face. "How can you send me off this way?" he laughs, his dark eyes flashing. "Now I will think of nothing but you, nothing but coming back to you, never mind all the gold and glory in Nubia!"

I am struck speechless, all my bravery used up on that one promise that I cannot believe I've just made. I am speechless before thousands of our cheering subjects, and Tutankhamun knows it, and he knows why. He takes my hand from his cheek and kisses it in one elegant motion, the laughter gone from his eyes. "I will make you proud," he says, his voice low and sweet and certain. "And then I will return, and I will make you the happiest woman alive."

Then Tutankhamun backs away; I hold my loose gown up and out of the dust as I bow slightly before him. He grabs the golden chariot rail, leaps into the cab, and drives his horses off to the barge.

He's sent off with proud, wild drums; the sails catch the

north wind and push the barges upriver, south towards Nubia. The golden Lady Ten Bows flies in circles above the barges as they set off for Tutankhamun's first war.

A week later, I stretch across my soft cushions and loosen the ties on my robe. The good sun beats down on my skin, heating the heavy gold and lapis bangles on my wrists and ankles. Two female fan bearers stand to the side in their fine linen and beaded necklaces, elegantly sweeping the hot air into a sweet breeze.

I close my eyes and smile, a smile so light and teasing that it stirs my heart as it dances on my lips. As I lie in the hot sun, I think of Tutankhamun at the crest of a cliff. He sits tall on his red desert charger as far below, on the rushing water of the First Cataract, the barges are towed through by straining, shouting soldiers. I see him riding through the stark sandstone canyons, his black eyes wary, his hawk cruising on the wind above him. I can see his enemies as well, tall and ebony black, quite as famed for their shot as the young king who hunts them. There are five tribes rebelling against Pharaoh, thousands of loosely united men living off the gold they steal and haunting an enormous range from the river to the Kurkur Oasis routes. They are fierce and they are frightening, but I know Tutankhamun will defeat them.

"Your Majesty-"

"Mutnojme," I murmur happily. She has come to laugh and tease me some more, I'm sure. She watches me stutter over my words when I talk about Tutankhamun, the way my cheeks flush, and she declares that I am in love at last.

But when I open my eyes, I'm greeted only with Mutnojme's despair. I nod to my fan bearers, and they shuffle away with the bright gold and ostrich feather fans tilting over their shoulders. Then I put my hands out to her, my heavy blue and gold bracelets clinking together like chimes on my wrists. "What's wrong?"

Mutnojme clutches my fingers and says in the tiniest whisper of a voice, "I'm with child."

I don't even gasp. It is far too dangerous, with all the women attending on me. I stand up and we walk to the edge of my balcony, facing the hazy cliffs of the Valley. I shake my head in dismay, but I hold her hands too, and I don't even think of telling her that I knew it was a bad risk all along.

"I'm not a complete fool," Mutnojme says, "I took care. But then I ran out of the medicine, and I couldn't get away... I think Teye knows I've been to see my wise woman, and I thought I'd wait until she came to court on her own..."

"You have to marry him now! When he returns from war, you'll just have to be his wife. You should write him immediately, so that he knows."

To my surprise, she shakes her head, snapping her favorite amber earrings. "I can't! My uncle would think we've forced his hand! It would be a disaster, for me, for Horemhab! I would lose my name and my title, and bring shame to my family, and because it is a family matter Pharaoh would not intervene. But what's worse, my love could lose everything he's worked his life for. He could not bear it, the loss of this life. He never wants to be poor and hungry-or nameless-again."

"No," I say, "Mutnojme, no, Tutankhamun would *never* dismiss Horemhab. Not because he fell in love!" I lower my eyes privately and murmur, "Not when we are in love, too."

"Ankhesenamun, Your Majesty... He is a king, and he will think that Horemhab insulted his Grand Vizier, and plotted to marry a woman related by blood to Pharaoh's wife without her family's permission, and worse, without royal permission. He will be irritated at the insult to my uncle. The discord's thick enough between those two; Horemhab knows Ay doesn't think he's good enough to marry me. Horemhab already thinks Ay doesn't value his friendship, or respect his station. Who knows what will happen now?" She makes a little moan of horror and cries, "What have I done?"

"But Mutnojme," I ask, "If you won't marry him, what will become of you? If you don't let him claim the child, what will happen to your reputation? You will suffer for this! You could find yourself unmarried forever!"

She bows her head. For a long while, Lady Mutnojme is silent. And then she says, "Come to the temple with me, Your Majesty. Come to the Temple of Mut, please, and lay my offering before the goddess Mut, in the Holy of Holies while I speak with the priestesses."

I recline in a curtained litter as soon as I leave the security of my barge. The gauzy fabric provides just enough of a veil between the bustling world of Karnak and me. Bare-shaven priests in pure white robes traverse the wide road with scrolls tucked under their arms, loin clothed gardeners tend the opulent gardens that bloom all through Karnak, in tight colorful corners and wide fields of blossoms. A steady flow of traffic, noble pilgrims and temple staff, moves up and down the processional way. We approach the Temple of Mut in the steady gaze of ram-headed sphinxes, and I wonder quickly, foolishly, if the wife of Amun bears me any ill will for my father's crimes, even as we pass under the very pylon that my husband gilded from his own treasury.

A haunting song drifts across the air. Far within the dark confines of the temple, they are singing for the goddess Mut. The priestesses have scrubbed and swept the forecourt to an immaculate state; even now, with visitors, they tend the row of myrrh trees brought in pots from Punt one hundred years ago, trimming the thorny branches and collecting the resins. Lioness-faced statues line the walls like fierce guardians. Gold and silver detailing along the walls and even the floors flash bright in the sun.

"Did you see this when you were a child?" I ask Mutnojme.

"Oh, yes. When I was a little girl, I came with the Great Royal Wife Tiy, your grandmother. It looks much the same now. His Majesty has done an impressive amount of work, and I can see he's used your face for the goddess. But who else would he use, I suppose?"

I flush, thinking of the Opet festival, when Amun and Mut are carried to Luxor Temple, known as *Ipet-Resyt*, the Southern Harem. The harem of Amun, of course, but then, Tutankhamun has shown himself as Amun as well. And even though I know I'm falling right into his arms, again I tighten like a bowstring at the thought of it. "I am not qualified," I say softly.

"You will be, when you choose it," she returns smartly.

I swallow at her dry truth, wishing fervently that I didn't have to let Tutankhamun have all of me to be his wife. I want to hold him, to care for him and kiss his pretty lips, but I don't think I can get into bed with him or anyone without screaming.

Mutnojme distracts me, talking about the goddess Mut. "I was born and named to be her priestess. My father Aanen wanted it so, and so did his sister, your grandmother. They had their plans for us from the moment Mother was pregnant: My sister was to be a king's wife, and I would be a priestess of Mut, perhaps the High Priestess here at Karnak."

"But it didn't happen that way," I murmur. My father ruined that as well.

"It was dreadful," Mutnojme says, a far-off look in her eyes. "Lord Ay came in one day and took my *naos* apart with his own cold hands: my shrine, my statue and all the flowers and perfumes I had given to the goddess. She was like my mother-she *was* my mother, because I had never really known my own. My aunt held me as I sobbed, and she told me they would let me have it but it was no longer safe."

It *was* terrible, I know this now. I always thought of *the heretics*, without realizing that they were all the people of Egypt, my people. Only Father believed in Aten alone, as if he had been born to become Amun's enemy. So, when this temple was attacked, and Amun's mansion stripped bare, and all the prohibitions laid down so that men could not even write the plural form of the word for *god* without a treason charge, the people were horrified. But where noble girls like my aunt had wept, and then washed their faces and bent their backs to Aten and Father, the men down in the villages and in the fields had picked up staffs and sickles and torched tax barges in the night.

And Tutankhamun put an end to it. It's stunning how quickly we had peace once Tutankhamun began restoring the temples! It's truly as if… as if it never happened, as if there was nothing but a smooth transition between Grandfather's gilded, peaceful reign and Tutankhamun's. I think of his wide smile and his dancing black eyes, and the way he grabbed me when I kissed him, as if he would pull me inside himself.

"Are you all right?" Mutnojme asks.

I realize I'm touching my throat in fear. I breathe, freeing myself, and then I turn to face her. "I think I must learn the mysteries myself, Auntie. I think I must be a priestess of the goddess as well. I must have her guidance."

"You must be her vessel in this world," Mutnojme tells me solemnly.

I look out through the curtains as my eight slaves stop walking, and the wide litter comes to a gentle stop in the pillared forecourt. I take my offering of sweet oil and Mutnojme clutches her flowers to her chest before giving them to me. And then I twitch my curtains back and step into the sun, and wait for the High Priestess of Mut to greet me.

"Welcome to the Temple of Mut, Your Majesty," she says, and all the priestesses who've managed to quit their work and line up behind her bow into a deep obeisance. "I am Lady Anat, the High Priestess."

"We are pleased to visit this holy place," I say softly. "This is the Lady Mutnojme. We have come to seek the guidance of the Mother. My lady shall make her offerings in the public court, and I shall visit the goddess in her inner chamber."

Anat bows, and when she rises she murmurs, "Please, follow me."

Anat is a tall woman with long cinnamon curls. She has a peaceful face and a wise green gaze. She's nothing like Lady Amenia, a noble appointee reveling in her role of Chantress of Amun. As Anat guides me deep into the sanctuary, I see devotion and mystery in her every movement. I find myself entranced by her, noting the grace of her walk, the proud set of her slender shoulders.

After purification, I am let to the inner chamber, the Holy of Holies. As always, I feel a small twinge of discomfort to enter such darkness. Though there are beautifully worked golden lamp stands, bearing wide, flaming saucers, I am enclosed in stone. The floor and the walls are black and the air is cool and thick. It reminds me of a tomb, of a cave, of a dark and threating place where no sun can penetrate. My father made temples without roofs, so that Aten could always look in on us. Here, the flashing electrum statue of the goddess emerges from the darkness, barely revealed by the dancing fire.

Anat attends the Mother every day and night. Her linen is the finest quality; her metallic brow is damp with sweet oils. Flowers hang around her neck and her feet are covered in offerings of fruit and bread and more flowers. Leaving Anat behind, I step towards the goddess to perform my obeisance. After I have honored Her and given my offerings, I pray for Mutnojme with my whole heart. She has had so much of her life upended because of my parents and her guardian Ay, and she deserves some happiness now. I pray that this baby brings her into marriage with her beloved, that her family relents and allows it. I pray for her health and her life, and then I press my forehead to the cold granite floor again, yielding my prayers to the Great Mother.

And, I pray inside my heart, in secret and silence, *please allow me to know you better.*

I can say no more of it. She must know what's in my heart. As we leave Her presence, sweet, soothing music drifts though the halls. I can hear the laughter of children in it, and I wonder if there is a nursery nearby for the babies of the priestesses. We go on, Anat leading me through a narrow passage that ends up in daylight, before the wide crescent moon lake that hugs the temple on three sides.

"It's beautiful!" I cry, gazing at the wide expanse of

shimmering, mirage like water. Bordering the lake are more whispering groves of myrrh, as well as a narrow band of papyrus marsh.

"The *Isheru* has been here since the waters covered the earth, Majesty. The Isheru was allowed to remain, so that the disciples of the goddess might enjoy its purity. Your revered grandmother swam here many times, for the *Isheru* can grant both fertility and peace of heart."

I lower my eyes, knowing that I require both, as much as my grandmother ever did. More, even, for grandfather had brothers and many sons. Tutankhamun has neither. I turn to Anat and proclaim, "I wish to be initiated, Lady Anat. I have had some basic tutelage in the rituals of Egypt's goddesses, and of course I anoint my husband when required. But I did not grow up knowing of the Great Mother, and I fear... I fear I cannot perform my duties without her blessing." I look to the priestess in horror, barely breathing my confession. "I want to be a true wife to him, I love him, but I don't want to give myself to him-as a woman, I mean. I don't want to give myself to anyone again. I... I used to get so sick and scared that I would faint, in my... in my first marriage... And now I have told him that I will be his when he wins his war, and I don't know if I can."

Anat doesn't even blink. "Then it is a good time for you to begin, Your Majesty. The Great Mother has long helped women in turmoil. I can anoint you myself, right now, and give you materials for study. But you are not to reveal anything to a non-initiate. And when your study is through, you shall fast until the day of your initiation."

"And then I will swim in the *Isheru*," I add, to the point. I need to be anointed by the waters that gave Grandmother such peace, and such love for her husband and people.

"Yes, Your Majesty. Then you may partake in the blessings of the sacred waters."

When I return to the temple courtyard, Mutnojme waits,

her eyes dark with sorrow. For once, I have found a measure of tranquility, and my usually cheerful aunt is in turmoil.

"Thank you for laying my offerings before her, Your Majesty," she tells me quietly.

"Please call me by my name, Mutnojme. We are kin, after all. I want us to be as sisters."

After a week of study, I am impatient. My studies seem not so much mysterious knowledge but botany and physical sciences, as if these things held the secret to some universal principal of fertility. Still, I push on, completing my assignments as quickly and succinctly as I once did when I was a child. I think of how clever Tutankhamun is. He would have figured it all out already, I'm sure!

Henutawy interrupts me, and I quickly cover my sheet of papyrus. "What is it?" I demand, irritated that she has broken my concentration.

"Lady Mutnojme is here, Your Majesty," the Amarna girl says with a quick bow.

When my aunt enters, she is driven. She clutches my arm and whispers, "The harem woman is delivered of a hearty, greedy little girl, my lady Ankhesenamun. Thank the gods, only a girl! She is most disappointed."

"Only a girl," I repeat. I stare down at my desk, unable to show my aunt the tears in my eyes. A girl, a healthy girl. Now we both have daughters outside of our marriage. "The lady should not be disappointed," I say. "She should be thanking the Great Mother, and thanking Amun. Her daughter is alive, and she will be beautiful." I wonder if she has Tutankhamun's bowed lips, or his dark, flashing eyes. I wonder if she looks like my little girl.

Mutnojme gives me a curious face. "Do you want to see her? I could speak to Madam Taemwadjesy, or perhaps Lord Pay…"

I smile over the pain, hoping I'm not actually grimacing. "No, Mutnojme. It would be most awkward for the lady.

And... well, they have stories of lionesses that lose their cubs and snatch the cubs of the others in their pride. I don't trust myself."

Mutnojme's light brown eyes mist slightly, and I remember her own matter, which I would have always thought of if not for the quizzing Lady Anat plans to give me tomorrow. "Mutnojme," I murmur, "What about..."

"I was mistaken. It's my time now. I was only late."

"Very late," I say, until she gives me an agonized look, one that begs me to ask no more. And so I tell her, "I am glad you won't have any trouble with Lord Ay."

Mutnojme laughs once, a ghoulish sound. "As am I, my lady. As am I."

I can't help but wonder, has she miscarried Horemhab's child? Poor Mutnojme! It is a terrible thing to lose a baby, I know better than anyone. How could such a thing have happened, after she spoke with the priestesses? And then I remember my mother so long ago, telling Nani she would pay for a service in gold. I lower my eyes to my aunt's pain-which must be very great indeed-invite her to sit beside me, and call for wine.

Chapter Sixteen

Winter, Year Four

The Grand Vizier Ay processes through the great courtyard of Malkata, in a litter held by four slaves who strain under the dignified bulk of his ridiculously gilded litter. A train of servants bearing ostrich feather fans and standards of his rank follow behind him. Scribes and junior noblemen rush out of the way; they all but bow as they would to Pharaoh. Heavy gold collars loop about his neck, the collars of favor given by Pharaoh for distinguished service. He wears a shoulder skimming wig of neat, thin black locks, oiled to a shine. Over his bright white robes, a sash blinks with thread of gold.

I lean over the wall and gaze down. His litter is lowered somewhat ungraciously to the limestone pavers. Ay reaches out and cuffs one of his slaves about the ear for the poor work. He then straightens himself carefully, so that the pleating on his voluminous robe swirls about most impressively as he enters the palace. I can't help laughing softly; Lord Ay reminds me of a great peacock, strutting about his well feathered nest.

"We are ready, my lady," Henutawy says, ducking her head out onto the balcony.

"I'm coming," I say. After six months of study, Anat says I am ready to go to Luxor Temple. All this time, she has drilled me in the ordinary things any fourteen year old novice priestess knows-the stages of womanhood, the cycles of death and rebirth, healing arts, and ritual. Anat says it's time to move on, though many women can dedicate their lives to further understanding of any of these.

As we row across the busy river on the High Priestess's barge, she says, "The Great Mother is like the black silt from the first Emergence, and every emergence thereafter. All things come from her. She is love and life, and she is merciless. She comforts the child and ravages the weak. She keeps the balance of life, above all things. She is *Ma'at*, even when her means are chaotic. Nothing is more important to her than keeping the world in balance, so that life may flourish. It is the same way for you. You must help Pharaoh to hold this land in balance, so that Egypt may flourish. You must hold the course with him." She smiles and says, "Sun gods above all are most given to extremes. They are hot-blooded and stubborn, and it is your place to give him shelter, to keep him steady. A good Great Royal Wife has no ambition, but confidence in her position."

"My grandmother said something like that," I remember. "She said she served Grandfather with nothing but love in her heart."

"Your grandmother was a wise and powerful woman," Anat says. "The old priestesses still speak of her greatness."

But we do not go to Luxor to learn of Grandmother. It is my great-grandmother, Mutemwiya, who gazes down on me during this lesson. The story of my grandfather's conception and birth line the walls, starting with the idealized depiction of the god Amun possessing the body of Tuthmosis IV and breathing life into Mutemwiya. Thus my grandfather was created, and born, to please Amun and Egypt, and above all, the immortal Mutemwiya, mother of the king. The line continues, and stability is presumably ensured for another generation.

"It is not as simple as all that," I observe, growing quiet and sullen. "Touch my lips with an *ankh,* and in the next register a beautiful baby plays on my lap."

"No, the histories do not depict the pain," Anat tells me as we walk along in torchlight, "But neither do they tell of the love, or the pleasure in loving."

I glare at the serene woman, my cheeks flaming.

"You will understand more once you are initiated," Anat says, and I bow my head and follow her, desperate for that day to come.

As we return, the winter sky grows grey and cloudy. Malkata harbor is full of bright, merrily painted barges, and I notice the Lord Grand Vizier now greeting one of them. When we disembark I can see that he has retrieved a slim young man, perhaps no more than sixteen years old, from a barge flying strange flags. He wears a crisp linen tunic and a red and yellow glass collar on his neck, but there is something distinctly ugly about his face. It is too... too strange. The bones don't match right, the nose is oddly large. His eyes are small and darting, like a desert fox. The youth falls to his knees as I approach, with far less flair and far more humility than any young lord at court.

"Your Majesty," Ay says, his voice washed with kindness. "Please allow me to present Djede. His father served yours as a foreign ambassador."

"Which one?" I ask. I couldn't give a fig about young men at court. I can't even believe I care enough to ask, but it bursts from my mouth uninvited. I dislike this boy already.

"Ambassador Tutu, Your Majesty," Ay says. This Djede fellow remains silent, prostrated.

I narrow my eyes. I hardly remember the name, or what I heard in connection with it, other than that Ambassador Tutu was a foreigner who retired before the plague. Foreigners were even less than outsiders in my house, I would not have acknowledged him if I saw him. "He is from Canaan?"

"The retired ambassador is Phoenician, Your Majesty, but

an Egyptian in his heart. His son is half-Egyptian, and a close friend of my own son, Captain Nakhtmin."

"Half-Egyptian!" I declare in astonishment. What man would give his daughter to a foreign husband? My father must have honored this ambassador, and helped him seek his Egyptian bride. "Well, Djede, on behalf of my husband, I welcome you to Pharaoh's court. His Majesty is away at war, as is your friend Captain Nakhtmin. But I hope you enjoy your time here nonetheless."

The youth just ducks his head a little, speechless.

"Young Djede is a hunter, and quite a proficient driver. He longs to be a warrior now, and so I have brought my son's former companion to court."

"I see." Young noblemen have been flocking here since word went out that Pharaoh would be raising another force of ten thousand men on his return from Nubia. All it means to me is more war in his future, war that he will thirst to partake in for many reasons; but the young men of Egypt are in a frenzy to join Pharaoh's army. I look over the bowed form of Djede. "As I said, you are welcome, sir." The wind whips along the harbor, drowning my words. I nod my head, offering a polite smile to Ay. And then Mutnojme and I, and my entourage, go on to my palace

"Djede," Mutnojme murmurs, as we climb up the steps. "I thought never to see him again."

"You know him?"

"Oh yes. Everyone knows Djede at court, or his father, anyway."

"The foreigner? My father's ambassador, Ay said."

Mutnojme gives me a long look. "You do not know? No, I imagine you wouldn't, nor would your husband. Ambassador Tutu was sent north to Amurru by Pharaoh Akhenaten, to assess the strength and intentions of the Hittites. Apparently they were able to deceive him, or he was unthorough. Perhaps he lied outright. But your father lost much territory, and his wrath fell on the ambassador. He stripped him of his rank, and would have done worse but for my sister's mercy. In the end, your father allowed the ambassador to stay in Egypt and keep his fortune, but he was a pariah at court after that. His Egyptian wife left him-and little Djede-almost immediately."

"So why should Lord Ay bring him here? If he is an outcast? Won't he be miserable? Court is not a kind place; it was difficult for Tutankhamun and me to feel at ease in Memphis, and it was *our* city."

Mutnojme shrugs. The wind whips her hair as we pass under the grand pylon. "Pity, maybe? Nakhtmin and Djede were companions before the scandal, and remained such afterwards, so my uncle knows him well. My cousin is a dog for the ladies, but there is no truer friend than Nakhtmin. He would put his own interests aside in the name of brotherhood. The poor boy was left by his mother, and his father is a reclusive drunk, so I hear. Though he will inherit a little wealth, Djede likely wants to make his own way, and restore his family's honor. It seems the Grand Vizier will help him along."

Three days later, Mutnojme bursts into my room just as Henutawy is washing my face in buttermilk, my atonement for the fierce winds on the barge. "He is trying to arrange my marriage!" she shrieks.

"Go," I murmur softly to my body servant. I rinse my face in rose water before I turn to Mutnojme. "What are you talking about?"

She grabs my hands and shakes her head dramatically, snapping the bronze beads on her chin-length braided wig. "Teye told me my uncle wants me to marry Lord Maya, the treasurer! They've all but set the date for the wedding feast! Even the servants know of it, and I didn't!"

I gasp softly at the horror of an unwanted marriage. "Oh, Mutnojme ... I'll say something to Tutankhamun when he comes back. I won't let them make you marry anyone you don't want."

"No," she says, "No! I will put an end to this myself! I will write to Lord Maya, explaining to him that I am satisfied to be a single woman in your service."

"Can you? Would you?" I could not imagine defying the head of my family in such a way!

"Oh, I shall. If my uncle disowns me, at least it would be my own disgrace. And he would know why..."

She means Horemhab, of course. "You will always have a home here," I say, amazed at her defiance. "Even if you are a fearful scandal of a woman," I add, smiling wryly.

Mutnojme laughs, high with courage. "I do not deny it, Your Majesty. I have given enough to my uncle's ambition, and I shall give no more."

And incredibly, she gets out of the marriage. No one even mentions it again, though I can tell that Teye is angry with her. The woman's eyes practically smoke with anger when she looks at Mutnojme, but Ay and Teye don't disown my aunt, Nefertiti's sister. Perhaps they think it would look ill to the rest of our court. Incredibly, Mutnojme wins this unbelievable victory, and I can't help but be thrilled that a woman, especially one I love, has escaped marrying a man she doesn't want.

Chapter Seventeen

Summer Year Five

Six months race by, and then I get the letter I've been waiting for. Tutankhamun has won his war. He's captured all five chiefs, killed many enemies and taken captives for the estates and temples. He's collected a staggering amount of plunder from these men who unlawfully seized the trade routes. He's run his chariot at the enemy, slipping through their arrows and firing his own. He's studied the arts of a general, sitting at the top of a hill with Horemhab and throwing his divisions into play, routing the enemy and winning the fight. I clutch his letter to my heart and thank the gods. Tutankhamun has done as he wished, bringing himself glory, and glory for our country.

The news roars through the city, and the people break into celebration. It doesn't matter that he's not finished yet, that he must invest his new viceroy at Fort Faras and reorder the Medjai in the western desert, to make sure a thing like this doesn't happen again. That is boring administration. Pharaoh's defeated his enemies and brought victory to Egypt again, and that's all anyone cares about at court and in the loud, jubilant streets.

But at night I lie in my bed, staring into the fire and tracing my fingertips over my arms, and I wonder what it will be like to be Tutankhamun's true wife. It will take months for him to get here, but we are intrinsically entwined, and already I feel him coming closer. And when he returns, I will do my duty, I will give myself to my husband, and if the gods will it, we shall have children to continue our holy line.

I clutch my body tightly, unable to forget how I was hurt so long ago. But this will certainly be different. Even now, months and months later, when I think of Tutankhamun's kisses my heart flutters and my cheeks grow hot, and I wish for him to kiss me again. Mutnojme assures me, as tactfully as she can under the circumstances, that not all women like all men, and that if I enjoy Tutankhamun's kisses I will surely like the other things he wants to do. And Tutankhamun-seconded by Anat, and actually my grandmother as well-tells me that we are made of one breath, that we are a sacred pair, meant to be lovers from before we were even born.

I bite my lips in the darkness, if only to stop the relentless beat of my thoughts, and the pounding of my heart. Tutankhamun has turned for home, victorious and blooded in battle, and he shall come back my true husband. I can only hope that it goes well between us. If it goes badly, I might hate him. I might lose not only my husband but my best friend as well, and I couldn't bear that. But what would it mean for things to go well? I cannot even imagine it. I sigh heavily and stretch out in my bed, pushing my cheek against the cool pillow. I close my eyes, knowing that I will see Tutankhamun in my dreams, sure that he is dreaming of me as well as he sleeps under the stars, with the desert wind kissing his handsome face.

Before the summer is over, my period of fasting ends. I stand on the banks of Malkata Lake at nightfall, squinting my eyes to be sure what I see is right. There are old men-old priests-rowing the barge through the darkness. Anat stands in torchlight at the prow. As I board, I do not ask her about the custom not to cross the river at night. The Nile shifts, especially at high water. The emergence is not yet complete, and the silt gathers in banks that can run a barge aground. But apparently, these ancient men can do it; they can cross the river better than Pharaoh's oarsmen.

We enter Karnak in utter darkness. The markets that spring up around the outer gates are all gone, leaving only a moonless plane. The trees sigh in the night. The torches flap loudly in the wind, casting wildly dancing shadows on the ram-headed sphinxes lining the path. Otherwise there is silence.

In the forecourt of the Temple of Mut, the priestesses stand in the shadows. One–a young woman with eyes slanted enough to be feline–offers me a cup. I look quickly to Anat.

"Right now, you are not the Great Royal Wife. You are an initiate. You must do as you are bid, without fear. Many have lost their wits trying to do otherwise."

I breathe hard already. I am not used to hearing such words from an ordinary woman, and I am never without fear. But something in the levelness of her gaze reminds me of everything I am here for. She would not poison me, or lead me astray.

I take the cup, and it is harsh and metallic tasting. I close my eyes and drink it down. I pass it off to the priestess with something less than humility, and instantly chastise myself. But it is to be expected.

Anyway, we walk on. In the second court, I am purified, and dressed in the loose yellow robe of an initiate. As I pull my hair out of the gown, I look over, to the lotus-blossom pillars. They sway in the firelight, and I look closer. No, they are still, and stone. The breeze blows over my cheeks, warm and sweet. How could I not have noticed before, how gentle it is, how my hair lifts softly off my shoulders?

"Come," Anat says warmly. She is kind to help me, I think.

No, it is the drug, making everything in the world seem a pleasure. Now we are in near darkness. The priestesses are left behind. It feels like we're walking into the very depths of a tomb. *Could it be?* I begin to feel frightened, because I know I'm not in control anymore. They've given me something hard, as I thought they would.

"They are waiting," Anat says. The path is black stone, and the torches have gotten smaller, or maybe I just fear that. Fear, she warned me against fear. I draw up what courage I can, and walk on. Still, I don't remember the entrance to the inner chamber being so far away.

"Anat-" I murmur, thinking I will ask her. I turn, and she is gone.

I stop, breathing hard. I am alone, and everything is dark. And suddenly, there's nowhere to go, the wall is against my hands. It's dark, and I'm alone in a tomb, and there is no sun and no air-

No, this is ridiculous. I'm gone off whatever it is that cat-eyed rekhyt *girl gave me. The wall can't bend this way!*

But I turn, running my hands along nothing but stone. And it's getting tighter. Now it isn't a question, but a terror. The space is getting smaller, crushing the thin cold air, pushing my straight arms to bent elbows. I hear myself scream as I feel about madly for a way out. And all the while it's coming, and I can feel it heating my breath against my face.

"No!" I shout, angry at the blackness, the coldness pushing down on me. I shove my arms out sideways just in time to keep from being crushed, and suddenly there is nothing but empty air on my right side. I fall into it, gasping, and there is the calm, orderly temple hallway. Anat is standing there, and I wonder incredibly if I just turned the wrong way looking for her, and made a fool of myself. And then, as I look on her, I get the growing feeling of disquiet that it is not Anat. Her eyes glow in the darkness like a predator. She holds out a deep-dyed linen.

I pluck it from her hands, and then she is behind me, and she ties it over my eyes. I touch my fingers to my neck, to feel my banging pulse. I know she will be gone again, and so I go on to whatever trial awaits. That is all it will be, a test.

I extend my hand, fingers spread. I can feel the wide sleeves of the primitive, gauzy yellow robe hanging in the wind. The air is cool before me, the hallway is wide open. And at the end of this, the inner chamber, and the path to the lovely bank of the *Isheru*.

There is something murmuring in the distance. As I get closer, it sounds like air rushing by. I must have gotten near the door to the gardens; I feel the warm wind on my cheeks again. I can feel the long sleeve dancing. *Why is the wind so hard?*

It's hot, blazing hot. The wind has become a roar, and as I step up my cheeks flame from heat. I gasp as I realize the path is full of fire, and I rush back into the cold. *No, it is all a lie!* I think, stopping immediately. I am running from nonsense, tricks and illusions. Aren't I?

I wish I knew what they gave me.

Something's coming towards me. I can hear it, footsteps, tapping down the hallway. It is one of the priestesses, surely. But she is dragging something. At the sound of metal grating on stone, I back up. It reminds me of when Tutankhamun uses his special stone to sharpen his swords. I reach for the blindfold, but as clear as a sistrum's ring I can hear Anat's warning. Women have lost their sanity through cowardice and disobedience. They disrespect the Great Mother.

I lick my lips, and turn to the heat. To go back the way I came would be wrong. Would it even be deadly? I don't want to find out, and so I go on, thinking that there is nothing before me to fear. But when I return to the roaring of the flames, and the burning heat on my face and arms, I feel faint. I stick my hand forward, and there is a quick singe; flames leap up the sleeves of my gown, and I scream, and screaming, I push into the fire. The flames lick around me, burning hot, but they do not consume me. They twine about my arms and legs as lovingly as pet snakes, brushing against my bare skin. And then they rush away, and there is cool air, fragranced with a blend of incense I don't know. The blindfold is pulled away, and I blink my eyes in the starlight. I am in the orchard, but something is off about this place. A flush of cold light casts shadows through all the leaves and branches of the trees, and I look up in surprise to see a full moon.

And then I am not alone. I hear the musical laughter of women, and then three are before me.

I look over them. The first is a woman in a deep, tawny gown. She is adorned with a thick collar and earrings made from an undulating pattern of blue and black feathers. Her face is older, matronly, and her gaze is both ancient and deadly, and as welcoming as the very soil of the earth.

The next stands like a coquette, her hand on her hips as she appraises me. She wears nothing but a sheer, turquoise diaphanous sheath that hugs her flawless body, shining more like the stone than any dyed linen. She laughs again as I look her over, as if she knows something about me that I don't. And then I see, surprisingly, that she wears heavy *shebyu* collars around her neck, as if she were bathed in Pharaoh's pleasure and favor.

Then I look at the final of the three, and my heart goes cold. Her eyes are the same, deep blue, lapis blue, bottom of the river blue. "Isis," I breathe, knowing at once. Now she wears a blood red robe, a robe stained by the trials of a woman, a robe announcing her dangerous magic.

She nods her head to me graciously. "Sister," she murmurs softly. "Welcome."

Only then do I realize that there is another there. He is in the shadows behind them, but I can feel the heat of him. He is hidden, but I can still hear the faint roar of the fire, and I know it is his. He is a god, Re, Amun; Aten, all of them even, and he watches me with a warm, curious gaze. Somehow, though I can't see him, I know there is a cobra curled up and ready to spit on his burning black brow. Frightened, I look back to the first woman, with her vulture adornments and cat-like eyes. "Go on, child. Take what they offer you."

I look back to the second goddess, the one of the turquoise. She holds a chalice of fine alabaster in her hands, where there was nothing before. I drink it slowly, watching her beautiful face for some clue of what will come. And then she laughs at me, because as I drain the cup, I can't help smiling. "You like it, I think," she taunts, whispering things in my ear that would make me blush, if only I were myself. Under her spell I feel nothing but lightness, yet also the madness of a wild dance, a careless madness that caresses me in the moonlight. Everything is beautiful, everything is sweet. The god in the background is pleased, I can feel his eyes on me as I bow delicately before him, and place the chalice back in Hathor's hands. I know it is she, the goddess of desire and love and intoxication.

"And my sister's gift," she says, twirling me towards the third goddess, Isis of the riverbank.

I take another cup, and this one is made of polished rose-gold. I drink again, waiting, wondering what sweetness Isis will grant me. I look to her, but instead I think of Tutankhamun, and how he would love to know that I had met her again.

"You cannot speak of this, not to anyone," Isis reminds me. "He has had his own encounters; he has told you nothing of it as well."

"He is a priest," I reply, knowing this already. And then I say, "Nothing has happened from your wine. There is no madness."

Isis smiles again, that same bewitching smile. "Snakes are rarely poisoned by their own venom. They never even notice it."

Suddenly, everything in me grows heavy. I want nothing more than to lie down. I look to three goddesses, and they are gone. I look down, realizing that my dress isn't burnt at all, and He is gone as well. But I don't care anymore, about any of it. I want nothing more than to sit, I feel sick, I feel like I might fall to the ground, and so I curl up beneath a sycamore tree. It is safe here. I close my eyes, and fall asleep.

"Your Majesty," Anat murmurs as I wake in a strange, small bed. She knows I am disoriented, and so she says, "Dawn approaches. We must go to a ritual, and then you will be permitted to swim in the sacred lake. Please come now."

Her apprentice stands behind with a diorite bowl, filled

with refreshing mint-scented water. I dress in the red robe she hands me, and follow them both back into the temple.

The rituals are edifying, and shrouded in secrecy. After it is all done, and I stand watching the eastern sky pale over the sacred lake, I feel as if my feet have taken roots to this place. I gaze out over Karnak, the tall, domineering pylons and temples shrouded in incense as thick as morning mist, and I know that every brick of this place was raised by my own people. I hear the wind whispering through the myrrh that the female Pharaoh Hatshepsut brought back from Punt and planted for the goddess. I know that there is magic here, deep and ancient magic; it is in me as well, and in Tutankhamun. I must fear it no longer.

I slip from my robe and step tentatively into the water. It is perfect, neither too cold nor too warm, and clear. I dip back until my shoulders are covered, until my hip-skimming black curls crawl through the water like a grasping river plant. There is nothing but peace, the gentle music of the water rippling off my arms and through my fingers, and the creamy light of dawn.

Chapter Eighteen

Late Winter, Year Five

"Bring my new rose gown," I repeat, snapping my fingers, irritated that I've let my wardrobe mistress camp down on the road with her clerk husband. Her replacement finally finds the special gown finished weeks ago, a deep, flushed rose pink. I can see the shadowed outline of my body beneath my sheer gown, and I turn a critical eye on my long bronze legs. I measure the sweep of my hips, the cut of my small waist, and then I catch my maids laughing behind their hands. My hairdresser comes in humming a love song, as if she were preparing me for a true wedding.

Mutnojme enters as my long curls are swept up atop my head and pinned in gold. "Brilliant," she says with approval. And then she gazes at my eyes and says, "Don't faint."

"I'm trying not to," I gasp, almost bursting with nerves. But I hold my calm, saying, "You look lovely as well." She wears a pure white gown with a collar and dangling earrings of beaded amber. Her sweet almond perfume fills the air. She is eager to see Horemhab, more than eager, and I don't care. How can I ask her to deny such a love? She has sat with me every day for over a year and listened to me babble about Tutankhamun, how could I deny her the man she adores?

"The crowds are restless already," she says. "And my maid says the barges are already docked."

"It is time, then." I wave my servants away, I dismiss the mirror. We turn to go, and I grab my aunt by the flowing sleeve of her linen gown. "Mutnojme..." I flush as rose as my dress, and look down at my gold gilt sandals.

She kisses my forehead and says, "Go steal his heart."

Ay and Teye follow me, and then Mutnojme, to the wide stone window overlooking Thebes's central avenue. The shadowy sky is dissolving into a sparkling ivory dawn. Tightly pressed, anxious crowds cheer in excitement when we appear above them. Fathers lift their children onto their shoulders; boys climb atop stone walls and carts for a better view. In moments, the far call of drums signals that Pharaoh's army is coming. Mutnojme and I exchange a breathless smile, and then we hear the peel of silver trumpets.

The army is an approaching shadow at first, but soon I can pick out the form of Pharaoh in his chariot, leading lines of marching men. Pennants and standards float like birds over the different companies, and I can hear the victorious soldiers singing down the avenue.

"Look how tall he has gotten!" I cry in surprise. "He must be as tall as Rameses now!"

Tutankhamun has burned mahogany in the southern sun. The golden wings of Horus cross his chest and his dark smile flashes under his blue war crown. Thebes showers him with flowers and cheering, the army marches victorious behind him.

I hurry away from the window and down the stairs to the palace entrance. Tutankhamun rolls loudly into the courtyard with his top ranking soldiers, chariot wheels rattling, their plumed horses stomping the stone concourse. How changed he is! I break a little in my rush to him, noting the size of him, the new hardness in his dark face, as if he'd been sculpted by a chisel. And then I see his eyes, and I can't keep myself away. I meet Tutankhamun just as he steps down, his cloak floating on the air behind him. His steady gaze drinks me in, and then he murmurs in a lower, deeper voice, "I've done it, *hapepy*. As I told you I would."

I wrap my arms around his waist and hold him tight, breathing him in after being parted for so long. His warm skin is still scented with the sacred incense he burns daily, but there is new oil anointing him, of frankincense and spikenard and the spices of the desert, yet as damp and potent as the flood. I breathe him in, and then I murmur, "I am yours now. I am ready to be your wife."

He says nothing in response, but his arms tighten around me. And then he takes my arm and walks us past the officials gathering on the steps.

His groom awaits him in the largest chambers of the city palace. "I'll be right back," he tells me, taking the towel from his man and tossing it over his shoulder. He goes off to bathe, while the men follow him with the immaculate robes of a sun-god from the wardrobing room. I clutch my fingers together, my heart stampeding, and wait for him to return. I pace the room, touching my fingers to my lips, clasping them behind my back. I jump when I hear Tutankhamun's voice behind me.

"Are you ready to go to Karnak?"

I turn, nodding. We are alone, tense. I bite my lips and turn my eyes down, so that he can't see how I've lost my breath. He comes closer, cautiously. I'm as nervous as a little rabbit, ready to bolt at the first misstep. Tutankhamun is bolder. He touches my cheek with his hot fingertips, but I turn my face and put my lips to his thumb. He brushes it over my mouth slowly, curiously.

"Your Majesty, the ceremonial barge is readied," Ipay intrudes.

Tutankhamun closes his eyes and smiles. "Yes, Ipay. I am coming."

When the man backs out again, Tutankhamun lets his hand fall to mine. "Better not keep them waiting."

We travel by barge to Karnak, and then we're carried by litter down the processional way, through more crowds full of high born men and temple employees. Bright sunshades hover over wealthy priests and their bejeweled, well-coiffed wives. Children cling to their mothers' legs, peeping out to watch us pass with wide eyes. When we take our thrones on the shaded pavilion, it is to the rustling of linen as everyone nearby jostles each other to make their obeisance.

A trumpet blows, and the parade begins. Tutankhamun displays an enormous amount of plunder for his rapt, enthusiastic audience. There are hundreds of tusks of ivory, exotic woods and fragrant resins, great hauls of copper. He brings home caskets of gold and snarling cheetahs. Two enormous yet incredibly graceful giraffes dance skittishly down the Avenue of Sphinxes. I turn to him in amazement. "You have brought all of Africa home for us!"

Tutankhamun tilts his head to me and murmurs, "You have no idea. These people had been robbing the trade routes for ten years. You should see what they had gathered around my stolen fortress. They had a good run of it, and so have I."

He has captives sent down the road, hundreds of captives. More gruesomely, there is a tally of near six thousand hands, the right hand being traditionally cut off each enemy dead to count them for the records. All of this is dedicated to the Temple of Amun, which Lord Paranefer, standing on a pavilion to our right and a bit below us, acknowledges with a bow to Pharaoh. The five captured chiefs are displayed on carts, chained but proud even though their names will be scorched from any record after they are ritually executed. Their blood, however, will live on... maybe. I note at least one princess among the captives, and for political reasons, she will have been made Tutankhamun's wife. Their child, if there is one, will be raised at court before being sent off to rule the rebellious territory. I drum my fingers on his palm lightly at this, as she drives her odd, cow-pulled chariot down our avenue. Tutankhamun's response is to lift my hand to his mouth, breathing his warm whispered kiss on my fingers. When he touches my knuckles with soft, hot lips, my eyes go wide with shock as I recognize the deep and frightening pull of physical desire for the first time in my life. It is a current, a hot and powerful current that wants to sweep me off to some unknown place. I quickly look away, to the fluttering white curtains of our pavilion, billowing in a northerly breeze.

The captives all march down, and it is very grand, but I can feel nothing save Tutankhamun's warm hand over mine. And when it is all over, we walk along in the midst of thousands of Egyptians cheering and throwing flowers and palms, yet we are the only people in the world. We cannot speak in all this screaming attention, but my shoulder brushes his arm, and he puts his arm around my hips. I can feel his palm against me, warm and strong, with only the sheerest of rose colored linen between our skin.

At dinner he says, "I never want to be away from you again," but I know he lies a little. He tells me about his war with a potent mix of an emperor's power and a child's love of adventure. Tutankhamun will go to war again. He adores the military. He is confident around his soldiers, who speak frankly and laugh loud, which is the complete opposite of the sycophantic civilian court. And the warriors love Tutankhamun back, because he lets them fight and win plunder, because he brings Egypt victory and glory, because they want a king who will stand up to the Hittites. He has sharpened his claws in Nubia; soon they will want him-and indeed he will want-to turn to the north.

But tonight, he is in Egypt, and the lights shine bright around the golden plate and flowers on our table. I have arranged this feast for him. I purse my lips in satisfaction as Tutankhamun dines on his favorite foods and drinks his favorite wines. I have beautiful dancing girls to please his eyes, but I know he loves acrobats and sword and staff dancers as well, and all are present. I know he loves the drums, and so I have many drummers. I have glowing alabaster lamps to give warm, soft light, and the sweet smell of frankincense fills the air. "You did this yourself?" Tutankhamun asks, charmed, and I nod with a small smile, wishing I was the sort of woman who could turn a clever and pretty phrase. As it is, I bite my lips shyly, flushed with pleasure that I have made him happy.

Tutankhamun smiles at me, as if he knows what I am thinking. "I've brought you gifts," he says. "Rose gold by the talent, ivory, and baskets of Red Sea pearls. And things for our house, incense and silks from the east and... Oh, this too." Tutankhamun reaches into his robe and pulls out a blue stone the size of a man's fist, the deep, clear blue I imagine the mid sea to be. As I gasp in astonishment he says, "A sapphire, also from the east. It's so rare their kings kill anyone caught smuggling one out of their land. But I guess one man got it through."

I take the glowing blue gem in my hands, marveling at the brilliance. It seems a thing too beautiful for this world, a thing stirred together by the gods, for their pleasure only. "Tutankhamun, this is extraordinary. I can't even cut it into jewelry. I just want it in my room, to look at."

"I knew you had to have it," he says, and I'm struck again by the depth and hardness in his voice. Tutankhamun tells me, "It's the second most beautiful thing I've ever seen."

I pass the stone off to Mutnojme, who wraps it in a linen napkin. I return to Tutankhamun as the feast softens to an ending, the melodious notes of harpists taking over for the drummers. He leans into me and says, "Now come to my party."

The throne room in Malkata palace is taken over with cushions and low seats. Elite warriors like Rameses and Horemhab mix with officers commended for bravery, served by a flock of young women with easy smiles and jingling beads in their hair. Young wives, young widows, and women with less formal alliances mix with the soldiers. Nakhtmin has one arm around Iset's waist, the other flung over the back of his half-foreign friend, Djede. Musicians drum hard and fast, and the dancing girls spin like flower petals in the wind, their long braids whipping around their shining naked bodies. I remember Hathor's sweet wine, and then I understand why such dancers are usually under her patronage. I feel Tutankhamun's arm wind around me as Nakhtmin catches his attention. I can hear nothing over the drums, the wild trilling of the women as the spirits move them into ever more breathtaking routines. Oh, he is introducing Djede. I am glad when Tutankhamun murmurs something quick, and we move on.

Once we sit, in haphazardly stacked cushions before Tutankhamun's golden, one-pair-of-sandals throne, a little entourage settles in before us. Tutankhamun laughs softly, and doesn't show his irritation. He wants to be with me alone, and they won't let him. They wish to gamble and drink, and now Iset's brought out an ornately carved opium pipe. The fashion is to carve them into *djinni* faces. She presents it packed to Pharaoh. Though Iset adores Nakhtmin, she looks up at Tutankhamun through her thick lashes as if she would go with him tonight as well, if only he would command it. Iset lights the flame for him.

But then he looks to me, holding Iset's pipe up teasingly. I nod, and he passes it to me. I take a long draw of the foul tasting, sweet smelling smoke. As I exhale, the familiar blurring warmth passes through my body, an old friend whose forgotten voice is easily recalled once heard again. Instantly, the gold inlaid furniture, the finery of our guests, gleam brighter in the firelight. The music rolls into my heart.

"Careful," Tutankhamun murmurs, watching me waver. He takes the pipe from my hands gently, and leans over me, to my aunt. The smoky sweet scent of his skin envelops me. My eyes follow as his gold and blue glass falcon pendant swings dramatically off his hard chest on a thick, woven wire gold chain. Blinking over the deep, dreamlike blue of the falcon is a blazing carnelian solar disk, protected by a gold spitting cobra. As Tutankhamun sits up again, one arm draped casually over his bent leg, the falcon falls back to his bare chest. Its two different eyes-one made of the sun and one of the moon-seem to wink mockingly at me.

"Are you all right?" His words whisper and curl around my neck, like caressing, twining serpents.

"Dizzy," I say, smiling. I hear my words as if I were underwater.

"Lean on me," he murmurs, and I back against his warm chest. Tutankhamun's arms come around me, as if we were one strange bronze-skinned animal, male and female, bold and timid, hard and soft. The muscles of his gold-cuffed forearms twitch and tense as he throws out the gilded knucklebones. I barely hear the good-natured complaints of the others when he wins. Tutankhamun's laughter is warm in my ear as he scoops a gleaming pile of small silver rings towards us.

I turn and look up at him. He is beautiful, fierce and polished at once, perfect in every way. His dark, flashing eyes pull me in and I am lost, unable to speak or think, swept off in this hard new current. When he puts his lips against mine the thrill of fear-and desire-rushes right through my heart. Senseless to anything but the scent of his body and the warm press of his kiss, I part my lips for Tutankhamun; I let him taste me, dizzy as this strange new touch fills my body with a warm, pulsing longing.

"Not here," Tutankhamun tells me, whispering against my lips. He grins softly, and looks out at all his guests. I flush, even though some of them are falling into other arms as well. Not here, not us.

"Come with me," he says, his hand cupping my cheek.

I breathe hard. If I go, there is no turning back. If I walk to Tutankhamun's bedroom, I will be his wife in deed as well as fact. He gazes into my eyes, waiting for my answer. He kisses me again, a slow, deliberate kiss that makes my heart pound and my blood race. "Come with me, *hapepy*, please," he murmurs, his eyes burning with desire. I hardly know myself as I nod. Tutankhamun takes my hands and lifts me to my feet, and dazzled by the rush of opium and new-born desire, I follow him from the throne room.

The tall gilded doors of his chamber bang shut behind us, and we stand in the light of a full moon, streaming in through his clerestory windows. He slips his robe from his broad, tanned shoulders, and then he sets his royal diadem aside. I run my hand along the immaculate white sheets of his wide, lion-footed bed. When he comes to me, I watch him with wide eyes, my heart thumping in my chest.

Tutankhamun brushes my gown off slowly. He kisses my newly bare shoulder, running his lips softly to my neck. I close my eyes to the gentle stirring of my blood; I sigh as my gown falls to a rose colored pool on the floor. Tutankhamun plucks the pins from my hair, letting my black curls tumble free over my golden fillet, running his hands through their length.

Feeling clumsy, I begin to unknot the gilded sash around his waist. My hands are shaking too much for me to manage his kilt as well. Tutankhamun takes my hands, kisses them. "Don't worry," he tells me, and I nod and breathe.

I lie back on his bed, and he snatches his intricately wound kilt off with hardly a twist of his hand. I look up at the thick ebony poles of his canopy, at all the fine linen netted with thread of gold that tumbles to the floor. I can feel him against me, hot and silky and heavy. I close my eyes, and Tutankhamun's lips are on me again. I try to feel how lovely this is, but it's so very frightening, it's just like having to walk into the fire of initiation knowing how badly it would burn… I know Tutankhamun can feel my heart beating through my chest. He murmurs in my ear, steadying words, soft promises. I nod; I want him to go on, I want to be his true wife. I run my fingers over his soft close-cropped hair as his kisses stray from my lips to my full breasts, which he cups softly in his hands, and on to my flat, quivering belly. Tutankhamun pushes my legs apart tenderly; I gasp at the warm surprise of his mouth, his deep and shocking secret kisses. I stare at him in astonished innocence and Tutankhamun flickers his dark eyes up and laughs at me softly. His warm lips and gentle, strong fingers uncoil something fierce and beautiful inside me, drawing it out until the exquisite pleasure shatters so incredibly I cry from it. I shudder as everything in my body and soul rushes to the center and then trembles away, leaving me breathless, stunned, shivering with pure pleasure. I catch his cheek in my hand and whisper, "How did you do that?"

Tutankhamun grins. He crawls over me and kisses me deeply in response, and I gasp to taste myself on his lips, sweet like summer oranges.

But then, as he's kissing me and whispering sweet things against my lips, I feel him push himself inside of me. I cry out in shock; the burning, the ache, it's all the same, and the beauty of only a moment ago is all gone. My slim bronze thighs clutch his hips in protest, and I shake my head frantically.

He murmurs, "Shh, it's all right, trust me," holding my face gently, seeking my eyes. "Let me love you," he pleads softly, the ache in his voice from his belly. "Love me," he whispers, his lips brushing my cheeks. He waits for me, still and eager, agonized as I pant in terror. But slowly-maybe it's the opium, and the crackling magic in the air-I realize that I don't want to stop this.

"Yes, yes," I say, realizing how thrilling it is that even now, at this final moment, he's seeking my permission. I offer him my quivering lips, and then, suddenly, amazingly, the pain lessens just like a miracle. Tutankhamun kisses me as he does his slow, winding dance; he finds my hand and we lace our fingers together. And then it becomes sweet, so sweet; and Tutankhamun-who knows the meaning of the little tremble in my breath-whispers with pleasure and rakish confidence that I can still run away if I want to. And as he whispers to me, his lips brush behind my ear and along my neck, and I can't hold back from him any more. With a soft cry of surrender, I give myself fully to Tutankhamun.

Chapter Nineteen

I blink awake, sure that it isn't light yet. And then I feel
him, I remember. Our bronze limbs are tangled together, our
hands clasped even in our sleep. I smile luxuriously, so full of
happiness I could drown in it. We sleep in a dreamy cocoon of
sheer linen and shimmering gold thread; the eight hour wicks
are burnt down to the nub, flickering lazily. Tutankhamun's face
is turned to me, his lips slightly parted, his eyelashes long and
black against his pretty cheeks. A moment later, Tutankhamun
wakes and laughs softly, pulling me up in his arms. "You are
really here," he murmurs with drowsy pleasure.

I curl into his arms and he brushes my curls back from my
face. "I won't let you go now," he warns me softly.

"Don't," I say. "Leave the curtains pulled and stay with me
this morning."

He bites his lip, considering it, his eyes flushed dark with
desire. But then he shakes his head and breathes, "No, no. It
must be nearing the first hour of the day. I must make my
offerings soon."

"So dutiful," I say, smiling, aware for the first time of the
blissful pleasure of my own duty.

Tutankhamun kisses my brow and says, "I have the sweetest,
most beautiful love to be thankful for."

I catch his hand as he climbs from his big bed. When he
looks down on me, I know I don't need to speak for him to

understand. He holds my hand up to his lips, and then he lays his cheek against my fingertips and closes his eyes in a deeply tender gesture. I couldn't possibly love him more.

And then Tutankhamun backs away. I wrap myself in one of his robes, and he walks me to my own quarters. Inside, I lean back against the door and close my eyes, smiling a secret smile as I relive our incredible night. I take a long, indulgent bath in water scented with rose oil, tilting my head back as my sleepy maids rinse my tumbling black curls. I can still smell Tutankhamun's fragrant body oil on my skin. I laugh aloud for the pure delight of it all.

Mutnojme waits for me, as if she had kept a vigil all night long. I take her hands, thinking I should say something, but I can't. I shiver when I think of Tutankhamun's touch, but I can't tell her-or anyone-any of these things. They are too deep, too much of the soul.

"Thank the gods," she says, laughing.

I smile and sit at my vanity, plucking up my golden mirror and gazing over my cosmetics and perfumes. "And how was the general?" I ask casually.

Her voice is flat. "I don't know. We barely spoke, and he left out with Rameses, drunk and singing war songs. I thought he might come to my room, but-" Mutnojme shakes her head. "It is good that he didn't. Teye arrived first thing in the morning, saying I should be ready to assist you, in case things... well, went wrong with Pharaoh. But I knew she was looking me over, to see if I'd had him in my bed."

I frown, first because of the embarrassment of the whole palace worrying over what bed I slept in, and then because I hope Horemhab hasn't given up on Mutnojme. He ought to know that she lost his child; and that before she lost the baby, she was making herself sick worrying for *him*, and how he might suffer if she had the baby! I can't stand the hurt in her face, and though I don't know if it's a lie or not, I say, "I'm sure he was just overwhelmed, and probably dead drunk after Tutankhamun's party."

We spend the day at sail. I go to the temple, still breathless with shock and delight as I lay grateful offerings at the feet of the Mother Goddess, in all her incarnations. When I see Anat, I bestow two chests of gold and one of silver on her temple, to adorn it.

When Tutankhamun finally comes to me in the early evening, he's wearing a plain kilt and a smart officer's cloak. "I have one more gift for you," he says. He brings a fragile alabaster box from behind him. "But don't wear them tonight. I want to go somewhere where we can relax a little, like everyone else."

"You are ever full of surprises," I tease in delight. I gently lift the lid, carved into lotus blossoms, and flip up the layers of soft, protective linen. And then, I can't believe it. I could weep in gratitude as I understand finally that the gods *did* make us for each other, and they had sent me signs all along. I lift a rope of shining purple beads into the firelight. "Amethyst. Tutankhamun... When I was a little girl, I thought I might have a necklace like this one day. I thought my true husband would give it to me, and you have..." I rest my head against his smooth chest and listen to the quick, steady beat of his heart, so much in love that I could drown from it.

Tutankhamun brings me into the starlit courtyard, to his waiting chariot, plain and wooden and entirely without insignia. To my surprise, General Horemhab joins us, flushed with wine and excitement.

"We have to hurry if we want to see Aha. He is fighting in the fifth match. Nakhtmin sent a rider to tell me his opponent, who fought in the second, might have a fractured wrist already."

"Where are we going?" I ask, thrilled.

"To watch the fights with the court. If you want to place a bet," Tutankhamun says to me, "Then place it on Aha. He is new to the matches, just elevated to an overseer of troops in our infantry."

"He feels no pain, Your Majesty," Horemhab tells me with a grin. "An ideal infantry man!"

"Pain is nothing to glory," Tutankhamun says decidedly. He snaps the reins and calls out to his horses, and we sweep out of the palace enclosure, cantering around the moonlit lake. We take a torch and palm lined road towards a harbor used by our workers. As we approach, a great cry of cheering erupts, but not for us. There are men everywhere in the square of the little mud-brick town sprung up to serve the harbor, shouting men surrounding what must be a fight. There are great rolling drums to accompany the scene.

"We are going in there?" I gasp, holding tightly to Tutankhamun. I am astonished that he would bring me around such men!

"Don't be frightened," Tutankhamun murmurs. "I'd never let you get hurt."

"I'm not afraid," I tell him as I take his proffered hand. "In fact, I've never felt so alive."

Tutankhamun's eyes shine in pleasure as he helps me down from the chariot. I'm delighted by the novelty of being so close to roughly clad commoners who shout bets and insults into the night. Tutankhamun brings me through some importer's warehouse and up onto the roof, where dozens of lords and ladies laugh and shout as they bet on the fights. I recognize a good chunk of the court of Thebes, drinking and laughing in torchlight and comparing the fighters below. There is no prostration, really no show of obeisance at all saving a polite deference, a clearing of the path before Tutankhamun. I squeeze his arm, overwhelmed by the freedom of moving about in a crowd. Of course, we are with Horemhab, and joined by Nakhtmin and a slew of retainers and entourage who would be loyal till death, but my pulse is quick all the same.

And then, like the bit of rotten meat that spoils an otherwise perfect dish, I see that Djede has accompanied Nakhtmin. I can't explain why I don't like him. Could I really despise someone for just his looks? His very presence here is jarring.

But Tutankhamun welcomes him into our circle. "Nakhtmin's been telling me that you can spin your chariot so tightly that you'll win any race on open ground. Is that true?"

Djede bows. "I like to think so, my king."

Tutankhamun nods at Djede's confidence, his eyes narrowing. I purse my lips in a smile, hearing Tutankhamun's secret thoughts: *I'll run circles around you, Phoenician.* But what he says is, "In that case we shall surely have use for you in our army."

The men make bets, and then a place at the front of the roof suddenly clears for us. We stand beside Horemhab and Nakhtmin, our men squared around us for safety, as below two dirty, bloody men grapple in the square below. "Which is Aha?" I ask Tutankhamun.

"He fights next. Shall I make a bet for you?"

I nod in delight. He turns to one of the men standing guard around us, snapping something about *deben*.

Aha takes the ring. He is a lanky man, and his opponent a bull of a man who shows no sign of injury. Horemhab eyes Nakhtmin suspiciously. "Have you turned and bet against us?"

Nakhtmin laughs roguishly, but assures Horemhab, "I saw his hand turn backwards, General. I nearly heard the crack with my own ears. You can see: he favors it. Before, his punches and grabs were right handed. Look at Rameses, who bet against us: he knows he's lost already."

I try to follow the fight, but the intoxicating freedom of being lost-somewhat-in the crowd is far more exciting. The warm breeze carries the scents of fertile soil, sweat, and roasting lamb. The spectators roar as the two men grapple, jeering and laughing and insulting the competitors. Moonlight and the light of a thousand torches mix, casting a ruddy glow over the little square. And of course, Tutankhamun is next to me, making my heart skip when his fingers brush my skin. He looks down at me every so often, as if reassuring himself that I'm really here, his wife truly by his side at last.

A great cry goes up from the crowd. Aha, held by the buffalo, threw him off and onto his broad back. Before our eyes, the fight transforms for the lanky young fighter. Horemhab cheers like a peasant, bringing the color to my cheeks. Tutankhamun looks sideways at me and laughs softly. We are as different from these people as can be, two smooth snakes in a pack of guffawing hyenas. But everyone, including Tutankhamun, enjoys Aha's unexpected success. He nods his head in approval as all around us men applaud and cheer the smaller man for his tenacity. Aha clasps hands with his bleeding opponent and lifts him out of the dust.

I laugh as Tutankhamun collects little leather purses of copper, which he empties off the roof onto the path below. The men wish to bet again, and we drink more honeyed beer. As the wind rushes around us, carrying the cries of the crowd, my lover-my lover!-slides his arm around my waist and kisses my cheek.

The next fight commences, with two bulky men with long, braided back hair. They circle each other again and again, and then rush into a furious embrace. I look back, through the veil of our guards to the lords and ladies behind us. They will have agents watching the fights, and they bet more than *deben*, as Tutankhamun probably has done as well. They spend their time drinking and smoking opium, and being seen. Every shared drink or pleasantry is a chance to make a connection, make a marriage or joint investment in one of Pharaoh's mining or trade ventures.

I hear Tutankhamun say in disbelief, "How many?" My attention turns back to my husband. He is talking to the untitled newcomer, Djede.

"One hundred and seven, Your Majesty. All at night."

"On a raft? With what bait?"

"Yes, Your Majesty; a raft, and baby goats, mostly."

"With what weapons?"

Djede smiles warmly. "I prefer my spear, and my man a heavy plank of cedar from my father's barn."

"You would spear him, and then pull him up and when he got close enough, your man would stun him."

They must be talking about crocodiles. Tutankhamun grins at the lanky half-foreigner. "You will show me, next week when my ceremonies are done. Nakhtmin can take a club, and we our spears. Nakhtmin? Horemhab, you want in? Spear or club?"

I gape in astonishment, and then bite my lips. Horemhab says happily, "I'm a club man, Your Majesty."

Tutankhamun says, "Excellent. We'll sail south in five days."

The crowd roars again.

When the fighting is over, we must cut through the throngs of peasants. They yield to us, staying on to drink and throw knucklebones. But some are already drunk, and those press close to us. Unlike the lords, they cry out in delight, "Pharaoh is here, Pharaoh!" They push and clamor to see us. I close my eyes briefly, and tighten my grasp on Tutankhamun's arm.

A man falls backwards, nearly knocking into us. Horemhab and Nakhtmin lunge towards him. Tutankhamun raises his horsewhip with a crack. The man's eyes are blurred with too much drink, but he too recognizes his Pharaoh. He darts his hazy eyes between Tutankhamun and myself, and he falls face flat to the floor, with Horemhab clutching his one arm and Nakhtmin the other.

Tutankhamun lowers his whip, tightening his grip on my arm even more. We walk around the drunkard, and back to the safety of the chariot. I am grateful for the smell of clean wind in my face. Once the rush of fear passes, I laugh and clutch his waist. The stars shine like scattered gems on an endless black cloth, and palms sway in the night breezes as we fly along.

"You will really hunt with him?"

"Him?"

"That ugly foreigner. I don't like him."

Tutankhamun laughs. "Poor Djede! You are a demanding goddess! The man seems to be brave, and of course, Nakhtmin claims he drives like the wind. I will put him to the test, if that is what he wants."

"You know of his father?"

"Of course, Ankhesenamun. I have the books, remember?"

Yes, that's right. Father instructs him from beyond the

tomb, as he could never do in life. I lean my cheek against Tutankhamun's back for a moment, as we go along in the chariot, gliding on the smooth path.

"Why else do you think he's trying to get my attention? He wants to win acclaim for himself, a title, and royal favor."

"Was his father a traitor, Tutankhamun?" I ask, my words clear in the night.

"No, *hapepy*. He was a fool. But he had to be dismissed, for he had failed Pharaoh, and that is dangerous enough."

"So dismiss Djede," I say. Send him back to wherever he came from.

"Ankhesenamun, I won't punish the man for his father's stupidity. He is Nakhtmin's friend, and if he is as good as he says and he wants to join the army he is welcome."

"But you won't give him any political post."

Tutankhamun laughs in the moonlight. "No, my love! I certainly will not."

Chapter Twenty

Five days later, the four of us, with Iset and my maids for my company, meet at one of Tutankhamun's smaller barges. Mutnojme, who is watched closely by Teye, pled fatigue to remain in the palace. Horemhab gazes over my shoulder for a long moment as I walk down to the lakeside harbor, as if he had hoped my aunt would follow. "General!" Tutankhamun calls; Horemhab quickly mounts the stairs to the deck. Never one to be under prepared, he has a slew of clubbing sticks bundled up like an overgrown quiver of arrows and tossed onto his broad back. Nakhtmin and Djede go up more slowly. Djede looks about like a boy on his first trip to the city, noting the gold-inlaid deck furniture and the two pillars of stone before the cabin, painted as lotus flowers. Cushions in shades of carnelian red-orange and bright blue are strewn about haphazardly, and simple rafts are stacked on the port side, next to a row of fine spears.

"How close they mean to get!" Iset murmurs, gazing ominously on the rafts, nothing more substantial than woven reed baskets smeared with pitch. She makes a quick gesture to ward off evil, and murmurs a prayer to her patron goddess.

We eat a simple, hearty meal-cheese and olives, bread and figs-as we sail south past Luxor Temple. The late winter sun is strong, giving a haze to the blue sky. Tutankhamun asks Djede to tell us some of his hunting stories, and he warms as he talks, growing more comfortable as he impresses the most powerful men in the world. He seems to love the hunt as much as they do; crocodiles and hippotamuses are his specialty.

Lady Iset sits beside me, eagerly chattering about her son Nebamun's education. I've told her that I plan to engage Senqed in creating a palace school for the children of Tutankhamun's closest friends, and surely she noted the way my fingers strayed across my belly as I said this. I can only pray that our own child will join this class before long, but I don't dwell on it, because the very thought of childbirth is enough to make me nauseous with fear.

My gaze strays over to the men, just in time to see Horemhab making eyes at Nakhtmin. The young captain stands up to stretch his legs, and says he wants to check the weapons and make sure the rafts have been smeared with enough pitch to water-seal them. When Djede joins him, the general takes a seat beside Tutankhamun, his face grim.

Iset speaks: "And then, next year our daughter will be old enough... Will you employ your old music tutors as well, Your Majesty? I think she has a gift for song..."

"Yes, yes," I say, wishing she would be quiet for just a moment. I can see anger firing in Tutankhamun's eyes, and Horemhab's voice is no more than a hiss.

Tutankhamun demands, "And the *Kenbet*? Have they taken their complaints to the court of elders?"

Horemhab nods, and I can just barely pick out his words. "They've taken their complaints, but they were never granted a hearing."

Tutankhamun drums his ringed fingers on the arm rest of his mahogany chair. He leans toward Horemhab and murmurs something dark, but I cannot hear it.

Iset cuts in, quite oblivious to the concerns of the men. "Of course, I've told Nakhtmin that Nebamun will need his own servant to accompany him-"

Horemhab stands just in time to welcome Nakhtmin and Djede back with mugs of beer. I turn to Iset with a warm smile. "Excuse me, Lady Iset. I'll just be a moment."

I stand and straighten my white diaphanous sheath, and then I go to my husband's side. Born in the viper pit of the court, he's already fixed the smile back on his face, but I know he is deeply troubled. The men's voices hush as I approach. "Can I steal you away?" I ask, like an eager lover.

"Always," he says, rising to take my hands. As we walk to the port side, a flock of sacred ibis fly overhead. Tutankhamun stands behind me and wraps his arms around my slim waist, resting his cheek against my braided hair. For a long moment, he stares out at his beautiful, prosperous land.

We've left the city behind, and the piles of mud-brick apartment houses pull apart into villages against the rugged desert hills. Papyrus and other water loving plants choke the riverbank, and sedge grass creeps overland behind it. Bees hum through, collecting nectar from wildflowers, and birds rush through the thick clutches of palms further back. Fields of wheat are cut into the land, mixed mindfully with watermelon, lettuce, and onions. The smell of baking bread carries across the river from the far off villages, and in the distance, we can see children playing in the shelter of an acacia grove.

Then he tells me softly, "One of Horemhab's infantry captains-a man from near his home village, who knew his father-has come to him with an alarming complaint. When last year's taxes were collected, the officials who came to the village robbed his wife for their meager savings. Others were robbed as well; the helpless, widows and old people who had no strong sons to resist. And those who did resist were beaten, some to the edge of death, and the taxmen used my authority to do it. And they say it's been going on for years, many years."

I turn up to him and whisper, "Tutankhamun, what will you do?"

His eyes linger on the villages, on the homes of the people he is sworn to protect as their father. "It might be worse than that. The peasants took their complaints to the court, and they were pushed off, avoided, neglected. Their grievances were buried."

"Someone in the *Kenbet* is corrupted."

Tutankhamun nods. "Do you remember the way it was when I became king? How Father had let the local strongmen do as they pleased? He made a mess of it, and now everyone thinks they can do what they want in their little villages. I'm going to straighten them out."

"How?" I ask softly, so as not to alarm the guests of our hunting party.

"I will investigate, and I will punish the guilty. I will send the lesser men to the Sinai desert, to the turquoise and copper mines, which is as good as a death sentence. And if the elders of the *Kenbet* are involved, they will have to die by the sword, as a warning to the others."

I flinch, gazing up at him. The headsman has not been called to Pharaoh's court since my father ruled, but back then, blood flowed freely through the capital city's square. I do not wish to relive those dark, terrifying days! But what else can Tutankhamun do? If he does *not* punish criminals, then this corruption, widespread as it is, will only grow worse.

"There they are!" Nakhtmin shouts.

We turn to see him motioning to a muddy stretch of the west bank. A dozen crocodiles bake in the sun, three more cut through the water to hunt. I straighten Tutankhamun's heavy beaded collar. "Put this to the side for today," I tell him. "There will be time enough to deal with it, after you catch your crocodile. Enjoy your hunt."

He nods, and kisses my brow, and goes off to join his men. I swallow hard, but my throat stays dry.

They choose a spot further down, where several sandbars push through the water to invite crocodiles to rest. At nightfall, the men prepare as Iset and I watch crocodiles slip into the water and shelter together against the night chill. The two largest males of the group, twenty cubits long at least, seem to disappear into the inky moonlit water as they continue hunting. These are the prizes my husband seeks tonight.

The men ignite torches and take coils of rope and nasty

chunks of bait with their weapons, bringing two crewmen along to hold the light. Three men-one spear, one torch, and one club-take two rafts and slip away from the safety of the barge. Tutankhamun works with Horemhab, and presumably the general is also murmuring in Pharaoh's ear about the unfortunate families of these infantry soldiers.

Instantly, I understand what the torch is for. The eyes of the beasts glow orange in the light, and finally, that is all we can see of them. I cannot imagine how Tutankhamun and Djede will aim with only two tiny globes of light submerged in blackness to guide them.

"I can't watch," Iset murmurs, coming out of the cabin in a thick, soft robe. "We can't see anything anyway."

"My lord is on the left," I say, gazing after the ball of fire hovering over the river. Tutankhamun's form is in shadow, the white of his kilt like smoke in the air. Iset stands beside me, fretting for Nakhtmin. After a long while, I hear the slightest whistle, followed by chaotic splashing, and then a thick, thudding noise. Tutankhamun and Horemhab's voices carry over the black water, mixed together, neither man's words comprehensible in the tangle. They stay out a long while, until the sounds are repeated across the river. Eventually the torches come together, and Tutankhamun emerges from the darkness, illuminated by fire. A taunt rope trails in the water behind their raft, towing a heavy load. Like the crocodile bites, stuns, and drowns his victims, so the hunters have done to him. Tutankhamun comes onto the barge quickly. He leans over the lotus flower stem, catching the rope that Horemhab tosses up to him. Once the rope is securely tied to the railing, Horemhab and the crewman come aboard, and it takes the three of them to tug an enormous river monster onto the barge. The crocodile's blood, black in the night, spills across the deck.

"Is he dead?" I call, coming down from the cabin.

Tutankhamun looks up, grinning fiercely, his teeth flashing white in the darkness. "Like a rebel chief," he says, and I approach Tutankhamun's kill cautiously. The beast's massive body is laid out in the moonlight; he is longer than the two of us lying foot to head. Two rows of giant fangs gleam white in his long, triangular jaw. He is bigger than the one Nakhtmin and Djede pull up by an arm's length, causing a bit of good natured ribbing. Tutankhamun speared him through the throat, right behind his menacing head.

The men take drink and smoke over their prizes. Horemhab and Djede and the servants bed down on the open deck, and Nakhtmin and Iset share my cabin. Tutankhamun and I shut his door to the world, and we tumble across the fresh smelling, tightly woven reeds of his camp bed, determined to please the gods with our love. Just before daybreak I collapse into his arms and we lie in blissful silence, listening to the calls of bullfrogs and the splashing of fish. Tutankhamun's fingers stroke my back softly, until I fall asleep.

Chapter Twenty-One

Every morning, I wake in Tutankhamun's arms. Sometimes, I wake up-halfway, at first, as if in a dream-to the delicious feeling of his lips and hands on my trembling body, because even in our sleep we're drawn together. We make love in the darkness before the sun rises, and he is gone from my bed just after, to purify himself and offer to the gods, to do his sacred duty as the intermediary between men and the divine. I ache for him when he's gone, even for a moment. It isn't just what we do; it's afterwards, too, when we lie together, breathless, seeing clearly into each other's souls. It's the way I lay on his chest and he curls his fingers around my hair, speaking softly about this or that, ordinary things when there's nothing ordinary about him, or us. But of course, it's the way he touches me, too. I go to my bath, and the water laps at my skin like my lover's lips. When my body servants brush my long black curls, I can feel Tutankhamun's hands lost in my hair. I am distracted and restless with anyone else, longing only for the moment when I can return to Tutankhamun, to hear his sweet voice murmuring in my ear, to feel his silky, fragrant body pressing against mine. I could die from the joy of him. It is as if there was nothing ever before our love, and nothing that will matter after. And I am grateful, oh so grateful, to have perfect happiness at last.

At midday, I hurry to his chambers, just to hear how his morning's gone. Most unexpectedly, there are five youthful peasant men in his inner chamber, drinking fine wine and gaping in wide-eyed wonder at the golden glory of Pharaoh's bedroom, and at the golden-brown hawk who glares at them from her heavy perch.

I take his hands, staring openly at the oddest strangers ever to assemble in Tutankhamun's chambers.

"Fishermen from Middle Egypt," he murmurs, kissing my cheek. "And one man who's been scribe-trained. They'll be assigned to the tax collection this spring, with the men accused of corruption. They're going to report on what they see." He kisses my hands and calls to them, "All right, go on. Enjoy yourselves at the banquet in the banquet hall, and then report to the treasury department. But remember," he says, his voice imparting the most murky shadow of a threat, "not a word to Lord Maya, or anyone else, about your true mission. When you return to me this summer, with your information, I will have your pensions. Do right by your king and you will go back to Amarna as wealthy men."

They make their obeisance, and scurry out of the room without raising their eyes.

"They are from Amarna?" I ask, once they are gone.

Tutankhamun puts his arms around me and murmurs, "Born and bred. They fought in Nubia with the division I plan to lead in my next battle."

"Oh! Don't talk about leaving me again!" I protest, laying my hands against his chest.

"Hush," he whispers, playful in his authority, kissing my mouth softly. But then he says, "There's something I must tell you... General Horemhab's made a request-"

"Your Majesty, the Grand Vizier is here to see you."

Tutankhamun looks over my shoulder, to Ipay. "Let him in." And then to me, "We can't tell Lord Ay anything about my spies, not yet. It's not that I don't trust telling him, but the fewer men who know about this, the better. I mean to let the criminals sink themselves this harvest time."

"Of course." I settle into one of his ebony and ivory chairs and take a glass of wine for myself, admiring the elegant simplicity of his ebony and gold décor as we wait for the Lord Grand Vizier.

"Your Majesties," Lord Ay says, swirling through the door in a voluminous robe. He makes a gracious bow to us, and allows Ipay to seat him and give him wine. Immediately, he turns on Tutankhamun. "I have had some disturbing news."

"What's that?" Tutankhamun asks, sitting beside me.

"General Horemhab will seek permission to marry Lady Amenia, the cousin of Lord Rameses."

I can barely contain my gasp of shock. Poor Mutnojme! Her heart will be broken!

"I know," Tutankhamun says, tilting his head to me. This is what he meant to tell me, as Ay interrupted us.

"And will you grant it?" Ay asks in wonder.

"I hardly see how I can refuse," Tutankhamun returns, waiting for Ay to crack.

As usual when it comes to Horemhab, old Ay bursts with agitation, the words pouring from his mouth. "Your Majesty, this alliance would be most dangerous to us! The Rameside clan is enormous and powerful, holding almost all the northeastern Delta. And with Horemhab as the Overseer of the Army... They would be unstoppable."

"I can't deny him, Ay," Tutankhamun says plainly, shaking his head. He even laughs a little. "There's no cause for it. He is a good man, my man, who has given me no reason to deny the bride of his choosing. Especially after you deemed it best to deny him once already."

"I don't trust him, Your Majesty. I never have. He wants nothing but glory for himself, glory and war! So: he falls in love, he says, first with a woman who's quite nearly royal herself, and then with a girl from one of the most powerful clans in Egypt? Quite delicate taste for an upstart commoner, don't you think?"

"He is my deputy, Lord Ay," Tutankhamun says, watching the Grand Vizier carefully. "And he has served me honestly and well. But I hear you, and I will think on it."

Ay pinches his thin lips and says, "But you will grant permission for the marriage."

"I will."

Ay sits still, and I wonder if he will press it again. It's quite true, I think. Horemhab aims high when looking for a wife, and the way he's left my aunt behind stuns me speechless. And if Mutnojme was pregnant, which she swears she wasn't, but if she was... could he have not hoped for that, as well? Might he have really wanted to force the old vizier's hand?

Lord Ay says nothing more, and he leaves politely. When he is gone, Tutankhamun looks to me and says, "He's right, you know. About a marriage alliance between Horemhab and Rameses, anyway."

"I know, Tutankhamun."

Tutankhamun sighs pensively, drumming his gilded fingers on his desk. "It's actually a *very* dangerous match, when you think that Rameses, with all his connections, is going to be training ten thousand new soldiers, and Horemhab trained the other five. But I can't deny Horemhab-really, if I don't trust him, why shouldn't I just have it done and replace him? And how could I, after all he has done for me? And it's also true that Lord Ay is a conceited old snake. He can't see Horemhab for anything more than a crafty peasant, and a rather brutish one at that. But Horemhab is just, and he loves his country like Ay loves his reputation and position. He cares for the people. He is a terror to the enemy, but he treats his captives well. He eats the same rations as his men, unless he has gone hunting. He is a solid man who doesn't shrink from being fierce and ruthless when he must be, nor is he heartless without cause. He is true Egyptian."

"You truly admire him," I murmur. Tutankhamun was raised to admire no one but his sires.

Tutankhamun nods. "So, I admire him, but I must outwit him. Both of them, Rameses and Horemhab. I'm sure their intentions are perfectly honorable, but I must take the teeth out of this lion before I set it free."

I laugh softly, and reach for his hand.

When the midday break is over, and the golden light of late afternoon showers through the clerestory windows, I go to Mutnojme. The curtains are pulled, and she sits in her bed as if ill, staring absently through the canopy around her bed. Her hair is undone, tumbling over her shoulders messily, and her eyes are red with weeping. I climb in beside her and she says in a hollow voice, "He's left me. He's given up."

I hold her, because there's really nothing to say.

"Why is it always this way? Why? I lost my sister to the throne, I lost the Great Mother for politics, for so many years; I've been denied a husband as my uncle plots to find one dumb enough to be safe and rich enough to make himself a profit, and now I must lose Horemhab because I am born too high for him. When will it be my time to have some happiness, something for myself?"

"It will come," I say, stroking her hair. "I promise, Mutnojme. One day, your uncle will be gone, and then you'll do what you please. Tutankhamun wouldn't have denied you Horemhab, you must know that! And you are like my sister, not my subject. When Lord Ay retires, you will do as you please."

"But it's too late! He has left me, and for *Amenia*! What will it matter, then, when I am free, if the only man I've ever loved has turned away from me? When I have lost so much already... What good will it do me then?" Mutnojme looks up at me and cries, "How could my uncle do this to me? He has stolen my life to advance his fortunes! I would have done anything for him, for my family! Horemhab said... he said he knew he had to find a wife when Nakhtmin was in his wine one night in Nubia, and he told him Ay would marry me to Maya. I hate my uncle now, I swear it! Love has turned to hate, like day to night."

"I know how swiftly it turns," I murmur, closing my eyes to it. "Truly, I know."

Chapter Twenty-Two

Spring

I bite my lips, watching old Pentju's thumb clasped on my wrist. It couldn't have happened so quickly... He lets go, and smiles into my wide eyes. "Your pulse is very high, Your Majesty. You'll want to choose a midwife soon."

I shriek happily and throw my arms around the tiny old man. "I must tell Tutankhamun!"

"You'll want to go out to the desert, then," Pentju says, shades of disapproval in his voice. He will fret until Tutankhamun returns from his sport, as he always does.

I walk down to the courtyard of idle chariots, and take a team of prancing greys through the western gate. Tutankhamun is just at the edge of the flat land before the mountains rise, and already I see a great cloud of dust under the yellow cliffs, puffing up to the brilliant blue sky. As we get close, I see Djede and another youth I that I recognize from Tutankhamun's inner circle, the younger Huy, the one Tutankhamun fought. They are cutting some pattern across the track, weaving through each other in a dramatic double serpentine, while Tutankhamun and Nakhtmin stand shoulder to shoulder like judges. Their own chariots wait with pageboys to the side, Aten's Fury faithfully pawing the ground.

I ride up to them and step down from the chariot. Tutankhamun looks over his shoulder and smiles his honey smile. "You will get all covered in dust and sand, my lady," he warns, but he puts his hand out and draws me close. "Look at Djede; he almost rivals my own driver, Huy. I didn't expect it, but he was telling the truth. I can definitely use him."

"You hate having a driver," I say. "You are better than both of them."

"But I like to shoot, *hapepy*. I can't drive and shoot in battle, at least not responsibly, no matter what the Wall of Proclamation says."

I pull on his fingers softly, tired of this talk. "I have something to tell you…"

He tightens his grip on my fingers in excitement as I whisper that I'm carrying his child.

Tutankhamun gives a cry of proud joy. He lifts me in his arms and spins me until I shriek and demand that he stops.

"Think of the baby!" I admonish, laughing.

"The *baby*," he repeats, trying the words out on his lips. "*Our* baby."

"If the gods will it," I say soberly, resting my face against his.

"They will," he breathes, "I swear it."

We linger at the track for only a little longer. Djede wins himself the accolades of his king, but Tutankhamun's lost interest in his sport. We rush back to the palace, to his chambers, where we step into his big bath. I wash the dust from his body as he kisses my face, my neck, my chest. Tutankhamun buries himself in my thick black curls, murmuring of miracles. An hour or so later, Ipay stands outside the door of the king's bedroom; Tutankhamun has a visitor. He grins and pushes himself off the bed like a spry cat. The sweet smells of frankincense and myrrh swirl in from Tutankhamun's antechamber as he opens the door. "Lord Hani! Come into my private chambers, and take a glass of wine."

I throw my curls back over my shoulders and rewrap my sash. By the time Tutankhamun brings his favored ambassador through the door, I am pouring purple wine into two golden chalices. They sit at Tutankhamun's *senet* table, and I retreat back to the bed, curling into the cushions.

"Is it done?" Tutankhamun asks, handing Hani the cup of wine himself.

Hani bows elegantly, and takes the proffered wine. "Done well, Your Majesty," Hani reports. He tastes the wine with a smile. "It is good to drink Egyptian wine again."

"You have just returned, then."

"I have come straight off my barge, Your Majesty, to tell you that there are twenty agents in place in southern Canaan, all whispering indiscreetly about a desired attack on the Delta. And another dozen of my own men, prepared to say they heard it in the taverns while spying for you."

"Beautiful," Tutankhamun says, raising his golden chalice in a toast. "One of Lord Maya's people will bring a package to your townhouse tomorrow. Go home, see your wife."

Hani rises again, giving another showy bow. "Thank you, Your Majesty."

Tutankhamun finishes his wine, and comes back over to the bed. I reach for him, murmuring "What was all that?"

Tutankhamun kneels down and curls his arms around me, and we fall into the pillows. "Rameses and Horemhab are two of the most powerful men in Egypt, both with thousands of loyal soldiers and retainers. Horemhab has the loyalty of everyone who works for him, because of his manner, and Rameses has one of the biggest, oldest families in the northeast. They were important when the foreign occupiers were expelled, under Pharaoh Ahmose. They are both good men, honorable, patriotic, everything they should be. But I will not give Rameses all those men and then all the loyalty of Horemhab's men as well. Not because I suspect them, as Ay does. I just don't want the balance of things upset."

"So what does that have to do Hani's trip?"

He grins at me, impatient for a kiss. "Wait and see."

Soon, the great men of court fall into worry. Centuries ago, the Delta was overrun with foreigners, and so it's a very sore wound, especially with northerners. Tutankhamun watches with his hands spread across the balcony wall as the greatest men in Egypt go running about the courtyard, exchanging frightened whispers. He turns from the balcony, his fine gold-threaded linen cloak spinning behind him.

The next day, Tutankhamun is outside the palace walls with Nakhtmin and Djede, showing them how he shoots from the back of his horse, when Rameses, Horemhab, and of course Lord Ay come to see him. I sit under my sunshade holding my breath, wondering how he can turn his horse with such a slight shift of his hips. On the last arrow, he takes the knot of reins from Fury's red mane and trots up to his officials. "Good lords," he says in greeting, pulling up beside them.

"Your Majesty must know why we have come," Lord Ay says. He looks like a snake, deliberately scenting a trail with a darting tongue.

"I'd imagine the content of Lord Hani's report," Tutankhamun says. He puts his hand on his hip, affecting a tired, thoughtful look. "It kept me up last night. Have you men any suggestions?"

Rameses steps up so beautifully, claiming his part in the pageant perfectly. "Your Majesty, this has particular concern for me. I think of my family in the northeast, I think of my lands. Long has the chain of northern forts been underfunded. I believe it is time to correct that. We must fortify and man our home line."

"Lord Rameses," Tutankhamun says, frowning, "You cannot leave now! I need you to train the new divisions! The Lord Overseer is a man of many talents, my first rate general, but his time is limited!"

"Yes, I know, Your Majesty," Rameses shakes his head. "But now we have an active mission, and there is no better man than me to lead it. We must defend the Delta."

"Yes, of course," Tutankhamun says, looking down on the

tied reins in his hand. His gold and leather wrist guard winks in the sun. He stares thoughtfully on Horemhab, who readies himself to accept yet another charge. But then, Tutankhamun looks over his shoulder. "Nakhtmin! I have given you the Nubian archers already. Do you think you can train infantry soldiers to fight and wield spears as well?"

Nakhtmin's eyes widen in disbelief, sparkling white in his sun darkened face. Of course Ay holds his breath. This would make his son a general in quick time. He must look like a cat with feathers on his lips, but I keep my eyes on Nakhtmin. "I will do it, Your Majesty! I thank you for your confidence in me."

"Well. There it is. Make it so," Tutankhamun says, satisfied with the solution. Horemhab and Rameses, slightly astonished, climb back into their shared chariot and return to the palace. They can have no complaint against Nakhtmin's ability.

But Vizier Ay lingers. He looks up at Tutankhamun and says quietly, "I had not heard of any plans to attack Egypt."

Tutankhamun sucks his teeth slightly. "For shame, Vizier Ay! And all that gold I have given for your spies! Young Lord Hani is not outstripping you, is he?"

For a moment, Ay stands very still. But then, Tutankhamun flashes a blinding smile at him, and wheels his horse around. "Dismissed!" he shouts joyfully, kicking Fury into a charge.

I look back at Ay, and he shakes his head at me, a little smile wrinkling around his eyes, a huffing little laugh rattling in his chest. "Clever," he says to me, and I give him an innocent smile, playing along with Tutankhamun's game. Ay sets his hands on his hips and stares at Pharaoh, galloping across the desert on Aten's Fury like an eagle sweeping down on his kill. "Rameses couldn't resist playing the hero, and now he'll walk off with one thousand spears when he could have had ten."

"It seems so, Lord Ay," I observe coolly. The lion has far less teeth now, and that is better for us all.

Chapter Twenty-Three

Summer Year Six

"You're showing already," Mutnojme says with a small smile.

I stand before my long silver mirror, turning this way and that to see the small rise in my belly. "Last time it looked gross. I was so small, my belly so big. But now…" I run my hands over my hips, pleased to see and feel the sinuous curve. I am still a diminutive woman, barely reaching Tutankhamun's shoulders, but at least I am a woman true. "Now I think it suits me."

In the moment of silence, I hear the humming of insects in the nighttime garden outside. The night is hot, so hot a haze hangs in the air even long hours after the sun has set. I leave off looking at myself and settle into my vanity chair, to let Henutawy untangle my wet hair with an ivory comb. I dab rose oil across my throat, and a bit of cream onto my lips to make them shine.

"You look beautiful, my lady, with or without a child," Mutnojme tells me, taking up a glass of wine. She swirls it absently in the silver cup before drinking, and I sigh for her. Horemhab is married to the stunning Chantress of Amun now, Lady Amenia with eyes the color of sweet wine and hair so black it's tinted blue. He has told Mutnojme a thousand times since that it is only for sons, and each time she looks a little sicker. But she never tells him her secret. Horemhab, at least, has the decency not to come to the feasts with his bride, and Amenia is content to rule her dormitory of girls at Karnak. My prediction came true: Paranefer runs a merry, well ordered camp at Karnak Temple, keeping the mansion of Amun lush with gardens and full of music and song. One would never think he was so dear to my father, or that they together designed a city just for a jealous Aten.

"I must go," I say, taking my aunt's hands. I wish I could do something for her, but it is nighttime, and I must go to my lord and love. "Shall we have breakfast on the lake tomorrow?"

"That would be lovely," she says, straightening the pleat of my sheer pink robe. I hug her tightly, with a prayer to the Great Mother whispering in my heart. Something wonderful must happen for Mutnojme, and soon. I know of no woman who deserves it more.

I leave my guard at Tutankhamun's doors, entering his incense-filled chambers with an anxious smile. Suddenly, I am struck with a terrible vision.

Ipay has swung the doors open, to reveal the smoky room where my husband is laid out straight across his bed. His left leg is propped up on cushions, his foot is tightly bandaged, and Pentju hovers over him like a winged Isis. I lose my breath at once, and I don't know why. It's nothing I haven't seen before-obviously, he's in pain again. But the tableau before me is somehow horrifying, as if demons were whispering in my ears as I look upon it.

"Tutankhamun!" I cry, sweeping past Ipay. I fall onto his bed and he turns to me, his eyes drugged and clouded.

"*Hapepy.*" His smile shows his exhaustion, and it's heartbreaking to see him in such pain.

"When did this happen?" I ask, stroking his cheeks.

"It's nothing, just a little ache."

"It is not nothing. He'll need six weeks, Your Majesty," Pentju tells me. "Three in bed, three on a crutch, and no exceptions. If my lord," he adds, looking to Tutankhamun, "you actually plan to fight and hunt again." Pentju shakes his head and says, "Though you should not. By pushing yourself so hard, you are undoubtedly hastening the day I have foretold."

Tutankhamun makes a disgusted little sigh in his throat, and waves his physician off.

Pentju performs his deep, subservient bow, and backs out of the chambers, his leathery old hands clutching his medicine bag before him. I turn back to Tutankhamun. "Shall I leave you?"

"No..." he whispers, running his cold fingers lightly over my wrist. He looks up at me with entreating eyes. "I need you now."

I bow over Tutankhamun and kiss his soft lips. And then I stand, and go around his bed loosening the gold threaded curtains. While he watches through that gauzy veil, I untie my beaded sash and shrug my gown off my shoulders. I slip inside the canopy, and lay down beside him.

One week after that, I stand on the balcony staring at the brilliant stars rising in the summer sky. The flooded lake has spilled over into the gardens of Malkata; it's as if the entire world was submerged in the Nile, and our palace alone is on an island. It is the highest flood of Tutankhamun's reign, perhaps too high.

I hold my hands over my stomach, trying to remember what it felt like when my first baby quickened. It is getting quite late for that reassuring sign, I think, and it's frightening. But I realize, day by day, that I can't remember anything from that year but panic and sorrow. It's as if this child is my first, and I'm an innocent again. Was that popping I just felt, like little fish blowing bubbles in the river, the first tiny kick? Is Tutankhamun's child-our child-well?

I pass through the billowing curtains in the doorway, and walk through the narrow, guarded hallway into Tutankhamun's

329

inner chamber. I hear Lord Hani's low, silky voice before the two spearmen at the door admit me. The towering gilded doors swing open. Tutankhamun lies in bed, enthroned in richly embroidered pillows, his long opium pipe to his lips. The northern ambassador leans over the bed with a stick of flame, watching as the brown, sticky resin crackles and sparks in the fire.

Tutankhamun flickers his shining black eyes to me. He breathes out the potent smoke, and it rises and curls over his dark face. He offers a half-smile, a smile strangled by pain, gesturing with his sharp chin that I should come to him. I curl up beside him as he looks back to Hani, murmuring, "What about the generals?"

"I could not turn any of them, my lord. They are Prince Aitakama's men. Many have Hittite brides and financial ties to the Hittite court. But Prince Nikkmadu despises his brother, and the Hittites who slaughtered his father. He is prepared to deal with Egypt. I cannot promise that he will deal faithfully, or that he won't provoke the Hittites to invade again. In fact, I cannot promise that the Hittites won't find a way to retaliate, Mitanni wars or no."

A small, angular smile creeps at the corners of Tutankhamun's lips, a carnivore's grin. "So you say for sure that there is finally enough discord sewn in Kadesh to strike," Tutankhamun prompts, his words languid and slippery from so much opium. My lips part in shock. Strike? He is bedridden, unable to ride his horse or even walk about his palace!

The graceful ambassador makes a pretty little gesture of uncertainty. "It is always a gamble, Majesty. But yes, there is enough discord to strike, and if Aitakama is taken hostage, we can be sure that Nikkmadu will have enough support to usurp his place."

"Take Aitakama hostage?" Tutankhamun hisses, scowling. "Why should I allow him to live? He is my avowed enemy!"

"My lord, Nikkmadu is young and ill-tempered, and his loyalty is far from proven. The threat of Aitakama's release will give us enough leverage over Nikkmadu to keep him dancing to an Egyptian tune."

Tutankhamun nods. "All right, Lord Hani. I am satisfied. I shall call the council to my chambers tomorrow. You will be here, to impress upon them the dangers of Aitakama's duplicity. You know the old viziers want Egypt to take a passive role in world events. More than anything, they want me to spend my wealth on the trade and infrastructure projects that make them rich. You must make them fear Aitakama more than the cost of war."

Another war... I clench my hands together, bowing my head until Tutankhamun dismisses Hani. I open my mouth to speak, but Tutankhamun sits up and swings his legs over the side of the bed. His sculpted jaw tightens as he sets his hurt foot on the cold floor, as he denies his pain and makes his way to his wall-mounted sword. He snatches it off the wall, and sits back down. His fingers caress the black and gold hilt as if it were a lover.

"Tutankhamun..." I say, shaking my head.

He holds his sword up, and pulls the hooked blade halfway out of the sheath. The bronze metal flashes in the firelight, reflecting in his hard black gaze. "Father lost Kadesh more than ten years ago, *hapepy*. Aitakama is the lawful prince-mayor of Kadesh, but he is nothing more than a Hittite dog. And you know, from our studies of geography: he who holds Kadesh can control all of the Biqa Valley." He closes the sword with a metallic sheer and click, and meets my eyes. "It is time for me to take back Kadesh."

"When?" I ask, heartsick.

Tutankhamun lays his strong hand on my small, round belly. "After our baby is born."

Chapter Twenty-Four

Two weeks later, the current bears us steadily towards Memphis. We sail past Denderah and Abydos, Akhmim of Ay's family and Asyut. It isn't too long before the land spreads out into the enormous vineyards and farms owned by the old Amarna barons, and the familiar eastern cliffs begin their steady march back to the river.

"You want to play *senet* in the cabin?" Tutankhamun asks, slipping his hand around my waist.

I turn in his arms and bury my face in his chest. "I did that last time," I say. "It has been many years... I am not afraid to look on it anymore."

"I'm glad to hear it," he says solemnly.

Slowly, on the great looming cliffs which nearly blot the sun, I see the deep, eternal engravings growing larger by the hour. At the boundary of Amarna, a sweeping, abstracted portrait of my father, my mother, and my two eldest sisters, was hammered into the sandstone just before my birth. Brave as I thought I was, when this looms ahead I pull Tutankhamun's arms around me and slide up against him, as if his embrace could protect me from the ghosts of memory.

And truly, the administrative heart of Amarna is a ghost city. The Central City is like an abandoned necropolis. There are no torches flaming in the palace harbor, no warm, dancing saucers of flame glowing from the high palace windows. The wind howls mournfully through the empty stone mansions. I close my eyes and hear the whispered laughter of my sisters, the roar of my father's banquets. I can hear the sweet music that filled the city each night. And then, as if it were all coming to life again, a glow rises from the Great Temple of Aten.

"What is that, Tutankhamun?"

"Meri-Re should be beginning the sunset service now," he says quietly.

I turn in his arms and exclaim, "Meri-Re is still here? Worshipping Aten?"

Tutankhamun nods soberly. The sight of his birthplace has brought a shadow to his eyes as well. "The simple folk stayed on, the fishermen and farmers... The mayor, Chief Mahu and the police, and a handful of noblemen stayed behind, for official reasons. And Meri-Re stayed, to worship Aten in his temple. Where else would he go, Ankhesenamun? Where else could he go?"

We reach the northern borders of Amarna as the sun begins to set. "Tell them to keep going," Tutankhamun commands his captain. "Push into dusk; we can tie down for the night once we've cleared the city."

The captain bows, but I see he is uneasy to navigate the shifting Nile in poor light. Tutankhamun and I decide to retire to his stateroom for a while, so that we can both escape the heavy sights. And then, as I follow his careful steps up the cedar staircase, I stop suddenly and gasp, "I finally felt it!"

Tutankhamun turns to me with alarm. "Felt what?"

I laugh with sweet relief. "Your son lives," I breathe, touching my round belly as Tutankhamun's eyes widen. "Our baby is alive. He is kicking me. Hard!"

Tutankhamun toys absently with a gilded walking stick, spinning it with his palms and anxiously looking towards the door. Finally, the boy comes into Pharaoh's chambers, and I hardly recognize him. He is shaved, for one thing, and in decent linen. He is no fisherman, part time spearman now.

He is a public official, a tax collector. The youth from Amarna drops into a deep position of obeisance, and Tutankhamun lets him remain there for a long moment, more than he would for any courtier. "Rise. Show us what you have brought."

The youth drops his bag, and produces scrolls. "These are from Shadi. I cannot write, Divinity."

"We shall change that."

He bows again, and passes the small scrolls to Tutankhamun. Tutankhamun notes the plain wax seal, and passes them to me. And then the young man begins to speak, and his tale is astonishing. "There are at least twenty of them, Majesty," he says, "All from good farming families. They steal and assault the people, but they do not keep what they steal for themselves. We believe they have been hired to work this evil."

"How do you know this?" Tutankhamun demands.

"Because some of them have loose tongues in the beer house. We have done Your Majesty's will, fully, and been useful to these criminals."

Tutankhamun nods, pleased.

"There is something else, Your Majesty," the boy says, now obviously pleased with himself. "One of us was able to witness a hand-off, something more precious than grain, maybe bronze *deben*. He gave it to a man on the *Kenbet*, I am sure."

"How are you sure?" Tutankhamun asks. I am sure I see the pulse in his throat quicken.

"Because my friend... He had gone to court for a dispute over some cattle he found and kept. He knew the face."

Tutankhamun raises his eyebrows at this dubious excuse, but he says, "Very good. I hope to read it all here, with more detailed information, and names."

"Shadi hopes-we all hope-Divinity will find these writings most useful."

"Excellent," Tutankhamun says. He produces a heavy leather sack that rings metallic, and tosses it at the boy. When the peasant is gone, he looks at me and says, "As I thought. Egypt will not tolerate this corruption any longer."

Chapter Twenty-Five

In the days before my confinement, Tutankhamun stays by my side. Then, as he watches on, Tanefrit my midwife proclaims that I must move to the beautiful pavilion just annexed to the palace. "Do you feel it, Your Majesty?" she asks. "The baby has dropped."

"I know," I say, with more confidence than I feel.

"What does that mean?" Tutankhamun asks, helping me sit up.

"It means your baby is getting ready to meet his father," I say, and Tutankhamun cannot help himself, he clutches my hand in a rush of excitement and kisses it.

"I won't leave you. Not until your women chase me out."

Tanefrit hisses a low *tsk* of disapproval, making Tutankhamun smile. He rests his cheek on my belly, and as I stroke the soft crop of his shaved hair, he sings a song of the river to his baby in a low voice. And then, grinning at me, he commands the baby, "Be good to your mother, little one, or I shall know why."

I watch from my feathered bed as my loose gowns are packed into woven baskets, as my gold and ivory combs and hand mirrors and my gilded glass perfume bottles are loaded onto trays. I sigh heavily and look up at Tutankhamun. "It's really happening, isn't it?"

He laughs and rests his hand on my ripe belly. "Yes, *hapepy*. Our child is coming soon."

"I hope I don't disappoint you," I say in a small, fearful voice. No matter how confident I am, how pleased to give Tutankhamun a child, I can never forget the trauma of having, and losing, my little girl.

"Ankhesenamun, you could never disappoint me! But we mustn't speak this way. The goddesses of Egypt will attend you; you mustn't forget it."

"And afterwards, you will go to war," I say, folding my hands over my stomach.

"Yes," he says quietly. "But not for so long as Nubia." He looks down for a moment, deciding if he wants to tell me more. "It's expensive to stay in the field. In Nubia, we paid with the gold we captured. Asia is not so rich, and their harvests have been poor lately. So, we're planning a quick strike, and we're going to take the city and the prince before a thousand talents are spent. You'll see. And you'll have our child to keep you company while I'm gone."

I nod, biting my lip, worrying over anything I possibly can. "And what about… your other matter?"

Tutankhamun waits until Henutawy and Akila carry the last basket out, and then he murmurs, "I'm going to wait until I return from Asia. Then I will have them arrested, and questioned."

"Couldn't Lord Ay finish your investigation?" He is the Minister of Justice.

"I don't need him yet. I'm going to catch them myself. Besides, he'll go through his office, and if anyone in his office is in on the scheme, they'll find a way to slip away from justice. That's why I'm going through Horemhab, and my own private agents. I'm sure Horemhab doesn't deal with any man who'd be involved in something like this."

A crash outside my room makes me jump in fear. My little maids have dropped my golden tray, and shattered my perfume jars onto the floor. "Easy," Tutankhamun says, stroking my cheek and smoothing my hair. He scowls at the girl when she enters my bedroom, bobbing a little bow of apology.

I begin to ask another nervous question, and he lays his fingers over my lips. "Enough. It is my business, and you must have strength for yours. I love you, *hapepy*."

I smile softly, just as my head midwife Tanefrit enters my room. "Are you ready to go, Your Majesty?"

I laugh a little, nervously, and let Tutankhamun help me from my bed. "As I'll ever be, I suppose," I say. "Take me to my pavilion."

I open my eyes slowly, awakened by the sweet trilling of the birds. The warm summer wind is lush with perfume from a thousand flowers. I stay in bed for a decadently long moment, my senses overwhelmed with luxury. This morning, everything is right in the world; I feel perfect tranquility. Soon enough, though, I realize that it wasn't the songbirds at all, but my own body that woke me.

I sit up from my lusciously soft bed of goose feather-stuffed mattresses and quilts, changed daily at great expense. My bed is large and carved from ebony, with the Eye of Horus engraved on head and foot to ward off evil. A statue of the ugly little dwarf god Bes stands near the door, to frighten away any evil spirits meaning to harm me or my child. Gold statues of Mut and Tawaret stand on pillars of ebony. My walls are marsh scenes also showing the animals sacred to the goddesses of childbirth. There is even an ibis, sacred to Thoth, wading in the thickets of green reeds painted onto my walls. It is all very pretty, like a story actually, and Tutankhamun has entertained me for days by telling me myths of the goddesses and their many divine children. Now he sleeps in certain discomfort in a low-backed chair, his head resting awkwardly on his knuckles.

"Tutankhamun," I call softly, and he blinks drowsily then brightens like the day to see me. I nod my head, and tell him, "I think our baby wants to meet you today."

Chapter Twenty-Six

My midwife and her three apprentices finally chase Pharaoh out of the pavilion, to my utter relief. He might not think I was so lovely, nor any woman, should he see the horror of women's work! Tutankhamun declares it is a foolish tradition. "Am I not a warrior, myself? I would not fear my wife's battles, but hold her hand through them!"

I can only think of that first time-the splashes of blood, my sweat soaked hair and sobbing face... I shake my head. "It is for women, only."

"I will be just outside," Tutankhamun whispers, relenting. He kisses me and goes out. When he is gone, I sigh deeply, and turn to my midwife. She is far younger than old Nani was, but she has borne thirteen of her own and brought hundreds more into the world. It is only now, with my husband on the other side of the door, that I ask anxiously, "Do you think it will be very much like last time?"

While the apprentices and maids ready my bath, Tanefrit tells me, "Second children can come much faster, Your Majesty. Much faster, and much easier. And it has been some six years, has it not?"

"I am not so much bigger," I tell her quietly. My delicate body is a curse for a woman who desires many children, and I am in terror from memories of my first baby. I am even haunted by the life changing accident at my own birth. Truly, this women's work is a dreadful business.

Tanefrit nods her head, but tells me, "There is a great difference between seventeen and eleven, Your Majesty. You shall see: this baby will come with much less struggle."

By midday, Mutnojme's joined us, dampening my brow with lavender water for my labor is already strong. The pain is nauseating. I cling to the ropes as if clinging to life itself, and Tutankhamun's child bears down hard and fast, eager to greet the world. By golden afternoon, in one last dizzying contraction, my baby is born.

I tip my head back and gasp. Mutnojme strokes my sweaty hair and my cheeks and tells me I have done it. I look down between my slim, bloody thighs, where Tanefrit holds up a big, hardy baby.

"A boy! A prince of Egypt!" Mutnojme cries in delight. Tears of joy rush down my cheeks. In moments, my son gives an angry, howling cry to complain of his ordeal, and I laugh through my tears at the strength in his scream.

"Is he healthy?" I cry, as I sit back and Tanefrit lays him on my chest. "Is he? Will he live? Is he healthy? Tell me!"

"He is a fine prince," Tanefrit proclaims, placing the bundle of this new person, my child, into my arms.

"He is so warm…" I say, cradling my new baby son. His cries quiet, and he peers up at my face with cloudy black eyes. His tan skin deepens and reddens with his first breaths, and I see he will be as dark and pretty as his father. I turn to Mutnojme. "Go tell Tutankhamun…" I begin, but my breath is ragged on my words. I realize suddenly that the pain between my legs has not gone away as it should. I look to the midwife, to tell her that I must be cleaned up to receive my husband, but a deep chill runs through me first and steals my words.

My little boy is taken from me, and I fall against the back of the chair. I hear Tanefrit say something about blood, but

I am suddenly too tired to care. I slump down, and fall into darkness.

I wake halfway in the night, so weak that the world is a haze around me. Tanefrit's apprentices take away dozens of linen strips soaked in my blood. Tanefrit presses her hands into my belly, making me cringe. It takes all my strength to ask, "Will I die now?"

I hear Mutnojme's voice, and her fingers brush my forehead. "No, you'll be fine! And you are blessed! You have given Pharaoh a healthy prince. But you must sleep now, and grow strong for them both."

"A hemorrhage. Just like my mother," I say, numb. "This means I can have no more children."

"No, Your Majesty, you are fortunate," Tanefrit says, "You should heal completely, but you must take care-"

I gasp in relief. I wipe my tears and steady my breath. "How is my baby?"

The midwife brightens. "Much plumper today, greedy for his wet-nurse, and his cry is strong. You may see him now."

"I will braid her hair first," Mutnojme interrupts, and I smile and wipe my eyes again.

I sit up carefully, propped by thick, soft cushions. Mutnojme also brings me a finer chamber robe, embroidered with flowers and gold thread. I wash my face in rosewater. She puts my heavy gold earrings back in my ears, and brushes cream on my lips so they shine. Finally, I am perfumed, and my ladies open the doors of the pavilion.

In moments, I see Tutankhamun coming carefully up the bright garden path. He holds our son closely, and I can see that he is whispering something to the baby. I know I am crying again. My fingers touch my lips, and then settle on my throat. This is certainly some beautiful dream. Tutankhamun comes in from the sun and breathes to me, "He is perfect. Thank you."

Tutankhamun sits on my bed, smelling of heavy frankincense. He passes our baby into my arms, and I love my son all over again, instantly. His black eyes dominate his sweet face, and his perfectly bowed lips curl into a yawn. A fine crop of black hair crowns his little head, peeking out of his swaddling as soft as feathers. "He is just like you. And so heavy!" I say with a breathy laugh of delight.

"He's strong," Tutankhamun responds with pride. "You gave me a fine son, like I knew you would. I want to use the name."

"Tuthmosis?" I ask shyly, flushed from his praise.

"It is fitting," he tells me quietly, and then he cups my chin in his palm. He lifts my face up gently and gives me a deep kiss. Tutankhamun puts his face against mine, and he whispers again, "Prince Tuthmosis. He is a perfect miracle, Ankhesenamun. Thank you."

Chapter Twenty-Seven

For two months, Tutankhamun and I spend much of our time in sweet, quiet bliss, wrapped up in his big bed with our son. Tuthmosis is as pretty as a gem, and he has us spellbound. Other than his rather quiet naming feast on the second day after I came back to the main palace, and Tutankhamun's daily obligations, we huddle in warmth and soft laughter in Pharaoh's chambers. I remember all the old precautions spat out by Nani: the lives of babies are uncertain, so it's best not to give your whole heart away in those early years. But it doesn't matter. Tutankhamun and I are the most adoring of parents, and our son stole our hearts from the first moment. Tuthmosis is the first child of our love, and we will honor him always.

But time falls away, even if I would cling to these beautiful days forever. If only the world go just go *on* for once, and leave us in peace! It seems that is the price that Tutankhamun and I must pay for our bliss; we can have each other, and now our son, but the world will always intrude and snatch at our time.

On a cool early winter day, Tutankhamun and I give our son over to the care of the Chief of Nurses, Sennedjem, the brother of Tutankhamun's trusted tutor Senqed. I cringe to let him go, even though he is still in the arms of his wet nurse, a priestess's daughter who will attend him for his entire youth. Immediately, as we ascend the royal barge-draped to signify

Pharaoh's departure for battle-I notice that my head is light, as if I were panicking again, but without any fear. Later, I notice it returns even when I am sitting. I am glad my midwife insisted on coming along with us. When I tell her of my symptoms, she says she foresaw this, because I lost so much blood, and promptly gives me an array of herbal teas, with a continued recommendation for as much rich meat and red wine as I can swallow. When we lay over for the night in a Delta town, my husband cuts calf liver for my plate, as I stare on with my lips curled up at the over-rich smell.

"Eat it..." he says quietly, more of a plea than a command "For you little body, for your health."

"It will make me sick, not healthy!" I protest, shaking my head.

"Maybe your belly, but not your blood. Eat."

In Tjanet I see my first of the great Byblos ships, long, deep hulled vessels with high sails and endless rows of oars, as they are hauled with care out of the dry dock and launched into the seaward channel. The harbor is filled with cries of laborers, hauling provisions aboard the enormous vessels. The fresh smell of newly cut cedar permeates the salty air. Just beyond the canal, the green sea shimmers like a mirage on the horizon and infects the marshes with brackish water. Hard wind whips the curtains around my half-shaded litter, northern wind that smells of winter storms. Horemhab is certain they can make a run for the coast, just before the seas ought to remain closed. They are all too brave. Nakhtmin boasts that they will fall on Kadesh like screaming eagles.

After Tutankhamun brings me along to inspect the ships-which we do briefly, with a scene, as all the workers fall into prostration-we retire into the fortress.

The noises of the street penetrate through the thick sandstone of Fort Tjanet's walls, and they go on into the night. Young Djede, who will be Nakhtmin's driver in Asia, has been named an assistant horse master, and given the task of seeing the cavalry ready to sail. The horses are loaded, neighing and screaming onto the ships, their cries echoing across the canals of the city with the shouts of their handlers. Djede's men will load the chariots as well, while the charioteers roam the city in droves, spending their wealth in the many bars and pleasure houses surrounding the coastal garrison. The laughter of prostitutes echoes through the streets as they troll about outside the fortress' walls looking for drunken officers. The infantry is here as well, though they have hardly any wealth at all, and they content themselves with gallons of Pharaoh's beer, unmarried town girls or what wives have followed them; they hold raucous bonfire parties on the outskirts of the city limits that infect the air with smoke, drumming, and the trilling calls of merrymaking women.

Deep in the Commander's House, I shyly push my warm robe down before the burning bronze brazier. Tutankhamun kisses my neck, his hands trailing down my bare arms. The night slips away against us, full of drums and wild cries that swirl around us, and the heady fragrant scent of Tutankhamun's deep bronze skin. He is insatiable after being forbidden from my bed for two months, and I don't want to waste a moment of our only true night together on empty sleep.

In the greying light, after our last lingering kiss, Tutankhamun climbs from bed. Still wet from his bath and oiled from his prayers, he suits up into ceremonial armor. I clip his falcon wing corselet into place and straighten the line of his white cloak, and then I burst into tears.

"Shh, shh," Tutankhamun murmurs, putting his arms around me. The gold covering his body is cold against my bare skin, and something about this feeling is suddenly hateful to me. I shiver and grip Tutankhamun tighter as he promises, "I'll be back before you know it."

"No," I breathe, closing my eyes. "Don't go."

"Shh," he whispers, rocking me softly. "I'm going and you know it. And you must be my regent, my strong and beautiful regent, watching over our home while I am away. This is our duty, and we do not hide away from duty. We are strong, you and I, strong and brave."

I nod against his chest. He tells me we'll be under the same stars at night, and he slips one of his golden rings from his finger and puts it in my hands, a gold ring with a round black stone. I hang an amulet around his neck, a *Wadjet*, the Eye of Horus, in glowing blue-green glass, engraved with words to keep him safe day and night.

We sacrifice and burn incense for his departure. Tutankhamun joins the thousands of other soldiers waiting on his great fleet of ships. I am proud, and I am agonized to be alone again, but this is what I am learning the life of a Great Royal Wife of Egypt must be. The young eastern light shines off Pharaoh's flagship as it pushes through the canal, and launches out to sea.

Chapter Twenty-Eight

As soon as we return to Memphis, I know that I'm pregnant again. I am overjoyed, but my midwife isn't pleased a bit.

"You'd best mind your health, Your Majesty. You're not nearly recovered yet, and you've complained of dizzy spells the whole way home from the coast. You are a small, delicate woman, who's had two traumatic births already..."

"But I feel much better *now* Tanefrit!" I look to Mutnojme for support, but her smile does not reach her eyes. No, how could it? She in her mid-twenties, of an age to have a great big boy or girl, yet she has nothing, no thanks to Ay and Horemhab! "If I have a girl, I'll name her Mutnojme, for my beautiful aunt and the goddess both."

My aunt purses her lips together again, an attempt to share my joy, but I fear her sorrow is very great indeed.

At night, Mutnojme accompanies me into the great hall. The high table is set, but Tutankhamun's throne is empty, and the hall seems so quiet now without his boasting warriors. The men who remain behind seem diminished for it, sitting in their little cliques and talking of nothing else but advancement or gossip. I am desperately lonely, and rather sore at the duties of loving a warrior-king.

I pluck candied dates from a blue faience dish, listening to Iset's mother prattling about the cost of tiles for her new loggia. Bored, I look about, my eyes falling on the Vizier of Lower Egypt, Intef, who sits with a pack of treasury men and mining officials around him. He the sort of fat man that scribe-types like to show themselves as in statue, plump under fine pleated linen and a great broad collar of malachite. His wife is too young for him, only a few years into womanhood but obviously content with her old husband's fortune. Henna shines in her hair and turquoise on her wrists, and her high, haughty laughter drifts through the hall, carrying an artificial ring.

"Lady Iniuia. Iset says she's intolerable, like a little desert rat clutching at anything shiny," Mutnojme murmurs, noticing my direction. "Much like Iset's own mother."

"Charming," I murmur. And then I look away from them and ask, "Is Iset almost ready to deliver?"

"Any day," Mutnojme confirms. "The poor thing can't get a moment's rest."

"Really? Why not? I wanted nothing but rest when my time approached."

Mutnojme smiles faintly. "She is cleaning everything in her mansion, herself. She's compelled to it. Iset's convinced her servants aren't doing a good enough job. But remember, she was like that with the other two right before they came."

In moments, Lady Teye approaches the table with a gracious bow. I indicate one of the empty chairs beside me. "Your Majesty, how do you do this evening?"

"Very well, Lady Teye," I say with a smile. "It is still quite early, but I believe Pharaoh and I shall have another child."

Teye's is astonished, as I thought she would be. My son is but a little over three months old. My own mother, with six healthy children, did not do so well! "Congratulations, Your Majesty," she offers me, bowing her head again. "Will you write to Pharaoh now, or wait until a few more weeks have passed?"

I laugh, leaning close enough in confidence to smell her modestly applied perfume. "Oh, I have written, Lady Teye.

There are no secrets between us, and he will forgive the error if that is what it is. But my midwife says so, and I know it for sure."

She wishes me health, and tells me that it seems Egypt will be blessed with princes. I'm grateful for her well wishes; yet though Teye is never anything but respectful, I sense that she thinks of me as a child still, even though I have lived as a woman for eight years now. There's something in the way she looks at me that makes me think she is comparing me to my mother always, something that makes me think she doesn't like me very much, even though I am her mistress. I offended her when I made Mutnojme the head of my chambers, I am sure. I muse idly what I might do to pay her some respect and mend any mistrust between us.

The treasurer Maya enters the hall late, his young bride on his arm. Like Intef's wife, she is startlingly young. "Look how lovely Lady Merit's linen is, Mutnojme," Teye observes archly. "Oh, and her necklace is Baltic amber, how fine. The Lord Treasurer must have given it to her when she bore him a son."

Maya and Merit take their seats at Teye's table, alongside Vizier Ay and the High Priest of Ptah, Iset's father. If Tutankhamun were here, they'd all be at his side, crammed in around his warriors and throwing dice. As it is, they are presently the most powerful men in Egypt, and a steady stream of noblemen and servants flock to and from their table.

"I don't regret turning him down, Auntie. I don't care if he's bought her the Baltic Sea."

"Your Majesty," Teye says, turning to me, "perhaps you will convince her to accept her family's assistance in seeing her married well before it's too late. Not only could she have offended a powerful man with such a vehement refusal, I am afraid my niece will live and die childless."

I press my lips together slightly as Mutnojme stiffens beside me. If only Teye knew the truth! Mutnojme has already lost her child, and I can feel her grief rise quickly.

"Perhaps if I had not been denied the man of my choice, you wouldn't be so worried!" She cries, turning a few heads.

"Let us have some more wine, ladies," I interrupt quickly, beckoning a servant girl. I look sideways at Lady Teye, surprised at her for making such a public scene. Her power and position have numbed her sensibilities. But I have had enough of this hurtful talk. I drape my hands lightly over my flat belly, hoping that my joy doesn't give Mutnojme sorrow. I cannot imagine her position, and I pity it, as much as I disagreed with her for starting the affair. She cannot marry Horemhab, at least not until Ay is dead, which could be years; but how will she ever have the eyes to see another man, when her sight is so full of the peasant general? And what man would want her when she's obviously in love with another, even if she won't admit it anymore? I fear that Teye is right after all, and Mutnojme will miss her chance to have a family.

I spend all my days with her that winter, passing our time sailing and gossiping in my garden. My aunt holds her sorrow very close to her chest, always keeping my rooms merry so that I do not dwell on missing Tutankhamun, always calling for music and wine and song. We attend the naming feast of Iset's new daughter; we attend the season's holy festivals and bless crops in the fields. And all the while, my son accompanies me with his nurse, and Tutankhamun's next child grows strong in my belly.

Of course, I must do my duties for the land. I exchange letters with the chief wives of the rulers of Byblos and Assyria, and I host visiting ambassadors. I sit in the audience chamber every so often, so that the lords might remember my presence, and I grant what petitions I can without deferring to Lord Ay. Between my appearances in the audience chamber, Lady Teye comes to see me every few days with her husband's written summaries of his work.

Lord Ay supervises Egypt while Tutankhamun is away, as he did before. He does not perform any rituals for the gods, nor fill any of Pharaoh's sacred offices. Even if he could the priests would not want it; for all his grandiose dreams of deification, Lord Ay is, as they say most respectfully, a man of the mortal realm. Truthfully, he switches his faith as he easily as he would switch a creased kilt, and no one really believes he offers to the gods with any sincerity. The only temples Lord Ay frequents are those most influential in Egypt; both the High Priest of Ptah here in Memphis and Lord Paranefer of Karnak are his customary dinner companions and the talk is purely business.

But there is no better man to minister to the thousand intricacies of ruling a mighty nation. I decide that I must see what he does, and so I stroll down with Lady Teye unannounced one day. I remember my mother doing this, usually with Mayati in tow. They would go about the palace enclosure, bringing small gifts like wine or honeyed date candies rolled in crushed nuts; this way they could see for themselves how Father's servants were employed throughout the day. This was long ago, before the nightmares of the plague, before my family fell to pieces.

"Your Majesty!" Lord Ay says. A range of surprised emotions flicker behind the polite mask on his face. I stand before him in a fine pleated gown, thick, beaded at the wide sleeves and hem, my curls pinned up around a golden diadem with a protective cobra on my brow. Henutawy presents golden wine from the northeast Delta, and Ay insists that we all share some. Naturally, he says, "But of course, you must forgive me. Had you come to my townhouse, we could drink in the loggia, but here I am at work."

He claps his hands and sends his servants scuffling out of his antechamber. There are papers everywhere. Maps lay open across a great mahogany table, detailed maps of the districts of Egypt, a long topographical map of Asia from the Negev in the south down to the wild, mountainous lands bordering the Hittite kingdom. Gilded boxes at both ends of his wide desk hold neat piles of scrolls, and one lies open beside his ink dish. Dozens of brushes wait, and the seals and stamps of his office stand in a neat row.

"Where is Kadesh?" I ask, looking over the enormous maps.

Ay walks around the table, plucking up a pointer of thin cedar capped in gold. "On the Orontes River," he says, indicating hilly land above a long valley on the loop of a river. In the background, I hear Henutawy pouring the wine into cups. "There is a good, flat plain to the west, and I imagine Pharaoh will make his camp behind it."

"Do they take the water of their river into the city? It seems to surround them." If they can draw on the river, the siege will last longer.

Lord Ay smiles and says, "Perhaps they do now. It's been some time since I've gone soldiering, Your Majesty. Of course, it is easy enough to debase a river, but that is a most unpleasant task."

I pinch my lips in disdain. "And are the Hittites far away? My husband said he would fight the men of Kadesh and perhaps some of their Syrian allies, but not Hittites."

"The Hittite king Suppililiuma is occupied with fighting to the east. During your father's reign, the great kingdom of Mitanni fell to the Hittites. But a resistance has formed in these late years, and so the Hittites have been kept occupied."

I look over the map, noting how Kadesh garrisons an immense natural highway called the Biqa Pass. Goods and armies that wish to avoid the more heavily traveled, and tariffed, coastal trade-routes can move down the gentle, fertile valley with ease. That fertile valley is a breadbasket for any army as well. "Will the Hittites retaliate when my husband seizes Kadesh and the puppet prince?" It seems that the two armies, Egyptian and Hittite, are not so terribly far apart. I clutch my chest softly; the Hittites were told to be monsters when I was a child. Tutankhamun should not fight them yet, while he's still so green.

"We shall make all efforts to settle the matter diplomatically," Ay says. "Kadesh has been an Egyptian possession for some two hundred years. It would be best if we made some deal with them, once we are again in a position of strength."

Finished with the map-and really, with Ay as well-I turn quickly. But I turned too fast; I think I saw the old vizier's gaze settled on my... on my hips... but I can't be sure. Horrified but unable to discover the truth, I dissemble; I look away and pretend I didn't see anything. I convince myself that I was mistaken. I look to Teye, and she offers a hard, bright smile, which surely she wouldn't if her husband had been leering at me... My fingers stray over the tiny rise in my belly, as if I could protect the baby from offense. When I look up at Ay, he smiles politely. His subservient bow makes him look very much like a loyal old servant again. "Henutawy," I say quietly, motioning for my servant to follow me. "Good day, Lord Ay, Lady Teye."

I return to my chambers in silence, horrified that after all these years and almost two children my hands are trembling once again.

Chapter Twenty-Nine

My pregnancy progresses easily into the harvest. With my son at my side, Mutnojme as a companion, and rallying letters from my husband, the days are warm and pleasant. My back aches sometimes, and the baby is a little dancer, always flipping about and kicking me. We laugh to feel his tiny heels thump our palms, no one as loud as little Tuthmosis, who is sitting and nearly crawling. Oh, if only Tutankhamun were with us!

Iset brings her children sometimes, and still I take more little toddlers into our royal school. I appoint an apprentice tutor as well, to help Senqed. And because I cannot help myself, I drag Mutnojme down to the harbor when I learn that the harem girl, her daughter, and other ladies are going to sail. The little princess walks alongside her mother, her black curls bouncing on her shoulders. She carries her little head proudly, as if she knew she was destined to play some great part in the world. "She is graceful already," I murmur. Her mother seems slightly older than me, perhaps twenty-two, and she is a curvy, earthy beauty.

But then I lose my breath. The tall, midnight black Nubian princess, wearing immaculate white linen and gold, carries a child as well, a little boy, a prince of Nubia and Egypt. He is only a few months older than Tuthmosis, with his thumb in his mouth, and Tutankhamun's eyes in a deep brown face. Lucky boy, who will have no rivals in this tiny court! Tutankhamun's

Nubian son will already have his throne, the empty throne of his defeated grandfather. "They are so beautiful," I say quietly.

"I should have known," Mutnojme laments. "I found out about his daughter easily enough, but I should have known there was a boy as well. But since you and he... I didn't even imagine there was another woman pregnant."

Palm over my own belly, I laugh. "It really doesn't matter. They are beautiful children, as I said. They are mine, too, in a way, and so I am glad for it." I am not like my mother, to scheme on and oppress my husband's other children!

"But there are no little ones," Mutnojme observes, pleased to claim this small victory for me.

"No, I see that."

"No, I want the gold. Gold for my harvest baby." I point to the gown, blended throughout with thread of gold and sparkling in the light from the high latticed windows. "And with that I want the amber perfume, and the thick gold bangles with the granulated edges and flower patterns."

My servant women rush about, packing my things into woven baskets and light wooden trunks once more. Mutnojme and Teye put their quarrel aside to assist me as I supervise the move to my Memphis pavilion, where our second child will be born sometime in the next two weeks. Once we arrive, we eat and drink as everything is put to order. The two room birth house, pillared all around and sweet with garden breezes from wide northern windows is immaculately fresh. It differs from the Malkata house where my son was born only in the deep purple curtains I had made with the dye Tutankhamun sent me from Tyre. The same protective goddesses make their appearances everywhere, in statuary and in the animals sacred to them on the painted walls. And I have given thanks and offerings to all of them, brimming with gratitude for this sweet life.

In a rare moment, Teye shares a confidence with me, though

it is not one a woman wishes to hear as she prepares to give birth. "I didn't think I would have a child. For nearly nine years, nothing; but just when I thought there was no hope, my Nakhtmin came along. Oh, it was dreadful! When women say they forget the pain of birth they must be lying. I can't forget it for a moment. The goddess never blessed me again, and honestly, I am not unhappy."

"Fortunately," Lady Tanefrit says, entering the chamber, "births tend to get easier each time."

I greet my midwife happily, feeling a wash of relief to see her assistants carrying in her medicines and supplies. I am eager to get through this, to be myself again and have both of my children in my arms. I don't care which it is, a boy or a girl, so long as the baby is healthy and strong.

When Teye finally leaves, I sit back in bed, and Mutnojme braids my hair over my shoulder. It takes several hours, for all the long, thick hair I have. Just as she is setting the first bead to a braid, the marsh scene on the wall blurs before my eyes, and I fall back into my aunt's arms. "What is it? Ankhesenamun?"

I shake my head. "I don't know. I'm so dizzy! Oh-" A strong contraction tears out of my back. I know right away it isn't one of the many false pains of the past month. I gasp, grinning through the ache. "I think the baby's coming now!"

But then it isn't right. "The baby hasn't turned yet," Tanefrit tells me, a look of alarm on her face.

"What does that mean?" I demand, breathless. My third labor is coming quick and hard, and my room is just barely set up. "Should I walk?"

"No, Your Majesty," Tanefrit says. "Lie still." And then she turns to her apprentices, and tells them to let down the ropes and bring the birthing stool, and prepare what she needs to deliver the baby.

And then, it is a nightmare. For five, ten, fifteen hours my body fights itself, and fights the baby. The baby's shoulder is caught in my little hips, because it wasn't in the right place when my body began to push it out. My screams echo off the walls until I can scream no more. I close my eyes and shake in Mutnojme's arms, unable to hold myself up another moment. Life fades and flickers once again, but before I drift away, Tanefrit gets the baby out, a girl, and she is broken, she is dead.

Chapter Thirty

"Are you sure you want to do this, Your Majesty?"

"Yes, Tanefrit," I say impatiently, standing tall as a Henutawy clasps a heavy lapis and gold collar around my neck in the pre-dawn darkness. "I must go, and I must bring my son." I glance at her from the corners of my eyes and ask, "You don't think I'm strong enough to hold him up?"

My midwife, who has not left my side in weeks, purses her lips and bows her head. "I am concerned, Your Majesty. You've not been out of bed for but a few days."

No, I haven't. But once the pain was gone, it was more from misery than weakness that I lay up day after day, trying to figure out just what I did wrong. How did I make my daughter come early? I have wondered, and sought guidance from the Great Mother, but I still can't understand it. She hadn't died; she was kicking the very morning before I lost her. Of course, trapped off in my hips for nearly a day, she couldn't survive. I press my hand over my belly and shiver, thinking of how bent up her poor back and shoulders were when Tanefrit finally delivered her, and saved my life. But then I think, my mother's midwife broke my foot, broke it so that I could never dance prettily, or walk very far; is there some curse that my daughters will have terrible births, like me? And why should that be, with who I am?

I draw a deep breath, and raise myself up. I collect my

son from his nurse, and take him by litter to the pavilion over the harbor. And then I wait, watching downriver for Tutankhamun's returning barge with all the expectant people of Memphis.

At sunrise, the peasants stand on riverbanks and pack onto the flat tops of roofs overlooking the harbor, waving palms and calling Tutankhamun's name. Flower petals rain down on the river. Cheering and laughter mixes with the pounding rhythm of the enormous drums on the shore. Tuthmosis is completely mesmerized by the celebration before him. His chubby little hands are pressed together in a suspended, forgotten clap, and he stares in awed silence at all the frantic, overjoyed people in their best and brightest clothes. I hold him tight against me, smelling the fresh lavender scent of his curls.

Then, my son jumps on my lap and squeals in delight. The barges creep slowly and steadily out of the horizon.

At the front, my husband's golden sails catch the wind and sun both. "Your *abi* is coming," I murmur in my son's ear. I have done everything to keep Tutankhamun in our baby's heart these long months. I have told him stories and shown him his father's image in stone and paint, and now my son repeats, "*Abi*," most seriously. I tighten my arms around Tuthmosis, thanking the gods for my little boy.

Suddenly, the cheering crowd goes wild, laughing and roaring with pleasure. Tutankhamun stands as a returning conqueror at the front of his barge, his hawk circling overhead, complete with the defeated Prince Aitakama dangling in a cage off the sidearm. The crowd shouts enthusiastically to Pharaoh and jeers his prisoner. Tuthmosis cannot understand that Tutankhamun has trussed up and abducted his enemy, but he claps his hands eagerly right along with it.

The barges dock, and Tutankhamun descends his barge amidst men bearing standards and flags, and finally, tall golden fans. He makes his way-with a polished palace guard just behind him-through an adoring crowd. But he isn't noticing of any of it. He looks up to the pavilion, to me. I catch my breath and rise, setting Tuthmosis on my hip. One look into

Tutankhamun's black eyes tells me that he received my last, tragic letter. Now he is bounding up the pavilion.

When Tutankhamun reaches me, he stops. His heart breaks in his eyes, and then he rushes to put his arms around us both. I shiver and melt into his warm embrace, crying, my cheeks staining with black kohl. "I'm so, so sorry, Tutankhamun."

"No!" he whispers fiercely. "It's not your fault. You got pregnant too quickly after you fought to have my son, it's my fault... Oh, thank the gods you are well!" His voice is broken with anxious sorrow. I press my face into his chest and grab the cloak over his back to steady myself. I'm sobbing in relief at his comfort, sheltered in his arms from the screaming, cheering masses.

"*Mawat* cry."

I gasp and look up. My son's little hand touches my face, and immediately I smile through my tears, so that he knows everything's all right.

"Let me have him, *hapepy*," Tutankhamun says. He takes his son from my arms, and then he takes my hand, and we return to the palace.

The officers cheer wildly as dancing girls rush into the banquet hall. Men laugh and boast of their victory over the rolling drums. They reunite with wives and lovers; they drink Egyptian wine and eat Egyptian food, and celebrate the victory that's made them rich in plunder and pay. Raised above it all, Tutankhamun sits at ease in his throne, picking over a gold bowl of sweet sliced melon. Vizier Ay sits at his other side, and I try in vain to forget that awful, lusty look on his face last winter. But he has no attention for me now; he furrows his brow as he tries to balance the figures Tutankhamun quoted in his head. "These bonuses-especially for the officers-will be difficult to draw from the public treasury right now, and the siege of Kadesh cost you over twelve hundred talents of gold. You currently have two temples under construction in Thebes, and Your Majesty wishes to keep the soldiers active..."

"I think you misunderstood me," Tutankhamun interrupts. "I mean to pay the infantry with *land*. Only the *seheny* will be paid from the treasury."

"Land?"

"Yes, I mean to settle them as landowners. I'm not talking vast estates, Lord Vizier, just modest tracks of irrigated land. It is a little thing to me, but for them, a farm that can carry a few tenants and be passed down to their children would mean their security. You look troubled, Lord Ay." Tutankhamun laughs and adds, "I am not taking *your* tenant farmers, am I? Perhaps I could exclude the men of Akhmim from the bonus."

"Hardly, Your Majesty," Ay says with a thin smile. "But where shall the cropland come from? It's already owned by other men."

"All the land-fertile and desert- is owned by *me*, Ay," Tutankhamun reminds him amicably.

"Forgive me, Your Majesty. What I meant to say was it is occupied by other estates. Surely, we cannot cast good men out for peasants?"

"That is a problem for Maya, not me." Tutankhamun smiles his most charming smile and says, "But of course, my friend, I will not deprive any of my most favored subjects. You are good to remind me."

Ay bows his head modestly.

"I've brought you back some of your favorite wine, from Cyprus. Did your stewards inform you?"

"Not yet, Your Majesty, but I look forward to it. I am most grateful, Your Majesty."

Down on the floor, a loud toast and cheer draws our attention. A great party of men surrounds Horemhab, soldiers and young palace officials. General Horemhab is loudly recounting a brilliant victory, retelling the story for those who lived it and those who wish they had. Horemhab has become a hero, not only highly esteemed by Tutankhamun, but by the enlisted men and officers alike. I gather that there was a glorious day on an Asian battlefield, but it must also be a bloody thing, because Tutankhamun doesn't tell me about it himself.

"I must congratulate you again, Your Majesty. The capture of Kadesh was no easy task." Ay raises his silver wine cup to Tutankhamun. "I suppose Your Majesty will want to continue to quietly fund the Mitanni resistance, to prevent the Hittites from trying to take back Kadesh, or striking somewhere else in the region?"

Tutankhamun narrows his eyes skeptically. "The old Hittite king will not ignore the loss of one of the most profitable and strategically important territories in Asia. I have ordered the garrison at Kumidi, as well as the other castles along the Way of Horus to remain battle-ready."

"But you have only just returned!" I cry, surprising them both with my unusual outburst.

Tutankhamun turns to me, his dark eyes shining. "It is a dance, *hapepy*. I take Kadesh, Suppililiuma will strike somewhere else. But when the old Hittite king launches his counter-attack, I'm not going to sit passively in Egypt as my father did. I'm going to meet his army in the field and teach him not to scheme on Egyptian territory!"

I sit back in my chair, burying my face in my wine. The Hittites were the monsters of our childhood tales. They stole Kadesh from Father years ago, they brought plague to our home, and they have thrown our family's carefully crafted Asian power structure into chaos. I don't think Egypt has ever had such a warlike, powerful enemy, and I don't want Tutankhamun to face them. "They are a dangerous people," I murmur quietly, looking at my beautiful, fearless husband.

"And I shall teach Egypt that Hittites bleed as red as anyone else," Tutankhamun declares. And then his leonine smile turns to one of honey and sweetness, and he lays his hand over mine. "But not yet."

While drums pound through the palace and parties go on all over the enclosure, Tutankhamun and I retire early to his chambers. I don't want to tell him how terrible it was, that his daughter died trapped in my hips and I almost died as well.

Wordlessly, I cling to him, pressing my palms to his, burying my face in his chest. He lifts me and carries my to the bed, and holds me in his arms as long as he can bear before his lips search out mine, and his hands pull at my loose robe. Entranced by his soft, hungry kisses and aching words, I let him wash away my sorrow. Only when we lie side by side and breathless do I think that I might get pregnant again, not but a little more than two months after losing my second daughter.

In the morning, the army marches Memphis's Royal Road in the brilliant sun, and Tutankhamun displays his prisoners and plunder for the priests of Ptah and Amun. Then, after the noblemen gather in the yard with the leaders of each platoon, Tutankhamun announces his gift of land for every infantry soldier. Pharaoh's words are drowned out by the roaring cheers of his army, but the courtiers in their pleated robes and perfumed wigs exchange wary glances. Tutankhamun is making landowners of peasants! The cheers of the soldiers merge together as they begin to chant Pharaoh's name. A satisfied smile settles on Tutankhamun's face.

Memphis erupts into festival as we enter the palace, and the smell of roasting oxen carries on the air. Once we're inside, the music and carrying on muffles behind the thick stone walls. I clutch Tutankhamun's warm arm tightly as Vizier Ay sidles up to us. "I have gathered your council in the audience chamber, as requested, Your Majesty."

"Good. But I will speak in private with you first, with you, and Maya and Horemhab. Alone."

Maya and Horemhab join us in Tutankhamun's throne room. Ay congratulates Horemhab, clapping him on the back and saying, "If I am not mistaken, you are now the greatest landowner in all of Egypt, General Horemhab. Your father would be proud of you."

"My father would be amazed," Horemhab agrees. "He was a soldier and a tenant farmer, and he never had anything to call his own but his spear and his sleeping pallet. Now I have thirty estates, and I'm planning to lay down emmer and barley of my own this winter. But truly, the soldiers are the greatest beneficiaries of Pharaoh's generosity." Horemhab bows sincerely to the throne. "I have full confidence that these worthy men will repay Your Majesty with their courage, and their blood. Together, we'll give old Suppililiuma something to fear."

Tutankhamun nods his head. "I know it. Now, I have summoned you all here to thank you for your dedicated and commendable service to me. Horemhab, who was at my side on that mighty day of killing when Kadesh fell, you have already received tokens of my appreciation, but there is something further that I will bestow on my three closest friends."

All three men look up expectantly.

"I've decided to grant you all tombs in the Saqqara necropolis, along with funds for generations of maintenance. Your worthy names shall be known for eternity." Tutankhamun smiles graciously at Vizier Ay and adds, "Lord Ay, you have served me as no other man alive could. I doubt I'd be here today were it not for your steady, constant guidance. Therefore, if you desire it, I shall permit you a tomb in the Valley, where your physical form shall rest among kings for all time."

Ay bows immediately. Once risen, he bows again, deeply, hand over heart, and declares, "I am most honored, Your Majesty. Your grace and generosity has made my dream come to life."

These are deep honors. I look sideways at my husband, knowing that he doesn't grant them out of love, or even generosity, though he is most generous. Lord Maya is plainly touched, and Horemhab is already swimming in favor. And Lord Ay-only Tutankhamun would know how close this honor strikes Lord Ay's deepest dream, as Father related in his Book of Days. It must benefit Tutankhamun to shore up support this way. A round of arrests and executions is coming, and quickly.

Tutankhamun looks over his shoulder and motions to the ever present, ever silent Ipay. In moments, we are served wine to toast eternity.

Tutankhamun dismisses his men, and Ipay opens the gilded doors. Just as Tutankhamun stands from his throne, Nakhtmin rushes in. "Your Majesty! You must see this horse that Mustapha's brought! She's just thrown Djede to the ground, and they are saying no man can ride her."

Horemhab laughs abruptly and says, "I'd like to see such a horse!" I quite nearly smile with him, as I wonder if he dislikes Djede as well.

Ay falls back as well, turning to his son and saying, "Is young Djede hurt?"

"No. He means to master the horse, one way or another, but I don't think he'll get this one."

Ay looks over at Tutankhamun, something like pride in his face. "Your Majesty ought to go down and give it a try. There is no finer horseman in the realm."

Chapter Thirty-One

The palace enclosure's grand courtyard is jammed with merry noblemen. In one corner, a giant cut of beef sizzles on the spit, and tables are set out, covered in flowers and wine, sweets and fruit, bread and cheese. Musicians throughout the wide yard gather groups of admirers, *seheny* officers with polished bronze on their leather cuirasses and noblewomen with flowers and bright beads in their hair. And in the forefront, a great circle has emptied out; I can see a bay horse with a star on its brow rearing up, its lead rope flying free through the air. We cut through the crowd of excited onlookers and Tutankhamun calls out, "Mustapha!"

A brightly dressed Bedu extends his arms before him and bows, a great smile on his heavy, bearded face. Behind him, three assistants in heavy robes stand with arms out, shielding the crowd from the skittish horse. Djede stands shirtless in a dusty kilt, gingerly examining his raw palm. The rope must have burned his skin away. I notice that a little group of noble daughters stands behind him, giggling and blushing at the Horse Master's bravery.

"King of Kings!" Mustapha calls merrily, as he rises from his gracious bow. Mustapha has sold horses to our house and our court for some twenty years, and Tutankhamun knows him well. His horses are the finest, gorgeous and proud desert horses that can run for miles, and require very little water.

"What have you brought to my yard, Mustapha? I can hear this animal screaming from my throne room."

"I have ten fine horses for Your Majesty, yearlings, down by the royal stables! But your young Horse Master here took a liking to this mare, even though I hadn't thought to sell her. She's been improperly broken by someone else, and needs retraining." Mustapha laughs and says, "But if he insists..." He spreads his palms in the air again, and shrugs.

"That's one of my best drivers, Mustapha," Tutankhamun says tightly. "He doesn't need a hoof to the temple."

"This doesn't look too good," Horemhab murmurs, stepping up beside Pharaoh.

Tutankhamun releases my hand, and strides over to Djede. "She ripped the rope away?"

Djede shows Tutankhamun his palm. "It's nothing," he says lightly. "I'll get on her back yet. If she can be ridden, I'll buy her, to match with my bay gelding."

Tutankhamun raises his brows but doesn't respond. Someone from the crowd cries, "That mare can't be ridden! Better take her down to the water before you give it another try! Save your skull!"

Laughter rings around the circle. Tutankhamun stands with his hands on his hips as Djede approaches the mare again. She's pretty, but her ears are pinned flat back and her eyes are wide, and I think it's quite stupid to try this before a gawking, shouting crowd. The horse is obviously terrified. Even Mustapha, who was amused when an untitled youth attempted the feat, starts to frown as he looks between his wild horse and the King of Egypt.

"Shh, shh..." Djede's saying, the words hissing through the air. The horse steps back, snorting, frightening some of the women in the crowd who now think better of being so close to a terrified beast. They try to push their way back, yelling for space, their bright sleeves flapping about. When Djede reaches out for the lead, still hissing like the wind in the trees, it's too much for the horse. She rears again; she makes a neigh like a scream, and backs quickly into a crush of people. Three officers jump away just before getting kicked, and others, safe, laugh at the spectacle.

"Enough!" Tutankhamun shouts, his voice low and hard. "Be calm, everyone!"

Djede turns with surprise, and Tutankhamun says, "Give her space. We have to catch her now, or someone will be injured. But give her space, let her breathe first."

Djede steps beside his king, a flush in his cheeks. Lord Ay-who must have crept beside me as quietly as a snake-murmurs, "What a damned fool that friend of my son is. He would have been better off left in the country!"

I tighten my hands over my arms and say nothing, but it is true. Now my husband is in danger, forced to catch a terrified horse in a courtyard full of half-drunk people. *Oh, Isis, protect him!* Tutankhamun steps toward the mare slowly, and I hear the low tones of his voice carry on a sudden wind. The mare's ears flicker at the new sound, and she stands still, her neck arched high and her tail streaming behind her. Tutankhamun sings to her, walking towards her with his palms up to show his empty hands. Mustapha and I both hold our breath; in fact, the entire crowd seems to. Then, incredibly, Tutankhamun is beside the mare, stroking her neck, still singing, holding the horse in his hazy spell. Even the giggling girls have gone silent, breathless, staring at him the way I do, ensnared by his magic.

The mare drops her head, and my husband's gold ringed fingers close around the rope. A muffled cheer rolls through the crowd, from those not still stunned into silence. The crowd parts up to the gate, astonished, and Tutankhamun leads the horse away. I stand uncomfortably beside Lord Ay for a long while, as celebratory laughter and the roar of one hundred conversations begin again. Djede stands in the center of it all, finally joined by Nakhtmin. I can't hear what they say, but Djede ought to be grateful that Nakhtmin got Tutankhamun when he did. I whisper a quick prayer of gratitude to Isis.

Tutankhamun returns to the courtyard, showered with applause. He walks up to Djede and asks, "Are you going to buy her now, after all that?"

"Maybe I'd better not," Djede says quietly. "I didn't mean to cause any danger, Your Majesty."

"Forget it," Tutankhamun says, holding his anger back. I can almost see smoke in his eyes, but he doesn't shout or scold his new companion. He turns to Mustapha and calls, "I suppose I'll buy her and break her myself. I might as well."

Mustapha, mortified, waves his hands in the air. "No charge, Your Majesty. No charge."

Chapter Thirty-Two

Summer, Year Seven

When the flood comes, it bursts so hard over its banks that the jumble of apartments just outside the walls of Memphis are washed into the river. Tutankhamun rebuilds for them, better than they were, and the peasants who lost their homes are so pleased they make a joke of it: Pharaoh is *too* good, they say. He is so full of blessings he drowns the country with them. The noblemen spend the long, hot days of summer on their pleasure barges, filling the air with laughter and music. At night, we have outdoor feasts in the sunken gardens of the palace enclosure. Afterwards, Tutankhamun and I retreat to private chambers lit by a hundred flickering lamps and scented with sacred oils, and we fill our nights with lovers' cries and dizzying passion.

Tutankhamun begins his days with sunrise rituals. Sometimes he takes Tuthmosis from the nursery and brings him along; when they return, my little boy is perfumed with frankincense. Sometimes his skin is warm from the sun, not cool from the dark temple, and I know that Tutankhamun is teaching his son to worship Aten, as he does. He does this discretely, of course. Though he insists on worshipping his god, he will not offend anyone with it; he does not wish to frighten anyone into thinking that the selfish, bloodthirsty reign of Aten will return. But he will share himself with his son, and pass our old ways on. I cannot deny him this; it's almost as if with Tuthmosis, Tutankhamun can reconstruct the bond of father and son that he was denied. And Tutankhamun is a sweet father, singing to his son in a low, dark honey voice, as tender and patient with the tiny boy as his own nurse, Maia, was with him.

During the day, I sail with Mutnojme while Tutankhamun sits on his throne. Tutankhamun sends musicians and dancers to accompany us, and we eat as well drifting along the river as we would in the palace. I keep my son with me constantly, my blessed only living child who laughs with joy at every swooping bird and every leaping fish. Tuthmosis is picking up new words every day, and his soft black hair is beginning to curl around his eyes. I can't help grabbing him and kissing his fat cheeks as he twists and squirms in my arms. Like his father, he wants to run; he can't bear being held back for very long. Mutnojme and I spread a blanket on the deck of the barge, lying in warmth as my dark, pretty baby plays in the sun. It is a sweet summer.

But then, I hear something that shocks me to my soul. One night, Huy and Djede, both loose from wine, talk loudly about the war in Asia. And what they say... I lean closer, to confirm this ghastly thing. Tutankhamun-sweet, passionate, enchanting Tutankhamun-ordered enemy soldiers bound and burned alive outside Kadesh. Tutankhamun is engrossed in his gambling with Nakhtmin and a young lieutenant from the northeast named Raia, and so I lean over to Huy and demand, "What? What are you talking about?"

They both gulp to see me in their faces. Huy says, "Saboteurs, Your Majesty, attacking our supply wagons in the night. Pharaoh executed them outside the walls of Kadesh, to show the enemy how such men are dealt with."

"He *burned* them?" I gasp, unable to hide my horror. "Alive?"

"What's all this?" Tutankhamun asks, suddenly behind

me, slipping his hands around my waist. I turn to his smiling face, meaning to confront him, desperate to know why-*how*-he could do such a brutal thing!

"Her Majesty was asking about the war," Djede says quietly, head bowed.

"Hmm," Tutankhamun murmurs, wrapping his arms around me and kissing my neck. "You don't want to know too much about that."

I lose my voice. I can't question him here, before his servants. I can't question him at all, it seems, because when we retire to his chambers, he kisses me until I'm dizzy and takes me to his bed. Tutankhamun is as full of passion as ever. I gasp in fierce, desperate pleasure as he twists his hips against mine, digging deep in my belly; I forget my fears as I rake my nails down his strong, silky back, arching my body against his as he holds me down beneath him.

Afterwards, his beautiful black lashes flutter shut. His dark, proud face is gorgeous at rest, his lips slightly parted. I can't help touching his angular cheek and running my fingers over his shaved black hair. I can feel my love for him surging in my heart and my belly, and all through my blood, but even still, I have horrifying thoughts. I press my cheek to the cool pillow and close my eyes, hoping they'll just go away, but soon they grow too powerful.

I climb out of bed, the tiles cold against my feet. I pour myself some of Tutankhamun's red wine and sit at his *senet* table and stare at the starlight outside the clerestory windows. The wine helps only a little; I still wonder about what more he has done on his campaigns. He will believe he must be ruthless to his enemies, and so he shall be. But I know what this does to a man, and I couldn't bear to see Tutankhamun corrupted by the unlimited power at his fingertips. I finish my wine, and slip back through the sparkling, gilded curtains. As I climb onto the bed, Tutankhamun stirs. "Where are you going? Come back here," he murmurs sleepily, smiling, eyes closed. He pulls me down beside him, and falls back asleep with his face buried in my neck.

In just a few weeks, I'm pregnant again. It is a horror, but not a surprise; Tutankhamun never goes to his harem anymore, and we never spend a night apart.

It is my duty to have his children, though Tutankhamun never reminds me. I would rather wait, but it seems I can't touch him without conceiving. I tried not to think of it when we'd fall into his bed or mine, but now I shudder in memory of the tearing agony of that fruitless harvest time labor. I pull my robe around me and hurry into the hall, because I have to tell him, I have to feel his arms around me before I crumple up in miserable fear. At mid-day, he ought to be finishing with his council, sending them off for the long break during the hottest part of the day, when most noblemen relax or sleep.

The servants preparing to scrub the halls and polish the lamps bow before me. I clutch at the gauzy blue sleeves of my gown, forbidding my tears. My servants act as if they see nothing, but I can feel their whispers at my back. Not for the first time, I wish Tutankhamun and I had our own house, so that our joys and trials would be ours alone, and not for the whole world to dissect and gossip over.

Tutankhamun is alone in his throne room, leaning back in his golden throne with his eyes closed. His gold sandaled feet are crossed at the ankles on a footstool depicting his bound and conquered enemies. For a moment I wonder if he is asleep.

But then, his stunning black eyes open and slide to me, and a warm smile crosses his face. "*Hapepy...*" he murmurs, standing up slowly. A gorgeous *nebti* collar spreads across his broad chest, the thick gold and cloisonné set vulture wings outstretched over his shining bronze skin. I drink in the sight of him as he steps down from the dais, I sigh as he takes me in his warm arms. "I needed you so much," he murmurs in my ear, "and you came. My councilmen are like little fish, always biting away at me, whining and fearing and insisting their concerns are paramount. This week they're lamenting the cost of my wars, as if holding Kadesh isn't vital to Egypt's empire! The Biqa Valley alone can provide all the grain for my entire army, and then some. And they worry about sending a couple more barrels of grain a year to my treasury!"

Tutankhamun cuts himself off, and tilts my face to his with soft fingers. "What is it, honey? What is wrong?"

"I'm pregnant again." I close my eyes and rest my cheek against his chest.

He cups his hand over my hair. He kisses my brow, and murmurs, "Come now, that is wonderful news!" This makes me cry harder, and we stand there before his throne, rocking as I tremble. I don't want this; I don't want to do it all over again so soon. But I can't seem to tell my godly husband this; the words stick to my lips. I don't want to be undutiful.

"I can't- Not again-" I stammer, frozen, desperate to share my fear with him, yet bound by my obedience to him, to our bloodline, to the throne.

"Come with me," Tutankhamun says softly. "I must meet with Lord Ay, but then I'm yours. Spend some time with me; let me care for you."

I nod against his warm chest, and he puts his lips to my hair. He brings me to his chambers, where Lord Ay anxiously waits in the anteroom, examining the unfinished game on Tutankhamun's twenty squares board. "Your Majesty," he says, brightening.

"In my private room," Tutankhamun says, breezing past his servants.

He sees me to his bed, brushing his fingers against my cheek when I sit. "Only a moment," he says, looking in earnest into my eyes. I nod again. He pushes his lips against mine and I catch his face in my hands, needing his love.

When he backs away, Lord Ay is standing in the doorway. I have the sudden and uncomfortable feeling that this man watched as I passionately kissed my husband. But the vizier's eyes are on his manicured nails, and I can't be sure. I cast my eyes down, and back into the throne of cushions crowning Tutankhamun's bed.

They are seated with wine, and Tutankhamun comes to it quickly: "I need twenty men arrested. Tax collectors, all. Here are their names and posts." He hands a copy of Shadi's scroll to his Grand Vizier.

Lord Ay takes it, looking on it with a furrowed brow. "Twenty tax collectors..." He turns his narrow face up to Tutankhamun and asks, "Will Your Majesty tell me why?"

"They are corrupted, Lord Ay," Tutankhamun says. "I have had them followed, the proof is all documented. And I have witnesses, willing to come forward."

"Witnesses?" Ay asks, plainly surprised. "There was an investigation? Who ran it?"

"I did," Tutankhamun says. "I had a concern, and it proved true."

Ay makes a little hum, and tucks the scroll away in his robe. "I shall send men out to apprehend these criminals immediately."

"Bring them here, Lord Ay. They might not have done this on their own."

Ay pauses. "Your Majesty, do you wish to have the men interrogated?" I don't like the way his deeply slanted eyes gleam suddenly at the thought of torture.

"Of course," Tutankhamun says quickly, looking hard at Ay. "It does no good to rip out a weed and leave the root."

"I will see to it, then."

Lord Ay makes a wiry, unnaturally nimble bow, and then he retreats through the great gilded doors. I turn my attention to Tutankhamun, who smiles warmly at me. I lower my gaze, knowing what he has just ordered. The men will be asked to give up their bosses, and if they do not, then they will be made to speak by Lord Ay's interrogators.

"It doesn't please me," Tutankhamun admits, standing over his bed. "But neither will I suffer corrupted lords hiding behind peasants. Those men should not have broken my laws; now they shall pay my price."

"If you must..." I murmur, looking down.

"I am doing my duty," Tutankhamun says, sitting beside me. "But I don't want to think about it now. I want to think

378

about you." He leans over and kisses me; his fingers straying to the knot in my sash.

"Tutankhamun," I protest quietly, putting my hand on his chest.

He makes a little growling murmur, pouting like a spoiled boy. I can't help laughing at him, and he sits back and slides my sandals off my feet. He takes my small foot in his hand and begins to massage it. "Don't be afraid of having another child," he says to me. "I'll be here; I'll take care of you. We're going to have another beautiful baby, just like Tuthmosis."

"Tutankhamun," I tell him quietly, "I don't know what I did wrong with our baby girl. How can I be sure it won't happen again? I can't live through another nightmare. I've done it too many times already."

Tutankhamun crawls over the bed and scoops me into his arms. I fit into them exactly, invoking an immediate feeling of safety and security. "Don't think about nightmares, sweet love," he tells me gently, kissing my forehead. He smoothes my curls and murmurs, "That's the trick of it. Think only of having another beautiful baby in your arms."

Chapter Thirty-Three

On a cool winter day, one of the imprisoned tax collectors chokes out the name of a man sitting on the *Kenbet* of Memphis, which is the last stop in the Lower Egyptian court system before Pharaoh's magistrates take over. Tutankhamun rushes through the halls to Horemhab's office, with me following in his wake. We find Horemhab behind a mountainous stack of paperwork, which he's obviously let pile up. Even Tutankhamun breaks his stride to marvel at it. But then he lays the written confession down on Horemhab's desk, grinning like a cheetah with a gazelle on the run. "We've got one. Send my best soldiers, quietly in plain clothes, and armed to the teeth."

Horemhab picks up the confession, grinning happily. "It will be my greatest pleasure to drag this thieving scum in, Your Majesty. And may the gods bless Your Majesty, for caring so much for his people."

"Just do it discretely, Horemhab," Tutankhamun says, his palm still on the general's desk.

"We will steal in like shadows on the wind, Your Majesty."

One week later, I sit at Tutankhamun's mahogany and ivory table, waiting for him to finish reading a royal messenger's scroll so he can move his white *senet* pawn. His black brows knit in worry, but then he dismisses the man and turns back to our game.

"What is it?"

"A small matter in the north," he says lightly. Tutankhamun shakes the throwing sticks. He moves his pawn four spaces, just missing the water trap that would send his pawn back to the beginning of the board. "Lord Hani tells me that Hittite troops have been seen coming out of the far north east."

"You will not go to meet them!" I cry, aghast. "Oh, please don't leave me now!"

"No, *hapepy*, I won't leave you now, don't worry. They're far enough from my land," Tutankhamun tells me, and then he seeks to distract me. "Look, I will beat you again if you don't pay attention."

"When I have three pawns off the board already? I don't think so," I retort, taking my turn. But as I throw the sticks, I feel my stomach turn over. I take a deep breath, and instantly my husband is alert. "It's nothing," I say quickly. "The tea is too strong, maybe."

He frowns. "You should lie down."

"No, let's finish our game." No sooner than I can say this, pain kicks me in the belly. I gasp and look up at him, and then it gets worse. I cry his name. I feel a sudden rush of warmth between my legs; my thighs are damp with blood and I know what it is, and I scream in sorrow and fear.

Panicked, Tutankhamun screams for Ipay, he screams for his physician. He lifts me in his arms, snatching me off the chair. A wide pool of blood soaks into the center of it. Pentju rushes into the room and my husband cries, "What's happening to her?"

"Put her down, Your Majesty. Let me see her..."

On the bed, I twist and cry in sudden pain. It is labor, coming fast and hard, and I am just shy of five months along. The physician says prudently, "We cannot move her, Your Majesty. You'd better wait outside."

"No!" Tutankhamun shouts. He pushes past his physician and kneels beside my bed, crying my name.

As I feel the cramping grow in strength, and another rush of blood, I grab his arm. "Please, Tutankhamun... Go."

"I won't leave you!" he cries, pushing my hair back from my brow. He turns to Pentju and demands, "Give her something! Help her!"

Tutankhamun's lifelong physician lays his hand on the king's shoulder. "Your Majesty, your wife is having a miscarriage. It's best that you leave the room, and let us care for her. There is nothing you, or anyone, can do to save this child. Let me protect the mother."

Chapter Thirty-Four

I lie like one dead in Tutankhamun's bed. Our second little daughter, so small and fragile, is wrapped in a cloth by the bedside. Tutankhamun sits at his gaming table, his head in his arms. He has never seen this before, at least not with his own child.

I am horrified when Ipay admits three men. I snatch the fresh blankets up around me, as if they could hide my humiliation. And then I know what they are here for, and I can't stop my crying, no matter how undignified it is.

The tall, well dressed master embalmer and his two apprentices come, appropriately solemn faced. Tutankhamun greets them in silence. He brings them to the bundle of our third child, a studied hardness in his face as he sweeps the cloth back and looks again on his lost daughter one last time. "Take her," he murmurs, heartbroken.

Yet they, the embalmers, balk. The apprentices look at each other, and the master raises one unnaturally smooth hand and says in a gentle whisper, "Your Majesty- I am afraid-" He shakes his head, and Tutankhamun frowns. "We cannot preserve one... not of age to be born. We ought not to... for anyone who hasn't drawn breath, who cannot even be named."

I cry in despair, pressing my fingers to my lips. Our tiny baby will be buried, buried in the sand? She will break up to nothing, as if she never were?

"But you *will* do it," Tutankhamun says, in a voice made rough with exhaustion and sorrow.

The embalmer's hand is still in the air, his fingers quivering, his color drained. I can hardly believe the man's nerve when he says, in a ghostly whisper, "Your Majesty, I *cannot*. It is against tradition, against our codes..."

It happens so fast. Tutankhamun seizes the tall master by his throat and drives him back to the wall. His teeth are bared like a raging lion, his lips are curled back. His eyes are so black, so full of rage he might be some creature come from another world to suck the very lifeblood out of the embalmer. As my stomach clenches in terror at his violence, Tutankhamun squeezes the breath from the man, trapping off his throat with his hard, gilded hand. "You *will* obey me!" he hisses. "Damn your code!"

Tutankhamun holds the man hard against the wall. The embalmer's face goes red, then purple. I scream his name in horror. "Stop, Tutankhamun, stop!"

Tutankhamun lets him go; the man falls to the floor coughing and gasping. Tutankhamun stands over him, breathless. He looks to the horrified apprentices and says, "Take my baby. Prepare her poor body..."

They scramble to it, and the master is up, bowing again and again like a child's toy on a string, repeating lamely *forgive me, forgive me, Lord of Life...*

Tutankhamun turns to me, shaking his head. "They will do it properly!" he cries softly. "I swear it to you!"

"Please, Tutankhamun, sit down!" I say, taking him in my arms. I ignore the lingering cramping in my belly and sit Tutankhamun down on the soft featherbed, stroking his back. He looks at me with wide dark eyes, and I don't know if he's frightened that he quite nearly killed a man with his hands, or if he's angry still, or simply grieving for our child. I wrap him in my arms and we rock softly, my tears streaming freely down my cheeks. "Shh, Tutankhamun," I breathe, because he is still shaking from the rush of his rage. I close my eyes and stifle my sobs against his shoulder. I cannot deny it anymore:

there is something dark and deadly in Tutankhamun. We escaped Amarna, and I have thanked the gods from that day until this one for it. But what if Amarna could follow us? What if it is in our blood, no matter what we do? I cling to Tutankhamun, as if I could hold him suspended in time, as if I could stop him from turning into the cruelest of all gods, despite the blood of that very god pumping hard through his veins.

A cold wind blows into Egypt. For two long weeks, I hide away from the world. When I finally rise from my bed, I go to the Temple of Mut and prostrate myself on the ground. But as I beseech the Mother, I can only think of my initiation. There were four there, beyond the fire. The Sun God, in whatever name he preferred; Mut, Hathor, and Isis. But only Hathor and Isis gave me their gifts. Not Mut, she only guided me. As I lie in the temple, I wonder in horror, could I not be blessed by her? I have Tuthmosis, and he is to secure our line, but perhaps I will never have another baby! And worse, I... I don't even want to try! How could the Great Mother have guided me to my love, but denied that love the blessing of fertility?

I flee the temple. As my driver brings me home, I think of my mother, who turned her back on all the goddesses of Egypt, and her six healthy daughters. Could it be that she-who defied all the ancient laws-would be so blessed, and yet I am cursed to near barrenness?

I take a deep breath as we roll through the enclosure wall. My armed escort dissipates, and I am left nearly alone in the courtyard. Dignitaries from the Double Treasury come and go, mixing with ambassadors and petitioners. Chariot officers newly elevated have traded their short kilts and leather armor for pleated robes, and they come and go to seek the king's favor. The court rumbles down the path of advancement, even as Tutankhamun and I choke on sorrow. I am quite grateful when they bow their backs to me; I need not look into their faces.

I pass through the whispering potted palms in the grand

387

portico. The smell of incense drifts along on the cool breeze. My maids are waiting for me, ready with a hot bath and warm, spiced wine. I take a long drink and sink under the water, and hold my breath until I can't stand it anymore.

Chapter Thirty-Five

I wake up to find Tutankhamun setting a mahogany tray on my bed. He brushes a stray curl from my face and murmurs, "Please eat, *hapepy,* you are like a little bird in my arms."

I sit up obediently, and murmur my thanks. Tutankhamun has been the most devoted husband these past six weeks, making every effort to see to my comfort, seeing me to sleep before slipping away to his own rooms in observance of custom. He doesn't speak to me of finding reasons for our sudden misfortune, he doesn't blame me; I don't speak of his murderous, agony-driven temper on the day our baby died, nor the embalmer he nearly choked to death.

He motions to the food. "I've brought sweet cream, and honey butter. The bread is fresh, and the pomegranate is from the best farm in the Delta." He pulls out his knife and cuts the big red fruit in two. The sparkling red seeds glisten like wet jewels. He takes one half for himself, gives the other to me, and I finally smile.

"That's better," he says quietly.

I touch his sculpted cheek and say, "When you were a baby, you gave me a half a pomegranate."

Tutankhamun smiles warmly. "Did I?"

"In the garden around the lotus pool, where we liked to swim. You were but a little older than Tuthmosis."

He sits back, looking down on me with brilliant dark eyes. "And you took it, didn't you?"

"I did. But Mayati stole it, and threw it away right after. You left with Lady Maia before that."

"I must have felt very brave that day. You were a goddess to me then, too. I always watched you, for as long as I can remember. I always heard you singing when I was in the library, and I would close my eyes and get lost in your song."

"Your Majesty..." Henutawy catches my attention, and then opens the door to reveal Ipay in my antechamber.

As Ipay enters in silence, I realize I'm finally hungry. For weeks I have eaten dutifully and sparingly, but suddenly I'm famished. I spread the whipped honey butter on my fresh warm bread, and sprinkle sweet red arils on top. Tutankhamun sighs visibly, relieved at my returned desire for food. Ipay tells him quickly that Nakhtmin has come again to his own apartments, in a short kilt and greaves.

"Tell him maybe tomorrow," Tutankhamun says, twisting a strand of my black curls around his finger.

I narrow my eyes suspiciously. He's turned away his daily ride for weeks now, just to be with me as I heal. I can see the restlessness building in his shoulders and burning in his eyes. "My love, if you want to go for a ride, or go shooting, then you should. I need to bathe anyway."

"Really?" Tutankhamun asks. "Are you sure?"

I taste the sweet cream pointedly, taking a determined sip. "Yes. I'm going to bathe, and maybe I'll go sit in the garden for a while. I'm all right, Tutankhamun. I mean, it's not all right, but I feel strong again. And you're wonderful, perfectly wonderful. Just come back, as soon as you can."

"But after I ride, I'll have to sit in the audience chamber, and then I must see Maya and Ay... We must raise the taxes to replenish the treasury, and the lesser men are already whining about it."

I lay my hand against his cheek. "Go race your horse, go run with the wind for a while before you have to do your duties. And I'll be here when you've finished, my husband, waiting for you."

"Will you wait for me tonight?" he asks softly. "I miss you," he says plainly, holding his arms around my waist.

I open my mouth to speak, but nothing comes. I bite my lips, and in the silence, he kisses me softly, he runs his lips along my jaw and down my neck to send shivers through my body. I close my eyes and turn my face up for his kisses, surrendering in silence.

But when he does come that night, I burst into tears as soon as he climbs into my bed. I can't do it; I don't want to get pregnant right away again. And where Mutnojme or any other woman would just say so, I can't bring myself to refuse my husband, and so for the longest while I can only shake and cry in Tutankhamun's arms. Thank the gods, he understands me, and he doesn't hound me with questions or worse, go on with his lovemaking; he just holds me until I can breathe again. And then he settles us back in my bed, tucking the long goose-down pillows around my body until I'm lying in a cloud. Tutankhamun draws the blankets up over us and wraps me in his arms.

"It's too soon," I finally manage, as I grow drowsy from his fingers gently gliding back and forth along my arm.

"I know," he says. "You're right. Forgive me, I'm hopeless for you. We must wait a little longer."

I sigh comfortably, nestling into his warm grasp, and falling into a deep, dreamless sleep.

In the morning, I decide what I must do. Like my mother, I will employ a wise-woman to protect me—and my unborn child—against a pregnancy before I feel strong again. But unlike Mother, I cannot deceive my husband. I tell him of my plan anxiously, aware that I am being undutiful. After all, I sent Tuthmosis to a wet nurse so that I could recover faster, and give my king more children, faster. It is duty, tradition. Yet I explain it to him, how Tuthmosis is so fine and strong because I had so much to give him; how when I got pregnant again but weeks after childbirth, both times I lost the baby, and in terrible ways. I tell him how my midwife said I have delicate health, and it is so obviously true. I tell him I want to wait with tears in my eyes, and Tutankhamun kisses me up and swears his love for me, regardless. "I am happy with our son," he promises. "I just want you, safe and healthy."

After he leaves, my ladies and maids enter my chambers. Blind male harpists play giant harps for me while I bathe, and when I step out of the steamy water, Akila wraps me in a thick, soft towel against the winter chill.

But once I'm back before my vanity, I send everyone away except my aunt. Mutnojme takes over for my body servant, dabbing perfume on my throat. I watch her, staring at the powdered malachite on her eyes, waiting for the right moment to ask her such a personal question.

"Mutnojme," I say quietly, and she looks down on me. "You have not gone back to Horemhab, have you?"

She shakes her head quickly, the green beads in her braids clicking together. "No. He would have it that way, but I wouldn't lower myself to it. He wanted Lady Amenia; he is welcome to her. He doesn't need the both of us. And I will not be his mistress, his whore."

"Of course not," I say. "I only ask because… The woman, the wise woman who helped you guard against pregnancy for so long. Is she still close by?"

"There were two, Ankhesenamun. One in Memphis, one in Thebes. I've not seen the Memphis lady in a long time, I do not know if she still practices medicine."

"You must find her for me," I say anxiously. I grab her hand, and she sees the fear in my eyes. "I can't go through it again."

Mutnojme makes a little murmur of empathy. She knows the horror of a lost child, a burden she has carried alone, in secret. She bows her head to me and says, "I will go straightaway."

Seven hours later, I drink a strong acacia tea, mixed with mysterious herbs and spells. My hand trembles as I set the cup down, and I sit very still, trying to feel anything. I eye the woman-a neat looking widow in soft white linen-with deep suspicion. "You are sure this will work?" I demand again. There is no worse feeling than putting your life so completely into the hands of another. This woman could have given me hemlock or a thousand other things, and like my mother, my life would gutter out in spasms on the floor.

Mutnojme reminds me, "I am proof that it does." She touches my arm lightly, with reassurance.

Henutawy comes back in the gauzy pink gown I gave her, saying apologetically, "Pharaoh's back already. What can I say to him?"

The wise woman's eyes widen, and I shake my head. "It's not what you think." My own thoughts run in the logical circle: her life is in my hands as well. It is probably treason to give me this medicine, or at least, many a king could work it out that way in his heart. But she cannot know that Tutankhamun is as desperate as me for this to work, so that I can heal.

I stand up, and there is no dizziness, no burning in my belly, and the fluted pillars don't start swaying like with Anat's drink either. I look down at the widow, who meets my eyes frankly and openly as I take her measure. She is fairly young, comely, perhaps thirty-five. Her name is Akasha, and she supports her three youngest daughters with her pharmacology. "You may stay here, with me. We will live between Memphis and Thebes commonly, with travels about the land. I will see to your daughters' educations and provide them with homes when they make their marriages. If it works, that is."

"I am honored, Your Majesty," she says, bowing her head.

Before I walk away, I look over my small shoulder and say, "Your profession demands discretion. If you are ever asked what you do, by anyone, you will say you are a healer, but no more. And then you will tell me who has done the asking."

She bows again.

I open my door, I pass through my antechamber.

Tutankhamun stands in the presence chamber, his back against the pastorally painted wall. He tosses a gilded staff back and forth between his hands. When he sees me he stands up and a torrent of questions tumbles from his lips. *Are you all right? What did she give you? What did it taste like? How do you feel?*

I put my palms against his chest. "I think it is fine. But let's walk, so the woman can get her pay and look at her new room. I think she is afraid of you."

Tutankhamun's neat black eyebrows rise curiously. "You will keep her here?"

"It's more convenient, I think. Should I not?"

"Do what you think is best," he says, putting his arms around me.

We walk out into the hall, and he puts the decorative staff to the floor every so often, using it as a light crutch, and only gingerly stepping on his left heel. "Are you in pain?" I breathe, knowing that he won't say anything unless asked.

Tutankhamun nods, falling into a thoughtful silence. We walk past a courtyard garden. The sunlight streaks the hall of the portico in swaths of light and shadow, and sparks off the gold inlays on the ebony lamp stands. Glossy wintering starlings swoop through the fig trees, chattering. "I'm always in pain now," he admits quietly.

I lay my cheek against his warm, strong arm. I am glad, now, that he has fought two wars, and killed his lion in Syria. I am glad he's painted his chapel with scenes of the Siege of Kadesh, and decorated his wardrobe trunks with motifs of frenzied battle. At least he will always have these things to gaze upon, to fill him with pride when he can no longer do them. "Are you done for the day?" I ask, hoping that now, finally, we can be alone together. I only ever want to talk to Tutankhamun. There is no one else for me.

"I am finished, until the sunset. Maya is preparing for the tax collection, and Lord Ay..." Tutankhamun looks around. Satisfied that we're alone, he says, "He is in the dungeon with that man they just took from the *Kenbet*."

The shrill, whiny call of a peacock echoes through the

garden, startling me. I lay my hand on my chest and look about for the bird, one of two from the markets of Punt. The male jumps down from the balcony above, a flash of blue and green.

"Who is the man, exactly?"

"Lord Herihor," Tutankhamun says, watching as the creature spreads his astonishing, many-eyed plumage. "His family has been in the priesthood of Ptah for generations, but he made his fortune running expeditions to Punt. And through stealing my grain, apparently."

"You will kill him?" I ask softly.

Tutankhamun looks down on me, his answer in his eyes.

"The courtiers will be frightened. They will think of the bad days, when Father killed high-born men every week."

"No," Tutankhamun assures me, striding along again. "This is different. Herihor has committed a crime out of greed, not principle or faith. Surely, no one can object to his punishment."

Chapter Thirty-Six

The next day, at midday, I stand on Tutankhamun's balcony with the sun on my face. Tutankhamun's arms are around my waist and his lips are playing on my neck. I sigh and lean back against his warm body.

The sound of galloping hooves startles us. A man on horseback rushes into the courtyard below, his horse covered in frothy sweat.

"That is one of Ay's informants," Tutankhamun says, backing away from me. He hurries inside and swings a robe on, and I know it is urgent by the way he takes no care for himself, no staff to bear his weight and keep the pain away. I want to rush after him, but I check myself at the door. It is not my place and the last person I want to see now, breathless and flushed from unquenched passion, is Lord Ay. I must wait, tapping my foot nervously, drumming my slim fingers on the ebony table.

Tutankhamun returns dark faced. He hurries past me, carrying a leather-bound book from his antechamber. It is his own Book of Days, and he flips through the pages quickly, his eyes racing over his indecipherable hieratic short-hand. "Yes, it's as I thought..." he breathes, setting his finger on a line of words. "Intef!"

"What has happened?"

Tutankhamun looks up at me. "We've arrested that man,

the one taking bribes on the *Kenbet*. But this morning, they've found another man from the court of elders floating in the river with his throat cut."

"Hideous" I say, compelled to touch my own soft neck.

Tutankhamun shakes his head slowly, his black eyes flashing. "It is much more than a bad death for one man! The man who was murdered was the very one Intef appointed to take his place on the court, when I made him Vizier of Lower Egypt. Everyone knows by now that Lord Herihor has been taken to my dungeon, and someone was scared of what he might be confessing. Someone thought this dead man knew too much about it, and they have silenced him forever. Who do you think that might be? Who led the very same *Kenbet* for years, and appointed this man to fill his place? Who had a fearful network of police and enforcers all over the city, and was allowed a free hand to run Memphis as he pleased when my father was king? Who has the power to kill a man in the night, and throw his body in the river without leaving one witness brave enough to come forward?"

"Lord Intef," I say, astonished.

"Lord Intef," Tutankhamun repeats, nodding his head.

That very day, Lord Ay himself arrests the Vizier of Lower Egypt, before all the courtiers, and brings him down into the dark palace jail.

Chapter Thirty-Seven

Spring

Finally, it grows hot again. The first of the tax barges begin to dock in the city, and great mountains of grain rise behind the walls of our treasury. In the palace gardens, white jasmine blooms in thick, perfumed swaths, which my gardeners cut and set in delicate faience vases to fragrance my chambers.

I have decided at last to make the Memphis palace truly my own. Tutankhamun, thrilled that I've shaken away the last of my melancholy, grants me a heavy purse of gold to make our palace up to my tastes. I oversee the painters with delight as they plaster over my grandmother's pastoral murals, and fill the rooms instead with bold colors and patterns. I choose deep, luscious reds, warm earthy orange tones, and vibrant cheerful yellows. Vivid fabrics and imported silks make the rooms inviting, and complement our gold and jewel inlaid furniture. In my private courtyard garden, I splash the walls with the most expensive of all pigments, deep blue; and then I order the heavy torches replaced with glowing alabaster lamps that warm scented oil as they burn. For the bathrooms, I select deep, soothing green, and then I fill the corners and line the walls with potted plants. The naked mahogany doorframes and doorways are polished to a high shine, and my jeweler purchases enormous chunks of Baltic amber to stud in gold settings into the doors.

And then I must go to Tutankhamun, because I cannot afford to pay my jeweler. Tutankhamun looks up at me with a sweet smile, setting aside the Grand Vizier's report. Lord Intef sits in stubborn silence in his cell, and Tutankhamun has yet refused to force him to speak. No matter how much misery the corrupted old man has caused in the land, I cringe at the thought of interrogation.

"I need to pay the jeweler," I murmur, shifting my weight like a nervous girl.

He laughs and stands up. "You have very fine tastes, little goddess," he says, putting his arms around me. He kisses my forehead gently. "You can have anything you like, Ankhesenamun. As long as you are not coating our floors in gold or silver..."

I bite my lip playfully. "Do I really have to send the goldsmith away?"

He furrows his brow anxiously. I laugh aloud and kiss his lips. "No, husband, I've not sent for any goldsmith to coat our floors. But the jeweler is in the garden, seeking payment like some merchant. Will you see him?"

"I will. I shall tell him to go to Lord Maya for anything else you might need."

Tutankhamun sends the man off quickly, and then he stands still, inhaling the fresh scent of jasmine. He pulls me by my hand into his arms, and I rest my cheek against his hard chest. The sun is warm and a green bee-eater trills a high, sweet song. It is a perfect day to be in love.

"Your Majesty..."

Tutankhamun laughs softly. They-whoever it might be at the time-always find us. They always break into our dream. Tutankhamun presses his forehead against mine for a long moment, and then turns on a young royal messenger. The boy is unfamiliar. He falls into prostration and hands Pharaoh a small scroll.

"Office of Royal Police, Amarna...?" Tutankhamun murmurs

curiously. He takes his dagger from his hip and cuts the seal. His eyes scan the papyrus, and whatever is written snatches something from Tutankhamun's guts. His eyes go inky black, and he gasps like he's been kicked in the stomach. He pushes the scroll into my hands.

My eyes scan the paper without understanding. *The Royal Tombs have been robbed and desecrated. We caught three men inside the tombs; they are in custody. There is great damage. We beg His Majesty to come immediately.*

Tutankhamun dismisses the frightened boy with a broken word. And then he turns away from me, and vomits.

Tutankhamun immediately orders our departure for the following morning. He wakes me at dawn, and already the palace is in a flurry of activity. It feels like the world is spinning out of control around me, and I sit paralyzed in my bed until I can remember how to breathe. As I go about my morning rituals of bathing and dressing, servants rush by carrying baskets, heading out to the harbor at double time. I am told that the boats with the soldiers are already loaded; three thousand veterans from Asia accompany the palace guard, and from this I can only assume the city of Amarna will be locked down.

Amarna. How can I touch my feet to her limestone paved avenues? I have done everything in my power to forget that awful place; now I must go back?

Mutnojme enters my chambers shortly after, her eyes rimmed with red and her face ashen. I know she is thinking of Mother, her sister, and how badly her body was violated in the darkness. To destroy a person's body is actually worse than killing them, because it will destroy their soul forever. If I thought about it, I would feel sick to my stomach. I would feel terrified, I might even think of being a little girl sitting at my mother's feet, back when she loved me. But I won't. I swallow hard and say, "We don't know anything yet. Let's not think the worst, let's just make sure that Henutawy and Akila bring everything we need."

"Has Pharaoh told you anything?"

"He knows nothing," I say quietly. "But we must hurry. Tutankhamun doesn't want to waste a moment."

Down at the harbor, Tutankhamun shouts at the overseers, waving his hand at them as if they were cattle. He rounds on the stunned servants who port dried meat and other provisions onto the boats. "Enough! We are not travelling through the wilderness!" He claps his hands behind everyone, ushering them aboard their barges. When he looks up at me, surrounded by my ladies, he shakes his head at the incompetence of his household.

"Hurry," I murmur to my women, and we walk down the crowded quay.

We are in silence for most of the journey. Tutankhamun sits in his cabin with his head in his hands, every so often looking up at me with dark, anguished eyes. "I should have spent more on security. I didn't want to be seen- I didn't think-"

I sit behind him on the bed, sliding my arms around his waist. "Tutankhamun," I murmur, resting my cheek against his back, "You did everything you thought you should have done. And we don't know how bad it is."

He makes a sickly moan and sinks his head into his hands.

This time, we reach Amarna in the hard morning sun. The walls of the city are yellowed with neglect. The harbor is empty but for a small vessel bringing supplies to the Great Temple, and a few rough fishing boats. Drifting palm trunks roll against the limestone quay, bobbing on the splashing water. I hug my arms around my body as the royal barge turns into Amarna's harbor, praying to Isis for the strength to enter my childhood home, which I have only done in my nightmares for these past eight years. I look to my husband for support, only to find that he is trapped in his own agony. "Everyone said it was the most beautiful city in the world," he breathes, clutching the golden deck rails.

As soon as the barge ties up, Tutankhamun tosses his staff with a clatter onto the polished granite dais, and he leaves the cabin deck. While I stand frozen on the deck, Tutankhamun walks alone into his father's abandoned city, the wind blowing his gold threaded cloak behind him.

Police Chief Mahu meets him at the end of the quay. Soon, chariots from the police barracks fill the harbor, and I can't delay anymore. Mutnojme appears beside me and I grab her hand tightly. We walk toward the deserted Royal Road, confronted everywhere with emptiness and neglect. Only around the Great Temple, where a skeletal crew of gardeners tends the sycamore trees, is there any sign of life. My father's proudest jewel, his shining city, is full of garbage-lined streets and graffiti-marred walls.

I clutch Tutankhamun's waist as he drives us into the dull yellow desert. The eastern cliffs rise in the distance, hazy in the heavy sun. A long line of policemen stand guard, and Tutankhamun drives his chariot straight through them. He reins the horses in before Father's tomb, and jumps down into the cloud of dust.

"Tutankhamun! I'm coming with you." I do not want to see what horrors await in the caverns beneath the ground. But I certainly don't want him taking in such unwholesome sights alone! My heart fills with ghoulish nightmares, and then, for perhaps the first time in years, I recall the faces of my family. If I let myself, I could remember my mother and father at their high table, my sisters' laughing banter and songs, and oh!- my own little girl, my very first baby, the first of three to die. I swoon in the heat, and tighten my grip on the chariot's hand-rail.

"No," Tutankhamun hisses. "There is no need for you to see this."

"I won't let you go alone," I say firmly, stepping down from the cab.

Tutankhamun puts his arms around me. He murmurs in my ear, "Obey me. I've never asked it of you, but obey me now."

His eyes are pained, liquid with inky black tears that must not fall.

Nakhtmin pulls his chariot up, followed by Mahu. I look from them to Tutankhamun, whose jaw is set bravely. I nod and fall back, ashamed to leave him alone yet deeply grateful that he has commanded it.

Tutankhamun takes a torch from the policeman, and with Nakhtmin and Mahu, disappears into Father's tomb. We stand silently in the heat, waiting anxiously. I keep my eyes on my golden sandals, or on the arch of the chariot yoke. I refuse to remember all the funerals, all the terrible funerals. I refuse to think of any of them, not here, where their ghosts are so powerful. I cannot begin to imagine that my family... that their corpses have been defiled. I have buried them-all of them-deep in my heart, and I want them to stay there, in peace, where they cannot hurt me. But someone, some foul, lowly creature, has resurrected them with this unthinkable crime.

Finally, the policemen and soldiers around me snap to attention. I look up and see the flaming torch reappear in the mouth of the tomb.

Tutankhamun emerges into the sun, his eyes as hollow as the tomb behind him. His face could be carved from black granite, and his courage is high as he walks from tomb to tomb, his scribes and policemen along to document the horrors within. I refuse to imagine it.

Tutankhamun returns to the chariot in silence. I barely have my hands around him before he cracks his whip and sends the horses into a fevered gallop. We break away from our entourage and run reckless for the city. Finally, the horses' hooves clatter down the limestoned Royal Road. The chariot's wheels sway and slide on the slippery surface, and I scream in fear. Tutankhamun wrenches the horses to a halt, and they whiny and rear in protest. He has brought us right under the bridge, under the window of appearances. The deserted Great Palace looms on one side, the shuttered King's House on the other, and all the memories inside stealing my breath as if I were a little girl again, helpless before a monster.

Tutankhamun drops the reins.

"What are you doing?" I ask, terrified.

"Going in."

"Tutankhamun, no! Please, no! Please take me back to the barge!" I shake my head hysterically. My husband looks possessed, gazing on our old home with empty black eyes. I fear that whatever evils he saw in the belly of the earth have broken him, but I cannot stay here! I can feel the ghosts reaching for my neck. I can't be here… "Please! The gates will be locked anyway. Take me back!"

Tutankhamun is still while his eyes trace the high ramparts of the palace. Then he snaps the reins, turns the horses in a wide arc, and drives us back to the harbor.

As soon as we're in the cabin, Tutankhamun begins to tear it apart. He throws a pricey, waist high alabaster vase into the wall; he smashes an ivory and ebony chair to bits. "Tutankhamun!" I shriek, reaching out for his bronze arms.

He is too quick for me, snatching a tall oil lamp and shattering it. He screams, "I want their blood, all of them! I want it to run like a river!" He sweeps the lamps and oil-burners off the desk, and upends that as well. I have never seen his temper explode this way; he doesn't even see me standing in the center of his raging storm, clutching my arms in horror. When I think of the last time I have seen a man with such violence in his eyes, my heart begins to flutter, and then to hammer away. I can feel my legs getting weak and my throat getting dry.

"Tutankhamun!" I cry, and thank Isis he stops. He covers his face with his gilded hands, and then clenches them to fists.

"I saw him," he moans quietly. "They tore the lid off the sarcophagus. They were looking for gold and amulets… they tore bandages. I saw him, I saw his face, what *was* his face. It was horrible."

Shocked, I go to him and put my arms around him, and I lay my cheek against his back. I console him softly, quiet words. I tell him it will be all right, as I would tell a frightened child. "Don't think of it, Tutankhamun…"

He turns in my arms. "It's my fault. He could have lost his soul, and your mother, and your sister… I did this, when I turned my back on Amarna. It's my fault."

"No, no," I say, shocked that he could think it. "You did what was right! If it is anyone's fault, it's his. He should not have mistreated so many people!"

Tutankhamun draws his breath tightly over the pain in his heart; it sounds like a little hiss. "He called me a coward, and what would he think now? I gave my faith and my name to his enemies, and look what's happened!"

"Tutankhamun! You can't think that! You believe in the gods! You made me as Isis on your throne! And a coward? You have become Egypt's greatest warrior-king in two generations!"

He looks at me miserably. "But still, I am the son who broke his father's laws! Don't you understand that? Don't you know I have worn chains around my heart every day since I became king, when I undid his life's work with my first royal decree?"

"You- you have never said that," I whisper, appalled. "You have never spoken of it."

Tutankhamun lowers his lashes, gazing at the floor behind me. "I didn't want to talk about it with you. Nakhtmin knows."

"Nakhtmin," I repeat. I back away from him, retreating to the comfort of wine, stepping gingerly over the remains of the stateroom.

Tutankhamun makes his own way to his bed. I bring him a glass of wine, and he drinks it down, watching me with luminous, sad eyes.

"You should rest," I tell him, and he nods and lies down. I take his sandals from his feet and pull the soft linen blankets over him. But when he finally chases his demons away enough to close his eyes, Ipay intrudes. As he pointedly ignores the mess, I call softly, "Go away, he is asleep!"

"Your Majesty, Chief Mahu craves Pharaoh's presence. He

has a man with him who claims to be the brother of one of the criminals in custody. I must have orders-"

"I'm awake," Tutankhamun says, pushing off the covers. He stands quickly and slips his feet back into his gilt sandals, and then he is gone. He does not return until nighttime, after I have bathed and gotten ready for bed. His cabin has been put back to rights, and I decide to sleep in his bed so that I can see him when he returns. But because I don't want to be alone in this awful place, I play *senet* with Mutnojme, which is almost as bad as being alone, because all she does is insensitively talk about her sister. I am beyond grateful when I hear Tutankhamun's footsteps coming up the stairs to the cabin, and the door swinging open.

He is surprised to see us both, and right away I can see why. In the dim light of small alabaster lamps, a dull red splash stains his white kilt. He meets my eyes, and then boldly walks on. He goes to the bedside table and pours water into a basin, removes his bloody rings, and washes his hands.

Mutnojme looks to me with wide brown eyes. "Go," I whisper.

She climbs off the king's bed with her head bowed demurely. "Your Majesty," she murmurs, bowing slightly before she leaves. I sit warily on Tutankhamun's bed, curled in my sheer indigo robe, toying with the small golden beads of my anklet. I've no idea what to say to him.

"There is another criminal, a fourth man. The brother has given a description, saying they all met together in his tavern. That's all he knows; the rest will have to come from the criminals," Tutankhamun says, drying his hands carefully on a linen napkin. He summons Ipay from his small chamber to clean his rings and throw the bloody water away. Then he looks at me, his eyes shining. "But one of them died of his injuries before I could have him questioned-a failing on Mahu's part-and the others are not in condition to speak yet."

"They were beaten," I realize. "So much that one died, and the others could not tell who their conspirator was?"

"They were caught in my father's tomb. What do you think happened to them?"

I purse my lips and nod. And then I wonder frightfully, "How long will it be before you can find out who the other criminal is, and this can be over?" I cannot bear to stay here much longer.

"I don't know," Tutankhamun says, unwinding his kilt and tossing it away.

I quickly put the pawns away in the little ebony drawer cut into the board game. As Tutankhamun gets into bed, I put the game down on the only table left in the stateroom. I snuff out the oil lamps one by one, and let the curtains down to protect us from mosquitoes. Last of all I shed my robe; a cold breeze wraps around my skin. I hesitate for a moment, my fingers to my throat, and then I climb beneath the blankets, and feel the warmth of Tutankhamun's smooth body press against mine. He turns to me like every other night, but for the first time in two years, everything in me tightens at the feeling of my husband's hands sliding along my hips. My fear rises quickly, not fear of him, but fear of memory, a fear so deep in my body that it is as thoughtless and involuntary as breathing. "Not tonight," I say shakily, my voice barely above a whisper. "Please. Not... not here."

"It's all right, *hapepy*," he says, seeking out my hand to lace our fingers. "It's just us here."

"Just hold me," I whisper. "Like you used to."

Tutankhamun sighs, disappointed; he had obviously hoped to lose himself in the pleasure of love, forgetting these awful things for an hour or so. But he tightens his warm arms around me protectively, knowing my heart, understanding the darkness of my memories like no one else ever could. "Of course," he breathes, "Of course, sweet love."

I turn and hide my face in his chest, desperate to hide from the ghosts just outside this barge.

Chapter Thirty-Eight

The sunlight is expansive, glaring, and a haze of heat hangs stale and suffocating over the city. I look out to the fields of golden wheat, combed and cut down into wide, square clearings. The fields have shrunk over the years, but I can walk through them blindfolded. I think of the ceremonies I have played a part in to bless those fields, and then I wring my hands together and turn my attention to this dreadful gathering.

Meri-Re and Mahu have just joined us on deck for an early midday meal. I don't recognize the two young acolytes with the priest, skinny boys drowning in pure white robes. The stone-hearted, low born police chief greets the soft spoken, aristocratic Seer of Aten with great respect; Meri-Re, on the other hand, returns a pinched nod. Mahu is beneath him, even though they are abandoned together in a city with no purpose.

"I swear to you both right now," Tutankhamun says fiercely, "I will return this city to her glory. In the beginning, I was advised to forego Amarna entirely, but I shall not abide this."

"There will be many people against that," Meri-Re observes. In his short black wig and *shebyu* collars given to him by my father, he looks exactly as he did when we left Amarna over seven years ago. Meri-Re is a kind man, but his presence here is sickening to me. And even with the silver shooting through his close-cropped black hair, Mahu seems the same as well. In his short, crisp kilt and leather tunic, and his hard brown eyes that were always devoid of compassion and light, he could be sitting before Father's throne, waiting for orders to tear the city apart in search of heretical evidence.

Tutankhamun responds darkly, "There is only one Pharaoh in Egypt, Lord Seer. If I had not turned so completely from Aten's holy city, this never would have happened."

"Your esteemed father put his heart into Amarna's creation," Mahu observes.

"Indeed," Meri-Re chimes in. "He was the greatest astronomer I've ever known. When I think of how he designed this city by the paths of the sun and the stars, and how he wished for Amarna to be the most ordered and beautiful city in the world... Well, it is a daily source of pain to see what has become of her."

"Perhaps I shall revitalize Aten's worship," Tutankhamun muses, as I turn to him with shock. He doesn't notice me, and so he goes on. "Aten could not stand alone, but there is no reason not to celebrate and learn from the god. I could begin a college, attached to the Great Temple and under your direction, Lord Seer. We could train Aten's priests to be the foremost astronomers in the world. Amarna would not be a capital city, as my father envisioned, but we could build it into a great center of study, of science and the arts..."

"It would be a fitting celebration of your father's passion for intellectual pursuits," Meri-Re says eagerly.

I can't stand this. But I am rooted in my chair at Pharaoh's side, unable to excuse myself, unable to save myself from the reminiscing on my father's brilliance and vision. Worst of all, Tutankhamun is equally tortured by and hungry for these words. And if I did not listen to his familiar voice, if I let my eyes unfocus, then time could shift and bend, and I would mistake the Pharaoh to my right. I might even remember my father for the man he was, I might even remember that I loved him too, before he turned so violently against me... Every word they speak is like a rope tightening around my chest, and it's getting more difficult to ignore the bulky stone walls and towering pylons of the city to my right.

"My father has been savagely attacked, Lord Seer, but thanks to Chief Mahu's alert guards, they could not inflict any lasting harm. Still, I know he felt the violation in the next world, and I know that he is angry for what has become of his city. I should like your assistance to create a special ceremony to appease his *akhu*, Lord Meri-Re, one that will be inserted into the sunrise and sunset services every day for a year. I mean to stay here for several weeks, Meri-Re, while we pursue the fourth criminal. During that time, I will function as Aten's High Priest. I will perform the new ceremony myself, in hope that my father might be pleased with me."

"What?" I forget etiquette and breathe my horrified question to Tutankhamun. He turns to me with a guilty look in his eyes. "We will stay here?"

Our guests busy themselves drinking wine or contemplating the ongoing harvest on the west bank. Tutankhamun tells me, "There is a fourth criminal at large. We must investigate further to find him; we must secure the tombs again. We must make sure our family is safe at their rest. This cannot be done from Memphis or Thebes! I thought we might stay in the Annex Palace."

"Oh-" I press my fingers to my lips before I speak the truth: I cannot stay there; I'd rather die than enter an Amarna palace! How could he ask it of me? I lower my gaze demurely, not wanting these men to see the rebellion in my face. My fingers fall to my tightening chest. I can feel Tutankhamun's eyes on me; is he angry that I questioned him before his servants? Or does Tutankhamun feel properly ashamed of asking me to sleep in the palace my father built for my sister when she became his wife, two years before the heartless man forced marriage on me!

Tutankhamun says, "Mahu, you must send your men out immediately to search for this fourth man. We can't wait until we've interrogated the prisoners. We have a description from the brother, who says the man was well dressed and soft-looking, perhaps a scribe of some sort, or worse, someone in my service."

The hard, hook nosed chief responds enthusiastically. "We ordered the city locked down as soon as our patrolman noticed the breach in the tombs. If there is truly a fourth man, he must still be in Amarna. He would have to have hidden anything he stole. Should I send officers into the city to search homes, Your Majesty?"

"Of course, and be sure to search the vacant houses as well, and the old workman's village."

"Your Majesty..." Mahu's voice pinches as he says, "No one has been in the old workman's village since the plague. The doors have remained sealed..."

"And the walls cannot be climbed over?" Tutankhamun questions. "Pay some of your men double and quarantine them for a week when they come out. We must check everywhere."

I snap my fingers at the nearest servant girl, needing water for my tight, dry throat. How many times have I heard Pharaoh order Mahu to search the homes of Amarna? And I will have to see it all! I will have to live here while the remaining peasants are terrorized in their sleep, their modest houses torn apart, the men and women full of fear and reporting on neighbors and friends to save themselves-

I cannot stand it anymore. I feel as if I am falling into a pit of hissing snakes, as if some dreaded thing were slipping like noxious mist all around my body. My hands begin to shake again, my stomach flips painfully. The air is too hot to breathe, too thick to fill my lungs.

Tutankhamun, in his anguished guilt, expresses to Mahu that they must do everything possible to secure the tombs from future violations. Mahu informs him horribly that, "The traditional manner of execution for a tomb robber should be a wonderful deterrent. When the stake is set properly, it takes days for the criminal to die, and if Your Majesty has this done in a public area it should leave no doubt how tomb robbers are dealt with-"

I gasp for breath, rocking forward in my chair. Humiliated,

I turn away from our guests, but when I look out to the fields the golden wheat sways and waves unnaturally under a liquid turquoise sky, and I know I'm succumbing to my long dormant panic disease. Tears rush down my cheeks as I struggle to breathe, and Tutankhamun is beside me in an instant but I don't want anyone touching me, I don't want to feel Pharaoh's hands in the shadow of Amarna's Great Palace. Mahu and Meri-Re pop up like frightened rabbits, but I can't stop this shameful attack. Tutankhamun lifts me out of the chair and I cover my face with my hands, sucking my breath through my fingers, sure that I will die.

Exhausted, I sit on Tutankhamun's bed clutching the blanket to my stomach. He's dragged a chair over to the bedside and now he sits watching me, a gilded silver cup in his hands. "Do you want more?" he asks softly.

I shake my head, still staring down at the swirling red and blue patterns painted on the floor where they meet the crisp white hem of Tutankhamun's cloak. I can feel the drugged wine warming my belly and coursing through my blood. I can breathe again. I can feel the sharpness of my life drifting away from me. And I cannot help but remember that my sister gave me poppy syrup when I was a terrified new bride; Tia used it often afterwards, to pull me back from my dizzy, shaking, suffocating madness.

"What can I do for you?"

"I can't be here," I tell him, my voice thready and weak. "I want to go home."

Tutankhamun says nothing. Out of the corners of my eyes I can see him sink his head in his hands. When he looks up again he says, "All right. I'll go home on Nakhtmin's barge when this is finished. Can you give me a day to make the preparations?"

"Yes," I say quietly. I look up at him, at the grave sadness in his dark eyes. "But won't you come with me? Can you not leave this to Mahu? You can't want to sleep in that palace!"

Tutankhamun begins to speak, but he swallows and looks away. "I must do this," he tells me. "I must... I have to fix this."

"You've done nothing wrong!" I cry quietly, tears flooding my eyes again. "You are a *true* king of Egypt! Why are you doing this?"

"Shh, be calm. You will get sick again."

"Why are you doing this, Tutankhamun?"

"I have to," he breathes, looking at me in anguish. "I told you. I have been a poor son, a disgraceful son."

"He was a disgrace of a father! This is madness! You want to live in Amarna, expand Aten's worship? Since *when*? What do you think your council will say? What will the people of Egypt-the people who suffered persecution and foreign death squads-think about this?"

"I don't care what they think! I care what I think of myself, and I care- I care-" He shakes his head, biting his words. But I know he meant to say that he cares what Father thinks.

"You never cared before! You knew he was wrong to banish the gods, and to use Egypt to feed Amarna! You knew he was wrong to butcher his people!"

Tutankhamun closes his eyes in agony. "Can you imagine what it is to be the son who broke his father's covenants? It is a horrible burden! I destroyed a part of myself when I destroyed his laws. And now this has happened, and I feel the guilt as if I had done it myself."

"But you didn't!" I cry. "Someone who wanted gold or revenge hatched a scheme to break into the tombs, not you! And you... you followed your heart! You cared about your people, and you felt the call of the gods."

"I was a child, Ankhesenamun! I did want those things, but everyone around me wanted them too, and perhaps I shouldn't have turned my back so completely on my own heritage! I... I relied too heavily on my council, I let them lead me, I let them take my name..."

For the first time, I see the tears welling in his black eyes spilling over his cheeks. I lay the blanket aside and reach for his hands, taking the wine and setting it on the floor. He needs no more encouragement to come to the bed and fall into my arms, enveloping me in his sweet-smelling skin. "I want to be a good king," he breathes, "I want to do right by my father; I want to be righteous, please understand…"

"Tutankhamun," I murmur, stroking his back, marveling how he can be so vulnerable underneath all his fierceness and his power. If only he had ever had his mother, if only Father had given him his due as a son, perhaps the world would not weigh so heavily on him… I kiss his cheek and he tightens his arms around me, and I know again that there is no other place in the world for me.

"What should I do?" he whispers against my long braids.

"You can't stay here," I tell him honestly. "You have chosen, whatever you think of it. You have made yourself into Tutankhamun, and you cannot be Tutankhaten again."

"But I must keep them safe," he says. "You must want me to keep our family safe! And what about the man who wasn't caught? He is my enemy! I must find him."

"Yes," I agree, "But you must do it carefully. You took your throne amid a rebellion, Tutankhamun, and you only kept it because you were able to compromise. You may not like it, but the eyes of your subjects will always be wary. Even my own eyes are, sometimes… You must take care not to seem like you'll go back to what your people are calling heresy and tyranny."

He sighs in my arms, searching for my lips, kissing me softly when he finds them. "I love you so much," he whispers. "Forgive me if I caused you pain…"

"I love you," I say, "You need no forgiveness," and I let him kiss me more. Then Tutankhamun wraps his arms tightly around me again, drawing a deep breath as he holds me. "I have to see to them," he tells me, and I remember the two servants from Amarna waiting anxiously on our deck.

"Go," I whisper, stroking his cheeks. "I'm going to rest here."

He leaves me, shutting the door to the dangerous world beyond. I won't go out to see my father's city again.

I must have fallen asleep, for when I wake again, Tutankhamun is standing in the doorway, his tall, athletic body framed by twilight. Still in the green gown I put on in the morning, I slip from the bed and quietly walk across the floor. I put my hand on his shoulder and he looks down on me, the golden cobra on his diadem winking in the lamplight. Tutankhamun encircles my waist with his arm.

"What are you looking at?" I ask, bravely casting my eyes out to the city. Light glows from far more windows tonight, as if Tutankhamun had ordered Amarna to come awake again.

"Meri-Re is finishing the new ceremony now," he says, looking towards the Great Temple of Aten.

"I thought you would do it yourself."

"I will go to the temple the day after tomorrow, to make my peace before we leave."

I draw my breath in surprise. Tutankhamun gazes down on me with exhausted eyes and says, "I will break his final vow, Ankhesenamun."

"What do you mean?"

"I mean... you are right. I cannot stay here, I can't be like him, I can't restore this city. I chose to become Tutankhamun, a traditional Pharaoh ruling with Amun's patronage, and I cannot resurrect Aten, not even to be side by side with Amun. And there will always be men who would wish to do harm to Father, and your mother, because of what they did to Egypt. I must move our family, Ankhesenamun; to protect them, I must rebury them in secret tombs in the Valley, where we shall be buried. Father vowed to rest in death in Amarna, but as I broke his laws, I shall break that promise. I can hear him screaming in my heart, and calling me a fool and a coward and every other thing, and I swear I hope that stops one day; but better screaming than silence. If someone breaks into those tombs again, we might not catch them. Father's soul might be destroyed, and then I will have failed utterly. So I will move him. It is my decision now, and I don't think he would have hesitated in making it were he in my place."

Such a reversal! I blink in astonishment, and ask, "But—what about the fourth man?"

Tutankhamun's eyes darken noticeably at the thought of his unknown enemy. "There is no one better to handle these matters than Lord Ay. He caught almost all of Father's enemies. I shall summon him to Thebes, and he can take custody of the two surviving criminals there. If anyone can find their accomplice, it will be Ay. The men can be executed afterwards, in whatever city I feel best to have it done."

I embrace him tightly, sighing in relief.

"Are you happy?" he asks me softly, kissing my hair.

I'm so happy that tears rush my eyes when I look up at his dark, handsome face. "Oh yes, Tutankhamun," I assure him. "I want to go home. Please, take me home."

"We will leave as soon as the arrangements are made."

Chapter Thirty-Nine

Summer, Year Eight

At Abydos our barge is met by a royal messenger on a snorting, foam-covered horse. The man comes on deck as we tie up for the night, dropping into a deep bow as soon as his feet touch the cedar planks. Ipay takes the message and brings it to Tutankhamun, who is dining on the granite dais before his royal cabin. He unrolls it, and then murmurs, "Intef has confessed. He created the entire scheme, and he murdered Setnakht, the elder from the Memphis *Kenbet*."

"Confessed?" I exclaim curiously. "I thought Ay said he was stubborn in his silence!"

"Thank the gods," Tutankhamun says quietly. "Now my justice can be done."

On the day of the execution, Henutawy slides a tight white sheath over my slender body. I sit before my vanity as Mutnojme paints my eyes heavily with crushed green malachite and a brushing of gold dust. She lines them in thick black kohl, extending the line in a thick wing towards my temple. Akila holds up my silver mirror, and I think how the effect of the make-up lends a preternatural effect to my light, hazel-gold eyes. Next, she refreshes the many hundreds of long braids in my hair with rose oil so that they gleam black.

Henutawy brings over the sacred ceremonial jewels that I must wear for this solemn display of Pharaoh's authority and justice. The heavy broad collar of Wadjet, the cobra goddess who, along with Nekhbet the vulture protects Pharaoh, is set with alternating bands of polished malachite and gold. She then brings the heavy vulture crown, done in gold embedded with malachite and carnelian, and sets it atop my braids. When Akila holds my full length mirror before me, I nod in satisfaction. My pleasure at my regal appearance is dampened by the nature of the day. In fact, I was so frightened to witness Tutankhamun's first civilian execution that Mutnojme gave me a half a cup of opium infused wine before painting my eyes, and my lips are still stained red from the calming potion. It would not do for the Great Royal Wife to faint at Pharaoh's justice.

Tutankhamun appears at my door only moments later. He is resplendent in his regalia. A banded corselet is crossed over his chest underneath his large and painstakingly worked *nebti* collar. His sculpted bronze abdomen is bare, and his long, pleated kilt sits low on his hips. A heavy gold, lapis, and carnelian sash wraps around his waist and swings down the middle of his kilt. His head is covered in a long, stiff *nemes* headdress, made of alternating cloth of gold and blue stripes. His kohl-darkened eyes glow with warmth as he takes in my appearance. "You don't have to go," he tells me, giving me one last chance at reprieve.

"No, Tutankhamun, it is proper for me to sit at your side," I say, taking his arm. We step out together and walk to incense-clouded portico behind Malkata's main courtyard, where the execution is to be held. Trumpets sing for us, and drums beat as we step into the sunlight. The dozens of viziers, lords, and senior palace officials come to witness lower themselves to the sandy ground, pressing their palms and brows into the dust. We take our thrones under a sunshade, and as soon as our court rises, the two disgraced aristocrats Intef and Herihor are brought out to their deaths. Earlier, as I bathed and dressed, Lord Ay's High *Kenbet* condemned the two for crimes against Pharaoh's Majesty and the people of Egypt. A handful of lesser men will die in the common square today, but these two are the peers of the most powerful men in the land. It's impossible to tell what the great lords gathered in the yard truly think; Tutankhamun believes that there are other schemes to snatch illegal wealth at work, because in exchange for support, Father allowed many men a free hand in their local matters. With the executions of Intef and Herihor, Tutankhamun is announcing to his country that he will not tolerate the corruption fostered by his predecessor.

Herihor looks the worse, for he has lost much weight, and his nose was obviously broken at some point. But Lord Intef seems only slightly less plump and well-oiled than he did the day we met him on the docks of Memphis, surrounded by his entourage. His eyes are darker and without his wig, his grey hair reveals his age, but a few months in prison have hardly made a dent in his well-fed physique.

And then the swordsman steps up, and the prisoners are made to kneel. A herald announces that Intef and Herihor are to die according to Pharaoh's law, and their lands and wealth are forfeited to the crown. But surprisingly, we are not informed that their wives and children are banished from the land. I think of the young and gaudy Iniuia and feel a moment of relief that she won't be driven into the deserts of the Sinai and left to make her way to Palestine with her babies. Still, it is unusual.

The moment of mercy is short-lived. Tutankhamun sits stonily still, wearing the impassive face of a remote god. His heart does not beat a fraction harder as the two men are made to kneel, but I desperately want to look away. I am not this hardened creature that I must appear beneath the dais; I am terrified of blood...

The sword swings and passes through Herihor's neck so quickly it is but a flash in the sun. "Oh!" I cry softly, tightening my fingers on the gilded armrests of my throne. There's a sinking dread in my belly and I could weep for disgust to see Herihor's severed head lying in the sand. His body falls like a useless, inanimate thing. I want to crawl onto Tutankhamun's lap and hide my face. Intef dies immediately after. It is done, so quickly.

The court goes off to the audience chamber afterwards, and Tutankhamun and I walk in slow state through the portico and towards our court. Any servants in the hallway fall to the floor at our passing, and they don't see that my quivering fingers are threaded with Tutankhamun's. I don't trust myself to speak yet, and so we walk in silence. As we enter the palace, Tutankhamun escorts me before him, and he lays his hand softly on my back for just a moment. I find a tentative smile, stealing a quick glance at him from the corners of my eyes. He smiles back at me, a tiny gesture of reassurance, not pleasure, appearing in the polished serenity in his face.

Horemhab approaches us at the open door of the audience chamber, making a little bow to Tutankhamun. When he rises, Tutankhamun takes his hand in a firm clasp and says, "The people should have some relief now."

"Your Majesty has done a great thing today," Horemhab affirms, warm with pleasure.

We walk into the hall and there is swift silence as men rise. Again, they go down in obeisance, not to the floor this time but into a deep, bent-back bow. They do not rise until we are seated, and only then do they return to their tables. Their conversations are far quieter now.

Tutankhamun beckons Ay, and the Grand Vizier approaches, silver flashing on his sash and around the hem of his robe. "Your Majesty," he says graciously, bowing.

"Well done, Lord Ay," Tutankhamun says, motioning for a servant to bring Ay an elegant ivory inlaid mahogany folding chair. "I had not expected Intef to break so quickly, but I am greatly pleased at the result. And to make sure that work is not in vain, I've directed Maya to train a special group of officers to go out with next year's tax collection and monitor for abuses. I will not tolerate any more of this."

Ay bows his head slightly. "I was as horrified as Your Majesty to learn that Intef was corrupted. He was so capable and hardworking... I am ashamed to admit that I was wrong about that man's character, but truly, he blinded me. Forgive me, my lord."

Tutankhamun motions for wine and wets his throat. "Don't worry, Ay. You made scores of appointments when I was too green to do it myself, and only one bore bad fruit. Now," he says, moving along, "I want you to resolve this disgraceful matter of the tomb robbers with all haste."

"From the information our suspect's brother gave us, I believe I know the man."

"Who is he?" Tutankhamun demands anxiously.

"There was a man named Ahotep who matched this description in the office of Royal Works. He oversaw the artisans hired to decorate the tombs. It would make sense. We have records of where he used to live. Now that this business with Intef is finished, I can look into his whereabouts in earnest. Now, Mahu's search turned up nothing, you say?"

Tutankhamun frowns. "Nothing. Chief Mahu locked the city down, but if this Ahotep-if that is who he truly is-has any stealth he could have eluded the police in the eastern desert. The searches in the city yielded a bundle of gold rings, but nothing else. I want them dead, Ay. I want them all dead in a month, before my family is reinterred."

Ay raises his heavy eyebrows as the tall order. "I shall certainly do my best, Your Majesty. The world will be a better place once these depraved men are gone."

The royal necropolis in the mountains of Thebes is a still, silent place. The purple of the mountains at dawn burns off into a dull yellow as we approach. My curtained litter sways slightly on the shoulders of eight immense Nubian porters, who bear me and my son behind Tutankhamun's chariot. As

Tutankhamun goes off with Lord Ay to settle on the secret locations for the new tombs, I lie back and play with Tuthmosis and his wooden horse. My son has just arrived from Memphis and he chatters away to me. Tuthmosis tells me that his horse's name is Glory. "He is my warhorse!" my son declares proudly, holding his toy up and flying him through the air. "He's the fastest horse ever!" I try to mind his princely dignity now that he is speaking and showing me a fiercely independent streak, but I itch to snatch him up and kiss his plump cheeks.

When I hear footsteps on the rocky desert soil I say, "Your father is coming," and Tuthmosis carefully sets down his wooden horse. I straighten my son's little red and blue beaded collar, and tuck his big black curls behind his ears.

Tutankhamun twitches the curtains back. "Are you ready?"

I clap my hands softly and hold them out, and Tuthmosis climbs into my arms. I step out of the litter and set my son on my hip. "If we must."

"*Hapepy*, this is important. We cannot fear it."

When Tutankhamun returned from Amarna, he became determined that we should visit his tomb as a family. He has told me that he has decided to build an addition to his tomb for me, so that we can rest together in eternity.

"Let me take him," Tutankhamun says, and our son gladly climbs into his father's arms. As Ay and our tiny security detail wait behind, Tutankhamun and I hike into the western branch of valley necropolis. The silence is so deep and potent that it could almost be alive, hanging in the sky and embedding itself in every *wadi* and crack cut into the mountains. When an eagle screams through the turquoise sky overhead I jump in fright, earning a rich, honeyed laugh from Tutankhamun. "Do you fear the spirits of our ancestors?"

"I don't like death," I say, and then I bite my lips because who really does? Yet Tutankhamun walks easily through these hills, knowing that they are carved through and out with the tombs of our ancestors.

With one arm cradling our child, Tutankhamun motions

towards the face of a golden mountain. "Our grandfather is rests there. He was a great king, who made this country rich and kept the peace for many years. I thought this place near him was fitting for my eternal rest."

Tutankhamun stops amid orderly piles of stone left behind yesterday when the workmen went home for the night. I look up at the spot Tutankhamun has chosen to for us be buried in, in the protected corner of a cliff near to our grandfather's tomb. "I see there's no one here to light the way in," I observe gladly.

"I didn't think it would be necessary for us to enter. Right now there are three unfinished chambers on a straight axis, but I'm considering adding a turn around the corner and a false hallway before creating your burial chamber. My engineers say it's possible."

"Sire, where is grandfather? And why is he sleeping here? And why will you and Mother sleep here, in the desert?"

Tutankhamun laughs softly. "My grandfather's body is at rest in the mountain, Tuthmosis. But his *akhu* is awake, and it can journey to the next world and back. One day, your mother and I will go to rest in the mountains as well. When that happens, you will be Pharaoh as I am now, and you shall make a tomb like this for yourself."

"Can your grandfather's spirit see us?"

Tutankhamun releases my hand and holds his son close. "If he chooses to visit us, he can. But during the day, he may travel with Aten across the sky, because he was Pharaoh as well. You come from a great line of kings, my son. Each had their appointed time in this world, to rule it as they saw fit. Now it is my time, but one day, it will be yours. And you must always honor your ancestors, Tuthmosis."

"I will, *Abi*," Tuthmosis says solemnly.

I cannot help smiling. Tutankhamun sets our son down so that he might walk around and explore a bit, and I lean into my husband's arms. "I will be glad to spend eternity with you," I tell him, reaching up to give him a quick kiss on the lips.

Tutankhamun brushes his fingers across my cheeks. "We

will always be together," he promises me. "As we always have been. The gods are kind." He looks to our son crouching to examine rough blocks of sandstone, and he smiles in satisfaction.

Three weeks after we return from Amarna, our family is reburied at night in all secrecy. I am not there, but Tutankhamun oversees it himself. When he returns, I usher him into a steaming bath; I sing to him softly as I wash his smooth skin, and he tips his head back and closes his eyes, forgetting coffins and broken vows for a few quiet moments. Afterwards he lies belly down on his bed and I crawl over his back, pulling the stopper from a bottle of silky spikenard-scented massage oil. Tutankhamun's bronze shoulders are tight; I knead my hands softly into the muscles of his shoulders, working in small circles all the way down his back. He sighs as his tension melts away, and then he turns beneath me and clutches my thighs, saying "Your turn."

I slip my robe off and lay on my belly. He oils his strong hands, and then I sigh in pleasure as he works magic on my small back. It is delicious, but then I feel his heavy warm body pressing down on me. He brushes my thick black curls away and kisses my neck, setting fire to my blood; he pushes my thighs apart and then pushes slowly inside me, and I gasp, frozen still beneath him, shocked by the sweet rush of pleasure. The hot summer night passes as a dream, ending far too quickly with the unwelcome approach of the sun.

And then, incredibly, at daybreak Vizier Ay brings us a messenger who delivers three *ushabti* from my father's tomb, as well as some of my eldest sister's jewels. Ahotep, the fourth tomb robber, was caught in Asyut, with all of the stolen property in his possession. But before Tutankhamun can rejoice, the messenger reveals that Ahotep resisted his arrest, killed one of Pharaoh's policemen, and wound up with a spear in the gut for his troubles. Tutankhamun drops back in his chair in disgust, robbed of his vengeance.

"Did I not give explicit orders that he should be taken *alive?*" Lord Ay demands angrily.

The messenger bows lower, not daring to advance any excuse.

And so it is over; not the way Tutankhamun would have wanted, but over all the same. The other two men are impaled on one of the tracks going out to the Valley of the Kings. I know they aren't dead just yet, and I try not to think of it, just like Tutankhamun tries not to think of Father, buried here in the western mountains of Thebes.

Tutankhamun's investigation into tax corruption is finished, and our family is safely reburied in secret tombs. Our son is beginning his studies with Senqed, and he can already identify the characters of the hieroglyph alphabet. Tuthmosis beamed with pride when Tutankhamun gave him his first writing kit, a handsome ebony box with reed brushes, a carved ivory ink well, and a supply of red and black powdered ink; Senqed assured us that Tuthmosis should be writing his name and simple words by the end of the flood. When our son is done with his tutor, and Tutankhamun isn't sitting in the audience chamber, we sail our barge along the swollen, sparkling Nile. Our people line the banks to wave and cheer as we pass by, our bright gold and blue pennants snapping in the wind, the great, low drum beating rhythmically to keep time for the oarsmen. On these perfect, peaceful summer days, I hold Tutankhamun's hand in mine while my son plays quietly at my feet, gliding all the while past the beautiful holy city of Karnak.

Chapter Forty

On a shining mid-summer's day, we recline happily in Malkata's courtyard. Three harpists sit in the corner, and most of the elite court gathers in the open air to play *senet* and drink wine, and gossip about each other. Lord Ay-ever at work-stands under a sunshade, dictating notes to a scribe. I relax on cushions with Tutankhamun; we watch our son run between the legs of courtiers with his little bow in hand and his black curls flying behind him.

Nakhtmin, practicing archery in the center of the yard with Djede, shouts out, "Almost! Look at that! Shaved clean off!"

An arrow, or really, a part of one, broken mid-shaft, shivers in the target. "What in the world are they trying to do?" I ask him.

"Mmm..." Tutankhamun looks over to his new General, Nakhtmin, and his new Horse Master, Djede. "Trying to split arrows, I think."

I laugh again, and grab his arm. "Go. Show them how it is done."

Tutankhamun grins like a boy. He pushes himself up. I reach after him as he goes, reluctant to let go of him. I watch as he saunters over to his men, noting with a twinge of sorrow that his walk is not nearly as spry or graceful as it once was, even months ago. But Nakhtmin claps him on the back, and tells Djede, "See how he does it."

Tutankhamun fits an arrow to Djede's bow, and shoots it off with ease and precision. I need not look to know it has gone straight to the heart of the target. "Now," he says in his sweet, lulling voice, "it is not the eyes that need focusing, but the heart. I will show you."

Tutankhamun exhales deeply, and I know in that exhale his very bones are remembering the exact way he held himself as he shot the first arrow. And to prove his point, and his flawless, lethal skill, he closes his eyes. He takes his stance again, and then, sightless, Tutankhamun shoots his arrow, splitting the imported ashwood shaft of the first right down the center.

Nakhtmin laughs aloud, clapping his hands. Djede narrows his small, frustrated eyes, staring at the split arrow. Nakhtmin cries, "This is why I follow this man, if man he truly is!"

"Is this a mortal skill, Your Majesty?" Djede asks. He's so unattractive that I never can tell if he's being sour or not. But why should he be upset? How foolish, for a commoner to be jealous of a Pharaoh! The two are not even the same species.

"I learned it through passion and practice, Djede," Tutankhamun tells him truthfully.

The merry laughter of women turns my head. Lady Iset holds my son by the hand, and Mutnojme follows behind. "Mother!" Tuthmosis cries. Iset lets him go, and my beautiful little boy tumbles into my lap, looking up at me with his father's deep black eyes.

"Your son will grow up to break hearts, Your Majesty!" Iset laughs, sitting at my side. "He was charming us with flowers, and showing off his bow."

"He is his father's son," I reply smiling, kissing my boy's plump cheeks.

My baby grins, batting his thick black lashes. He sinks into my lap and puts his finger to his mouth. Suddenly, Mutnojme draws her breath. I follow her gaze to General Horemhab, entering the courtyard at a brisk clip, Lord Hani in tow. She loves him so much, even now, that the mere sight of his heavy frame is enough to turn her heart. But I know that the two of them together, Horemhab and Hani, always means one thing: war in Asia.

"Iset," I murmur, looking to Nakhtmin's wife.

Iset is no fool. She purses her lips tightly and murmurs, "It is a joy and a misery to have a warrior for a husband."

"Will you take Tuthmosis?"

Iset's face warms. She adores children, and Tuthmosis and Nebamun are dear friends. And Tuthmosis adores Iset as well; when she holds out her arms, he gleefully goes to her. He doesn't crawl into her lap as he did mine; he sits precociously at her side, running his plump little fingers over her beaded bracelet. "Would you like to hold this?" I hear her ask, as I push myself up.

I note that Lord Ay has looked up from his scribe's tablet, to watch the general with quiet eyes. Tutankhamun welcomes Horemhab and Hani, directing a servant girl to bring wine. But Horemhab is in a single minded mood. He murmurs quietly to Tutankhamun, and Tutankhamun narrows his eyes. As I slip closer, I hear Horemhab say, "They're south of Kadesh, looting and burning any cities and villages that pay us tribute and refuse to switch allegiance. But the Hittite king is still in Mitanni."

Lord Hani's voice sounds like silk over Horemhab's gravel. "Likely the Hittite king will know nothing of this if an envoy was sent to complain. He will say that his men were attacked as they rotated home from Carcamesh, even if they are out of their way. He will say they were only defending themselves. It will be like when he stole Kadesh; he will say he was provoked, he violated no treaty. Egypt will be on shaky ground again."

"Shaky ground with whom?" Tutankhamun asks, laughing. "I have no peer to question my behavior. That treaty is long dead! Lord Hani, you did not return to Egypt without dispatching to the garrison at Kumidi?"

"They are ready with provisions and soldiers, Your Majesty."

I put my hand to my throat, and my heart. I had almost forgotten that Tutankhamun would return to war! I could wilt

with disappointment, and worse, I know he isn't well. I know
he is sharper with his servants, I know he gasps when I rub his
foot; and I know he will ignore any pain to chase the glory of
a victory. And these are the Hittites, not a rag-tag band of city-
state militiamen defending a single garrison and some fields.
He must want this fight so badly he can taste it.

"We must prepare immediately," Tutankhamun decides.
"The fortresses at Kumidi and Beth-Shan should send their
soldiers north as soon as a rider can reach them. That is a
combined total of one thousand men. Rameses is ready at Fort
Tjel; he can take his men out and march the Way of Horus.
Once he passes Gaza he can replenish his provisions at the
Palestinian cities on alert. Nakhtmin, prepare five thousand of
your men. We will go by sea as soon as possible. Horemhab,
order a thousand charioteers including my personal company,
see to the supplies and the weapons for our army, and meet me
later to discuss planning." Tutankhamun turns to Hani. "We
shall meet over dinner, to discuss our business. That is all."

Once dismissed, each man goes off to their duties. Djede
lingers behind a moment, as if he would receive some special
command from Pharaoh. But Djede takes his orders from
Rameses' immediate subordinate, who moved in to fill his place
as Overseer of the Stables of the Two Lands when Rameses
went off to command Fort Tjel. Finally he turns away from the
archery targets and melts into the crowd. Tutankhamun and I
are left facing each other.

Surrounded by other courtiers, there's nothing we can say.
He extends his hand to me and I take it, and we walk off,
only to come face to face with Lord Ay. Tutankhamun puts his
hand on the old vizier's back. "I must leave you to your own
devices again," Tutankhamun tells him merrily, like a little boy
ducking his tutor to run and play in the fields.

"I did manage to hear most of it," Ay concedes.

"And you are going to say it will be too expensive, that we
want to avoid all-out war with the powerful Hittites…"

Lord Ay offers a small smile. "I was going to tell Your
Majesty that your people will be deeply proud of their king,

for achieving a victory over the Hittites and restoring Egypt's glory in Asia."

"I'm glad to hear it," Tutankhamun says, grinning. He takes me into the shadows of the portico, away from the laughing courtiers and breezy music. "I know what you will say as well," he murmurs, taking me in his arms.

"That makes it no less true. You are unwell, which will make it doubly dangerous."

"If I have too much pain, I won't fight; but either way, I intend to general this battle."

I look up into his handsome face, the luminous black eyes that I know so well. "But what if something happens during the fight, when you are already in the field? I'm not just worried about pain; I'm worried about your bones breaking. Pentju said they are as brittle as glass now, Tutankhamun! And you know it as well. Why else are you so cautious these days? Why else did you not hunt last winter?"

Tutankhamun kisses my brow. "I will go, Ankhesenamun. There is nothing that can be said to stop me, not even by you."

"And I will be worried sick each day!" I cry softly, truly dismayed. It is not a lie, I can worry myself sick, I shake from fear and I can't eat when I'm too upset. And I had a true attack for the first time in years in that wretched city of Amarna! I couldn't breathe and my heart was beating like it would explode, and I would have fallen to the ground if Tutankhamun hadn't picked me up. "Please!" I say desperately. "Please don't leave me."

Tutankhamun can feel my pain as his own when he wants to, and now his sadness is written on his face. "*Hapepy*," he murmurs, holding me against his chest, stroking my hair soothingly. And then he says something I would never have expected in all my life. "Why don't you come with me?"

I look up at him, blinking in astonishment, sure that I have heard him wrong. He grins like a lion and says, "Come to Asia with me! I can keep you at Beirut castle, where you will be safe. And then you need not worry, for I will ride in between engagements to see you, and when I have my victory, we will return in triumph together."

"Me! Go to war! I could be captured!"

"No, you'll be protected, believe me. The king of Babylon brings his entire harem on campaign, why should I not bring my only beloved?" And then he leans down, kissing my cheek and breathing in my ear, "You have never made love to a warrior fresh from battle. You'll like it."

I shiver at this light touch, these heady words. "Will I?"

"Oh yes, I am sure. I know you very well."

"You're impossible," I tease, looking up into his handsome, fierce dark face. "And conceited and stubborn."

He bites his pretty lips and laughs, his eyes flushed with delight.

"Swear it will be your last battle, Tutankhamun. You have proven yourself as a warrior and made your name. You cannot keep punishing yourself this way! I love you so much that it punishes me as well, please…"

He wraps his arms around me, fitting me perfectly against his hard chest. "I don't want to stop," he murmurs, sounding more a boy than a king. "I love to fight."

I dig my fingers into his back, agonized that I must be the one to beg him to surrender his passion to his affliction. "But I will, Ankhesenamun," he says, and I gasp in relief. "I swear by Amun himself that this will be my last battle."

Chapter Forty-One

Our ship splashes forward and I laugh aloud as the cool, salty spray hits my face. "This is incredible!" The wind whips us more fiercely than drag from the fastest chariot. Our sailors are running Egypt's fleet up the coast of Palestine, somewhere between Gaza and Ashkelon. Tutankhamun calls me over to the port side, where dolphins dash just beneath the surface of the blue water. They flip through the waves and race the ship like an acrobatic escort. "Will they take us all the way to Jaffe?"

"All the way to Beirut," Tutankhamun says. He leans out over the water, his fine white *nemes* headdress blowing back from his strong bronze shoulders. "Here, get a better look; I will hold you."

With his arms secure about my waist, I stand on my toes and lean over the wall of the ship, watching the waves break on the hull as we lift up and splash down again and again, the dolphins leaping and riding the crests of water made by our wake. Delighted, I look up at Tutankhamun. "Thank you," I say, kissing his lips. "I never thought to see such a thing in my life."

"You are not afraid?" he asks admirably, brushing my whipping curls away from my face.

"I ought to be!" I say, thinking of how unimaginably deep the water beneath me is, and what sort of creatures fill it. "But no, this is wonderful! I'm so glad you brought me! We shall have a true adventure together, at last."

"You are brave," he tells me, his gaze growing serious. "You're so brave I thought I might ask you..." He looks down, gathering himself.

I stroke his cheek and murmur, "What could it be? Just ask me."

"I want you to stop taking that medicine, Ankhesenamun. I want to have another baby with you. I love you so much, and I love Tuthmosis, and I want our family to grow. And you are so beautiful when you're carrying my child."

Tutankhamun searches my eyes hopefully, his own filled with raw love. I whisper, "I don't know... It's terrifying, Tutankhamun. It's like battle, maybe worse, because it's my babies who are killed. I don't know if I can lose another child, or endure another bad labor."

"Will you think about it?" he asks softly.

"Even if I stopped right now, it would still take time, Akasha said. I might not conceive right away."

Tutankhamun smiles winsomely. "That's all right," he says quickly. "As long as one day soon..."

I wrap my arms around him. I never stopped wanting more children; I only wanted the pain of it to end. Perhaps now, after my body has taken a break, I will be stronger, I will be able to give Tutankhamun another son. Maybe I could even have a little girl of my own, a daughter who would grow up knowing only love and happiness. "All right," I say quietly. "I'll try again, for us, for our family." I turn my face up for the kiss I know is coming. The wind beats my hair around our faces and Tutankhamun's lips taste salty from the sea. How could I not feel bold and hopeful here, soaring over the waves?

At night, we glide through the calm onyx seas, only broken up by the small crests of white foam lapping against the hulls of our ships. Our flotilla is enormous, with five thousand of Egypt's soldiers broken up fifty to a ship, along with crew, horses, and servants, and all bedding down under the stars. The wind, which had gusted from the north-west all day long, now reverses itself, becoming a gentle breeze that blows off the Palestinian coast. The sails are turned and rested oarsmen take the place of those sailors going to bed.

Privacy is quite nearly impossible to find. Tutankhamun and I share his three room cabin, of course, but the walls are thin. Several of my ladies have come along, and they must share our accommodations as well. It is clear that the soldiers and sailors are uncomfortable with women aboard.

I sit in a bronze basin while Henutawy dabs tepid water on my shivering skin. Akasha and Mutnojme sit together sharing warmed wine and the simple, dried foods available for our journey. Akasha is excited to reach Beirut. The port city, she says, is known for its well-stocked markets, and she is anxious to collect some of the herbs uncommon in Egypt. Especially of interest are the more potent plants, which can bring harm as well as healing. "Not only hemlock, my lady, which we have, but also Syrian Rue, and a host of others. Syrian Rue is useful to bring a trance-like state in which we can hear more clearly the murmurs of the gods, but it can also bring severe illness, even death when extracted improperly."

"Or properly, as the extractor desires," Mutnojme says wryly, casting me a smile. "I for one have no interest in such nasty things. I only hope to purchase some of Asia's famous purple dye." She is in high spirits as well. The further we traveled from her domineering uncle the lighter she became, even admitting to me her desire to speak to Horemhab once more. To resolve those things left unsaid between them, she claimed, but I know better, and she should. Surely old Ay must retire soon, and Nakhtmin will be the head of that family, and Mutnojme will do as she pleases.

"You speak truly, Lady Mutnojme," Akasha says. "The powers of such herbs can be employed for good or evil, depending on the intentions of the user. I will collect what I can, for our use at home."

"You should speak to my husband," I tell her. "He has long studied herbs and their more nefarious properties. Although I must admit, these days he is far more concerned with swords than plants."

Akasha bows her head. I know she will not speak to Pharaoh, at least not of her own volition. Like many of our servants, she is timid around the man who is said to have the blood of the gods flowing pure through his body.

After my unsatisfactory bath, I join Tutankhamun at the sweeping lion-headed stem of his flagship. His eyes are again skyward. "Pleiades," he murmurs, staring at a cluster of bright stars rising in the heavens. "Soon the sea will broil with storms, closing the shipping lanes."

"How will we get home?" I ask, nestling into his arms. I feel quite small indeed under the wide night sky, with only narrow planks of cedar between myself and all the monsters of the deep water below. The cold air chills my wet skin and hair, but Tutankhamun's fine body is warm, as always.

"They will open again, *hapepy*, at the end of the planting season. And if we win before that, then we will march down the Way of Horus, and enjoy the hospitality of our Asian allies. Our ships can follow, once it is safe."

"You are so confident," I marvel. Never in his life has Tutankhamun concerned himself with defeat, not even when he took his throne amid a rebellion. "You know the gods love you."

He makes a little murmur of affirmation, kissing the top of my head. "I should hope so, but I must always strive for their pleasure. They like war, and they love victory."

"You are not worried about the Hittite iron? I am told it can smash through granite in a single strike." I shudder to think it, wondering how our peasant infantrymen ever find the courage to charge headlong into a wall of iron swords.

Tutankhamun laughs softly. "You must listen to warriors, not women, when you wish to know about weapons. You have seen my iron dagger. I assure you it cannot split through granite, and it is heavenly iron, meteoric iron, not that common substance found in the northern soils. But I hope to gather a few hundred iron swords in this battle. It's about time we added some to our arsenal. Thus far, only the Hittites employ it, and even then not as much as they use bronze. But I must admit I am drawn to those swords. I have never seen one close up, and I long to. They are indeed quite strong, stronger than bronze. I believe they will have much influence in the future."

"Do not wish to see them too closely, Tutankhamun," I tell him softly.

We turn landward, stopping to pick up provisions in Jaffe on a bright, fair day. The rocky coast around Jaffe juts into the sea and apartments and towers clustered together on the hilly landscape. Mud-brick apartment buildings sprawl all about that hill and the land is studded with tall palm trees and deep green pines. Everywhere there are splashes of scarlet and saffron and deep blue, canopies over roof-top dining areas, curtains catching the salty sea breeze and dancing from windows or balcony doors. The gently curving city wall comes directly to the water, and long rock walls go out into the sea and make their harbor. On either side, miles of beaches stretch into the distance. Pale brown boys in loincloths cast wide fishing nets out over the water. As Pharaoh's fleet pulls into the harbor, they quit their work and jump and run in the sand, calling their friends to see us.

It is ridiculously hot-a sucking, clinging, wet heat-and more than anything I long to leap from the ship and into the sparkling blue water. Pharaoh goes ashore to confer with his generals and supervise the loading of water and grain. Once again, I note that his walk is cautious, slower than ever before. He hid his pain away as we reclined on the deck of his ship, but as soon as his feet touch land it is obvious that each step sends a breath-snatching stab through his left leg. I stand beneath the sail's rigging with Pentju and Akasha, who lament the unhealthy, humid air together. "This is a swampy, vile place," Akasha mutters, swatting at a pack of mosquitos that cluster around the mast.

"Pentju," I say softly, interrupting them. "It is much worse now, isn't it? He denies it to me."

The old physician turns his wizened face to me and says frankly, "Much worse. He should not be here at all. You should entreat him to remain behind, in the command tent."

I look out to the rolling turquoise waves, breaking just beyond the beach. "I could sooner entreat his hawk not to fly," I say quietly. "But he promises me that this will be his last campaign. After this, it will be left to Horemhab, Rameses, and Nakhtmin to defeat Egypt's enemies."

Pentju's sharp eyes cloud, his sight suddenly gone behind a milky veil. I know that what he sees now is not that which is before him, but whatever it is beyond this, whatever his deified father whispers to him. "It must be Rameses," he says plainly, the old man's voice suddenly as clear as the bright sky. "It must be Rameses who picks up Tutankhamun's sword."

Tutankhamun's rich laugh carries over the water. He walks between his generals, Huy and Djede trailing behind. For certain, he is confident of victory, confident of his own prowess and the skill of his men, no matter how the pain in his foot burdens him.

"You said Rameses?" I ask, looking on the stocky General Horemhab, who casts as wide a shadow on the beach as a great Lebanese cedar. "Do you see some... some tragedy befalling Horemhab? Will he be struck down in battle?" Pray it shall not come to pass! Mutnojme's heart would break to pieces, especially as she denied her love these past few years.

The old doctor narrows his eyes, blinking them clear again. "It is gone," he murmurs. "My father will say no more."

After three more days at sea, we finally land at the rich port city of Beirut and disembark in an exotic new world. The people line the streets and cheer for us as ever, but their clothes are heavy and their beards are long and curled, just like in Tutankhamun's murals. Their women have scarves covering their hair. I look down on my sheer linen gown and hip-length, gold-beaded braids, and feel like an exotic bird on display. It seems both the men and the women are staring at me rather than Pharaoh. "They've never seen anyone so beautiful before," Tutankhamun murmurs with pride as we follow our silk-capped escort to the city's castle.

The Princess Dowager of Beirut, Ashera, is a dark, bewitching woman with attractive shots of silver in her luxurious black hair. Even though she is a foreigner, she reminds me a great deal of my grandmother. I admire the straightness of her shoulders, the graceful tilt of her neck. But she is but the mother of a prince-mayor, and she makes no effort to cross the barrier of servant and god's wife. I'm deeply grateful that Mutnojme came with me. When Tutankhamun goes off to see his troops settled and the princess goes off to see to her servants, a giddy Mutnojme takes me by my hands and we rush out to see the balcony. The princess's chambers give a view of both the land and the brilliant blue sea, and the setting sun is streaking the deep blue sea with orange and gold. The wide stone harbor is packed nearly full with Egyptian ships and more are landing, and all along the beach tiny fisherman's boats lie belly up and abandoned for the day.

"I wonder that they dare take those little boats out there!" I say, thinking of the vast, rolling emptiness just off the coast.

"I would do it," Mutnojme declares. "I think it would be marvelous to skip over the waves, and run my fingers through the sea."

I laugh at her boldness. "They would get bitten off by some hungry creature," I predict. "Right at the hennaed tips. It is beautiful here, but I will be glad to be back on the river with Tutankhamun."

"Your Majesty!" Princess Ashera calls me in her thickly accented Egyptian. I expect some foolish problem with my servants, but her face is grey with horror.

"What is it?" I demand. "Have the Hittites attacked?"

"No, Your Majesty," she cries, shaking her head, her eyes wide with terror. "The Pharaoh is sick! He has only just arrived, he could not have gotten ill here-"

"Sick? How is he sick?" I demand.

"With fever," she says grimly.

By the time I rush through the castle, Pentju has walked Tutankhamun into Ashera's late husband's chambers. I grab his arm immediately.

"It's nothing," he insists, brushing Pentju away as the old doctor tries to help him into bed.

"Nothing!" I gasp. "Pentju, what is wrong with him?"

"Not enough to keep me off my chariot," Tutankhamun hisses.

"You must be delirious with your fever!" I snap angrily.

Pentju tells me quietly, "He let himself get bitten up in that filthy coastal sewer. It's malaria."

"Malaria!" I run to his bedside and lay my hand on Tutankhamun's burning brow. "Oh, my poor husband…"

"It's not that bad," Tutankhamun says dismissively, but he moans at the coolness of my hand. Then, quietly, "Everyone has had it. Grandfather himself had it six times. Is that not right, Pentju?"

"I attended the god myself," Pentju says, "when my father was the royal physician. It is not in your blood to succumb to this. Nonetheless, Your Majesty, I shall make you my remedies."

"Do your worst, you old witch doctor," Tutankhamun murmurs, and then he turns his head away, and closes his eyes.

Tutankhamun lies in bed for two long weeks, while our restless army takes the city over, filling every tavern and brothel in Beirut. Some of the soldiers whisper that it is a terrible omen for us that Pharaoh starts his war already ill. I pinch my lips, knowing that he was not well when he stepped onto his ship, nor for some while before that. But our subjects have never seen that. They have seen only his power, his riches. They do not know of his suffering. They have never seen him burying his face in my thighs and gasping in pain as Pentju tended him, and he would not want them to.

And so after twenty days, the Pharaoh of Egypt rises from his sickbed and suits up in his new golden armor, and then he dashes off in his chariot, reckless and beautiful, to hunt and punish Hittites.

Chapter Forty-Two

Winter Year Eight

The winter storms are fierce and frightening. Thunder cracks above the palace, and the small windows flash with broken blue light. The princess says it is their great god, Ba'al, who rides his chariot through the clouds and hurls brilliant, jagged bolts of lightning into the sea. Akasha makes a gesture to ward off evil, murmuring privately that Ba'al is no more than Set, the evil-doer who murdered Osiris to steal his throne. I stand for hours, watching the exotic sight of water from the heavens pelting the cold grey sea. I wonder anxiously how Tutankhamun will circle his enemies with his chariot wheels bogged down by mud. On his last visit, he told me that more Hittites are pouring out of the hills. In turn, Tutankhamun has called up more warriors stationed in the garrison cities along the Way of Horus. Every day, Egyptian casualties stream into Beirut, bleeding and screaming and stinking from rotten wounds. War is a disgusting business, and I cannot understand how our men love it so. But still, I am sure that Tutankhamun will win, and I hope then the Hittites will keep to their own land, or at least expand in some other direction.

"Mutnojme," I say, turning away from the stinging rain, "is Princess Ashera still at her embroidery?"

"She left just moments after we did, Ankhesenamun. I think she's carrying on with the city's high priest."

"The dowager princess?" I ask, amused. "She is a grandmother!"

"A handsome, rich, lonely grandmother," Mutnojme clarifies, grinning.

We are cut off when Henutawy rushes into the room. "There is an army approaching, Your Majesty, from the southeast this time. The maids think it is the Hittite Army!"

"Tell the silly little hens that the Hittites will not break our line." I straighten my thick blue robe and push my heavy curls over my shoulders. Mutnojme and I follow Henutawy into the Ashera's large antechamber, where both my and Ashera's maids bunch up and peer out the slit of window like anxious chicks.

"Get out of the way!" Mutnojme orders; they all fall back. I am too small to see, but Mutnojme peers out and says, "It looks like a black snake, winding through the mist."

"It's definitely an army," I decide. A rush of excitement courses through my body. "I must bathe and find something to wear. And order the kitchen to boil extra tubs of water. Pharaoh will want to bathe as well."

For a moment, as I sit in my steaming bath, I wonder if it could be the Hittites after all. Tutankhamun's army rides in from the northeast, not the southeast. But for the Hittites to come to Beirut, where I am kept under guard... I dismiss that thought immediately. Tutankhamun would never let it happen. He would move heaven and earth before I fell into Hittite hands! I remember Nakhtmin mentioning small rivers on their march, and surely they are only swollen with all this rain, necessitating another approach.

My servants wrap a loose, gauzy rose gown around me as the castle's guard trumpets out the call to open the gates. I tap my foot as Henutawy dabs rose oil on my throat, and then I rush down to the courtyard, just as the great wood and bronze gates pull open. Tutankhamun rides in on the back of Aten's Fury, glowing brilliantly in his golden shirt of ring mail. Behind him, a division of chariots rushes into the courtyard, carrying standards indicating that they are his personal soldiers from the district of Amarna.

He pulls Fury up beside me, smiling jauntily in the fine mist of rain. And then I see the bloody gash across his left cheek, and my eyes widen in shock and anger. "Tutankhamun! What happened to you? You are bleeding!"

He jumps down, and I see his jaw tighten as he hits the ground, as he smothers a grunt of pain. I take a hard breath, suddenly frightened for him, frightened that he is badly injured. But he has a brilliant smile on his face when he turns to me. Tutankhamun kisses me quickly, letting his hot fingertips linger on my cheek. "It was an arrow, but I'm fine. It'll make a nice little scar to show Tuthmosis."

"Someone shot at your *face*?" I demand, appalled. When he his page takes the steaming red stallion away, Tutankhamun takes my arm and brings me out of the rain.

"It is war, little goddess. They aren't trying to be nice. But it could hardly touch me. It whistled as it flew past, leaving just this little bite. Now what is that I smell? It cannot be steak!"

By the gods, he does not care. It has gone well beyond high courage. I realize with a start that I know just when this look in his eyes was born: when a boy lay on the floor between Tutankhamun and Father, dead with the Diadem on his head. Tutankhamun is fearless, but he ought not to have had to have been. He ought to have been allowed to be a boy, just once in his life. I take his hand and murmur, "I had an ox slaughtered this morning. I could not eat another lamb."

"Your timing is flawless," Tutankhamun says as he savors the good, strong scent of beef.

"There is hot water in your chambers for your bath as well."

"Show me yourself," he says, his eyes warm.

In the torch lit chamber, Tutankhamun stands while his grooms pull away his golden armor. He had the suit made after capturing Aitakama, after his body got too thick and strong for the old one. The gauntlets and greaves are covered in gold, the gold itself worked with tiny, painstaking detail into gorgeous patterns of flowers and birds. But under his greaves, which cover just above his knee down to his ankles, I see he's bound up his foot like a wrestler. "I'm fine," he murmurs, watching my eyes. Behind him, Pentju purses his lips and carefully says nothing to contradict Pharaoh.

"Pentju, while my lord is bathing, can you order a small basin of water? And bring me some of your soothing herbs and unguents."

Tutankhamun settles into the near boiling water with a happy laugh.

"Camp life is not so fine?" I ask, picking up a soft cloth. I dip it into the water and squeeze it out over his strong shoulders and smooth chest. As I wash his beautiful body, I watch the water beading on his tight bronze skin. I marvel that even soaking wet, Tutankhamun's body smells of sacred incense.

"Battle has its own pleasures," he murmurs, closing his eyes. "But nothing like this. And you are never there, which makes it all rather cold and empty."

After his bath, I drape a thick robe over his shoulders. Pentju brings me what I've asked for and disappears. I sit Tutankhamun in a low-backed chair and lay the basin at his feet. I shake the potent, minty herbs into the hot water and stir them with my fingers. "Soak," I command, smiling into the sweet steam. "And tell me about your battles."

Tutankhamun leans back at ease, stepping his feet into the water. "My battles… We are facing a worthy opponent, that's for sure. They may be barbarians, but they are fierce and brave. Because of the damned malaria, I've not fought them as much as I want to. But my men do well, and the Nubian and Greek soldiers are a blessing."

"You've fought enough to get shot in the face," I point out, pouting in dismay.

"Yes, love," Tutankhamun teases, looking down on me with a playful black gaze. "But I've not fought enough for my liking, seeing as I shall retire after this campaign. I will surely lead my

men in the coming days. The Apiru have crawled out of their
rat holes and taken sides with the Hittites."

The Apiru are a nomadic people who live outside the laws
of decent society, raiding and harassing their neighbors like
pirates of the land. They are somehow related to the Amurru
people, and occasionally play cat's paw for the despicable
Amurru prince. "I wonder why they should take interest in
the Hittite's ambitions."

"Whatever it is, I must defeat them all, and leave enough
Egyptian soldiers to keep the peace while the innocent villagers
put their lives back together. And of course, I must collect my
tribute."

I massage his feet, his calves. He winces when I touch him
along his arch, up the tight cord along his shin. Meaning to
distract him, I smile and say, "Akasha thinks there are demons
in the mist here."

"I haven't met any demons," he tells me, his voice rough
from pain working away under my hands. "I have met heavy
chariots with spiked wheels, and swords that tear through bull
hide shields. But we are faster than they are, better equipped
and better organized. We like to corral their infantry with
our chariots, and shoot them like fish in a tub." Tutankhamun
touches his finger to his cheek lightly, brushing some of Pentju's
honey and willow bark paste off. "Sometimes these fish bite
back."

I laugh softly, shaking my head. "No one can shoot like you,"
I murmur. I rinse the oil from my hands, and pull the basin
away from the chair. And then I kneel before Tutankhamun,
and take his smooth hands in mine.

He isn't thinking about battle anymore. He lifts me up and
pulls me onto his lap. I lean down and taste his warm, sweet
lips. Tutankhamun tugs off my sheer gown. His fingers brush
my bare skin slowly, so lightly. I bite my lips at the delicious
rise of passion and push his robe aside. Tutankhamun grabs
my hips to guide me onto him. I moan in pleasure, arching
my back deeply as he thrusts up inside me. My long curls
brush over his feet and sweep the floor. When I straighten up

I kiss him deeply, hungry for him after all the days of anxious separation. And then I cling to him, drowning in a sudden rush of pleasure.

Tutankhamun grabs me tight as he stands. "Not so fast," he murmurs. He tosses me easily onto the bed and falls over me. Our laughter echoes through the damp, cold chamber before giving way to sighs and soft cries of passion.

Afterwards, I lie breathless in his arms, our legs tangled in the fine linen sheets. I reach up and touch his pretty lips with my fingers, shivering as he bites my fingers softly. We face each other on the pillows, sharing soft kisses, breathing each other's breath. I touch the raw, red skin around the gash on his cheek and make a murmur of empathy. "Maybe you gave me another child tonight," I whisper, running my fingers over his soft lips again.

Tutankhamun's dark eyes flash. He kisses my fingertips, one by one. "You stopped taking the medicine."

"The day we spoke of it," I tell him, kissing his smooth chest.

"My perfect love," he murmurs, drawing me up against him so that we might wring every bit of happiness from the short while we have alone.

Horemhab has joined us tonight-along with Nakhtmin, Huy, and Djede-and finally, Mutnojme can no longer deny her love for him. Perhaps it's the wine, or the exotic surroundings that free her, but finally, she goes to him, stunning us all when she slaps her hands down on the high table and struts down to the crowded dance floor. Horemhab twirls a Phoenician girl about, laughing as he spins her. Mutnojme-her sea blue gown swishing around her ankles-strides boldly up to the general and takes his hand. Horemhab is stunned, breathless. He turns his back on his partner; though she pouts, she dissolves back into the crowd of hip-shaking women, eclipsed by Horemhab and Mutnojme's great and long denied passion. Their hands join together as if pulled by invisible chains, and then their bodies. The drums beat wildly around them, but they move slowly, oblivious to the world around them. My aunt lays her dainty cheek against his wide chest. He places one thick hand on her braided hair, and then he closes his eyes.

"Look how he loves her," I murmur to Tutankhamun. "This is not ambition. This is something from the soul."

"*Hapepy...*" he returns, sliding his hand over mine. "I never thought it was ambition with her. We men talk as well, you know. I have been sick and dizzy with love for you my whole life; you think I cannot recognize the symptoms in another man?"

"What can we do? She will be thirty soon! We must help them, before it is too late for children. You must talk to Ay; you must make him see reason!" Even as I say it, a chill creeps over my neck as I remember Pentju's entranced prophecy. Ramesesnot Horemhab-will finish Tutankhamun's battles. Oh, dear Isis, I beg you to protect Mutnojme from further sorrow! She has born so much already.

Tutankhamun lifts my hand to his lips. "When I return, I shall speak on their behalf once more. But I cannot force Lord Ay to do anything. He is as an uncle to me. I will speak for them again, though, I promise."

The party goes long into the night, and Mutnojme and Horemhab do not split apart again. Before the music dies down, they disappear together. They have gone off to his bed, obviously. And not long after, Tutankhamun and I slip away as well, leaving the soldiers and the local girls to their sport, sport which pales in the light of true, deep love.

In the early morning, I help Tutankhamun suit up in his armor. I kiss his calf as I strap his greaves to his shapely but aching left leg, wishing that I could take his pain myself. I cannot bear to see him suffer. He slips into his linen corselet, and then his groom drops his gorgeous tunic of gold ring mail over that. Just as he fits his blue war crown to his head, a messenger comes to the door.

"Lord Huy is violently ill, Your Majesty!" the boy says, not daring to take his eyes off the floor.

Tutankhamun makes a face. "What? How is he ill?"

"He… His belly, Great God… He is in agony, and-and-he is vomiting bile."

"He is your driver!" I cry, a surge of selfish hope rushing through me. "You cannot go to war without your driver!"

"By all the gods," Tutankhamun mutters, scowling. "The fool has drunk too much wine! I saw him guzzling away at it last night, with those girls on his lap! Tell him to ready himself, hangover or not! We must go back to the front lines, without a moment's delay!"

But it is not to be. The younger Huy is desperately, frighteningly ill. When Tutankhamun and I go to see him, he is crawling across the floor, pitifully-and futilely-reaching for his own leather armor. He's so sick that he's sputtering nonsense about the war goddess Sekhmet; he claims she is begging him to return to the fight and plucking white flowers from his chest.

"This is no hangover," I murmur. I grab Tutankhamun's arm softly and whisper, "It is poison."

The young Egyptian military doctor attending him bows his head and says, "I have found nothing to indicate any poison I have ever known. And this is not fatal, painful though it may be. But he will need some days to recover."

"Tutankhamun-" I breathe softly, shaking my head. "He is your driver, why would someone want to make him sick?"

Tutankhamun clenches his teeth over his fury. "To keep me out of the fight, that's why! Cowards! I will *never* be stopped." He whirls on his servant. "Tell General Nakhtmin to have his second prepare himself. And tell Master Djede that he will take over as my driver, until this fool has fixed his guts. I can wait no longer; the Hittites surely do not wait!"

"Tutankhamun, no!"

"Ankhesenamun, I must! I lost weeks from the malaria, I was too weak afterwards to throw myself into the battle, and now there is precious little time for me to take the field! Don't worry! Djede is a skilled driver. Whoever meant to keep me from the fight should have considered that!" Tutankhamun will hear no argument, he will not be constrained. His great vision is now singularly focused on only one thing: performing feats of bravery in battle, winning glory against the Hittites. No matter what I say, my imperious, determined husband hears nothing.

And so they go off to war this way, with Aten's Fury and his match hitched to Tutankhamun's chariot, and the ugly but talented Master Djede at the reins. The half-foreign boy is finally in his glory, rising from obscurity and family disgrace to share a chariot with no less a man than the Lord of Life, the Living Horus. The rain pelts down hard and cold, but I stand shivering on the ramparts to watch Tutankhamun, glowing like a god in his golden armor, until he disappears into the hills.

Chapter Forty-Three

In the early morning hours, my sleep is fitful. I see Tutankhamun in my dreams, but he is not shooting from his chariot with furious precision. He is on the back of his red charger, swinging his heavy hooked sword through the air. His horse rears and stomps on a mountain of vanquished enemies, but more come rushing on, like locusts, like swarming black beetles climbing over each other, moving as one terrifying creature. The double uraeus on Tutankhamun's brow glows like a beacon, inciting their ravenous thirst for a Pharaoh's holy blood. For moments, there is chaos, horrible blackness, but then Tutankhamun breaks free and Fury runs like the wind, carrying him away.

I wake up breathless, the cold air hitting my sweaty skin like needles. The sea hums outside, and I hear a soldier's call from far below my chambers. Mutnojme enters my room with a vaseful of tiny winter wildflowers and bright berries on branches. In Egypt, our gardens are always in bloom with one flower or the next, and suddenly, I am painfully homesick.

"Look who's finally awake," Mutnojme teases, setting the flowers down beside my bed. "Here's a bit of color for you, my niece, to remind you of home. One of the local goddesses is having her feast tonight. I thought we might watch the pageants. It's better than staying in *again*."

I grab her arm anxiously. "Is there any news from the front? Has anything happened?"

"No, why?"

I close my eyes, measuring my breath, stilling the pounding of my heart. It was only a dream, after all. And he got away. He got away, even if-gods forbid it-this was no dream, but a vision. "I cannot bear it anymore. Tutankhamun must quit this madness, Mutnojme!" Oh, Tutankhamun! If only he were sleeping beside me, safe in my bed.

That night, as we head off to watch the rites of a foreign goddess, two Egyptian soldiers burst into the courtyard on horseback, their horses covered in foamy white sweat. I stop at the top of the winding stone stairs and grab my aunt's hand.

The soldiers-dusty and travel worn-dash up the stairs two at a time.

"They have won-" Mutnojme breathes. I cannot respond. I am frozen once more, even as I can feel my blood rushing, churning, as if it were draining from a gaping wound. I dare not even breathe. Oh, Tutankhamun! Do not let him be hurt! Would I not know it, if he were-if he were-oh! I cannot think it. I am sure I would feel it, though...

The soldiers reach us quickly. I draw a trembling breath and step forward. They drop to their knees.

"Quickly!" I bid them.

"His Majesty was injured in battle this morning. General Horemhab requests that you return with us at first light, to be at Pharaoh's side."

Horemhab has sent for me? Tutankhamun cannot? The world spins around me. But at his side, at his side, he lives... I cannot speak sense, but only manage a pitiful, "Injured... How?"

Of course, their tongues freeze, fattening in their mouths. I rock back on my heels, and I manage to shout, "How!"

The taller soldier raises his head from his bow. He turns

his eyes up to mine, and they are low and mournful eyes. "We were cutting the enemy line-rushing through with our chariots to separate them. Pharaoh insisted on leading us in. We were moving so fast... Master Djede must have lost control. He flipped the chariot, in the thick of the enemy. His Majesty... he was injured badly by the fall, but he got up anyway. He freed the horses, but it was too late for Djede. The Hittites ran him through."

"And my husband?" I gasp, but nothing reaches my lungs. The panic is back, the vice-like crushing of my chest... Crushed, as Tutankhamun was in the fall? "Did he reach his horse? Did he get to safety? Please, tell me!"

"He did, Your Majesty," the soldier says, his jaw tight with pride. He nods his head, and repeats, "He pulled himself onto his great red horse, but the dishonorable enemy rallied and mobbed him. And His Majesty swung his horse around, trampling them and cutting them down with his sword. He was fearless, Your Majesty, utterly fearless. But then, one of them got too close... Pharaoh was struck in the leg by a Hittite sword, Your Majesty. By the grace of Amun, His Majesty found the strength to stay atop his horse-"

I can't help screaming. I hear Mutnojme's voice, swirling in this nightmare. "Will he live? Do we have time?"

The silence is horrible. It is the silence of fear, of dread to tell me a thing so awful it will tear apart the very world. And then he dissembles. "His Majesty made it back to the camp. He made it back and then fell to the ground. He is terribly injured... His physician told General Horemhab that Pharaoh's knee is shattered and his thigh is broken from the sword. There are other injuries, too, I've been told. Forgive me, madam."

I clutch Mutnojme's hand, ready to be sick.

"Will he live?" Mutnojme demands again.

The soldier bows his head, "I am not a physician, my lady. I only know the Great Royal Wife must ride out with us at first light."

The night is unbearable. Though Akasha tries to help me, there are no herbs, no potion that could dull this pain, this gut terror. And how could I try to dull it? To sleep, when even now, my other self is in agony, bleeding perhaps to his death? His death? How am I even thinking of it? How could this be? Tutankhamun is a force of nature; he cannot die so arbitrarily, so suddenly!

As soon as the sky turns grey, I wake Mutnojme. She insists on coming with me, as does Akasha; the three of us, ladies of the palace, riding with a tiny escort through the Lebanese wild. Even the sight of the horses is a sharp, piercing sorrow. How many times did I ride with Tutankhamun, clutching his waist as we cantered along, the wild wind in my hair? How many times did he sit behind me, holding me steady as I learned to ride on my own? Tutankhamun taught me to ride the sleekest horses in his stable. Yet now, I am terrified to ride by myself, but I climb onto the mare's back. If I fall, if I die in the effort, I have to go to him.

"Don't think the worst yet," Mutnojme says, shaking her head. She too is breathless with fear to ride horseback, one of many who took some token instruction out of fashion, because Tutankhamun did it so much. Tutankhamun could have made that chariot dance across the field, but he wanted to hunt and scream and kill, and so Tutankhamun let Djede hold his life in his shaky hands. Djede, rot him! How could this happen?

The taller soldier, Kheti, watches me dubiously as we trot out of the gates with the lightest guard imaginable. He can see the terror plain on my face. "Your pardon, Majesty, but we must ride hard. Are you and your ladies up to it?"

"We will manage," I say, my voice shaking, failing me. But I cannot fail Tutankhamun. I dig my heels into my mare's flank. She bursts into a gallop, far ahead of the soldiers, and we race for the hills.

The rocky hills leading up into the Lebanese mountains give treacherous footing. When we are forced to descend a hill at an agonizingly slow walk, I ask Kheti, "Was it like this, where his chariot overturned?"

Kheti narrows his eyes. "No. It was flat enough. It must have been the chaos... Or perhaps that foreign Master Djede wasn't able to steer that big red horse Pharaoh has."

The other soldier, Anhouri, says, "It was the horse that saved His Majesty from worse! The beast reared up on the Hittites, striking out with his hooves and crushing men underfoot. As soon as the way was clear, he bolted for the camp. He knew the way to safety, I saw it from across the field."

Aten's Fury saved Tutankhamun. It was just as I saw in my dream. My father's snorting, rebellious stallion saved Tutankhamun's life. But if the sword has taken his leg...

By sunset, my body aches from the long, hard ride. I look up, around, sucking my breath in shock as the signs of war become apparent. The tall, fresh scented pines suddenly become black, scorched skeletons. Tucked into a small valley off the road, the charred remains of a village stand like an evil shrine. I wonder if Akasha was right about the evil spirits. I shiver, and rein my horse back to Mutnojme.

"The Hittites passed this way in the spring, Your Majesty," Kheti announces. "But there's nothing down there now to cause Your Majesty concern."

"Nothing but ash and bones," his partner intones softly, earning a sharp look from Kheti.

Our lead scouts call to us. They have stopped ahead on the road. Beyond them, the road seems to drop off, as if it simply falls off a cliff.

When I reach them, I look down and see another sky spread before me, full of glowing stars, snug in the foothills leading down to a wide valley. The Egyptian Army's camp stretches out in all directions, like a piece of the heavens fallen to blanket the earth.

"There it is, then." Kheti nudges his horse's flank with his heels and trots on, down the winding road.

We ride into the huge tent city under a black, star studded sky. Soldiers in kilts and rough, homespun cloaks line the road

459

as if I were in a procession, and they bow in a long, snaking wave as I pass by.

"Where is he?"

Kheti pushes his horse ahead. "In the center, Your Majesty."

A wall of elite soldiers surrounds a huge felt tent directly in the middle of the camp. I jump down from my horse and hurry past them, into the tent.

Inside, oil lamps burn dimly. Incense and thick opium smoke choke the air, creeping out of the innermost partition. Nakhtmin rises, his face ragged with misery, only to drop to his knees before me. "Your Majesty..." he cries, gazing up at me. "Forgive me..."

I have no time for this. And forgive Nakhtmin? Why should I need to forgive Nakhtmin? I lay my hand on his shoulder-an attempt to comfort, when all I want to do is get past him, and to my love. I can hear nothing from the inner room. Tutankhamun does not scream or weep in his pain, and I am momentarily hopeful. But then, the silence feels ominous.

"Your Majesty, I must speak to you!" Nakhtmin cries out.

I turn back to him. I try to respond, but my words break. "Later," I manage. Later, after... After what?

I push my way in, and there is my love, flat on his back, laid out across his narrow camp bed. His beautiful face is wet with tears, and it is this I see first, breaking my heart. But oh! My eyes wander down his body, to the most hideous sight imaginable. His thick, strong thigh, held tight with a bandage to stop the flow of blood from his heart. His lovely bronze skin, washed but covered in a slick red sheen. And then, beneath the bandage- It is beyond awful. His heavy femur is cut in two, and the lower piece has torn through his thigh, revealing all that what should be within, all that made up his leg. The sword wound is a great red slash, wrapping around the middle of his swollen leg. His knee is also swollen, swollen to deformity. Beneath this, his quivering, blood-soaked calf, and then his foot, also distended, blackened with bruising, and shattered. I think immediately: there is no man in history who has survived such injuries. I cannot help it; I choke his name out in a sob.

Tutankhamun-I don't know how-is awake. He moans at the sound of my voice, and tries to turn his head to me. I rush to him and fall to my knees, seizing his hand. *"Hapepy..."* he breathes. Foamy, frothy blood sprays on his lips, and I shudder, feeling his pain as my own for one brief, unimaginable moment. "I knew you'd come..."

"Yes, my love, I am here," I say, weeping, kissing his hand. I lay his fingers against my cheek, stunned by the weakness in his cold hand.

"I'm sorry, I'm so sorry love..." he says, desolate, pained, a rumbling wheeze behind his words. His broken ribs are grinding on his lungs, abrading them, tearing them with each agonizing breath he takes.

"No, my love, you've nothing to be sorry for," I say, sinking into misery. "Shh, don't speak, save your strength..."

"The chariot flipped... I could not save Djede..." he tells me quietly. "I called to him, but he took fright, he ran away from me instead of to the other horse. The enemy cut him down fast."

"Don't think of it, Tutankhamun," I insist, caressing his face softly. "Just think of getting better."

He tries to laugh, but it is a ghoulish, grating rasp. "Better?" he asks, his eyes dull with pain and medicine.

"You will fight, my lord," I say softly, forcing myself not to sob. "That is your duty. We do our duty."

"Yes, I will try..." Then, before my eyes, the pain overwhelms him. He gasps, grinding his teeth, looking down at his mangled leg. "It's so bad, though. The pain is too much..." His tears fall, and he is ashamed of them, but they can't be stopped.

I snap my head to the physician, who grinds herbs in the corner, in the judging gaze of Tutankhamun's old, silent hawk. "Give him something!"

Pentju pours some liquid into an earthen cup. He comes to the bedside. I lift Tutankhamun's head in my hands, and Pentju pours the tonic down his throat. Whatever it is, in only moments it rocks Tutankhamun's eyes back, and his thick, beautiful black lashes flutter shut. So, all this legendary doctor can do is drug him to sleep?

I summon all my strength and turn to the physician. "Tell me now. Can you heal him?"

Pentju faces me with a thousand sorrows in his eyes. When he doesn't speak, I moan in agony and bury my face in Tutankhamun's neck. The sweet scent of his skin, the warmth of him, all the things I love are now a torture to me, taunting me with their threatened loss. No! If he goes, I shall go with him. We shall walk through the Twelve Gates of Night together; we shall enter the Court of Truth hand in hand, as we lived our life. We must not be parted, not ever.

But then I think, what of Tuthmosis? Our son, waiting at home, playing in Iset's garden with Nebamun, praying dutifully for his father's victory. The pain is like a knife, the realization staggering: I cannot go so soon into the shadows. I must raise my son, the last heir of a most ancient, proud line. Oh, let me not think this way! It is not over yet.

Pentju finally whispers, "There is some hope... He was in shock yesterday, and now he's lucid, so that is something. He will not die from shock, like many men might, and the worst of the bleeding has stopped. And he is very strong, in body and soul. But it is a disastrous wound, Your Majesty. A disastrous set of wounds. I will do the best I can for him, but your husband is in the hands of the gods now. May they preserve him."

I bow my head in prayer, such a prayer as I have never prayed before. And then I lay my face delicately against his shoulder, and close my eyes, washing my beloved's body with my tears.

Chapter Forty-Four

It is a night of horror. Sometimes Tutankhamun screams until his face is purple and blood drips down his chin. Sometimes he's so gone on opium that he cannot string one word to the next. He begins to shake from the pain, the relentless, merciless pain, and Pentju fears that his shock is returning. I try to soothe him, to keep him warm and push more medicine on him, while Pentju washes the nightmarish injury with antiseptic herbs, and-agonizingly-fits an open splint around his thigh. The specter of infection, that greedy beast who feeds on warriors more ferociously than their enemies ever could, crouches menacingly like a demon lurking in the shadows. But by mid-morning, Tutankhamun collapses into true, exhausted sleep, and Pentju suggests that I do the same.

"I couldn't," I murmur, lifting my head from my numb arm. My temples and eyes ache from crying. My eyes water and my senses are dazed from all the opium smoke. "I will watch over him."

But then, there is noise outside the tent, and a servant boy rushes in. "Divinity is asleep?"

"Yes," I say, rising. "Be quiet."

The boy bobs his head obediently, and whispers, "The Overseer of the Armies is outside, Your Majesty. He says it is urgent. He says he must see Pharaoh."

"I... I will see him myself, and give his message to my husband when he wakes."

I can hardly tear myself away, not even for duty. Still, I slip out of the inner tent, and find to my shock that General Nakhtmin still squats on the floor, his face in his hands. I try as best as I can to think of his sorrow, which pales so much against my own. But he is Tutankhamun's closest male friend, and he obviously shares my agony. I kneel beside him, and whisper, "He is sleeping now, Nakhtmin. He has found a bit of peace, thank the gods. And he has defeated his shock, and his bleeding. All may be well yet." *Be well...?* I wonder, even as I talk. *How, exactly?*

Nakhtmin looks at me, as I have never seen him before. His eyes are blackened from exhaustion. He tries to speak, and cannot find his tongue. Finally, he reaches into his sweat-stained tunic, and produces a small pouch. "This- I found this in Djede's pack! He has deceived us all, and I vouched for him, I brought him into Pharaoh's circle... foreign traitor! May Ammit tear his flesh for eternity!"

"What?" I snatch the pouch, and dip my little finger inside, withdrawing a black powder. As Nakhtmin cries, *my lady, no!* I touch my finger to my tongue. Immediately, there is a harsh burning, a burning beyond fire, as if fire held stabbing knives within it. I spit it ungraciously on the floor of the tent, and only then do I understand fully. "The poison! *Djede* poisoned Huy!"

Nakhtmin nods miserably, and I fall to the floor, clutching my knees. "Oh, I knew!" I gasp, beaten by grief and guilt and horror. "Oh, Tutankhamun! He thought- he thought someone meant to keep him *from* the fight, and I didn't think any further either... Oh, this could have been prevented, so easily! If only he had listened!" I round on Nakhtmin and cry, "Why did you bring that awful foreigner so close to us? Why didn't you know he was evil? This is your doing!"

"I lay my life at your feet, Majesty. I will gladly die for failing my king."

I can only sob, muffling it with my hand in a desperate

attempt at dignity. I don't want Nakhtmin's life! I push myself up. "Oh, Isis, give me strength!" I cry softly. I spot a jug of water and flee Nakhtmin, splashing water into my face. Now I must deal with Horemhab.

I step out into the sun. It is a glaring, cruelly bright day, cloudless and fair with a warm, gentle sun; the sort of day to beckon Tutankhamun to his sport. General Horemhab stands before me, looking even more massive in his short leather kilt and corselet. His pale, tawny eyes look like the eyes of a lion, alert and cunning.

"I must see him, Your Majesty."

"He is asleep finally," I say, refusing.

"Truly, Your Majesty, he would want me to wake him. There are more enemy soldiers en route, and I have had intelligence that the enemy commander has sent for reinforcements, presumably to destroy our army and force us into surrendering all of our Syrian territories! Pharaoh has battled his entire life to *prevent* this very thing!"

"And he should not have battled at all, Horemhab!" I hiss suddenly. "You pushed him to it! If you had not trained him, he wouldn't have been in the field, and this never would have happened! Damn the Asian territories, Horemhab! If, *if* he survives-" my voice breaks and I furiously shake my tears away, "Tutankhamun will never walk again! He should never have been here to begin with! But none of you cared about that, you only cared for glory and riches!"

I shake as I accuse him of these things. I have never spoken so to any man, not even a servant; and I am but a little bird of a woman before the great, hulking shade of the general. Yet he humbly bows his head and replies, "My lady, you know your husband. Can you tell me, truly, that he wasn't born a warrior?"

I bite my lips on my tears, on the things I would say. Yes, Tutankhamun is a warrior. Whether it was his blood or his destiny or his harsh upbringing that led him to it doesn't matter; Tutankhamun is a warrior, and I love him for all that he is. But the pain is no less bearable for that.

"Majesty, something must be done. Pharaoh is badly injured. If the enemy takes our camp, he will be captured. No Egyptian king has ever been captured before; your husband would feel the disgrace so greatly that he would prefer death. If we do nothing, the Hittites could inflict a humiliating and devastating defeat on your husband's army. Pharaoh would not abide it. You must let me speak with him."

With Tutankhamun injured all other threats pale. It is difficult for me to force myself to grasp the severity of the situation, the chance of capture and the other evils that Horemhab warns me of. "What... what would you suggest we do?"

"We must give them battle, of course. We will split the army, sending enough men with Pharaoh and you to bring you both safely to Beirut, where you can join with the other soldiers. You can garrison the city until the seas open in the spring. My men will remain here; we're expecting reinforcements to arrive by land in under a week, and I have several strategies which might give me the advantage over the superior numbers of our enemy."

"Horemhab, how can I ask him to move? The pain would be... You cannot imagine his suffering. It kills me just to see it."

Horemhab looks down on me with that pale, unflinching gaze. "There is no choice now, Your Majesty. It is flight, or capture."

I close my eyes and bow my head.

And so we must move him. Tutankhamun doesn't want help to get onto the board. He bites down on leather strips not to scream, his eyes water from the pain, but he's so terribly bull-headed and proud that he shuns the aid of the six soldiers standing by. "Tutankhamun let them help you!" I cry, grabbing his cheeks as my heart breaks and bleeds for his suffering. He shudders then, his head heavy in my hands, gasping from the pain and the effort, his eyes full of misery and agony. "Let them help you," I whisper, kissing his quivering lips. I stroke his beautiful cheeks, and then I back away, and nod to the soldiers.

We get Tutankhamun into a wagon pulled by four strong horses. The ever-faithful Aten's Fury, gashed on his belly but still pawing the earth and snorting like a beast, is led behind his master. Before we quit the camp forever, Tutankhamun speaks softly to Horemhab, giving him orders, and then the final, most pointed command, "Don't let them come any further south on the coast. And keep Kadesh!"

"I will do my best," Horemhab replies honestly, looking down to the rocky dirt beneath our trail.

Tutankhamun breathes sharply through his broken ribs, and waves Horemhab away.

On the second night of travel, I stand by the fire, waiting to take the prime cuts of sizzling meat for my husband's plate, hoping I can entice him into eating. Across the fire, Lady Mutnojme sits with her arms wrapped around her knees, staring blankly into the flames and fearing for Horemhab, who remained behind to face the Hittites. I turn away, unable to comfort her when my own husband suffers so wretchedly.

I slip into the tent, saying, "Tutankhamun, I want you to try and eat some of this tonight. It will give you strength."

He is sleeping, beautiful and peaceful, as if his head were on the pillow beside me in our own bed. I don't want to look away from his face, to see how Pentju has bound and sewn him up; I set the plate down next to his narrow bed, and sit beside him. I murmur his name softly, and reach out to stroke his cheek.

His skin is fire to my touch. "Tutankhamun?"

Nothing. Nothing but his breathing: shallow, thready.

I lay my hand over his head. He is burning with fever, burning like fire. I shake his shoulders and call his name again, and he is like a rag doll in my grasp. I scream, "Tutankhamun! Pentju!"

The physician rushes into the tent, and I cry, "He won't wake up! He's burning up, Pentju!"

I step back while the old physician hovers over Tutankhamun, checking his breath and his pulse, and finally, pulling the thin sheet back on his injuries. Pentju sighs heavily, and I grab him and cry, "What is it? What's happened to him?"

Pentju takes a breath; and then, "There is an infection, Your Majesty."

"Well, give him something! Some herbal drink, some of your magic! Why are you just *standing* there?"

"Your Majesty, the infection will progress quickly. I cannot treat this condition, Your Majesty. No mortal can."

"But Tutankhamun is no mortal!" I scream, grabbing the man, shaking him as I would shake a naughty maid. Why doesn't he understand? I nearly slap his face. "He is Pharaoh! He is stronger than other men! We must only help him do it!"

And then I hear his voice, a frighteningly calm whisper. "Ankhesenamun, my love."

I gasp, and drop into the chair at his side, staring at his beautiful face and trying to hide my horror for his sake. How can all the fire that is Tutankhamun go out? It's obscene, that such a man, in the first rush of true manhood, could be so suddenly snatched away. We made love not but days ago! How could it happen? How will he die, right now?

Tutankhamun smiles at me: my stubborn, brave, beautiful boy. I kiss his hot face; my tears roll over his cheeks. He looks at me with dull black eyes. He looks at me through the delirium of fever. I lay down beside him, taking him in my arms, clinging to him as if I could pull him out of the arms of Anubis. "Don't leave me," I beg him. "Oh-*gods, please*-Tutankhamun, you can't leave me! Please fight, please, oh, please don't leave me here, without you!"

"I'll wait for you," he murmurs, smiling as if this were any day, as if he were perfectly well, which makes it all so much worse. He raises a hot hand to my cheek and says, "I'll wait for you across the river." And then his hand falls away, and he closes his eyes. Fearless in his last moments, my sweet Tutankhamun lies still in my arms, and waits for his tortured body to die.

Chapter Forty-Five

My screams rise from my belly, tearing through the camp and echoing up into the hills. The pain-I can't nearly describe it. It is as if someone had slit me throat to belly and torn everything out, and then lit a fire in the emptiness of my body. Tutankhamun is me, and without him, I am a shell, a wraith, a thing without any substance at all.

"My lady, my lady, please... Ankhesenamun..."

Mutnojme's hands are on me, but I scream again, clinging to Tutankhamun. I cannot let him go. He is warm yet, hot even, and somehow his body still smells of the incense he's burned to the gods at sunrise and sunset, every single day of his reign. I wail again, clutching his face as the stabbing pain strikes my heart over and again. It will never end. If I live to one hundred years old, it will never end.

Mutnojme and Pentju stand behind me as I wash Tutankhamun's body with perfumed water. I moan in horror, my hands shake as I hold them on either side of his handsome face, as I touch his eyes and plead in whispers for him to open them. Oh, my love; my best friend, my teacher, my baby brother, my other half... The man who pulled me down in his arms and held me until my fears whimpered away, the boy whose cheeks I stroked until he could bear his pain and loneliness. Tutankhamun was my laughter, my song, my strength. And he seems so serene now, lying on the narrow bed of woven reeds, a linen sheet pulled up to his hips. The horrifying pain he endured in the last hours of his life left no trace on his beautiful face. I dampen my soft white cloth in the fragrant water again, and touch it to the thick fringe of black lashes pressed closed against his dark bronze cheek.

This makes me sob. How often did I wash the ceremonial kohl from his eyes? How many times have I dressed this body, washed it, tended to it merely to see the pleasure in his face? I could not count the times I rubbed sweet oil into his muscles or cream onto his hands. But this is to be the last time I care for Tutankhamun's sweet body. I turn to his physician, and my aunt. "Leave me," I murmur.

They disappear, and I place the cloth down and raise my arms to Isis. And then, drowning in agony, I wash my husband's lifeless body.

Chapter Forty-Six

We set sail from Beirut, risking the wrath of the winter storms to hurry Tutankhamun home for his embalming. Just as I noticed nothing about the journey from the battlefield to the port, I pay no attention to the world outside my cabin. The pain is too great, as if my arm and leg were tore off yet I was forced to live on, split in two. I sob until I am sick, and because I cannot eat, my stomach is torn apart from the retching. After the second night of this, when I cannot sleep from the misery, Akasha enters my room. I lift my head from my arms, barely seeing my wise-woman's face. "Drink, Your Majesty. It will lessen the pain."

I obey her. The brew is strong, full of heat and spice. It could be poison and I wouldn't care. I drop my head again, expecting nothing to help this. But soon, the hammering of grief softens, leaving in its wake a hazy relief.

"Please honey, try to eat something." This is Mutnojme, speaking to me, a steaming bowl of lentils in her hands.

I wave her away listlessly, weakly. She helps me to the narrow bed, tucks the blankets over me to guard against the frigid night air. The potion is strong: I hardly recognize her. She could be my mother, or the goddess Isis herself attending my grief.

"Go, Mutnojme," I murmur, hearing my voice under water, as if I were drowned.

"Honey, no… You should not be alone."

As Akasha's brew works through my blood, mist from the sea fills my cabin. I want it to cover me, to numb my heart and hide me from a world that has the audacity to go on as if the very center has not fallen out. "I wish to pray," I tell her, rising from my bed. I weave from the powerful drugs. My loose white robe swirls around my ankles as I cross the cabin to the small golden shrine that has accompanied me on this ill-fated journey. Behind my back, my lady obeys me and retreats. I stop at a wide diorite bowl and pour water, watching it splash into the smooth stone. The sound is soothing, reminding me of a sweet summer night when I ran my fingers through the waters of Amarna's sacred lake. I wash fresh tears from my face before I fall to my knees, entreating Isis to comfort me. When I close my eyes, lost in the haze of the drug, I am standing on the riverbank again, listening to the screaming of a woman whose very heart had been torn out. But when I look into the water shining like a mirror before me, I see only my own pain-ravaged face. Still, I can feel the goddess around me, and I know she will not abandon me. She is my sister in grief, after all.

Horrifyingly, when we stop to take on provisions in Jaffe, Huy boards my ship and falls to his knees on the deck before me. I so am distraught that I want to kick him, but I don't. I can't speak, and so he begins to beg at my feet that I will not hold his crime against his family. I know he means his father, the Viceroy of Nubia, his baby brother Paser, and his young wife and daughter. By this time, Mutnojme has come up behind me.

"What are you doing?" she demands. "What ever made you think to approach the Great Royal Wife? To board her ship? Report to General Nakhtmin if you have something to say!"

"Forgive me, Your Majesty," Huy says, spreading his arms out in obeisance.

It is too much, and I dig my fingernails into my arms not to strike him or order him arrested for treason. But Djede deceived him as well. "When did that criminal poison you?"

"It must have been at the banquet the night before... before the Pharaoh's division rode out. We were sharing wine," Huy admits softly.

I close my eyes and return to the darkness of my cabin. I can't believe that Djede despised Tutankhamun so much he was willing to end his own life in order to kill his king. Or perhaps he truly was seeking the high honor of becoming Pharaoh's First *Kedjen*, and he just couldn't handle Tutankhamun's horses. Could my love really have died for something so foolish? Oh, if only Tutankhamun had not wanted to shoot, if only he had not hungered to prove himself in battle against the Hittites! There are a thousand things I could say *if only* to, and none of it matters. Tutankhamun is gone, and I am left to find a way to live each day without my beating heart.

Egypt. When we reach the Water of Re, we transfer to barges and make for Memphis with such haste that the sailors are ordered to open the sails *and* row us. All along the beautiful branch of the Nile, sparkling in the eternal sun, my people come through the green reeds to wail and beat their breasts in sorrow. Their faces are shocked at the death of their young and loving king. Men's mouths go slack as they see us, the royal barge hung with cloths of mourning. Women tear their hair as if they too had known and loved Tutankhamun as I do.

In Memphis, the embalmers meet us at the waterfront. It is the man Tutankhamun choked, and as I expected, he and his partner exchange worried looks when they learn of our long travel. I grip the man's hand-flustering him, when I need him to be sensible, genius even-and I ask him if he can do his job. He knows that the army priests will have done what they could, but no proper embalming was possible in Asia. I hold my breath with a desperate prayer, waiting for his answer.

The master embalmer places his hand over mine. It shakes, as if he was touching Isis herself, but nonetheless he says, "I will use every bit of my craft to escort your majestic husband to a dignified final rest. His Grace is worthy of all diligence and honor."

"Do not fail me," I whisper, so that none of the fifty or so servants-armed escorts, fan bearers, and officers-can hear me. "As a wife, not just your king's wife. As the woman who loves him, do not fail me."

He bows his head and makes his pledge, and I release him. Their braying donkeys pull my husband away from me for the last time in this world. Tutankhamun needs to be taken to Thebes for burial, of course, but because their work should have begun more than two weeks ago, they must start their horrible process here. When Tutankhamun is returned from their devout care, it will be as a *sahu*, dried and cut and bandaged... I fall back against Mutnojme as they leave, gasping against her shoulder because every part of me wants to run after them and protect Tutankhamun from their awful tools. When I remember how horrified Tutankhamun was at the sight of Father's mummified body and face, I am sick with anguish that he will make the awful transformation himself, so many years before he ought to.

"I want my baby," I cry to her softly, finally. I need my child with me like I need water.

"Come on, Ankhesenamun. Let's go home. Tuthmosis will be anxious to see you as well."

We take chariots from the harbor and drive through the thick white walls. Memphis palace looms above the city, casting a dark shadow onto the road as it did the first day I ever saw it. The soldiers stand on the ramparts behind billowing white, red, and black flags. The tips of their bronze spears flash blindingly in the sun.

Mutnojme and I share a chariot. Nakhtmin rides a bit behind us, with another commander named Kha'em. We ride through the quiet, sorrowful crowd, the men shaking their heads and spreading their arms to me in obeisance, the women and children crying. It is a torture, this outpouring of grief. Tutankhamun, with the arrest and execution of Intef, earned the love of the people, the ordinary people, those who sweat all day for their bread. He was ripped away from them as well, by the selfish, evil actions of a half-foreign boy.

The gentle keening of the crowd suddenly becomes sharp. "No, no!" A woman calls, a woman in the back rows waving her headscarf in the air. "No, Goddess, no! Do not go in!"

Somehow, the sobbing rises over this. My terror rises sharply, a miserable, overwrought terror. "Tuthmosis..." I breathe to Mutnojme.

The great bronze gates groan open. My driver, a young captain, brings us beneath the shadow of the pylon. I look up anxiously to the sentries walking along the ramparts, bows strung and quivers of arrows at the ready. Who are these men armed against? Who do they belong to? Are they mine still? What did that woman warn me against? I clutch the chariot rail and scan desperately about for any sign that someone has seized the palace in my absence. My heart sinks; Tuthmosis is not standing in the center of the courtyard, clutching his nurse's hand. Our horses stop in the forecourt, and the mob of palace retainers and officials bend their backs in prostration. I cannot see their faces for any sign of discomfort or fear. And beyond this sea of obeisance is Vizier Ay, standing tall on the granite steps leading into my home.

PART THREE

1325 BC-1324 BC

Chapter One

I step down from my chariot and look immediately to Akasha, putting out my hand to summon her. Mutnojme stands on my other side, her breathing hard and quick. "Be calm," I say, without so much as moving my lips. We know nothing. *We know nothing. Tuthmosis is likely asleep. The woman outside was screaming foolishness...*

I approach the Grand Vizier, but Ay does not bow to me as he should. My tears rise, and I blink them away furiously. I continue up the stairs as if suspecting nothing, longing more than anything to run to my son's chambers. *Oh, please, Isis, Mother of Horus, Mut, Great Mother of Heaven, do not take my child from me!* Not my baby, not Tutankhamun's baby boy...

Lord Ay stands under the portico in one of his monstrously voluminous robes, layer on layer of linen pressed into thousands of delicate pleats to hide his wiry, lizard-like body. His head is bare, shaved; the way Tutankhamun wore his hair.

"I have prayed for your safe return, Your Majesty," Lord Ay says, speaking first. His clever eyes run over me; he quite nearly sniffs the air to see if I suspect him. There are guards everywhere, and I know the faces of my palace guard; new men have been slipped in here. My eyes blink at the horror, fluttering my lashes. My son is dead. Tuthmosis is dead. Ay has killed Tuthmosis. Ay wants to be king.

And then I see Lady Teye emerging from the portico. She

481

should have been in the line of palace servants in the courtyard, bowing. They must think me a great fool to believe I would not notice this disrespect. She regards me with particular venom, as if I had wronged her greatly, showing me the full horror the trap I've walked into. Ay will marry me to claim the throne. I choke back my sob while desperately guarding the expressions of my face. I am sure they can see the depth of my fear as I ask, "Where is the prince?"

"We will bring you to him, Your Majesty," Ay says warmly, extending his hand toward the dark interior of the palace.

My baby... I waver in the horror as I attempt to walk unknowingly into my own hallway. As I enter the centuries old and lovingly maintained Central Palace of Memphis, my own appalling personal tragedy takes on even greater dimensions. I think of the tales of my ancestors, kings for two centuries back, kings who became emperors on the strength of their will and the blessings of our gods, a line from father to son unbroken for generations. If Ay has killed my son, my-our-great line is extinguished. Could he possibly be so evil? The man who guided Tutankhamun through rebellion and restoration, the man who served my father so faithfully? Could he murder Tutankhamun's son? Could he have plotted all this in the short time-certainly less than a week-since my letter reached Memphis, informing him that Pharaoh had fallen in battle?

And then, like a flash behind my eyes, I see Djede on his knees before me, his plain headscarf blown about by the wind over Malkata's lakeside harbor. I see Lord Ay at his side, smoothing his way. And then I want to vomit, I want to die from agony and fear. I want to rip the man to pieces, but I can't so much as raise my voice. He planned it all, certainly playing on Djede's jealousy and resentment, maybe even getting the old drunken ambassador involved. He told Tutankhamun that his people would adore him for a Hittite victory, and he sent us off with blessings and an assassin in our midst. I feel Nakhtmin walking behind me. Was he involved as well? He, who was Tutankhamun's confident, his closest friend? How many people does it take to murder a Pharaoh, to destroy a dynasty?

We pass through a gallery honoring our great-great-grandfather, Amunhotep the Second. He had been a formidable king who, like Tutankhamun, found great pleasure in battle and was one of the first of our family to favor the horses of the Bedu people across the Red Sea. I think with bittersweet sorrow that Horemhab was right; Tutankhamun was a warrior born. Though Father did not fight, love of battle runs heavily in Tuthmosid blood. And now, that blood has left the world, all because old Ay wanted to feel the crown on his bald, leathery head.

But then I remember Tutankhamun's other children, and tears well in my eyes. Maybe they aren't dead yet! After all, the Nubian prince couldn't take the crown because of his heavy foreign blood, and the other child is only a girl whose claim is far less than my own. Perhaps Ay would even mean to save her as a pawn in the marriage market! Oh, it is something. If I could save those children, even to know that they were in the world, that our blood carried on, would be something...

"On second thought, Lord Ay..." I call out, hoping that he is still in the mood to play along with his ruse. I gather he doesn't want the court, though surely those present are all in his favor, to see me manhandled, and he will try to get me into private quarters before telling me of his crime.

He turns to look at me, his heavy eyebrows raised in curiosity. I stand tall and declare, "I should not see his highness so travel worn, even to soothe my own grieving heart. Perhaps you will wait a moment? Lady Teye, would you be so kind as to attend me?"

Ay gives a gracious little nod. "I am ever at your command, madam."

So we go up into my room, and I collapse before my vanity. "Lady Mutnojme, Lady Teye, please find me a suitable gown."

Once they are gone, I snap at Akasha. Akasha quickly retrieves water so that I can I rinse my face and refresh myself as I claimed to want to do. She bends low as she combs my unbound curls. "Yes, my lady?"

"There are two children in the harem. One, a Nubian prince, must go home with his mother. Perhaps one day he will find a way to claim his grandfather's throne, but for now he should hide. The other child is a girl, about five years old. I believe her mother is akin to the High Priest of Ptah somehow, and her people are from Memphis. But do not take her there; Hebnetjer is Ay's man through and through. Do you have anyone you might trust with a child?"

"One of my daughters lives in the Fayoum, Majesty. She has many children, and one of her husband's sisters lives with them as well, with her own babies. No one would notice another."

In desperation, I agree to this. It is better than certain death for the girl, or whatever marriage old Ay forces on her in a few years. "Take a chest of my spare jewels and bribe Lord Pay and the harem madam Lady Taemwadjesy; they will keep their silence, perhaps even without the bribes. Give the rest to the women, but make *sure* they understand the danger they are in."

By the time Mutnojme and Teye return, I am slumped, staring thoughtlessly into my mirror as Akasha combs the last wind-tangled knots from my hair, and then rubs my favorite cream scented with rose oil into my long black curls. I make some small murmur, sending her off to check on Henutawy and Akila, and wonder if it is the last I will ever see of Akasha. I will have need of her, and I pray she returns.

For a moment, I hold my breath. In the polished silver of my golden mirror, I peer at the gently floating curtain around my bed, the linen as thin as a ghost's breath. Then, I set the mirror down, and listen as Akasha's footfalls get farther away. All is still. Mutnojme lights some delicate incense, and the smoke drifts through my chambers. I close my eyes, imagining that all is well, that my son is studying his lessons just down the hall. I can feel the lightness beckoning me from another life, a beautiful life as sweet as a dream, and just as fleeting. For the shortest of moments, I knew perfect happiness; I, who had suffered such fear and sadness as a little girl, was granted a deep, soul soothing love, a divine love. Perhaps we in this world, even the royally born, can only have so much joy before it must run out.

And then, heavy feet tramp outside my door. At least twenty men rush to my room, all stopping at once as if on command. One pair rises over the rest, slapping the stone and tile work as if to smack it into obedience. I sit a little taller, and when he finally enters my room, only then do I rise.

The miserable old man actually revels, his thin lips pinched into a grimace that can't quite pass for a smile. His cold eyes flash with delight. "My son?" I ask, as calmly as I can.

"Gone to his ancestors."

Though I expected it, to hear of the death of my little son is a blow stunning in cruelty, in finality. I must turn away from him, not to give him my grief. Mutnojme's arms surround me at this moment, and she shouts, "He was a sweet baby! How could you be such a monster?"

"He was a threat, my niece. Lions do not tolerate the cubs of other lions in their dens. But it was not painful for him."

I cry against Mutnojme, unable to stop the rush of horrible thoughts. Who did it, and how? Was he scared, in that last moment? Confused, terrified, crying for *Abi* or *Mawat*... Stop, stop, I must be strong. I have only to look at Ay's wizened face, and his slanted, cold eyes to feel a rush of hatred.

I hate the terribly polite look on his rotten face. "I shall explain what is going to happen here. I own the court; the most powerful men in Egypt are in my debt, and those who would oppose me are all going to die in Asia. I own the Great *Kenbet* and the lower courts will follow me; I control the gold mining, I control mining for bronze to arm your soldiers, and I have enough gold of my own to raise fifty thousand soldiers tomorrow. In a few weeks, once the shock of your husband's death has softened, we are going to marry and sail south for Karnak, where you will walk me into the Great Temple of

Amun and anoint me Pharaoh. And I should like to have a son from you."

I shake in Mutnojme's arms, from a crippling mixture of rage and terror. "Never," I manage.

"I thought you might say that," Ay says casually, as if he were reacting to a trader quoting a price on ivory from Punt. "I had also thought that you might want to do your duty to your husband, and see him properly entombed. These things have a way of going bad, you see. Things get broken during the embalming and wrapping, spells are forgotten, without which the *akhu* of your husband could not cross to the other side..."

"You would threaten me with my husband's afterlife?" I ask softly, stunned by the depravity of this man before me. "And my son- What have you done with my son?"

"Do you wish to know? I bear you no ill will, Ankhesenamun. On the contrary, I have a great esteem for you. If you behave as a well-bred King's Wife should, and give me what I want nicely, then you can order your husband's funeral just as he planned it for himself-"

"I cannot be your wife," I interrupt, aghast, afraid that he would truly do something to destroy Tutankhamun's funeral arrangements. I break away from Mutnojme and face Ay full on. "Please, I cannot be your wife. I- I am in mourning." I seize on this, praying that a man who can murder a king and his son might respect the simple request of a grieving royal widow. That I am bargaining with the man who killed my husband and baby!

Ay makes a little noise of carelessness, as if he were debating the worth of my request. He has no conscience at all, I realize, to stand here torturing me this way. No matter what he says, I won't be able to trust it. "I would not want to grieve you any more, dear lady. Behave yourself pleasingly, and you shall find me quite favorable. Attend to your husband's funeral. You may have unrestricted access to his rooms, to royal scribes who will send your instructions to the workers in the royal necropolis, and of course you can send for whatever artisans you might need. You've only to send a note to Lord Maya at the Double Treasury, and he will release what funds are required."

"And my son's funeral?"

"Yes, of course. For tonight, however, I shall desire you to remain in your chambers. And if there is nothing else...?"

I stare at him through a wall of thick tears. No, there is nothing else. I shake my head, and then I put my hands to my face to hide my agony.

Chapter Two

I collapse in a pile before the gilded *naos* in my room. The still face of Isis looks over me as I sob. My son! My hearty baby, who greeted the world howling in anger before his milky black eyes focused on my face and he knew me for his mother. How he loved me! He never cried when I held him, he only smiled the honey smile of his sires as he gazed at the world from my arms. How like Tutankhamun he was! He followed his father so solemnly, clutching his little offering for Aten at their private morning worship. Tuthmosis, running through the flowers with his streaming curls and his little gilded bow... What was his end? Where is he now? Has Tutankhamun found him?

"He will try to be my husband!" I cry in horror, wrapping my arms around my outraged body as if that could protect me.

"You could kill him," Mutnojme murmurs softly, stroking my hair back from my face. "I would help you kill him."

I turn my face to her, examining her carefully. "He wouldn't give us a chance," I decide. "He wouldn't eat or drink anything I gave him, and I don't know what servants I could employ yet..."

"Perhaps there will be an opportunity."

"If only Horemhab could return!" I say, knowing that I voice Mutnojme's thoughts as well, even if she is too tactful to say anything. "Horemhab would have his soldiers, and the support of the northeast because of Rameses…"

Mutnojme looks down, concealing her sorrow. "Ankhesenamun, I know in my heart that there is no way he can return to Egypt. You heard Ay: he can raise a great army, and he will to keep the throne he stole. And that isn't even considering the Hittites and their allies, who must surely outnumber Horemhab's forces by now!"

I nod, gazing on the bed where Tutankhamun and I spent such precious little time together as man and wife. In the silence, my aunt and I both contemplate our cruel losses. Of course I want vengeance for Tutankhamun and Tuthmosis, almost more than I want to protect myself. But I heard that beast's threat clearly; I am paralyzed by the fear that he will murder my husband and son again, in the soul. I close my eyes before I cry. "I must focus first on my duty, Mutnojme. I must see that my husband and son are properly interred. I can only pray that Ay respects my mourning, and so long as he does, I will do nothing to threaten either the sacred ceremonies to set free my husband's *ka*, or the ceremonies for my son."

The next few days are nearly impossible. I miss Tutankhamun from the deepest parts of my body and soul, the pain greater than a soldier's who lost his limb and still writhes with the ghostly ache. My sorrow for my son is shot through with desperation, because there are so many unanswered questions. I need to know how he died and what he felt, what his last words were, and where he has been taken. I need to know who is to blame, but Ay denies me any information about my baby's death. In part I wish I had stayed behind to protect him. But I could make a thousand wishes, and none of them would come true. With the death of my son, Ay has robbed me of my life, and when I bleed that week I know that there is no hope for new life, either. There can be no future, no children, and certainly no love. Even if I had some choice in a husband, I could never want one. After having Tutankhamun, to take

490

another man to my bed would be like mating with a beast. My only partner is gone; life can be nothing but an endurance of lonely days, each moment spent mourning for what was and what might have been. The loss of Tutankhamun is brutal, the loss of Tuthmosis senselessly cruel.

Thankfully, Ay leaves me alone in my misery, locking me in my chambers while I sicken from grief. I turn half my great golden *naos* into a shrine for Tutankhamun, full of flickering alabaster lamps, flowers from my garden, and perfumed oils. I offer his *akhu* the bread, oil, and salt from my meals, and of course the strong, dry red wine he loves. The sapphire he gave me, as big as a man's fist, adorns this alter. But Tutankhamun already has the greatest jewel of all with him, which he gave to me that very same day as the sapphire: our son, Tuthmosis.

In another week, the monster opens Tutankhamun's chambers to me; my lost love's essence rushes over me as mightily as a *khamsin* wind. I gaze miserably on the enormous bed where we lay in such happiness; it's cushioned with goose-down and strewn with gorgeously embroidered pillows, and the sheer gold-threaded curtains are invitingly clasped back with carnelian pins and gilded ties.

I turn away, to the rich red walls detailed with ebony and gold. A collection of swords is hung on the wall the way other men hang decorative plates and silks. I take the biggest in my hands, feeling its weight as I remember how easily and artfully Tutankhamun wielded it. I make no effort to dry my endless tears as I sit on Tutankhamun's bed, clutching his sword and wondering how the gods could be so cruel to give him that tortuous death. I hate his beautiful *khepesh* sword, as much as I love it for being Tutankhamun's prize possession. He would want it with him in our tomb. Our tomb-will it even be finished to include my chambers now? I will not lie with him, as we wanted.

I shake my tears away, desperately focusing on work. There is so much more here, so much to catalogue. All in total, Tutankhamun has hundreds of weapons in his various collections here and in Thebes. I decide to send all of his weapons to his tomb, along with the many board games we passed our time with, each more painful to regard than the last. I sort through these, and then, reaching into the bottom of the trunk, I come across something I had not expected: the five heavy volumes of Father's Book of Days. For some reason, I cannot bundle these with the rest of Tutankhamun's belongings. They are his, surely, and I have never cared to look in them before. Yet when I return back to my apartments that night, I add these to the stack of possessions I bring along under the pretense of continuing my work. I set them aside, covering them as if they had some awful power of their own, and must be bound up for the safety of all.

I must also deal with the matter of Tutankhamun's death mask, his coffins, his sarcophagus. The mask will be molten gold, poured into a mold of his beautiful face. I know the gold, the statue, none of these can capture his true beauty. That his features were perfect is one thing, but a peasant can be lovely. The heart that drove him, the luminous, fertile black glow in his eyes, the brilliant force of his *ka*, these can never be captured by human artisans! Oh, Tutankhamun!

I tilt my own face back for the mask-maker, so that I can manifest Tutankhamun's creation: the golden canopic shrine he designed, which will use my face and body as the model for the guardian goddesses at the four corners. Above the oiled cloth, the heavy wax coats my face, stealing my breath. And for once, the artist Bek does not rave about my superb cheekbones, the delicate straightness of my noise, the budding of my lips. He is blessedly silent.

Planning the funeral is exquisitely painful. To touch all that Tutankhamun touched is to feel him again, yet it is to salt my wound with the reminder that I will not touch *him* again until I have left this world. I sort slowly through his soft linen clothes, his gorgeous collars and bracelets, his jars of cologne and sacred oil. I admire his sandals, some decorated with his bound enemies, some with ornate beadwork, some so heavy and thick with gold they could purchase food for a year. I gather up his walking sticks, some just subtly different from the staffs of office and power, because he would not broadcast his pain. And of course I must collect his beloved books, thousands of sheets of papyrus in his own hand, near twenty years of copying from the land's most sacred and informative texts, all precisely catalogued and constantly studied....

I must include his favorite foods. Tutankhamun loved garlic and olive oil on almost all he ate. He loved those little baked sesame sticks; he loved pomegranates and dried figs and honey. He loved wine; we must have wine for him...

It is a terrible agony. I can hold myself well enough in the day, but before long, the nights become intolerable. Sometimes I wake drowsily in the darkness, unaware, sure that I have felt Tutankhamun's fingers tracing up the curve of my spine, his silky body pressing eagerly against my back. Sure that I have felt his lips on my skin, hot, soft, whispering of love and hunger. As the nights pass one on the next, the pain mounts, the hideous, empty ache pulses with a life of its own. I douse my pillows in his cologne in hopes of influencing my dreams. Sometimes he is there, wavering like a reflection in the water before me, always breaking up when I reach to touch him. Never is the deep longing fulfilled, never is my heart at peace. And then I wake fully, sobbing for him, twisting in my hot sheets. I rake my nails up my inner thighs, raw pain to dull another, more brutal agony. *Tutankhamun...* How can I bear another night without him?

Chapter Three

"Oh, my lady…"

I blink in the brightness of daylight. Mutnojme stands over me, her face twisted in dismay. I follow her gaze to my bloody, gashed thighs, and then I shake my head. I cannot begin to explain the depth of my pain, and I cannot be free of it.

Mutnojme sits beside me, sweeping my curls from my swollen eyes. "Akasha has returned, I think. Henutawy saw her on her way to the kitchens for your breakfast."

"But will he let me have her, with her knowledge of potions? I doubt it." I can only pray that her mission was successful, that Tutankhamun's other children have been secreted away to safety.

I rise from my bed. I go to my bath, the only place I am permitted beside my garden. The water stings my cuts, but I barely feel it. Instead, I think of Tutankhamun's thick thigh, gleaming red with blood, mangled by a Hittite sword. There is no pain I could feel to compare to it, nothing I could even imagine.

That evening, just as I finish with Tutankhamun's preparations, I receive a frightening letter from the embalmers. Responding to my letter requesting the date that my son will be ready to bury, they tell me that they do not know, for Tuthmosis is not in their care. Perhaps, they suggest, he is with their competitor?

But there is only one other fine House of Beautification in Memphis, and this one is used by the lower aristocracy. Immediately, I tell the servant who brought the letter to tell Lord Ay that I must see him at once. As I watch him walk away, I think how this servant, and all the other new faces in the palace, is but more proof that Ay convinced Djede to throw Tutankhamun's chariot over. How could he ever have arranged a coup so fast, if he had only killed my son when my letter came a week ahead of my arrival? But if he has done something with my baby boy's body... I roll the letter tightly, holding it in my hands like a talisman. Perhaps is only at the other house of beautification. Please, please let him be at the other house!

The guards keeping me prisoner in my chambers open the doors for Ay. The sight of him in his *shebyu* collar-given as a reward by either Tutankhamun or my father-makes me sick; worse is the slight smile on his leathery face. "You're looking very well, my dear," he tells me, striding into my inner chamber, my bedroom. "Go on," he dismisses Mutnojme and my maids. Reluctantly, they leave me alone.

"Where is my son being prepared?" I demand immediately. "He must be buried with his father, my lord..."

Ay regards me for a long time, his cold dead eyes tracing my face. "Come now, Ankhesenamun. You cannot have thought, truly, that your boy would be accorded a public funeral! How would that look to the mob?"

My heart-what is left of it-shatters like glass. Dumb with horror, I whisper, "What? What can you mean?"

He steps closer still, so close that I can smell the rank mixture of wine and onions on his breath. "Your son will not be buried with his father, Ankhesenamun. I made other arrangements."

My hands begin to tremble. "What other arrangements?" I whisper in horror. "You have had my son embalmed..." Dear Isis, let him not say he buried my child in the dirt!

"He has been embalmed and buried already, my dear. He has been buried in a secret place, an unmarked tomb, with one cartouche to identify him to the gods. No one else will know him. Tutankhamun had no heir."

I stifle my sob with the back of my hand. How could anyone be so cruel? How could it even be possible? Mad with grief I cry, "Why did you do this? You murdered Tutankhamun! You murdered my son even before Tutankhamun fell in battle, and now you deny my son his place in history? Why? After everything my family did for you, why would you betray us so foully?"

"Do you truly wish to know? I see no reason not to tell you; I don't keep many secrets from my wives, you know."

"I am not your wife!" I cry. "I will never be your wife!"

"But you are, beauty," he insists, grabbing my wrist, digging his fingers into my soft skin. I can feel my flesh bruising from his hard grip, an aggressive touch so at odds with the cold, calm tone of his speech. "And I have waited a long time to make you my wife. You truly are the most exquisite woman of your family, and you shall be mine, just as the crown shall be mine. Now, we were discussing motive, I believe. Shall I go on?"

I cry softly, wishing he would let go of me, wishing I did not have to endure the closeness of him and the hissing of his foul breath. His threat to make me his own has my hands shaking, and holding my wrist, the horrible old man can see it. But as much as I want him to release me, I feel that I must know the truth. I nod my head.

"Very good. About the time your Tutankhamun was born, I realized that your father was going to destroy his family, and anyone connected with them. Well, to be entirely truthful, I saw glimpses of it before that year. Your father was never truly sane, you know. I think you, of all people, know that."

I flinch away at the lascivious light in his eyes, which is as cruel as it is repulsive. He only squeezes my wrist harder.

"Pay attention now, darling. As I was saying, your father had determined to destroy the priesthoods of the land, without realizing that the people of Egypt would see Pharaoh drowned in the Nile before they forswore their gods. But I knew I could save the throne for your family, even with your father's wild and erratic actions. For almost ten years, I controlled this land with a fist of granite. Me! Not your father, me! They were my spies, and my policemen, and my allies who held down the rebellions in their districts. Truthfully, the local rulers did as they pleased, and only paid service to Aten when Pharaoh's eye was upon them. That was my plan as well, to keep the lords happy, so that they would not rebel in defense of Amun. But in the end, your mother and I both knew that we were fighting a battle destined to lose. And so when your father died, your mother took power. Eventually, she would have realized that she couldn't have ruled without me. She would have married me, you know."

"Never," I breathe, shaking my head in disgust. I could almost laugh at the idea, were I not so terrified. My mother would not have let Ay launder her linens, let alone touch her as a husband.

"Why not? After all, I was the one who ruled Egypt! I should have been king, more than anyone, for I was the only one who knew how to rule! But then your sister, that little spider, murdered her own mother in greed and cold blood, and all my plans were thrown down. I thought, perhaps, that I could kill her and take the crown myself, but not while my name was linked to your father's genocidal commands, and not while his son breathed."

"You murdered Mayati," I say softly, tears spilling over my cheeks. Oh, Mayati! That this horrid man took your life! "And Smenkhare, and my niece, and even poor Panhesy! How could you kill so many?"

Ay waves his hand at his deplorable evil. "Your beloved killed more men than that, Ankhesenamun. Didn't you know? He had a ferocious temper; but of course, it was in his blood."

"He kept *Ma'at*, he was a king and a warrior! You did this for greed!"

"No! Not for greed, Ankhesenamun! I did it because I *deserve* to be king. I'm the one who kept your father from being swallowed by rebels, I'm the one who made peace in this land!

Is it so wrong to want a little recognition? The crown is my due! It is my destiny, my reward. I've earned it."

"And so why wait so long? Why let Tutankhamun and me live?" I demand, my anger burning through my tears.

"As I said, the time was not right. Actually, it's still a bit too early. But Tutankhamun... He was born to die."

I fight as hard as I can to slap his face, but he easily holds my arms down, laughing at the little effort it takes. "Oh, if he had kept to his hunting and his battles, perhaps he could have lived another year or two, but he should never have interfered with the workings of this land. I had set up quite a system under Intef; your husband cost me several thousand talents worth of grain, which I would have sold to foreign lands. A great many men lost their livelihoods when Intef was arrested, and those are the men who turned on you, who would not support you if you ran to them right now and told them everything. Tutankhamun could make as many soldiers as he wanted to, but truly, if Djede hadn't done him in, someone else would have."

I turn my head away and close my eyes, refusing to acknowledge any more of this evil. But he goes on, enjoying his confession. "I promised Intef that I would spare his wife and child, and I did. When Tutankhamun was safely away in Amarna, I convinced Intef that he would not be believed if he accused me of any crime, because I controlled the justice system. He knew he would die anyway, and I told him that if he confessed-"

"When Tutankhamun was safe in Amarna..." I breathe, stunned into speech. "You... *You!* You are behind the Amarna tombs being robbed? You violated my *father*? My mother, whom you claimed to want to marry? Tutankhamun suffered for that!"

"And quite nearly turned back to Aten, I believe. A pity he didn't, it would have made my work easier. And so, now you know it all. I will be king in name, as I deserve, as I have been king in action for all these years. And you will be my wife, my prize, my sweet princess. You must obey me in all things, as you have ever obeyed and pleased your king."

Now, he steps into me completely. "No!" I shout, but he ignores me, he pulls my gown from my shoulder. I scream and smack his hand away.

Ay catches my hand, sneering a warning. He leans down and kisses my cheek with his wet, stinking mouth, and I nearly die of fear and disgust.

"Please..." I cry, falling quickly into that helpless place, a little girl hidden away in her own heart, powerless to fight. "Please, I am in mourning..."

"So mourn," he says, and horribly he is touching me, his bloody hands are running all over me and I can't stop him. "I care not," he hisses, and then he adds, "You will make me Horus, now, tonight."

"No, no," I cry sickly, as Tutankhamun's killer paws at my body. Suddenly, as if a spark ignited a heap of dried wood, anger bursts red-hot from inside me, and I find the strength to shove him back, shrieking, "No! Never! I will die before you touch me again! You killer, you beast! You are no Pharaoh! Sooner make a dog in the stable Pharaoh, a monkey in the marketplace!"

Ay strikes out to slap me, but I duck and trip away, searching desperately for some weapon I can use to kill him. Let it be now! Let me spill his blood, his life, all over this floor. Let Tutankhamun and Tuthmosis, my sister Mayati, and all those he twisted and destroyed have their revenge!

My head jerks back. The monster has grabbed my hip-skimming curls; he pulls me furiously backwards, with more strength than I could ever have imagined the wiry old man to possess. I have no balance, no escape. I fall against his chest and he clutches me around my tiny waist, propelling us both towards my bed, the bed I shared with my love. I scream and kick, and he clamps a hand over my mouth, hissing viciously, "Not that I don't enjoy your cries, pretty little goddess!"

There is no shame now, no care for dignity. I bite his palm as hard as I can, piercing flesh, tasting blood. Ay screams a foul curse, dropping me just long enough for me to rush away. I scramble across my bed and seize an alabaster lamp, hurling it at his head, missing by only a breath. I think to escape, and realize just as quickly that these guards are loyal to the usurper. He will have spent a fortune buying them. There is no one I might even scream for, no one who will help me. I look to my desk, where my dagger sits to break the seals on my letters. If only I could run swift! But that is the only weapon I can remember, in my panic. And he has seen me look, the cunning jackal. We leap off at the same time, seeing nothing but the gold and ivory handled knife on my writing table. My fingers curl around the handle, and I can imagine, I can *feel* as sure as any warrior, how delicious it will be to plunge the cold bronze into old Ay's traitorous guts.

And then, his hand-as hard as granite-seizes on my wrist. He smashes my hand on the mahogany table, sending searing bolts of pain through my entire arm. I scream, clutching the weapon with all I have while desperately wrenching my arm around in his grasp. But a shocking blow hits the side of my face, blinding me with bursting darkness and popping blue lights. Pain explodes through my cheek. Another punch stuns me, a third throws me down. The killer grabs me before I fall, his wiry arm tight around my waist once more. Delirious with pain, I twist and scream, kicking behind me like a mule, anything to get free.

Ay's other arm wraps around my throat, choking me, pulling me back, lifting me up to his stinking mouth. "Enough! Hear me, you mad bitch! You will please me, you will do it now, or I swear to you I will burn your Tutankhamun! I will burn his corpse and put a butcher boy in that pricey golden coffin, and your king will die again forever! You will never see him in death, he will never walk in *Aaru* or cross the sky with the sun, and he will be nothing! I will *burn* him, Ankhesenamun, do you understand? I will burn him, and burn your son, and I will have you all the same!"

The fight rushes out of me instantly. "No..." I gasp, blood on my lips. "No, no, I beg you..."

He says no more, at least nothing I can understand. I hear nothing but the pumping of my own blood as my face hits my desk, scattering my carefully laid scrolls. I feel his hand desperately yanking at my pale blue gown and I scream in horror, no, no, this cannot happen. That this common man, this servant, this killer of my family should take me; it is too terrible for words. The monster gets my gown up around my hips, and I die, I die, the desk rocking and groaning in protest beneath me.

Chapter Four

There is nothing that can take this pain away, nothing that can scotch it from my heart. My throat is torn from screaming, my hands are numb because I clutch them so hard to keep them from shaking, and still they tremble. The shame has seized around my neck and it won't let go, and I do not trust myself not to fall into a fit of panic. And throughout all of it I know one thing:

He must die.

Who could have imagined such a beast? How could he have dared such an outrage? He seized on my father's death to slowly tighten his grasp on the throne of Egypt. He seized on the instability my father created to build a web of allies with illegal wealth, and Tutankhamun-and truthfully, Horemhab-discovered it and crushed it. And he used Tutankhamun to clear his name, to be effective in bringing the gods back to Egypt. He could not have done this ten years ago, he admits it himself. And then... and then, he killed my love, only after attempting to destroy his restoration. Thank all the gods that Tutankhamun remained true to himself.

I am sick to know that he confessed to me for one reason only: he thinks I am powerless. He thinks that he can spit so clearly in my face; he can show me my husband's and my son's and my sister's blood on his hands, and he is sure that I will do nothing but cry and beg and hide away.

The water of my bath can't be hot enough. Oh, I am sick, sick to my stomach. I feel impure, befouled, and it shows on my face. Mutnojme tells me in my ear, brushing my hair, "It is *his* crime, his. Not yours."

"I know," I tell her quietly. I know it very well. I pick up my silver mirror with a lotus flower handle, and examine my blackening cheek. "I have never been struck before," I murmur. "Mayati slapped my face a few times, but I've never been truly hit."

"It looks broken," Mutnojme says quietly. She meets my eyes in the mirror, and I can tell she is frightened.

The old pig sends me a physician on the next day. A middle-aged man with a heavy braided wig and a sour little mouth, a man I have never seen before. I look to Mutnojme and she tells him, "Get out."

And then, the day after that, Akasha returns to me. "Your Majesty," she cries softly, touching her heart in disbelief when she sees my face. "He summoned me, he said you were injured, but I did not think..."

I must remind myself to breathe at the sight of her. "Did you succeed in your mission? Are Tutankhamun's children safe?"

Akasha makes a small bow. "They are far away from here. The Nubian prince is headed home with his mother; the little princess is hidden in Egypt. And you have Lord Pay's loyalty, without any payment. He will not alert Ay to the children's absence. Ay has sent men against his brother Rameses, after all. General Horemhab and Rameses are rumored to have clashed with Ay's troops already, somewhere outside Gaza."

"Horemhab is alive?" Mutnojme asks, breathless. "He has defeated the Hittites?"

"He won a truce, my lady. I believe he is more concerned about matters at home than victory. I pray no Egyptian territories were lost, but I am glad for the safety of Pharaoh's army." Akasha turns her attention back to me and asks, "May I examine your face?"

I nod, closing my eyes and imagining Tutankhamun's Nubian son, and his graceful little girl from a royal scribe's daughter given to the harem on Tutankhamun's coronation. They are safe, they are alive.

"Horemhab couldn't fight his way home..." Mutnojme breathes. When I look at her, she has tears in her eyes. The pain in my heart is sharp, sudden. "Ay is sending such an army against him..."

The rush of hatred almost makes me vomit. I want Ay dead, the very earth he walks on must be crying for his death. Such a creature should not be allowed to pollute humanity. I wonder if Nakhtmin betrayed us as well, if his anguish in Syria was all a ruse. At this point, I couldn't doubt it. Looking at Akasha, I wonder if there would be any way I could poison Ay. He would never take a drink from me, or eat any of my food. Could I poison his garments, as my father's diadem was laced with poison?

"Your Majesty," Akasha says softly, "Your cheek might be cracked. The swelling should go down, but it will be sore for a few weeks."

"We should do something to stop him at least from doing *that*," Mutnojme says angrily. "As tiny as you are," she tells me, shaking her head in disgust. "He has no respect for you, though you are his better in countless ways!"

"Perhaps if the people wanted to see Your Majesty, that man would be afraid to hurt you," Akasha suggests.

Mutnojme nods in agreement. "We will be in Thebes by the time Your Majesty is healed. When we get there, Akasha must pay commoners in the city to cry for Pharaoh's wife. They will want to know you are safe. They will want to know you are still their mother."

Akasha looks to me, and I approve of the plan. I cannot kill Ay locked away in my room, of that I'm sure. He'll never trust me enough for me to attack him successfully. If I am going to kill him for his outrages against me and my blood, and all of Egypt, then I must do it secretly, like a snake in the grass beneath his feet appearing only to strike. But how? "Horemhab would kill Ay," I muse, casting my eyes to Mutnojme.

"He would, Your Majesty. And though Ay is paying

peasants-perhaps even in gold to do this dirty work-Horemhab *does* have the support of the people. Out of the country, he can be portrayed as the man who lost the war *and* the king. He can be portrayed as a man who means to steal the throne. But once the army fights its way into Egypt, would he not have support?"

"Ay has legitimacy on his side," I say quietly. "Horemhab does have a very high rank. Tutankhamun vested him with the title of King's Deputy, along with the hereditary title of King's Son to be carried by all of his children. Tutankhamun granted it to him in Asia, when they took Kadesh." I must close my eyes, take a breath. The wounds are too deep, too fresh. "But he is still an outsider, and base-born. And Ay has bought the powerful men of the land over a period of perhaps fifteen years. But still, if he *could* defeat Ay's army, and return to Egypt, he would surely have support."

Mutnojme shakes her head hopelessly. "How could he defeat so many thousands of men? Ay will throw all of his wealth behind his wicked gamble. He told us, he could buy ten armies if he wanted to."

I frown, paining my cheek. It would be perfect justice for Horemhab to defeat and execute Ay. Not some private death, where Ay's body is found and he is mourned and Amun forbid revered, but an outright attack on his false claim to the throne. If Horemhab could defeat Ay's army, if he could seize the palace, if Ay could watch all of his allies slithering away to join his enemy's cause in hopes of keeping their heads... If Ay could be captured and killed and his name destroyed, buried as he buries my son's name... That would be the vengeance that he deserves: nothing less than terror, betrayal, and pain. Nothing less than what he gave Tutankhamun and me, and our innocent child.

But how could it be done? To help Horemhab achieve this great revenge, I must cut Ay's army in half, at least. Accounting for the men who will desert to Horemhab once he enters Egypt, just on the strength of his legend among the soldiers, I'll guess there would be at least fifteen thousand men left at Ay's disposal. He certainly could raise no more than this in such a short while. Horemhab will have perhaps seven thousand.

Akasha gives me a mercifully high dose of opium in my wine, and so I am able to lie in bed without shaking myself sick. As Mutnojme organizes my cosmetics to keep busy and not fear for Horemhab, I stare through the glittering silver threads in the sheer curtains of my canopy, wondering the impossible. Ay must pay in blood for what he did to me, to Tutankhamun, to all of us. But how can it be arranged?

Chapter Five

That night, I take another long, steaming bath, watching the water ripple through eyes opened with Akasha's magic. I always have great quantities of sacred oil in my possession, and tonight I touch my brow and my throat with frankincense. With my ladies Mutnojme and Akasha and my maids waiting in my antechamber, I go down on my knees before my gilded *naos*. Terribly, I cannot find the required peace, and I cry softly to the goddess Isis. I pour out my tears as if they were an offering, and the calm that comes after isn't comforting. It is only still, the stillness of the tomb. But in the quiet, I find the Lady, and for the first time in my life, I can sense her husband as well. The god of death, of darkness, of seed growing in secret in the earth, of the child forming in the womb. Osiris, the lord of death and rebirth.

I see Isis behind my closed eyes, with her piercing midnight blue gaze. She wanted revenge as fiercely as I do, long ago when she walked the earth and Set killed his brother for his crown. It was her magic that saved her husband, allowing him to have a life in death. I know then that I must do my duty for Tutankhamun, above anything. I must see him through his journey. I must beseech the gods to embrace my son, even if I cannot anoint the brow of his coffin. Tutankhamun and Tuthmosis must live on, in death.

And then my vision breaks up sharply. I open my eyes,

509

thinking someone is entering my room. But no one comes. In the silence that follows I feel myself rocking softly with each breath I take. I extend my upturned palms again, out from my bent elbows, and I close my eyes. Now, breaking my heart, all I can see is Tutankhamun on his rearing, stomping horse, Aten's Fury, the sunset behind them. I think of Tutankhamun's laughter as he won a hand of dice or game of *senet*; I remember the way his dark eyes would suddenly and obviously flush with warmth when I spoke to him. I sit back on my shins and cross my arms over my aching heart, unable to meditate any longer.

Missing him, I go to the last trunk of his possessions, the things I have not yet sent along for the funeral. I know I will not be able to sneak these things past Ay, for what they represent: the golden suit of armor that Tutankhamun wore on his last charge, including the badly mangled left greave; documents of all sorts from his two victorious wars, from his political victories and pet projects, things that tell about the parts of his reign that Ay will likely want to take credit for. With these things are the collections of both Tutankhamun's and my father's Book of Days.

I don't know how it happens that I am compelled to read my father's words. I stare at the rectangular wrapped bundles and bite my thumbnail, my heart pounding as if my father had just entered the room and called me by name. At the same time, I wish that my father could have heard that bastard Ay claiming fifteen years' worth of victories for his own! He would have had Ay torn to pieces; he would have probably done it with his own hands.

But Father did not love me. I take a book on my lap, running my hands over the dark cloth as Tutankhamun did so long ago, my fingers shaking. I have lit frankincense and myrrh incense, but for some reason, I can smell the sunset *kyphi* that my father grew to favor towards the end of his life. I clench my fist one time, to stop the trembling of my fingers. And then I push open Father's heavy book, and his neat, elegant handwriting leaps off the creamy papyrus in shades of black and red.

I know the hieratic shorthand immediately, because it is
so close to the abbreviated writing Tutankhamun used just
for himself. I turn through the pages that encompass Father's
eleventh year of reign. There is nothing about me at all, or any
of his other children. There is much about the Nubian Medjai,
Horemhab's bravery against the Ayukati in the northeast of
Nubia, and the High Priest of Amun's whereabouts. Father
thought he was running for Punt, and he ordered General May
to put a fleet in the Red Sea to blockade his enemy's flight. It
is difficult to read his words. I stop and draw my breath more
than once, but the effects of Akasha's brew are strong: my fear
and sorrow are blunted, unimportant.

And then, I turn the page, and Father abruptly switches
his attention to the northern lands at his back. Father thought
himself above every other ruler in the world, and so he was,
and naturally he had a bit to say about all of them. He talks of
the limpid mayor of Byblos, Rib-Addi, who could not tell that
he was sacrificed by Egypt in an effort to retain the far more
lucrative ports of Beirut and Tyre. Father's politics surprise me.
He was a far more clever man than I ever knew, a man who
pulled foreign rulers about by strings as if they were children's
poppets.

*These lesser princes-who have such delusions of their own
greatness, for all their groveling-can perhaps one day be brought
to bear on domestic matters, as I have used their peasants for hired
soldiers. Foreigners are generally so covetous of Egyptian grain and
gold-and our women-that there is no end to the foolishness they can
be encouraged into when any of the three are dangled before them. The
Hittites of all men have the least subtlety, sparing perhaps the princes
of Troy to the far west of Anatolia. Those are cousins, after all: one
barbaric and one effete, but both possessing the depth of intellect of a
puppy. Suppililiuma is a savage brute of a man, who has terrorized
the lands from Mysia to Mitanni, but he is a baited bear, and his mad-
dog sons will tear the land apart in no time. They will never be able
to attack Egypt out right, despite what my court fears. They can do
us great harm in our Syrian holdings, and there will have to be some
compromise to avoid the expenses of a defensive war. But the Hittites*

will never be strong enough to attack Egypt outright, and so I can use them as weapons, pointing them where I will.

I look up into the blue and orange flame dancing over my alabaster lamp, seized by an idea so outrageous that it would be madness to consider it a moment longer. I couldn't use a foreign army to neutralize Ay's forces, could I? If Egyptian territory were attacked with enough ferocity to make Ay fear great losses, then he would have to send some of his troops to meet this enemy! But which state could I provoke? And how, when I am a prisoner in my own palace?

I wonder if I could possibly get Aitakama executed. He is still our guest, after all. If Aitakama were killed, it would certainly enrage factions in Kadesh, and perhaps even Aitakama's ally Aziru in Amurru. Even better, it would anger the Hittites, since Aitakama is their dog. But would it anger them enough to retaliate with the sort of fury I would need to engage Ay? And how could I get a prisoner executed anyway?

I shake my head, and stand, and pace the room. It would have to be the Hittites. Kadesh could not raid so far afield as to give us worry. Their defection certainly wouldn't provoke stolid old Ay into sending men, thereby opening his flank to Horemhab. Only an extraordinary threat could make Ay take such a risk, and only the Hittites frighten Ay. Was he not ever concerned about provoking them? Pray Isis, there must be some way *I* could provoke the Hittite king. I could accuse him of killing Pharaoh, condemning him in the international world as a dishonorable coward. But that would entail revealing to the world that Pharaoh died in battle, which is not an admission my family would care to reveal, when Egypt is supposed to be unconquerable and Pharaoh immortal. My family has spent two hundred years crafting that reputation, a reputation that is partially responsible for our empire. Many foreigners will not even *face* an Egyptian army. Not only do they throw their weapons down, they bring out their wealth to enrich Pharaoh's coffers; they bring out their daughters and wives to give Pharaoh for his slaves. I wouldn't destroy that. And I will not credit Suppililiuma with a crime Ay committed.

I throw the tall, gilded double door open and beckon my ladies. "Akasha," I say, as we retreat into my bedroom, "What does the world say of this? Do they know Ay has seized power?"

"Well, the Overseer of the Army is racing for home, but I believe that is because he has had no word from Your Majesty. Lord Ay has not announced anything, if that is what you mean. I believe-" she bows her head, ashamed. "I believe he will not claim the throne until he announces your wedding, Majesty. Though he has bought much support in the court, in order to be Pharaoh he must at least pretend to follow protocol. He must pretend that you chose him for a husband, making him the legitimate king."

"I thought as much," I breathe, excited for the first time in weeks.

Mutnojme brightens, noting my sudden interest. "Will you fight?" she asks, her voice nothing but a hopeful whisper.

I cannot believe the audacity of it all. I think I may have a way to strike the Hittite king, taking something from him only a touch less agonizing than what he took from me. If a wolf can love a wolf, that is! "I think..." I say, biting my lip slowly, hardly daring to say it aloud. "I think I shall propose marriage, Mutnojme."

Her hopeful gaze becomes bewildered. "Marriage?"

"To a Hittite prince," I say.

"But... How? The Royal Widow-of all Egyptian women-cannot marry a foreigner! A cook's daughter would not even marry a foreigner! And you cannot make a Hittite of *all* foreigners into Pharaoh!"

"He will be killed, Mutnojme," I predict softly, fully aware of what I will do. But blood for blood; the Hittite king did not directly kill my husband, but I know for certain he sent plague infested men into my home when I was a little girl; my sisters died with thousands of my people, it was the end of my childhood. The Hittite king has also killed scores of Egyptians in battles on supposed treaty lands. This must be just one more strike in our war, which my father claimed would never truly threaten Egypt proper. "The Hittite prince will never make it into Egypt. I will get a message to Horemhab as well; if I can send a man to Hatti, surely I can send a man to a camp in Palestine. Horemhab will kill the Hittite, and Suppililiuma will go to war in retribution."

Mutnojme is breathless, but disbelieving. "How will you convince him in the first place? The Hittite prince? When everyone knows that Egyptian women never marry foreigners, least of all you?"

I am earnest now, shaking my head. "They know, but they do not understand it. They let their women marry with foreigners; perhaps they are not as proud as we are. Princelings even unite their little kingdoms this way. Is there not one among the fifteen sons of Suppililiuma rash enough to believe that the wealthiest widow in the world is offering herself to him, even though it is against tradition? A tradition he cannot understand? Perhaps the king himself would jump at the chance to make Egypt his. And then his son would be killed. He would declare war, and Ay would fear Suppililiuma's revenge. Ay would even be blamed for the prince's death. Ay would have to send some of his troops against the Hittites, and Horemhab would fight his way through the rest."

Mutnojme's eyes fill with tears of hope, and I finally smile despite the pain in my face. She adds, "This false marriage with Ay would have to be delayed. We could find a way, I'm sure…"

I nod. "At least the coronation must be. And I would have to have a man I could trust, to be my emissary." I think I know the man already, Lord Hani, Tutankhamun's close friend. But I must get into the court to be sure that he is still faithful to us. "You go ahead with your plan to get me back in public, and for the love of Isis, Akasha, see that I do not conceive from that beast. I shall do the rest."

Mutnojme and Akasha agree, but then my aunt cries, "No, you can't! You cannot do it! Ay would have to know of your proposal to the Hittite at least, and he'd likely suspect the rest! He would make you suffer for it, terribly!"

I inhale sharply, unsure whether it is the drug or my anger lending this courage. "He will probably kill me. But I can see no other way to avenge my blood, Mutnojme. And can you really think that I don't long for death every waking hour? If I didn't have my husband to bury, and my son to pray for, don't you think I would have taken hemlock or arsenic by now?"

"But what if you needn't die? What if we could find some other way to bring Horemhab back? What if he didn't want to be king and you could be Pharaoh-"

"No," I say. "Horemhab will want to be king, or someone else will. If I were a woman like my mother, perhaps, but I know myself, I am shy and quiet and I would not wish to command a council of mighty men. And I know what men think of me. They will not believe that I have the strength to be a king, and there will always be one or more among them who desire me, who would be willing to throw this land into chaos to marry me and become Pharaoh. And Horemhab will be the first of them. When he rescues me, he will expect me to reward him with marriage." I put my hand up at her quick refusal.

My aunt stares at me with horrified, tear filled eyes. "You mean, you will wish to die even if you kill Ay? Even if you win? Ankhesenamun, my niece, please! You cannot want this!"

"Oh, but I do!" I cry, wishing I could make her understand. "You can't imagine what it's like, to have such a marriage as I had with Tutankhamun, truly a marriage since before we drew our first breath! You can't imagine what it is to love a man who is your twin in every way, your perfect match... I could feel his pain, I could cry his tears and feel his pleasure, and he spoke straight to my heart with his every word and breath. No one will ever know me as he did and I could not wish to be known that way by anyone else now that he is gone." I touch my aunt's loose, pretty henna-tinted waves tenderly, wishing that I did not have to cause her this pain. "I must go to him, Mutnojme. Once I do my duty to him, see him buried and avenged, there will be nothing left for me but to go to him."

"Pharaoh would not want you to die!" she objects fervently. "I know that. Your husband would not wish for you to die, if you could live a life free of harm and *then* go to him. If Horemhab were Pharaoh, and you a dowager princess, you could have a rich life without the responsibilities of the reign. Anubis comes soon enough on his own time! You need not summon him!"

"Mutnojme-" I shake my head. Though she has lived at court for these past eight years, though her beloved sister was a Great Royal Wife, she still does not understand it fully. "I am bound to the Horus Throne. Perhaps if I were past childbearing, or if Horemhab had any royal blood, I could be free, but as long as I am alive and young, no unblooded man can rule without being my husband. The gods blessed my line, Mutnojme. Amun himself made my blood divine. The people of Egypt will want me to give Pharaoh a child. They will want me to anoint him, guide him, make him a real king. But I want to go home; I want to go to my husband. I want to lie in his arms beside the river in the next world. This world is but a shadow now for me; the next one is the only world that is real to me. But I must do my duty first. I need you to help me, please."

Chapter Six

9 Epiphi, 1325 BC
Valley of the Kings

The heavy drums begin to beat, and a great cry rises from the mourners. The tall peaks of the Valley loom before us, pink-grey in the creamy morning light.

"Good morning, beauty," Ay says with cruel cheer as he steps beside me, making a thoughtful adjustment to his fine linen robes. His silver-bristled head is bare, and capped with a golden diadem. I recoil at the sight of this killer posing as a prince. It is a topsy-turvy world; everything is twisted. Proud young Horus is dead, and old Set is measuring his head for a crown.

"My lord," I respond neutrally. It is as polite as I can be, for I have resolved to destroy this man, even if I lose my life to do it. In order to succeed I must lull him into believing he has defeated me completely, as much as I can without tasting bile in my throat.

"You are looking quite well today. Serene, almost," Ay says, glancing down at me. "What mischief are you working?"

I do not miss a beat, because what I say is the truth. "I am pleased to free my husband's *ka*, Lord Ay. His *akhu* will always cross between worlds, and his *ba* will live forever in the mouths

517

of men. I have done my duty." *As I pray was done for my son*, I think. No, I mustn't torture myself with that. There is nothing I can do about that. I must do what I can for Tutankhamun, and then do what I can to get free of this nightmare. Then I will know; then I will surely see my boy, in his father's arms.

The procession is a mile long at least, snaking for hours into the desert. It is the first time in my life that I have ever walked so far, but the old man would not think of my comfort the way Tutankhamun did. With my eyes blurred by tears, I remember the day that Tutankhamun brought Tuthmosis and me to see his tomb, the tomb he thought we would share. But just as Lord Paranefer turns up the path to my husband's tomb, a burly man rushes past us from the back ranks. I watch in shock while he seems to argue with Lord Paranefer. Beside me, Ay watches with a narrow glare. And then, to my complete horror Paranefer backs up and turns to his right. We are going into the catacombed Main Valley, where hundreds of years of tombs clutter the cliffs.

"What have you done *now*?" I breathe. I am numb to terror; I am learning to expect it.

"A simple change."

"False servant, traitor," I hiss, shaking my head. I cannot hold back. I should beat his face, I should have a servant beat his face, I should have him stabbed right here. How can I bear it? How can I be calm when this beast commits such atrocities? Why does the sun god not burn him to death, right here in the desert?

"Careful, little princess," he snaps in a fierce whisper, "I will destroy all of this, with the snap of my finger." We stop before the small tomb my husband meant to honor *him* with, and Ay murmurs, "Your father rests just nearby. So does his mother. It is fitting."

"Where?" I demand at once.

"Perhaps one day, little kitten. If you are sweet."

"And if I am not?" I am disgusted and insulted before my deceased family. "Where will *I* rest?"

"In pieces, my pretty darling," he murmurs, passing off his pleated white robe. I shudder, imagining a painful death. It will only be a few moments of pain, I think determinedly. Only a few moments, or at worst a few days, of pain, and then I will be in Tutankhamun's arms again.

Ay steps up, donning the leopard skin that indicates he is now the highest priest in the land, and the heir to the throne. I watch the rigid old man in his glory, the eyes of Egypt on him as he takes the place of Pharaoh's heir. The common people at the back of this line-honored mayors, merchants, the like-will know next to nothing of his crime; they will only see this display, and mark its meaning.

The priests purify the area with water and oil and incense. Priests from the temple of Osiris, the Guards of Horus, now flank my husband's coffin. It is brilliant, it is shining gold in the sun; it breaks my heart for a millionth time. "Oh, Isis," I rock softly, and in a moment, Mutnojme is at my side. I feel her slim, strong arm holding up my back. Is this happening? Is this truly happening?

Now, the Grand Vizier, false Prince of Egypt, makes his great performance. I choke as Ay steps up as Horus, with a sacred adze in his oil-anointed hands. I won't watch it. I turn my head before these worthy men, all chosen by Ay in the end, sparing Nakhtmin. And Nakhtmin might well be a traitor, too.

I turn against Mutnojme's shoulder, only looking back when they sacrifice the animals, because I must. In fact, as Ay kills the bull that represents Set-ridiculous, yes!-I pray as hard as I can to Osiris, begging forgiveness for this mockery. I beg him to take my husband with him anyway, because Tutankhamun deserves his peace.

When it is time for me to anoint Tutankhamun's coffin, it is a battle to blind myself to my husband's enemies, standing around his coffin like a pack of hyenas over a killed lion. I touch his golden brow with quivering, oil dampened fingers, but as soon as I do I can feel him, and I pray with my whole self that his journey to the other side is triumphant, and that he rises with his father in the morning, shining with the sun.

And then, Tutankhamun's pallbearers bring him down

into darkness, where he will never feel the sun again. We-the few allowed-descend into the tomb. I did not expect anything great; it is a commoner's tomb. But still, it is stunning to see the jumble of his possessions in unpainted chambers. I see the golden shrine, with its four goddesses bearing my body and my face. It was meant to stand in a pillared gallery of stone, but instead the shining piece is insulted, packed up as in a store room. The two black granite statues of Tutankhamun stare through me, flat and sightless, their headdresses in gold. I think of his strong, warm bronze arms, and how they wrapped around me, how I always felt welcome and protected tucked against his chest. I could die now to know that I will never hear his heartbeat again. I will never spread my fingers across his chest and walk them over his flat belly. I will never hear his soft laughter, or see a flush of delight in his dark eyes. If only I *would* die, right here in the darkness of this common tomb.

And then, in the small burial chamber, I see the incomplete painting where Lord Ay's image enacts for all time the ritual he just abused outside. Most telling of all, he has painted the blue crown of my family on his head. I think of whatever artist put his brush to the stone to paint this monstrosity, which is not nearly fact yet, and I curse him. Only after this do I realize that my image, my name, is nowhere to be found. I turn to Ay at this hideous omission, my eyes full of tears.

Even Ay is overwhelmed by his own blasphemy, striking him full in the face. He turns away from me, gives everything a perfunctory glance and rushes out again, up into the light of day. Teye trots behind him like an obedient dog. Suddenly, I am alone. They have not shut the sarcophagus yet, nor set the shrine. I walk to the golden Tutankhamun. No metal, not even the flesh of the gods, could hold a drop of the glowing beauty of his skin, the lush fullness of his mouth. Black glass lined in lapis lazuli is nothing to Tutankhamun's endless black eyes and lovely dark fringe of lashes.

"You were too beautiful for this nasty world," I murmur, caressing the cold, sculpted gold. I draw a small wreath of flowers from the folds of my voluminous pale mourning gown, kiss it, and smooth it over the uraeus on this golden Tutankhamun's brow, and then I whisper to him. "I will join you soon, my only love."

"Your Majesty…"

"Paranefer," I say softly, unable to pull myself away.

"It is time, Your Majesty. Time for him to begin his journey."

"Of course," I say, nodding, my tears slipping along the golden face of my husband. *How could I be ready to leave you here, my love?* For a long time, I cannot move.

But finally, I know I have to leave him. I turn to this priest of Amun, my father's dear friend, and look him full in the face to know his part in this evil. Paranefer parts his lips, and looks over his shoulder. He shakes his head, closing his eyes. He cannot speak the words. "An outrage," he murmurs finally.

"But you will anoint him Pharaoh."

"What else is there to do? He will have me killed. Forgive me, but I am no warrior, madam, just a weak, spoiled man who loves life too much. Poor Egypt; what will he do to this land?" Paranefer's eyes trace the painting of Ay's victory-for that is what it is-and he looks away in scorn. "Come, Your Majesty. Let us go now, before there is talk. Your husband is at his peace."

It must be now. One moment will be as wrenching as the next, and he is right. I can only pray, from my deepest soul, that I won't live this half-life much longer. My broken heart begins to pound as I realize the opportunity before me. I look to the priest again. "Paranefer, you *can* do something for your true king. For him, and for me. You must draw on that courage that I know my father saw in you, Paranefer. It would not be dangerous for you."

"Madam?" he breathes, his delicately handsome face hopeful.

"Delay the coronation. Use some excuse, and get it qualified. The priestesses are having visions; the sacrifices gave bad omens… He cannot go against the High Priest of Amun, not on a matter of divinity. Not if he wants to rule in this land."

Paranefer's eyes gleam for a moment. "You have the look of your mother when you say that."

"Then do what I tell you to do. Delay the coronation. Give me some time, Paranefer, *please.*" If this is all to work, this insane scheme hatched in the depth of my mourning, then Ay cannot be named the true king just yet. He is not in line for it, he has no blood. The world cannot know, for sure, that he will be king. They must believe, in their ignorance, that I have some choice in a husband, in the succession.

Paranefer bows. "I will do my best, Your Majesty. May Amun-and Aten-protect you."

I nod my head observantly, with gratitude for his blessing. But I tell him from my truest heart, "Tutankhamun, Osiris, and Isis protect me now."

We must feast with Tutankhamun's *akhu*, just outside the tomb. The plates will be destroyed afterwards, buried in the ground nearby. Though my heart pounds at what I have done, I sit at a shaded pavilion eating and drinking in deep silence, seeing nothing but Tutankhamun's flawless face: Smiling, laughing, eyes full of tears. Screaming with joy to run down his prey, murmuring in my ear in that intimate way he had of letting his lips brush my skin on every word. Holding Tuthmosis in his arms, eyes alight with pride and hope for the future. My husband, my son...

As we turn to waiting chariots, I bite my knuckles and hide my face against Mutnojme's shoulder. "I can't leave him here," I cry softly. "It was dark down there. He loved the sun, he loved the wind! How can I leave him in that cold, dark mountain?"

"He is not there," she whispers, holding me up. "Not unless he wants to be, now that this is over. He must be journeying to *Aaru*, to meet his mother."

"Oh- Beketaten..." I let this comfort me; I let my heart warm with the thought of Tutankhamun finally embracing his lost mother. How proud she must be of her fine son! She gave her life to give him his. I will end my life to avenge his death. I dare not look to Paranefer, riding off in his chariot, his impeccably fine priestly robes streaming behind him.

Chapter Seven

I cannot bear it. Oh, Isis, I cannot stand it, I should pitch myself over the balcony now and put an end to this... He has come back, and I can't breathe, and worse he *knows* I have this problem, he has watched me all my life and he knows where I am weak. Mutnojme urges me to drink the warm tea; she has to hold the cup for me, because my hands shake so bad my wrists hurt. I don't even try to hide it. I watch them like I used to, half amazed, as if they were in rebellion from the rest of me.

The tea is artificially soothing. I can't endure life without the aid of some quieting, dulling potion. Ay knows this, too, and he doesn't mind giving Akasha access to whatever she needs to keep me calm. He does not know that she can prevent the child he so desires from me this way, which is a mercy.

"The peasants have been gathering at the docks crying out for you, Majesty," Akasha reports, as she sorts little leather pouches of crushed herbs and powders and roots into a long ebony box. "This is third day of it."

Perhaps this is why Ay did not beat me this time; he did not need to, actually, because I am tiny compared to him. Perhaps he will take me out of my prison, to show the world how well we get along. The courtiers will not see the bruises on my small wrists, and if they did, they could hardly object.

Mutnojme begins to brush my wet hair gently, and I tilt my

head back and close my eyes, trying in vain to forget. "It was awful," I say, because I think I will die if I swallow this, if I keep it to myself. I turn and look at Mutnojme, almost gasping with the horror. "He is awful. I can't do it. I can't play sweet, I can't try to trick him into trusting me, I know my sister would but I cannot-"

She makes a hushing noise, and puts her arms around me.

"I have to do this," I cry, more to myself than anyone. "I have to end it, no matter what."

My antechamber doors open, and there stands Ay, tall and wiry in his pleated robe, slack-cheeked and sallow faced, his eyes as cold as the black granite floors. "Are you ready, my dear?"

I cringe, I can't help it. I pull my indigo shawl tighter, and for a long moment I can't make my feet step forward. In that moment I doubt everything; how could I ever get to Hani? Ay will intercept any message I try to send, he'll lock me away. I'll never get revenge and Horemhab will never kill Ay, and I will live this nightmare until Akasha is merciful enough to poison me.

When I can walk, he insists on gallantly taking my arm. This is so that everyone in the palace can be made to believe that I lean on him, that I choose him. I think I am a traitor for even doing it, and my eyes are full of tears as we walk along. But I am not too blinded to see that he is invigorated and thrilled when he experiences the deep prostration our servants greet me with. This makes me believe that he has not yet commanded it for himself, a slight breath of hope. It also tells me how much he is using me, how much he needs me.

We go into one of the smaller courtyard gardens, where the wall is painted with a scene of my grandmother offering incense and blue lotus flowers to Amun, Mut, and their child Khonsu. My grandmother, Ay's older sister. He pauses a moment to consider her old-fashioned, stylized portrait; he looks down at me and smiles before releasing my arm. "Please, sit," he says, inviting me to the benches of my own garden.

Immediately, Teye and Nakhtmin enter. Teye is in the most provocative gown of sheer pleated linen that I've ever seen her wear, and her long braided wig is capped with long golden beads. She glares at me from painted eyes with open hatred, as if I have stolen her cruel, nasty, common husband.

I cannot look at Nakhtmin. I already feel cornered by enemies, and I could not bear to see any sign of victory in his once faithful eyes. His betrayal would be the worst, I think, for what he was to Tutankhamun.

As I stare out at the clusters of white jasmine, Ay speaks to us all as if we were now a happy family. While his new servants bring us a light breakfast of fruit and cheese and watered wine, he takes the opportunity to tell us what he means to do. "Lord Paranefer has sent me a messenger, and later this week, Ankhesenamun and I will travel to Karnak. I shall set the day of my coronation, which will occur at the time of the Opet festival." He catches my hand in his like a suitor, and I look at him in startled horror. "I have taken the liberty of ordering commemorative rings joining our names to be made casted of faience, for issue at our banquets and to worthy persons throughout the land."

So soon? I do not know what to do, and I lose all my cunning. I look about like a frightened gazelle, briefly seeing Nakhtmin's appalled face. I flush with guilt, and though I know I ought to play on the old man's desire and his veneration of my blood, I feel sick, far too sick to manage him. I snatch my hand away and rub it, as if I could remove the stain and heal the injury. Ay studies me coldly and announces, "The forthcoming child of our marriage shall be my first heir if it is a boy. If Ankhesenamun gives me no sons, then her daughter shall marry Nakhtmin and Nakhtmin shall be king after I die. In the meantime, Nakhtmin shall take over the post of Viceroy of Nubia." He looks at his son expecting Nakhtmin's pleasure, but Nakhtmin only offers a tepid *yes, my lord* and returns to his wine. Could he be innocent of this? Could he be as furious with his father as I am? Even when his father offers to make him a prince?

"And what shall I be, my lord?" Teye demands suddenly, her voice shrill. "You promised that you would never place another woman above me. Am I to be second wife now?"

"Yes," Ay says plainly. "There can be no other way. But you shall enjoy the benefits of a good private income, your own palaces and barges, and anything else you might desire."

"But I have all that," she protests. "I have been a Person of Gold for almost twenty years, and I have more income than I could ever hope to spend. I shall be ashamed to give up my seat beside you, my lord, and I do not deserve such treatment after thirty-five years of faithful service."

"My darling Teye," Ay says, reclining back on the bench. "You have been a wonderful wife, at my right hand since you were a lovely little girl. You have always known my mind, and been effective in my service. But Ankhesenamun is my destiny. She is the king's wife, darling, a born king's wife of ancient blood, and I have become the king. You must accept this, Teye. As you accepted your title and pension as a Person of Gold, and all the other rewards marriage to me has brought you, you must now accept this. Ankhesenamun is now my Chief Wife."

I am wrapped up in my own shame, but I cannot fail to miss the burning, hateful stare that Teye gives me as we depart the garden. I feel crushed by my first day out of my chambers, crushed and terrified. Ay seems to have such control of my palace; he has placed many new men in positions of power, and those who served Tutankhamun or my father who remain are utterly obedient to Ay. They bow and scrape to him, yet he is still called *my lord*, and not prince or king or anything else. But Ay leads me along through my palace like I am his pretty little doll, showing me how the guards are all new men, his men, bought with the gold my father and Tutankhamun gave him. In the main courtyard where the chariots come and go as they ever did, he shakes hands with the powerful Mayor of Thebes, who he recommended that Tutankhamun appoint years ago.

He issues commands to several viziers of Upper Egypt and Theban treasury men; they obey as if he were still speaking for Tutankhamun. Ay's massive network of allies and contacts, which he employed to break and then restore Amun's worship, is now employed to make him Pharaoh, to pretend that he is legitimate until everyone forgets that he isn't and the crowns of Egypt no longer look strange on his head. Ay takes me to the balcony overlooking my grandmother's wide lake, and I gasp to see hundreds of barges crawling through the canal and along the river, as thick as locusts swarming in the sky. "Those are my new General Kha'em's barges. He is taking more men north to secure our borders against the rebels."

"You mean Horemhab," I say softly, as I stare with mournful eyes on the additional thousands of men gliding down the Nile. They will attack Horemhab, my only hope, long before I can do anything to help him. And what if he dies? What if he dies, and Rameses dies, and there is no one left to oppose Ay?

"Horemhab will never return to Egypt, Ankhesenamun. I have charged my generals with bringing me his head on a pike." He says this easily, with such certainty that the deed could have been done yesterday in secret.

That night, Lord Ay returns me to my chambers to wonder if there is anyone in Egypt who did not betray Tutankhamun. I am certain that everyone in my palace will spy for him, that I have no friends here. Thankfully, Ay doesn't stay, but he leaves me in such a state of helplessness that I wonder how I ever thought to challenge him.

But the very next day, as we are retiring from another tortuous breakfast meeting, a familiar, bashful messenger offers Ay a deep bow and presents him with a small scroll. Whatever it says irritates the usurper, and he storms off, leaving me alone outside of my chambers for the first time. Teye almost runs in his wake, seeking an opportunity to be of service before she is publicly displaced as a first wife. I am left alone with Nakhtmin-and countless servants who will report how quickly I returned to my rooms. I walk off without acknowledging him, and as I step away I hear him say softly, "Your Majesty!"

I have no use for Ay's son, but he quite nearly throws himself in my path, bowing his head because he dare not throw himself down at my feet. "Your Majesty, please!" he says with a shaking voice and when I stop walking and glare at him in silence, he looks up, and he has never appeared so wretched. His face is gaunt and his eyes are dark, and his long braids are in desperate need of tightening. It seems he has no pride in his new station.

"Did you know?" I demand softly, aware of the gardeners filling back in to tend the sprays of blue cornflowers and the early Damask roses, pink petals shivering in the wind.

"Nothing, I swear it," he breathes, shaking his head. "But I found out soon enough. He has filled the court with his men, greedy men who should have died with Intef. But I am no traitor, Majesty! I beg you not to believe that I was involved in this evil thing. He was my best friend-"

"It doesn't matter," I say with sharp cruelty. "Done is done, and you shall be a prince of Egypt. In fact, you shall be Pharaoh. I will die before I give that creature a child." I do not say that if I succeed, he will likely be killed by Horemhab as well; I don't tell him that Horemhab will not believe in his innocence when he barges into the court to find Nakhtmin sitting at his murderous father's side.

"I could not be Pharaoh!" Nakhtmin gasps, horrified. "By Amun, no! And frankly, my father is not finding it so easy to become one. He has old General May, and that Commander Kha'em who he's promoted, and he can buy many others. But there are enough great men of Egypt-not that collection of greedy criminals who support him-who will not bend their backs to the Grand Vizier as if he were a prince born. Lord Maya will not open the treasury for him, he must spend of his own wealth until he is coroneted, and the honest nomarchs around the land hope that you will choose a husband and put an end to my father's peacocking. And best of all, there are rumors that Djarmuti is arming men in the northeast to help his cousin Rameses come home."

"But Ay has Thebes under his control," I say, refusing to be swayed by Nakhtmin. It could be another trick; he could be testing my loyalty to his horrible father. "And I can hardly choose a man to marry when your father commands my palace and holds me prisoner in my chambers. Besides, there is no one left to choose from, even if I were inclined to marry, which I am not. How could I marry a man who was my servant?"

Nakhtmin shakes his bowed head slowly. He holds his palms up to me in appeal, and there is true agony in his eyes. "I am not a traitor," he repeats again, as if it were everything to him that I believed him.

Beyond the portico, I notice two of Ay's guards standing together, watching this exchange like dogs guarding a farm yard. "I must go, Nakhtmin. If you say you are no traitor then do something to prove it. Your words are as empty as this life your father has inflicted on me."

The very next day, Ay arrives at my chambers impatient and agitated. I am ready to go, anxious that Paranefer has sent for Ay. The usurper claims that he will be made king in the summer, during Opet, but that is too soon for my plan to succeed. I have heard nothing from Paranefer after he accepted my charge in Tutankhamun's tomb, to delay Ay's coronation. I don't know if has helped me. He might even expose me.

"Hurry," Ay mutters, "We are late already. The harbormaster will spend the rest of the month in the palace jail, to consider where his allegiances should best lie!"

I look curiously at the leathery old man, and he snaps peevishly, "You will tell them all that I am to use Tutankhamun's barge whenever I wish it. And you will write to Lord Maya in Memphis, telling him that the Double Treasury shall be at my disposal!"

"It would make no difference," I reply quickly, seizing this unexpected blessing as I follow him out into the hallway. "He will think you wrote yourself, in my name. He will think you appropriated my royal seals. I've not sent so much as a note to my sister empress in Babylon, I have no secretary, I have no ambassador. I have not been able to attend to my religious duties or any of the other functions of my station. How will Maya or any other Egyptian heed my command when they know I am kept prisoner in my rooms? When I have not so much as sent letters to the foreign rulers announcing my husband's death, or held one feast of mourning in my own great hall? It does not surprise me, my lord, that our... our arrangement is doubted or considered illegitimate by those whom you have not... cultivated." I almost said, purchased. "You have not allowed me to function as a Great Royal Wife in any way."

"By the gods, you shall!" he barks his decision, pulling me along. "You shall write your letters straightaway. You shall appear at banquets at my side, and today, you will enter Karnak with me and tell Paranefer, from your own lips, that I am your choice of husband! Or I shall lock you away for the rest of your life, come what may!"

My throat has gone so dry with excitement that I can hardly speak. I am sure the old reptile can hear the pounding of my heart. I can hardly breathe, but I manage to ask, "And my ambassador? I must have my ambassador back."

"Who is your ambassador?" Ay asks. "I don't recall you having a personal ambassador."

This is true; I rarely sent letters to foreign princesses, I never involved myself in matters of state, which unlike my mother I considered to be in my husband's domain. But I say clearly, "Lord Hani carried all my correspondence."

As we step up on Tutankhamun's hastily prepared barge, Ay suddenly turns and grabs my arm. His clawlike fingers press painfully into my skin, and I gasp and look at him with wide eyes. "My lord, you are hurting me!" I cry, drawing the sharp, astonished, angry attention of several oarsmen.

"Keep quiet!" Ay hisses, lightening his grasp and pulling me along. I very nearly trip over my feet. Once we reach the

shaded dais before Tutankhamun's gilded cabin, Ay pulls me
into the chair beside him and mutters, "I shall give you the
freedom to fulfill your office, so that the people can see that
you choose me without duress, so that there is no doubt of my
legitimacy. But if you attempt to slander me in any way, I will
destroy you. I enjoy you and I want a son from you, but I can
be king without you just as easily, especially since there is none
of your line left. There is no man powerful enough to defeat me
on his own, Ankhesenamun. They may grumble and cling to
protocol to frustrate me, but no one will rescue you, not even if
you offered them the throne. There are none who could defeat
me if you happened to die. I will give you some freedom, but
I will be watching you," he says, brushing his hard hand over
my face until he catches my chin in his palm, "I would not wish
to harm such a lovely, pleasing creature. I have been gentle
with you so far, believing that you would see reason and obey
me, but I can just as easily make you beg for my mercy."

I quiver slightly, but I forbid myself to imagine what he
might mean, especially since he's already cracked my cheek
and shamed me to the ground and he claims that is gentle
treatment. I force myself to keep my gaze forward, as if I were
honest indeed, as if I were not scheming this very moment.

"I will be watching you, always," he tells me again, "but
your ambassador may serve you. You can send letters to your
fellow princesses in Nubia and Asia, and you can also send
letters to the wives of the prominent Egyptian nomarchs and
priests, informing them of how grateful you are for my loving
guidance and experience during these unfortunate, difficult
weeks. You may praise my high birth, my blood which even
runs a touch in your own veins, if you remember. You may
prepare them for the news of your choice in husband, and be
sure, Hani will be instructed to show me all correspondence.
I have other methods of knowing what is said and sent out, so
be warned."

I lower my eyes demurely. "Yes, my lord."

He releases me and takes his own seat, raising his chin
haughtily as he crosses his feet on his footstool, as Tutankhamun

once did. My husband's stolen barge casts off for Karnak, where we are met by the immaculate, serene visage of Paranefer.

He bows deeply to me, and then Ay clasps the hand of the High Priest of Amun. "You are looking well, old friend," Ay says.

Paranefer bows his head again, and says, "We have had a good harvest this year, as well as some very promising pressings at our vineyards in the Delta. I shall send you some, with a very nice smoked cheese. Please, come, eat."

In the aromatic myrrh groves surrounding the Temple of Amun, where the small silver-green leaves shiver in the river breezes against long and sharp thorns, Paranefer has arranged for a small picnic. Tutankhamun always dined in Karnak's star-studded hall, with Amenia's singers serenading him. Paranefer's servants lay a good table. There is minted lamb, good sesame bread, and Palestinian olive oil with roasted garlic set out on a low table; there are bowls of salad and dates and figs but no grapes, and no pomegranates, which are considered the food of the gods.

Ay escorts me to my seat, tucking it in after I am in it. "You must eat well, my darling bride." He turns to Paranefer and boasts, "We are anxious to have a child. Are we not?"

"Indeed," I manage to say, as if it were nothing.

"Well," Paranefer says, getting stuck, because he must be as revolted as I am. "May the great god bless you," he offers ambiguously.

"The food is delicious, Lord Paranefer, and your garden is immaculate. But let us come to it. Is Karnak prepared to make me king during Opet?"

Paranefer draws a little breath. "My lord, there is a difficulty with that date."

I sip my wine, staring safely down at its interesting golden color. It makes me think of Amarna wine for some reason, though we had all kinds. How truly amusing, after all, that Paranefer is the High Priest of Amun, and the boss of Karnak. The peasantry might not be as amused if they knew of Paranefer's early career, but how could they ever? This city within a city is tightly run, and the peasants keep behind their markers.

"What difficulty?" Ay asks, setting down his knife and napkin.

"The prophets have gathered together, my lord, and we have consulted the oracles, taken auguries and read the omens, and we fear the great god wishes to venerate the last king of the Tuthmosid line this Opet. Frankly, it would be disrespectful to their late majesty to crown you at such a sacred time."

"Opet is for *living* kings," Ay says, his voice filling with quiet menace.

"Nonetheless," Paranefer says reverently. "But it is not all bad news, my lord. The great god Amun shall bless your new line when the wheat is high. You shall be king at the end of *Peret*."

"What mischief is this?" Ay demands. "Oracles, auguries? Are you telling me that your signs are against me, Paranefer?"

Hiding behind my lashes and my wine, I see Paranefer bowing his head modestly. "I am telling you that we priests of Karnak believe it is Amun's will that you are made Pharaoh in the winter. The great god does not say why."

"Who do you think you are toying with?" Ay demands. "Do you expect me to believe that the boy who designed temples for Aten is consulting oracles now? Pharaoh Akhenaten's pretty errand boy, first on his belly to praise the one true god?"

"That was another lifetime, my lord," Paranefer says smoothly. "I have spent nearly ten years in this place, Lord Ay, and I have come to know the truth and the might of Amun, the King of Gods. I am his first and truest servant in all the land, after only Pharaoh."

"Oh, certainly!" Ay snaps, tossing his hands in the air like a haggler in the marketplace. "What is it, then? You want gold? More estates? What is your price, you hustler?"

"I require nothing, my lord. Our temple sustains itself once again, thanks to the good god Pharaoh Tutankhamun, True of Voice, and the many vast estates and restitutions he entitled us with. And I am sworn to protect this land from catastrophe and chaos, as would be any man who seeks the Horus Throne. It cannot be bought, Lord Ay. Egypt would not tolerate another period of disrespect to Mighty Amun."

I nearly gasp. Paranefer's brown eyes flash with triumph, because he knows he has Ay on this point. Paranefer can command a rebellion now, as my father's old nemesis did when he was the High Priest of Amun.

"I shall remember this," Ay says coldly, resuming his meal.

I could cry for joy, but I keep my head down. I remain timid before Ay's ugly, cold rage on the barge. He mistakes my trembling for fear, and leaves me in peace, but I am shaking for excitement. Everything has fallen into place on one dry and dusty day, as if Isis herself reached down and moved everything along in my favor like pawns on a *senet* board. As the barge creeps back across the river to Malkata, I watch the clouds of sand blurring the distant cliffs, and I silently rehearse what I will say to Hani when he comes.

Chapter Eight

I have watched Hani on his past three visits, and each time he is utterly respectful, and quite mournful. He tells me that he misses Tutankhamun more than anything in the world, that they had brilliant plans together that would now never be brought to life. But we are accompanied by two young scribes, Ay's men, who must read and copy everything I dictate; consequently Hani never says anything that can be construed as critical of our new master. But on the fourth visit, in the beginning of summer, I hold my hand out as if I would be escorted through my private garden. Hani steps to my side, and I ask softly, "When did Ay murder my child?"

"Madam," he sighs, gazing at me sadly. "I was not at court at the time. As you know, I had just returned from Asia when I discovered the Hittite army in Amki, though I wish to the gods I had said nothing of it! Your husband sent me home, and I passed the winter and beginning of the harvest with my wife on our Delta estate. I returned only for the funeral. But it is a disgrace," he says, in a low whisper of a voice. The two nasty, spying youths trail us too far away to hear what we say. I can only hope that Hani is cultivating them, turning them to his service the way he would a malcontent maid in a foreign court.

"Would you help me?" I ask him simply, gazing at his handsome face. I feel a moment of sorrow thinking of how

535

Tutankhamun prized Hani's service, followed by a moment of fear. Hani is a natural courtier, a consummate deceiver. He could easily betray me to Ay, and then I will die with nothing accomplished. But if not Hani, who?

"Anything," he says easily, keeping his face light and merry for the spies behind us.

"I want you to go to the Hittite court," I say. "I want you to press for a son of Suppililiuma's, a son that I can marry and make king."

Even Hani stutters over this, as Mutnojme did, as any Egyptian would. For a moment he thinks I have gone mad, but I explain it to him as softly and quickly as I can. The Hittite will be killed, and there will be war. I say no more than that, but he understands. He knows that Lord Ay must pay for his crimes, and Horemhab will surely be a willing instrument of justice.

"He could not be king, though," Hani murmurs softly. "You could not marry Horemhab."

"I will marry no man," I say. I look sideways at Hani and say, "I don't expect Ay will let me live after he discovers the catastrophe I have brought down on him. And if you try to persuade me against doing this, I'll slap you, I swear."

Hani bows obediently, but not before he shakes his head ever so slightly. He cannot understand why I should wish to die before my twenty-second year, but as my servant he can't presume to object.

"Why can Horemhab not be king?" I ask in a whisper.

"Because he is so terribly common, he has no support outside of the military. Rameses would be a better choice. His blood is old; there is even a sister of your ancestor somewhere in his blood, three generations back. Egypt will accept Rameses, and the priests will anoint him."

I shrug a little. "It doesn't matter to me. The gods will have to indicate their choice once I am gone." For a moment, I wonder if I could have Mutnojme marry Tutankhamun's daughter to the new king, whoever he might be. I wonder if she could be made a Chief Wife, and have a son to inherit. I could die happily to know that my blood will sit on the Horus Throne, even if it is not a child of the line of my sires. As we return to the starting point of our walk, the polished stone stairs of my portico, I ask, "You can memorize a dictation, can you not? To commit to paper only after you are safely out of Egypt?"

"Of course," Hani says, naturally because it is one of the necessary skills of an ambassador of his caliber.

"Is the Hittite king still at war?"

"He is in route to his capital city, I believe. The Mitanni rebellion is weakening."

"Perfect. The next time you visit me, you shall take my spoken letter, as well as the other letters that the usurper has had me write praising him. You shall go to the Hittite king and bring him my proposal, and do everything in your power to make him agree to it."

"As you command, Majesty," Hani murmurs obediently.

And so my deadly plot is hatched, and flown off to the court of Hatti. There is no turning back.

Chapter Nine

After the Opet festival, during which Paranefer dedicated a ceremony to Tutankhamun attended by the upper echelons of Theban society, the number of people hanging on in Ay's unofficial court dwindles. Gone especially are the fathers of those soldiers trapped over the border in the malarial swamps of the Phoenician coast. Iset's father is here from Memphis and-tellingly-the entourage of lesser priests and bureaucrats that always hung onto Intef's cloak hem. There are men from Thebes here who I don't recognize, perhaps Ay's old friends or noblemen who felt so slighted by my father than they did not strive to reach the heights of Tutankhamun's court. But that is all. I see fewer men every day. Even now as I take the sun on the promenade beside my grandmother's lake, I can see great empty spaces where only a week ago there were barges. Ay is losing men like a vexed cat drops fleas.

As I stare out at the turquoise water, noting the standards of every traitorous barge at the quay, I catch sight of a small, swift moving craft entering the lake from the canal that connects it to the river. "What is that?" I ask Mutnojme, motioning so slightly with my chin that my heavy gold earrings don't even rock.

"Military," she says, shielding her eyes with her long, manicured fingers.

Eight oarsmen push the fast boat along, up to the quay. One

of the men, in a short, netted leather kilt, leaps from the boat and runs towards the palace as if Anubis were chasing him, a package in his arms.

"Let us return," I breathe, my throat going dry.

A hard wind out of the desert pushes us along as we return to Malkata. Once inside, we greet the usual commotion of servants, scribes, and courtiers, all who pay me their obeisance, even though they will not take my commands or fight for me. I think to go into the great hall, perhaps to catch some gossip, but my servants would be better placed to hear anything, and besides, whatever message being brought will go straight to Ay before anyone else.

I pace my chambers anxiously. Clouds have gathered outside, and the light is an ill grey-yellow color, the color of a coming storm. Though we are surrounded by my empty chambers and safe from spies I whisper to Mutnojme, terrified of being heard. "Do you think they caught Hani?"

She tries to deny it, but Mutnojme's frightened, too.

"You had no part of it," I tell her, as reassuringly as I can, but it doesn't comfort her. She was against the plan from the start, and now she nips her nails with her teeth, curled up in my ivory and mahogany chair as if it were a plank of wood in a roaring current.

"If could be anything," she says, sketching a fine hope. "It could be Horemhab. He could have had a great victory. He could even now be marching for Thebes, or Memphis."

I nod, I even try to smile, but I doubt it greatly. Old Ay would not have let his carefully worked plan fall apart so easily. There will be tens of thousands of men waiting to kill Horemhab if he even enters Egypt, along with anyone who supports him.

As it grows darker, I hear the stamping of feet outside my door. It can only be soldiers. Ay has sent his soldiers to arrest me. I touch my neck softly, as if catching my breath in my hands. Mutnojme and I exchange a frightened glance, and then my doors swing open and ten of Ay's guard barrel into my chambers without any pretense of respect or honor. Dear Isis,

I will be tried for treason against a false king. There will be a fake trial, with handsome young Hani tortured into confessing against me, and then an execution before anyone in Egypt can shout a word of protest. And Horemhab will never reach Ay, never kill him, he will never face justice...

The newly promoted captain speaks. "Your Majesty, the most excellent and revered Lord Ay requests your presence."

I lick my dry lips ever so slightly, and follow them.

I'm surprised to see that Ay has still not claimed the king's chambers. I am brought to his apartments, large and ornate but filled with the clutter of his work; then into his antechamber, his work room, where the large map table is surrounded by boxes of scrolls and broken down shelves, ready for transport. As I stand there, guards flanking me as if I was a criminal, I realize that Ay has appropriated my father's red granite desk, the one Tutankhamun kept in his map room. His seals of office -all presented to him by Tutankhamun- are pushed carefully to one side, ostensibly for the royal seals of Egypt. He will take four more throne names, he will write his common name-which should be spat on by all good men everywhere-in the ring of eternity, he will have it raised on golden rings to adorn his fingers. He will stamp my execution warrant with one of these rings.

Ay enters the room with a chilling, icy calm. He circles my father's desk and leans against it, crossing his arms over the heavy broad collar gilding his chest. He studies me, and I try to seem innocent as I wait for him to tell me that he has Hani in the city jail across the river, where Hani is weeping out the truth as Ay's torturers work him over. I couldn't blame him.

"What do you know of my son, Nakhtmin?" Ay asks me, staring through me as if I were standing accused before his Great *Kenbet*.

The ignorance on my face is real, full of surprise. "Nakhtmin? Your son, my lord? What should I know of him?"

He remains silent, by which I understand I am to keep

speaking. I shake my head slightly, and tell the truth. "I saw him last with you, I'm sure you remember. Has he not gone to Nubia to replace Lord Huy?"

Ay stands up again, approaches me ferally, circling me like a hyena. "No, Ankhesenamun, he has not gone to Nubia. He sent me a gift to signify his refusal of Huy's office. Go on, open it if you like." Ay indicates a leather-covered woven basket, less than a cubit in length and height. It is the package the soldier brought in.

"Surely it is no concern of mine," I say as lightly as I can. "Have your servant open it."

"There is no need." Ay walks to the basket. He lifts the top and a rancid smell blasts into the room, sickly-sweet and noxious. I cover my mouth and my nose, and Ay says, "My son has sent me the head of General Kha'em's second in command, and he has seized the garrison guarding the road to the sea."

Ay drops the basket top, closing the foul thing away again. He stares on it for a long time, as if it truly confounded him. Well, yes, loyalty would amaze him, and Nakhtmin, bless him, he has proven loyal. I could shout for joy and relief, but instead I look right into the killer's eyes and say, "My lord, I am as surprised as you are! I was certain your son had in some way supported your... cause."

Ay scowls at me as I accuse his son of being a conspirator in his regicide. "You wouldn't have encouraged this, Ankhesenamun, would you? Did you know that he planned this? Did you offer him my throne? Your self?"

"No, my lord," I say firmly. "I did not. If you have lost your son's loyalty, it is on your own account."

"I do not keep you here to scold me," he says shortly, and I relax, I know that I will not die for this. But then he crosses the distance between us, and he raises his hand-the one he touched the wretched parcel with-to my neck. I flinch away from the threatening touch, but he catches me, holding me about the throat as he runs his thumb along my skin. "If you ever did try to take my throne from me, I would cut this pretty neck in half." He bends and kisses the vein running up my neck, and I close my eyes and shudder at the horror of his cold mouth, his murmured threat. "Run along," he tells me, and I back away, and then turn to flee into his outer chamber. The greedy thugs in the rogue palace guard remain behind for their pay.

I am still reeling from his words, the sight of the head no doubt shown to terrorize me, and his awful touch when I feel a hand grab my arm. After a lifetime of physical seclusion from nearly everyone I gasp and spin to face my attacker. Lady Teyewig in disarray, black tears streaking her face, sobs, "I know it was you! You- you seduced my son!"

I try to shake her arm off, but she grips me tightly, spitting in her rage. "You have cost my son his life, his inheritance! My husband may be blinded by your-your *charms*-but I am not! You seduced my poor son and sent him to a shameful death!"

"Take your hands off me," I breathe in cold fury.

Teye releases me, but she leans forward to hiss in my face. "You may think you have won, pushed me from my rightful place and turned my son against us, but I swear to you, I will see you fall! Once Ay is coroneted, he has no need for you, and I will be sure to make him know it."

"What did you think he would do with me?" I demand, whispering just as fiercely as she. "You planned this wicked thing with him, what did you think would happen?"

"I did not think he would be besotted with a fair face after all my years of faithful service! You are nothing but a pretty little toy, Pharaoh's toy, and you will pay for taking my place beside my lord!"

I open my mouth to tell her she is welcome to him, but the antechamber door swings open again, and the guards file out. Teye doesn't miss her chance to run inside, leaving me alone.

I slip out into the hallway, and for a long moment I am still. There are few guards here. I could try to make an escape; I could slip out the western gate, and disappear into the desert. It would be treacherous, but at least I wouldn't be trapped in Malkata palace, waiting to be murdered! I could try to walk to Denderah and find someone, anyone who was still loyal...

The thudding of a door behind me spooks me into motion.

As the doors to Ay's outer chambers open, I can hear Teye within sobbing wildly. I tighten reflexively, thinking the usurper, the killer, is walking behind me, his eyes all over me as his wife of thirty some years weeps within his inner rooms. But it is only the old man's butler, his head bowed in shame as he passes me by.

Chapter Ten

Once again, it is winter. A year has passed without Tutankhamun, and each day has been worse and more painful than the last. But Hani is not discovered; even now, he could be returning from Suppililiuma's court. Even now, the Hittite entourage could be under attack, and for all his spies Ay knows nothing of it. He is too busy planning his coronation to do much else, and too certain of my defeat to consider that I might rise against him.

Nakhtmin has lasted longer than anyone could have imagined. His men are like the heretic rebels of years past: they hit the enemy quickly, striking supply lines and burning warehouses of weapons, and then they dissolve back into the southern deserts that he knows so well. The city of Thebes is in terror that he will attack, but I know better. He will harass Ay's troops, eating away at them bite by bite until they are weak enough to fall under Horemhab's sword, or until they surrender to him. Ay has had to direct an entire division back from our northern border to chase his rebellious son, and I count that as a victory. My victories are few and far between, though, and I am crumbling under the pressure of maintaining an obedient front to the man who murdered my beloved husband and son. I thank the gods for the old age that saps his vigor and keeps him away from me far more than he would wish.

"Drink, Your Majesty," Akasha murmurs, handing me a hot

mug of herbs mixed with wine. I sigh and cup her potion in my hands, knowing that the drink has little effect now. My pain is like a dull knife, hurting more as the sorrow is dragged out, day upon lonely, hateful day. But there is some relief, and I close my eyes and press my cold fingers to my temples. Mutnojme brushes my hair with long, soothing strokes, and Akasha hums softly as she crushes the herbs to prevent conception. They attend me as they would attend a woman who was deathly ill: in near silence, stepping softly, making little comforting murmurs but knowing better than to seek my conversation.

On the year anniversary of Tutankhamun's death, Ay denies me the right to go to his mortuary temple. For the first time in months I bridle against this, demanding why. What purpose could it serve to keep me from honoring my husband? What plot could I hatch at a mortuary temple? It is deliberate cruelty, but he holds firm, and I realize that I cannot win. Instead, I keep vigil with Mutnojme through the long night, remembering the awful death, the grotesque infection, the maddening pain that Tutankhamun endured. I stand on my balcony under the stars, watching them slide from east to west as the night drags on, wondering if my husband is among those stars, and why I cannot feel his presence, why he never comes to me in my dreams. I seek him and never find him. He is across the river, as he promised, but the banks are always shrouded in mist and I cannot find a boat, and always he fades away when I call to him. I cannot even see his handsome face, and I wonder in horror if I am forgetting it. Why does he not come to me?

"It's because he knows I have... I've submitted to that man," I whisper, staring down at my feet. "He must hate me now."

Mutnojme puts her arms around me. "You're speaking madness. He could never hate you! What else could you do?" she soothes, holding me close.

"No..." I breathe, shaking my head. I should have died first. I should have been a lioness, fighting until my death before I surrendered to him. I should kill myself before I walk him into the Temple of Amun, where Paranefer will blasphemously make him a Pharaoh. I am no good wife to Tutankhamun, I am no warrior. I am not even much of a woman.

The sun rises slowly, and the cliffs lighten from dusky purple-orange to golden yellow. Tutankhamun died at sunrise. Tutankhamun died in horrible pain, his victory stolen from him, thinking he had lost the war and failed to defend his driver; he died in the terrible culmination of a plot that had tightened around us for every year our love got sweeter, as if we had been living a borrowed life all the while. Ay measured our life like he was Anubis himself!

I walk towards the edge of my balcony and look down, to the limestone walk underneath, where kilted guards stand like statues with their spears in hand. The deep green crowns of tall palms shiver in the desert breeze. Beyond them, rows of royal blue irises border the path, their lush and cool color a brilliant contrast to the warm cliffs bordering the Valley. I put my hands on the whitewashed sandstone wall of the balcony and lean forward, thinking, *Is it far enough?* The last thing I would want would be to be broken from the fall, but not killed.

"Ankhesenamun!" Mutnojme cries softly, rushing to my side.

"Leave me, Mutnojme," I say, defeated, disgusted with myself. "You've done your service. There is nothing more you can do for me but let me go." Ay has made sure that there are no weapons I could use to kill myself, no ropes, no knives, nothing but this balcony. Can I do it? Can I pitch myself over the side, come what may of my Hittite plot? Can I do it, even if it would be a slow, brutal death?

"No, Ankhesenamun, look! It is Lord Hani, returning to court!"

"He is hot for it, my lady, but he's a wily old king, and he is cautious. He seems to know that no Egyptian woman ever gives herself in marriage to a foreigner, and he wonders why a princess might want to. Especially you."

"You have come back without success?" I cry, despondent. I

look to Mutnojme, who blocks the entrance to my garden, and I lower my voice. "How can he be so hot for it, yet refuse to send me a prince? I cannot endure another day of this! I have sold myself to seek revenge, I have held my tongue when I could and shut my eyes to my life, so that I might bring justice for my husband and son, and a better king for Egypt. I must have this!"

"Madam," Hani whispers sadly, "I cannot imagine what you suffer." He shakes his head, and leans close. "I have bought a man in Suppililiuma's court, and he says that the old king believes that if you are true, you are a great fool indeed. With just a little more pushing, he will send you a son, and behind that son will come the Hittite army. The old king thinks that he might conquer Egypt without bloodshed, and so own the land from the Hellespont to the third cataract of the Nile. He lusts for this the way men lust for pretty girls! We only need coax him a little further."

"Then why did you *leave*?" I demand. "Why did you not coax!"

"Because he must have a letter from you, my lady, in your own hand. You must write him again, beseeching him, outraged that he would doubt your suffering, your shame in asking a foreigner for a son. You must speak of the great honor you would give him, as if you were oblivious to the fact that you would be relinquishing your country to Hittite control. I can buy more men-the Hittite court is a terrible, fractious place-to tout the virtues of such a match, and to laugh at the naivety of the Great Royal Wife of Egypt. But I must have another letter from you, playing the part, begging him for a son."

"But the coronation will be soon! Surely Suppililiuma will know-"

"Not if I go now, madam. I have a man who will be willing to set sail, even in winter. If I go by way of Cyprus, I could reach Anatolia in a week. The prince could be on the road in two. But it is up to you, and how persuasive you can be."

I frown at this terrible setback, but Hani, ever prepared, produces a scroll and a writing kit. I close my eyes and pray:

Oh, Isis! Let my words turn the heart of the old Hittite king! You must want revenge brought down on the man who murdered Pharaoh, the man who follows Set the Destroyer! Let the foreigner fall into my trap, so that this vengeance may be done!

I dip the brush into the ink, and write.

Chapter Eleven

Year One Ay

When Ay is coroneted, he holds my wrist so tightly that his fingerprints bruise purple into my flesh. Afterwards there is feasting and acrobats, fire-eaters and dancers, just as if it were a grand feast day. Were it not for the opium I smoked, I could hardly endure sitting beside the usurper with the cobra and vulture of Egypt on his brow, and all of his minions toasting his success. It feels like salt rubbed into an already mortal wound. I sit with little concern for my reputation, slouching in my throne, my eyes heavy and drooping from the joy flower's potency. We have been officially wed for three days now. Let the court know I can hardly bear it!

Suddenly, a soldier comes rushing down the side of the hall, and I sit up anxiously. He bounds up the dais and leans over to Ay. I hear his hissed message, "The traitor in the north has done a strange thing, Your Majesty."

"What has he done?" Ay asks mockingly, grinning too hard over his victory to care for Horemhab any longer.

The soldier furrows his brow. "Our scouts saw an Asian messenger enter the camp. The next morning, the traitor set out with Rameses and a few other men. General Kha'em set a reconnaissance party to follow him, and what they saw was... disturbing."

Ay now looks up at the soldier, slightly concerned. "What did they see?"

"It seemed there was a party of men from the Hittite court travelling under a banner of peace. As they approached the southern portion of the Way of Horus, the traitor's men fell upon them. There were signs that survivors got away, but many Hittites were killed."

Ay leans back in his throne, murmuring to himself, "Why should they be coming here?" Then he asks the soldier, "What men of worth in the Hittite lands were among them?"

Now the soldier grimaces, and I hardly dare breathe. He does not even have to speak, but his words send a shiver straight through my body. "It seemed there was a prince among them, and they were bearing many precious gifts."

"It *seemed*?" Ay hisses as his cunning heart begins to understand. "Did Horemhab kill a Hittite prince, coming to Egypt to do me honor?"

"There is something more, great lord," the soldier says in a painfully boyish whisper.

The look Ay gives him is enough to wilt him in his leather sandals.

The soldier bows his head and says, "The traitor left your seals behind, Majesty; as if he had been following your orders when he killed the prince and his emissaries."

Ay turns to Teye with a foul glare. He takes a long while to master himself, and then he says, "The Hittite king will take his revenge. Horemhab is clever."

Teye replies icily, "It is as if the gods granted him this gift."

"Indeed," Ay agrees, and then he rises from his throne. "I will make preparations."

As he steps down, letting his cloak billow with artful imitation, I look at Teye, and her eyes are on me. The faintest hint of a smile is on her lips.

I am not long in my chambers when Henutawy slips into the sight of my mirror. "The vizier's old wife is here," she says disrespectfully, despising my enemies loyally.

I look to Mutnojme as if to tell her to keep her faith, and be calm; even so, I feel a trembling in my belly. I wonder how Teye might have discovered me. "I will receive her in my antechamber, Henutawy. Serve the black plum wine."

I make the woman wait, since she could not hate me more. It is cold today, and I change into a thicker gown of white linen with blue lotus flowers embroidered at the hem and wide sleeves. As ever, I wear Tutankhamun's amethyst necklace. I rub my fingers over the sunset-purple beads, and then I go out to greet Teye.

"How did you do it?" she asks, her voice dripping with satisfaction.

I sip my wine slowly, hoping that it quiets my pounding heart. Ay will be drafting letters to the Hittite king now, and sending orders to his generals to head north, towards the borderlands of our empire. Suppililiuma is sure to wave my letter as he accuses Ay of murdering his son. He is sure to speak of Hani's visits to his court. I lower my gilded cup and say, "I did nothing. Horemhab is the killer. Is that not what the messenger told us?"

Teye laughs softly. "Very well. I'll get to the bottom of this. You've killed yourself, little madam. I'll have my husband, and your crown."

"You've run mad," I say, hoping she cannot hear the quiver in my voice. Ay won't believe her until there is proof, but when he does find out, she'll press him to be merciless, and he will listen. I have only a little time left to prepare.

The High Priestess of Mut is rowed towards me on a clear, bright morning, a beautiful morning three weeks later, a morning full of birdsong and sweet breezes over the water. The banners of her ceremonial barge snap and leap like silver fish in the sky. The priestess comes ashore with her white robes billowing around her slim ankles and her loose cinnamon curls streaming behind her.

I stand on Malkata's quay, on a shining blue harbor made in the name of love, and take the hands of the priestess. "Your Majesty," she says, bowing her head. "I've come as you commanded, bringing you the blessings and good wishes of my priestesses."

"I thank you," I say softly. We are both aware of the spies, the guards, the ladies of the court who follow me as if they weren't going to run to Teye when I leave the harbor. I feel like a hounded creature, stalked and hunted in the desert.

We walk back into the palace enclosure together, and I can feel old Ay's cold, godless stare falling on me from high above the pylon gate of the enclosure wall. Men entered the palace this morning, determined men off a barge out of the north. They might have carried a letter from an outraged Hittite king.

With a chill still in the air, I bring Anat to my bath, which is full of soft, hot steam. Anat lines her unguent jars along the granite bench. I step into the waist-deep water and try to clear my heart of all thoughts, even though they beat like drums. Ay will kill me. Will he rush in with a knife, or send me before his court as a traitor? I resist the urge to stroke my soft neck, that spot his thumb touched that I cannot stop holding as if it were injured.

Anat begins her low chant, calling the goddesses of Egypt to witness. I splash my face-and my consciousness-clean. The musical water drops slowly back into the bath, creating perfect circles that ripple far out across the still surface. There will be water in *Aaru*; it is a field of reeds, eternally green and lush.

From far down the hallway, I can hear sandals stomping against stone.

Anat murmurs on, her dialect thousands of years old. She pours water over me from a vessel made of earth, and rubs frankincense oil over my brow. I can smell Tutankhamun in that oil. I smile, picturing him standing tall and beautiful on a papyrus raft in a clutch of reeds, calling to me that the water is clear and calm, and the duck are plentiful. It will be so sweet to see him again, to feel his arms around me!

Now the shouting of men echoes into the hall outside my chambers. Anat looks at me with alarm, but her words do not stumble. I purse my lips in a determined little smile and hold my palms up, closing my eyes, and she finishes the ritual.

In my presence chamber, my maids shriek as soldiers intrude without warning. I turn to emerge from the pool, purified and blessed, just as the captain of the guard bursts into my bathroom.

"Majesty!" Anat cries.

The captain, Ay's man, looks stunned at my nakedness. Recovering, he barks savagely, "Madam, I am here to arrest you for high treason against his divine majesty Pharaoh Ay! You are ordered to return to your inner chamber and await further command."

The water hides my legs as my knees weaken and buckle. I draw my breath and remind myself that I wanted this, that I knew it would come to this. I step out of the water slowly, feeling it slip off my skin luxuriously. A tear slides down my cheek, hidden by my splashed face. This might be the last bath I ever step out of. Will Ay really cut my head off, like that man whose head was in his basket? Like Intef, with that great gout of blood gushing over the sand? My chest tightens abruptly, snatching my breath. I force myself to stand still as my servant drapes my soft white robe over me. She pulls my long black curls out and arranges them precisely, and then I nod to the guards, and walk towards my bedroom.

Chapter Twelve

Before Ay comes to me, I am in a terror that he will touch me, that he will spoil my purification rite. But when he finally arrives-in the night, likely on his way to a lavish banquet-he has Teye on his arm. He has closed ranks with her again, and she is in her glory, the faithful one, gloating over me like a woman half her age might and as weighted in gold as the shrine of Mut herself.

I sit at my vanity, which is festooned like a bride's with big, bright winter blossoms. Mutnojme combs my hair slowly, burnishing my obsidian curls to a high shine. I watch the two of them only from my mirror. If I am a traitor, if I am to die, why would I deign to speak to them? I need not hide myself anymore. In fact, I close my eyes, ignoring my tormenters and inhaling the musky-sweet scent of the flowers. I am sorry that I will die before the roses bloom again.

Ay speaks, quite calmly. He always was a cold fish. "You didn't mean to marry a Hittite, did you?"

"No," I say, as calmly. I want to know, I *must* know, how he found out, and what will happen next.

"I thought not. But you know, that is what people will remember. That is what they will think."

I narrow my eyes. He means to frighten me with this? "I am not my mother," I say. "I am not a commoner, and I don't care what they think. The gods will know the truth, and so will my husband. My *true* husband."

"So brave," Ay says with mock approval. "And such a clever kitten; who would have thought it? I can hardly bear to kill you. But you are a dangerous beauty, and I'll be satisfied when you are safe and dead, except for in my perfect memories."

This is so disgusting a thought, so outrageous, that I cringe and curl my fingers around the ivory handle of my mirror, as if I would strike him with it. I steady myself, knowing that would only please him and dishonor what might be my last day in this world.

"So, you have nothing to say in your defense. Well, I came here to tell you that your little intrigue will fail. King Suppililiuma and I are exchanging letters, and I hope to find a diplomatic solution to this unforeseen tragedy. Nakhtmin the traitor will be dead and gone in a month, and Horemhab will die before he sets a foot in Egypt. You have gambled all, and lost, Ankhesenamun."

"I have lost nothing but the chain of mortality, Ay. You will die and become nothing; Ammit will eat your wicked soul. But Tutankhamun and I will live on together, forever, no matter what you might do to us. I know that now. I trust that. You think I will ever be known as the woman who tried to make a foreigner king? You shall be known in all ages as the killer of a king, the man who destroyed a holy dynasty, father, mother, and son, who married an unwilling woman forty years your junior, for nothing more than greed and lust and a few months on the throne. You wanted immortality, and so you have it: immortal shame."

A quick glance in the mirror shows me that the veins in Ay's neck-under his heavy, outdated wig-are bulging. Teye clutches at his arm and quickly says, "Nothing you say means a thing. You're going to be beheaded in the courtyard the day after tomorrow, and I am to be Great Royal Wife."

I shiver in involuntary fear, immediately wishing that I hadn't because Teye smiles a hollow-eyed smile. I will be glad to be rid of these evil people, who watched me as a child and decided I should be the linchpin to their ambitions, and who have now ordered me to death. But oh! I don't want to do it! I don't want to lay my head down and feel the stirring of breeze on the back of my neck and then-

Mutnojme sets the comb down, moving naturally and gracefully though she is near shaking with fear and anger. She dispenses a few precious drops of my vanilla and amber perfume, and when she brushes the oil over my pulse gently, I can feel the tremor in her finger. The delicious scent warms and sweetens the air around me, and I regain my breath. Now I look over my shoulder and say, "My lady shall be released. She is your niece, who came to my side as I bid her. She is innocent of any wrongdoing, any knowledge of my planning."

Ay lets Mutnojme hang in her terror for a long, cruel moment; but he finally issues her reprieve. "You will go back to Akhmim," Ay commands. "You will live on the family estate in the country, in obscurity, knowing that the shadow of my axe will hang over you always."

As they go, I waver in my chair, grabbing my aunt's arm. The blood rushes from my head and everything spins, and Mutnojme is weeping as she holds me up. Dear Isis, I thought it would be a sword, a sharp sword. "He said an axe," I gasp, horrified. "He said the shadow of his axe."

Mutnojme cannot answer. She takes me to my bed, and Akasha brings me opium, and I try to make the incontrollable quivering in my guts stop.

I spend the following day gazing at the beauty around me, feeling the warm wind on my cheeks. Truly, there is nothing but beauty in this world, if only men would stop their evil long enough to see it! I could have been a happy woman with Tutankhamun and no throne, just a garden and a warm, brightly painted house; but there is no point in thinking of this. At sunset, I make my final prayers to the sun god, beseeching him to know his true daughter and bring me home, no matter what sort of burial I receive. The late winter sky ignites in color, gold and scarlet and fuchsia. So quickly, the silver stars pierce through the veil of the heavens, sparkling in their eternal dance. They are the last stars I will see in this world, and I don't know if they will become clearer or fainter in the next one. As I lie on my balcony that night, watching the sky over the mountain cemetery of my ancestors, I envision the next world. Once my journey is complete, I should find a river like the one I've known my whole life, banked with thick reeds and lush flowers. I think it would always be twilight in that next place, but not gloomy. The very air will be full of magic, and I will be with Tutankhamun, and there will be no boundary of flesh between our souls. I mustn't be afraid to go where he has gone first.

Mutnojme has gotten a hard, snapping fire going in a wide bronze brazier beside me, and we sit together and drink wine, talking about better days when Tutankhamun and I were newly in love and blessed with a strong son, and every hope in the world that more babies would follow.

Suddenly, Akasha emerges from my chambers. She bows, and I bid her not to waste any more time on formalities. And so she says, "One of the guards wishes to speak with you, Your Majesty."

Mutnojme's eyes widen, and she grabs my hand hopefully. "Perhaps he will help you escape," she cries gently, my true sister.

Surprisingly, my heart leaps with desire. I can hardly stop the tears of relief, but I say practically, "No, Mutnojme, please. It couldn't be." It is better not to hope, better to think only of the place I will go.

He is a handsome young man, actually, this guard who comes before me in my audience chamber. He drops to one knee and I say, "I hope it is important, I have very little time left."

He tells me, balefully, as if he were a boy who had ripped the wings off a butterfly, "I thought-your humble servant thought-that you, my lady, should not die without knowing what is coming for the man who orders your death."

"Tell me," I breathe. What a blessing, at this late hour!

The man nods his head and says without scruple, "Pharaoh Ay sent five thousand men after his son the general, and the entire division defected to General Nakhtmin. They are marching north now, to join the fighting in Palestine on General Horemhab's part."

I laugh, looking at Mutnojme. Nakhtmin might be the one to bring justice, after all! "If Ay's own son rebels against his illegitimate rule, what can the common people do?"

"There is more, great lady. They say the Hittites are sacking Amki, and they are terrified in Beirut, they have shut up the city walls and closed the port. Since so many Egyptian soldiers have rushed south, the Hittites and their allies are preparing to take over our northern territories."

I cannot help but frown at this. "That is displeasing. I pray this matter is resolved quickly, so that our attention can be turned to holding the north."

"It will mean a great war, my lady. Pharaoh is sending four divisions to deal with the Hittites alone. He has lost the northeast; Lord Djarmuti has refused to send him taxes in the spring, scorns him as illegitimate from his Delta fortress. Already his section of Egypt calls secretly for their patriarch Commander Rameses to take the throne, and so they will obviously fight for it. And General Nakhtmin now commands nearly ten thousand. It will be a long fight, my lady, but everyone thinks you have cost him the crown of Egypt. You do not die in vain. I pray the generals will make a good peace for Egypt once Pharaoh Ay is dead."

Tears rush to my eyes, but I attempt to remain serene before this brave young commoner. On my tiny signal, Mutnojme attempts to give the guard bronze, but he will not accept it.

"I have taken his gold, my lady. I tell you this for Your Majesty's sake, but also to lighten the weight in my heart."

"You may leave me," I say softly. He bows deeply, and I turn my back on him.

When he is gone, I take Mutnojme's hands. "You must do

something for me," I tell her, as we stroll back out to the stars and the bright waning moon.

Mutnojme nods, and so I say, "When Horemhab returns, you will marry him."

She stammers, "He may not ask me-"

I click my tongue softly in disbelief, and then I say, "He can't breathe without you. You just need to remind him a little, I think."

Mutnojme laughs softly and says, "You've come a long way when you give me advice about love, little niece."

I close my eyes and smile wistfully. "I'm going to see my love tomorrow, Mutnojme." If only I weren't so afraid of how I will go to him… I can't waste my time thinking of it. "You have to marry Horemhab, because he will need you if he is to be king. But he cannot fight Rameses for it. You have to make sure he doesn't. Egypt will lose everything to the Hittites if a strong succession isn't established and supported right away. They must make peace; they are soldiers first, they will all understand this. And then, somehow, you have to fit Tutankhamun's daughter into the next ruling family. Our blood must mix with the next dynasty's blood. I can die happy knowing that I have done that much for my family."

I cannot sleep. I watch the stars spin across the sky, and then, all too soon, the sky lightens. Black goes gray; gray softens to a misty blue haze. I rub my hands across my neck, and offer to Anubis that it will be a quick death. I shudder to think it would take more than one strike of the axe. Akasha comes with a pungent tasting drink, and I say, "This will not dull my wits, will it?"

"Not terribly, Majesty. And it is only a precaution. There will be no pain."

"It is easy to be confident when it isn't your neck," I say wryly. I go my bath, breathing in the sweet steam from hot water saturated with rose oil. My bath is almost as sweet as the garden at the Temple of Mut. I stare at the sparkling bits of pink and red and black in the polished Aswan granite tub, running my fingers along the warm buffed surface. The beautiful black-haired servants who replenish the hot water wear white linen so light it floats on the steam.

I lean my head back for firm hands to wash my hair and massage my scalp. I refuse to cry, but I really don't want to die today. I'm barely twenty-two, I've barely tasted life! Save a hateful trip to Asia I've never truly been anywhere outside a royal Egyptian palace.

But Tutankhamun didn't want to die either. Certainly not on the field of the battle he had waited all his life to fight! I have to go to him. I have to take him in my arms and feel his mouth against my neck, feel the warmth of his breath, hear his words murmured in my ear. I resign myself before I leave my bath, and while Mutnojme dresses me in a sheer, bright green gown with a narrow waist and wide, pleated hem and sleeves, and combs my curls out until they ripple in black spirals down to my hips, I smile at my reflection in the mirror. I am going to my love again, and if it is frightening, he will comfort me as he always has. I can feel the potent magic and power of the golden *seshed* circlet and rearing cobra that Mutnojme sets on my curls; I know I will have my place in the next world. I will die like my grandmother, sure that her reward and happiness were awaiting her in death. I will die like Tutankhamun; quiet, in acceptance of my fate.

The drum beats steadily as I walk into Malkata's courtyard. The witnesses Ay has called form a three sided square around the usurper's pavilion, and behind them rise high white-washed walls. There is a block in the center of the courtyard, in the very place I once leapt into chariots beside Tutankhamun. Beside it stands Ay's hired thug, a wiry-looking fellow who doesn't look strong enough to do the job. My eyes dart to his hands, and I actually cry in relief. He has a long, polished bronze sword, flashing naked in the sun. I can walk to my death now, knowing it will most likely be swift.

The witnesses all stare. Surely they will never again witness a thing like this, a Great Royal Wife put to death by a treacherous councilor. I see Iset's father, looking puffed up and self-righteous, terrified that he will be tainted by his son-in-law's rebellion. But the other men, older, lesser officials bought by Ay, don't look very pleased at all. Some of them can look at me only for a moment, some not at all. Ay sees this too. When I reach the block and the herald begins to call out my titles and my guilt, Ay waves his hand from his solid gold chair and stands, like he was a vizier still.

"This woman is a traitor to Egypt, a traitor to her blood! She plotted with the Hittite king to make an enemy prince our Pharaoh! She must die, there is no other choice. Ptah himself demands her death."

The crowd looks to Hebnetjer, and he nods complicity. No one misses that Amun doesn't call for my death, and Paranefer is nowhere in sight. But Ay is anxious to have this done. For once, I can see the emotion clear in his face, and he is outraged, yet he is afraid, too. He is murdering the last living true heiress of a sacred line, and he is misjudging the crowd. Each accusation he spits points to his own guilt, and the lords in Malkata's courtyard grow more uncomfortable, more burdened with shame as they stand under the hot sun. Ay condemns me to death, and his audience stands horrified, knowing that he is murdering me solely for trying to escape him. I thought to shout at him, to call him murderer before his allies, but it is plain to see that they already know. Ay will kill me, but my death will cost him support. His own supporters weep now; they weep with disgust and sorrow that he should kill me this way. He cannot be long for this world.

I turn to Mutnojme, who follows me. I take my heavy gold earrings from my double piercings, and the lightness feels strange. She tucks them away in her robe, crying silently, and then takes up my long curls and tucks them into my diadem in the way we decided upon last night. She comes before me, and she is supposed to bow, but she flings herself into my arms, crying. "I can't do it," she sobs, "I can't play along. I love you. I hate him. I will dance before his tomb, and then hack his name out of existence."

"Name your daughter for me," I say, and then I kiss her cheek, and she mine. I try to smile brightly. "I'm never going to let him go once I find him again," I tell her, and Mutnojme nods, crying. Finally, she backs away.

The drums stop, and I breathe hard, wishing one last time that I didn't have to do this. I refuse to look at Ay. I look over the high enclosure walls, and up to the brilliant blue sky. I can hear my breath in my throat.

A cool breeze stirs my hair, and maybe it's just the drink Akasha gave me, but I think I hear laughter on the wind. No one else seems to hear it, and my heart pounds in my chest. I lower myself to my knees, to the embroidered cushion someone has so thoughtfully set out. No sooner do I touch the ground, the smell of frankincense and spice permeates the air. It is the smell of Tutankhamun's skin, and suddenly I can feel him as sure as if his warm brown arm was against mine. I cry for joy and relief. I want to go now, I want to be with him, I want to hold him again. I bow ever so slightly, exposing my small bronze neck. The wind sings, and it bites, it burns-

In a blaze of light, Tutankhamun grabs me into his arms. "It is over, *hapepy*. It's all over. I'm taking you home."

565

Epilogue

14 years later

Pharaoh Horemhab paced nervously outside the birthing pavilion, his sandals beating the limestone path in a furious rhythm. Every so often he looked towards the portico, where General Seti sat consoling young Nebamun, the son of Nakhtmin. He shook his head again, wondering if this was all a great mistake. He had never understood the will of the gods, those mysterious forces so easily deciphered by his predecessors. But the girl-to tell the secret truth the princess and rightful ruler of Egypt-had been battling with Nebamun's child for hours now. Her shattering screams tore through the Memphis palace enclosure like a jagged knife, setting everyone from the mighty king to the lowliest servant on edge. If she died, and the child with her...

No, he could not think of that. The gods must love him, and they must certainly love the black-eyed girl within the sandstone pavilion giving birth. Yet had Horemhab not learned in all his long life that the love of the gods was no guarantor of life? Through the clouds of incense drifting through the lush garden, Horemhab could see his dear battle-brother Rameses clutching the hand of his three year old grandson. If the girl within died, if the child died, or if it was a boy, then all of their plans would be dashed to nothing.

Another ear-splitting scream and Horemhab sunk down onto a black granite bench, his face in his hands. "Forgive me," he prayed softly, thinking of another divine black-eyed child, a student he trained to be a warrior and then failed to protect.

And then, silence. Horemhab turned to Rameses, both old

warriors' eyes shining with a mixture of fear and hope. The gilded doors of the pavilion swung open, and the Great Royal Wife Mutnojme appeared, her own forty-three year old body swollen with a long awaited child. Horemhab blinked, his sun-dazzled eyes unable to see into the darkness of the pavilion. But yes, yes, there was a baby in her arms! And his beautiful wife was smiling, that magnificent smile that lit up her whole face, the smile that never failed to melt the rugged old warrior's heart.

Mutnojme stepped down from the portico, her soft white robes swirling around her ankles. "A daughter," she breathed, unfallen tears in her eyes. "A daughter for the throne of Egypt."

Horemhab leaped up, but then he checked himself. It was no longer his concern; his duty was done. Just as he could not claim the throne for his own blood, he could not be the first to greet this baby of the most holy blood. "Has Maia survived?" he asked hopefully, and when his wife nodded, he gave a deep sigh of satisfaction and sank back down to the bench.

He watched with relief and awe as Rameses, his heir even though his own sons by Amenia were strong, led his grandson to the Great Royal Wife. Seti's three year old son made a graceful bow, and Mutnojme, who adored young Rameses, lowered her swollen body to the ground. "This is your wife-to-be, my child," she said softly, her voice breaking from a sorrow many years old. "You must love her as your true sister, always."

The child, precocious beyond his years, wrinkled his face up in confusion. "She doesn't *look* like a wife," he said with endearing reluctance. "Not like you, Auntie!"

Mutnojme smiled again, and Horemhab sighed as the brilliance of her smile illuminated the garden. He could hear the birds singing again, he could feel the north wind, Amun's breath, on his face once more. Mutnojme said, "But she will be a great beauty, Rameses. And you must adore her, and care for her always. Will you promise me?"

"Yes, Auntie!" Rameses said, eager to please as always. "What will her name be?"

Horemhab held his breath. A name was not formally bestowed until a child had lived for fourteen days. But the name of *this* child would have even more significance. And if it was too like the old names, the priests would balk, the people would not accept her on the day she finally claimed her destiny. Still, it must have *something*, some hint... After all, it was the grandchild of Tutankhamun that Mutnojme cradled in her arms.

"I think we shall call her Nefertari, young lord," Mutnojme murmured, issuing a challenging look to Horemhab and the elder Rameses both.

"Beautiful Companion," Horemhab mused, finally standing to look at the child. Though she was only moments old, he could see that the baby had eyes as stunning and black as her mother and grandfather. Her tiny features were perfect, so much like the brave woman who had given her life to grant him the Horus Throne. No one who saw this child would doubt that she was a Tuthmosid! But was that not what they wanted? Was that not the essence of everything that Mutnojme had made him swear to, before she agreed to be his wife? "I think it is fitting," the old warrior-king decided, nodding his thick head.

Young Rameses, nothing more than a baby but already possessed of a strong sense of his destiny, peered down on the infant again. "Nefertari," he said in his baby voice, smiling winsomely. "I will love you forever, my sister, my beautiful wife-to-be."

The End

Author's Note

The Amarna Period is one of the most fascinating, mysterious parts of Egypt's long history. While recent years have seen remarkable progress in our understanding of this time, so many parts of the record have vanished, and it is nearly impossible to fully reconstruct the reign of Tutankhamun.

In creating Tutankhamun's character for this novel, I relied most heavily on two sources: what the young king revealed about himself, and indisputable DNA evidence. Tutankhamun saw himself as a hunter and a warrior. Of all the equipment in his small tomb, his 300+ weapons stand out as a collection. He had bows and arrows, daggers and swords, and armor. There were multiple chariots in Tutankhamun's tomb, both the ceremonial and practical kind. And apparently, the king was not wasteful in his sport. One of Tutankhamun's golden fans is beautifully illustrated with a scene of Pharaoh hunting his own ostriches, to collect feathers that once adorned the very fan. Hunting was obviously a passion of the young king; many trunks, buckles, and other personal items are decorated with scenes of the chase.

Because of discoveries in the general and later pharaoh Horemhab's tomb, we know that at *least* two major campaigns took place during the reign of Tutankhamun. We also have Horemhab making reference to "sitting at his lord's feet on the day of killing Asiatics," a clear indication that Pharaoh had taken the field. The greatest enemies of Egypt were in Nubia, and "Asia," which meant everything from the Palestinian coast to Babylon, and up to the land of the Hittites in present-day Turkey. Tutankhamun was quite devoted to the domination of these enemies. His sandals are decorated with bound prisoners of both Nubian and Asian variety, so that he might always walk on them. As in the novel, Tutankhamun also carried walking sticks whose handles were crafted to represent the broken backs of his enemies.

In modern day Luxor, the remains of Tutankhamun's temple bear the details of one successful Asiatic campaign, with both chariot and siege warfare employed. And, as in the novel, Tutankhamun depicted his defeated enemy returning to Egypt in a cage hanging off Pharaoh's flagship.

But even with all the evidence that demonstrates Pharaoh as a warrior, Egyptologists are hard-put to list the young king with his military forbearers. For many years, his age gave them pause. However, it is well known that in the Bronze Age, boys became men far earlier than they do today, and it would not be rare to find a young man of Tutankhamun's age on any field of battle, even in a position of authority.

Today, there's another reason causing speculation on the king's fitness for battle. DNA tests prove that Tutankhamun was afflicted with a rare bone disorder which cut off the blood supply to the bones in his left foot, leading to their eventual necrosis. At times, walking would have been impossible without mild to great pain. During the periods when his affliction flared up, he would have used one of the many gilded staffs found in his tomb to keep his weight off his foot. This surely would have affected Tutankhamun's training and participation in warfare, as I demonstrate when Tutankhamun fought Huy and sparred with Nakhtmin. Though it would not have precluded him from fighting, eventually he would have had great suffering and difficulty. In my research, I was struck again and again by the conflict of a young, hot blooded king who was obviously devoted to glory in the hunt and on the battlefield, yet handicapped by an affliction that threatened his mobility and everything he loved. For the purposes of this novel, I decided to show Tutankhamun as a young man who fought tirelessly and tenaciously to overcome his physical pain in order to become first a hunter, then a warrior, in the short time he felt he had to do it.

How Tutankhamun felt about his father, and his father's

failed revolution, is unclear. We know that he embarked on his Restoration early in his reign, changing his name and the state religion back to the "orthodox" format. At the same time, however, he bore both names on his famous golden throne, as well as countless symbols of his office. And neither Aten nor his father suffered any *damnatio memoriae* as became popular in later years. It is highly possible that Tutankhamun did his duties to his nation's god and his father's god with an easy conscience. However, it would not be easy for any young man to undo the life work of his father. We do have one small piece of information that might be telling about what stresses wore on the young king: according to Horemhab, Tutankhamun had a hot temper. But considering what we know, Tutankhamun was no tyrant during his brief tenure. Tutankhamun led his land back into prosperity, and tragically died before his true potential could manifest itself.

Concerning Ankhesenamun, we know much less. She was the third living daughter of Akhenaten. Her mother was the Nefertiti of legendary beauty and ambition. Ankhesenamun would have been raised with utter loyalty to her father's new laws. At some time before her father's death, when she was quite young, she bore her father a daughter who appears only once in the record, and then vanishes. She married Tutankhamun shortly thereafter, but because of the vague details of the ephemeral ruler Smenkhare, who reigned briefly once Akhenaten was dead, we cannot know if she was made to marry that king as well. Certainly, this very young princess was bound to the throne, and the property of whatever man sat on it.

During her marriage to Tutankhamun, the young queen is demonstrated as a supportive, nurturing partner. Dozens of pieces of art reveal her touching Tutankhamun softly, straightening his collar, or holding his arrows while he shoots. In other works, Tutankhamun is giving her flowers or pouring oil into her hands. Pharaoh obviously adored his wife, and she him, but even though she knew happiness with her husband, she struggled to bear him children. Ankhesenamun lost at least two babies, both girls. There could be many explanations for this, including trauma from the baby she bore as a child to the closeness in kinship with her husband. What we don't know is if they had any surviving children. A particularly intriguing statue appears to have been reused by Horemhab, who "recycled" many of earlier Pharaohs' statuary, as was common. It details a Pharaoh, Great Royal Wife, and a very young prince who holds his finger to his mouth like a toddler. It is done in late Amarna style, the standard for Tutankhamun's reign. The only other man to create art in the Amarna style was Pharaoh Akhenaten, and it is known that his Great Royal Wife bore no sons. Of course, in the power struggle after Tutankhamun's death, a son of Tutankhamun's would have been utterly defenseless, and could easily disappear from record.

As for the Hittite affair, we cannot know Ankhesenamun's motivation. It is generally accepted that she sent Hani to the Hittite court to beg for a son to marry. Hani arrived in the fall, as the king was returning from battle in Mitanni. Ankhesenamun was desperate and frightened, but could she really have meant to marry a Hittite Prince? Such a thing was unheard of. Egypt never gave away its daughters. In the novel, I decide that the young queen knew she was in a hopeless position, and so she played the only card she could to create chaos for Ay. This is Ankhesenamun's last appearance in the historical record. As this book first went to the publisher, her body was finally identified. She had been buried in a spare tomb with one of her sisters, possibly the tomb her sister was given in secret after the Amarna tombs were violated. Her head was unattached, and is now missing, but was said to bear long, beautiful black curls. There were no items bearing her name or title, and nothing has ever been discovered through archaeological efforts or in private collections belonging to her. We can only assume that her burial was quick and unceremonious, as befitting someone killed by a king.

What we do know is that within four years after Tutankhamun's sudden death, Horemhab became king. Ay's monuments and even his tomb were savagely attacked during this period. Horemhab had at least two known wives, and so it seems quite bizarre that he would have had no children to pass the throne onto, even if he gave one of his daughters in marriage to a man outside his blood. We know that he married Lady Mutnojme, and that she died either in childbirth or of complications in late pregnancy around age 43. Before Horemhab died, he named old Rameses his heir, and created the Nineteenth dynasty.

Some names in this work have been altered for clarity. With so many royal names in Amarna being honorific to Aten, I thought to set the eldest daughter of Nefertiti apart by playing on a name she is referred to in the collection of international correspondence found on the Amarna archeological site. So, Meritaten becomes Mayati. The real Paranefer changed his name to Wennefer when Tutankhamun changed his name, but for artistic purposes, I left it the same in the novel. Also, Rameses is thought by many to have been called Paramese, but I have chosen to call him Rameses, as that is who he became.

CPSIA information can be obtained at www.ICGtesting.com
Printed in the USA
BVOW08s1147290616

453952BV00001B/6/P